Gray Matters

Dolores Arden

About the Author

Dolores Arden has resided in the San Francisco Bay Area for more than three decades. She currently calls Vallejo, CA, her home. She lives there with a pocket-sized Great Dane named Remy and a back garden the size of a national park. *Gray Matters* is her first novel.

Gray
Matters

Dolores Arden

BELLA
BOOKS

2020

Bella Books, Inc.
P.O. Box 10543
Tallahassee, FL 32302

Printed in the United States of America on acid-free paper.

First Bella Books Edition 2020

Editor: Medora MacDougall
Cover Art & Design: Audrey Gilles

ISBN: 978-1-64247-196-0

Dedication

My everlasting gratitude goes to the ones who offered their unfailing words of encouragement, who so generously stepped in to help in the unique ways that they could, and who so dutifully and tirelessly read the early drafts—even though they weren't very good! Your friendship and support are everything to me.

CHAPTER ONE

Despite Remy's best intentions, the conversation had not gone well. For the twentieth time in an hour, she stole a glance at the wall clock, then focused her gaze back on Erica before the other woman could notice her audience was less than rapt. Christ, it was nearly two a.m.

In retrospect, it was hard to imagine an occasion where one might consider it a good idea to open a discussion with: "I think we should see other people." Yet, inexplicably, Remy had done precisely that. And she had waited until well past midnight to start down that particular rabbit hole. With a prosecuting attorney on the other side of the kitchen counter, no less.

The situation would be laughable if it weren't so depressing. Stifling a groan, Remy rolled her head from side to side, trying to loosen the band of tension at the back of her neck. It wasn't like she'd been sleeping much anyway. The dreams had returned several months ago, more vivid than ever. Or rather, the dream. It was always the same—immutable and inescapable, repeating on an endless loop. Remy wondered briefly if she'd done this to herself on purpose. As if spending half the night bickering with Erica were preferable to what awaited her once her eyes were closed.

She took an objective view of the woman standing across from her. They were going on two hours of fruitless debate now, and Erica did not appear to feel the strain. Her face was fresh and unlined. Her short blond hair fell across her forehead in that intentionally careless way it always did. She was still talking even now—in the midst of litigating her case—and it looked as though she was prepared to go several more rounds.

"...perfectly willing to own my part of what's happened between us, of course. But more importantly, I think you need to stop and take an honest look at what's holding *you* back."

Remy had missed the first part of that sentence, but she didn't need to ask for a clarification. She'd caught the gist of Erica's argument. She'd caught the gist of it hours ago. Her only defense was to reiterate the fact that they had come to an understanding—right at the very outset. Remy had stated her intentions clearly, and Erica had agreed. Apparently, however, this was a minor detail, with little to no bearing on the case at hand.

In the few months they'd been seeing each other, what had started out as casual had morphed into something else. Remy could admit that. Even accept some of the blame for it. But only to a degree.

"I mean, what are you really afraid of?" Erica went on. "Can you ask yourself that and give me an honest answer?" She paused, her eyes wide and unblinking.

When they'd first met, it had been those eyes—the stunning, mercurial quality of them—that had impressed Remy the most. They could turn softly seductive, when there was something Erica had her heart set on, or sharp and calculating the moment she sensed an opponent's weakness. And they could slip from one permutation to the next in an instant.

Right now, they were enormous. Tumescent blue splashes, brimming with unshed tears. Erica was pulling out all the stops, resorting to the most lethal device in her arsenal. Remy recognized it immediately because she'd fallen prey to it too many times to count. But it wasn't going to work this time. Not at two a.m. on a Monday morning.

Remy pried her gaze from Erica's beautiful face, steeling herself against the woman's talents. "Look, I'm not afraid of anything, all right? I just think we need to admit that this thing isn't working between us. That it hasn't been working for a while now. And just, just…"—she motioned in frustration—"move on."

Remy let the silence drag out as long as she could stand it. Reluctantly, she looked up again. Yep, there it was. Not a torrent, just a solitary tear. Bright in the glare of the kitchen's overhead light. Tracing a silken path down the curve of a very soft, very smooth cheek. The urge to reach over and brush it away was almost overwhelming. Remy wanted to use her lips to do it, and then her tongue. Inhaling deeply, she shook the thought from her mind. It would be the end of the discussion if she did that. And then they'd wake up naked a few hours later, Erica sated and nestled up against her, Remy bleary-eyed and defeated, furious with herself for having allowed it to happen again.

Determined not to give in, she watched and waited. The dull metallic clicks of the clock marked the widening gulf between them. Then finally, abruptly, Erica relented. "Well, okay then."

Remy felt her own eyes widen in surprise—before they quickly narrowed again in suspicion. She kept her mouth shut.

"I can see you've made up your mind." Erica's tone was suddenly light, almost brisk. "So I suppose there's no point in arguing about it any longer, is there?" Her features shifted into an easy, vaguely unsettling smile. Remy felt the elation of a runner at the end of a thousand-mile journey. Right before she steps off a cliff.

Erica stuck out her hand. "Friends?"

It was a trick. Erica Forsyte, U.S. Attorney, Northern District of California, had never given up on anything that easily in her life. No, she was merely shifting tactics. Staging a retreat in order to reevaluate and alter her line of attack. In a few days—or a couple of weeks at the outside—she'd be right back at it again, guns blazing. Remy knew this with a cold certainty only achieved in the smallest hours of the morning. But she was too goddamned tired to do anything about it now.

Drained, she leaned against the doorjamb and watched as Erica clicked down the stone pathway to the tree-lined street in front of the house. It was a dark and moonless night, but it might as well have been the middle of the day for all the energy coiled in that high-powered step.

Erica's vehicle chirped to life as she opened the driver's side door and slid gracefully into the sleek interior. Moments later, the engine awakened with a low rumble, and Erica paused to look back. She gave a small wave, then steered the car away from the curb and disappeared down the street.

Remy let the air escape from her lungs, her chest like an old deflating tire. Like she'd been holding her breath for hours and had only just realized there was fresh oxygen in the room. She threw the deadbolt on the door and headed for her bedroom at the back of the small house, closing windows and flipping off light switches along the way. She refused to allow herself one more glance at the clock. Her alarm was automatically set for five o'clock every morning—no need to fixate about how little time remained between now and then.

The sheets were crisp and blessedly cool when they struck her skin. The pillow still held the scent of jasmine. Erica's scent. Remy wondered groggily how long it would take the aroma to completely fade from her linens—and whether she was certain she really wanted it to. Erica was a gorgeous, intelligent woman who obviously cared a lot about her. It should have been as simple as that. And yet, for whatever reason, it wasn't.

As the night rose up to wrap in an ebon shroud around her, one of Remy's last coherent thoughts was to hope, and then doubt, that she and Erica could be friends. That, and a desperate prayer to the powers that be. That they grant her this night, for a few hours at least, a merciful and dreamless sleep.

He set the cereal bowl down with a thud, causing the spoon to clatter and the milk to slosh out on the table. There was no concentrating behind that incessant sniveling. He got up and crossed the room to the radiator and stood there staring down. He nudged at the flesh with the toe of his boot, then he squatted to check the bindings. The ankles were still snug, but the wrists had loosened up a bit. He yanked at the sheepshank to draw it tight again. Then he straightened and hawked a spit. He crossed the room and resumed his position in the recliner, but the whimpering sounds were louder now than before. He snatched up the remote and stabbed at the volume until the television noise swelled to fill the corners of the room. But he could still hear it. Chafing at him beneath the din. Mewling, like a polecat caught on a wire. He exhaled and dropped the remote on the table. Then he picked up the hunting blade and stood to cross the room again.

Remy snapped awake and sat upright, automatically reaching for her service pistol on the table next to the bed. She rested her hand on the firearm and waited, straining to hear anything besides the drum of her own heart in her ears. The bedroom was silent, as still and empty as the rest of the rooms beyond. If there had been anyone present in the small house with her, she would have sensed it immediately. But there was no one.

She blew out a breath and sank back against the cooling sheets. The remnants of the dream still played in a fading montage across her mind. The shabby room. Poorly lit and sparse with rundown furniture. The woman. Bound and gagged, with the man standing above her. The glint of the steel blade in his hand. Remy could never make out his face in the dream, nor that of the young woman who made those terrible, piteous noises. But she knew.

Samantha Kaye Willard was an elementary school teacher and mother of three. Her body had been discovered three months ago—nude, with its throat cut, in a dumpster in the Tenderloin district of San Francisco. Samantha Willard was 32 years old, coincidentally the same age as Remy, born in the same year and the same month, only a few days apart. Remy had started having the dreams a few days after they'd caught the case.

As of now, she and her partner Cookie were three months and eleven days into it. Three months and eleven days without a suspect. Three months and eleven days without a lead.

Remy glanced at her bedside clock and groaned. The glowing numerals read 4:58 a.m. She turned off the alarm before it could sound, slapping at the button harder than she needed to. Stiffly, she climbed out of bed. Unable to bear the thought of turning on a light, she squatted half naked and groped through the inky blackness of her closet, stepping into socks and sweatpants and running shoes as she happened upon them. Waking now, she made her way unerringly through the dark house. Splash of cold water in the bathroom, earbuds and house key by the front door.

Outside, the neighborhood still slept. Remy leaned on the railing of her front porch and gently stretched her calf muscles. The shadowy street lay empty in both directions. No movement. Barely a sound. She hit the play button on her phone, and Fatboy Slim's "Rockafeller Skank" struck up a throbbing chord in her ears. Bobbing her head in time, she cranked the volume a little higher, then skipped down the steps and headed up the street at a rapid clip.

CHAPTER TWO

Panting, Giana leaned her weight against the cardboard box and shoved. The heavy carton barely budged at first, but then it suddenly gave way with a gritty scrape across the concrete floor, nearly throwing her off balance with it. She should've taken Lena's advice and donated the damned books to the library. Someday, she'd learn to listen to her aunt, she really would.

Giana stepped back to catch her breath, surveying the wall of packing boxes that now rose from the floor to the ceiling of her aunt's garage. It was a humbling experience to look at the entirety of one's own life, wrapped in crumpled newspaper and tucked away in a corner.

A lump was beginning to form in Giana's throat when her aunt Lena strolled into the garage and stood beside her. With slender builds and dark, shoulder-length hair, the two women were carbon copies of one another, separated by thirty years. The older woman placed an arm around her niece's shoulder and squeezed. "It'll all be here waiting for you, sweetie. Whenever you decide you want to come back."

Giana exhaled and nodded. The truth was, she couldn't care less about the stuff in these boxes—it was her auntie she didn't know what she would do without.

As a child, Giana had shown the typical young girl's adoration for her father and her big brother, Tony. But it was her aunt who had always formed the true cornerstone of her universe. The closest thing to a mother she'd ever known, Lena was her best friend and her most loyal confidante. In a house dominated by strong-willed men, she was her biggest defender. When Giana had "gone away" to college at nearby U Penn, her aunt was the one who'd helped her decorate her dorm room. Four years later, when she'd moved off campus to complete her postgraduate work, Lena had helped her find an apartment. And then, some years after that—when Giana was devastated to discover that her fiancé was in fact a lying, conniving, shitheel of a cheat—it was Lena who'd been there to pick up the pieces.

"What about this one over here?" Lena kicked her toe at a lone open box, sitting apart from the rest.

Giana walked over and stared down at its contents. A scrapbook and various picture frames. David's favorite cable-knit sweater. A stuffed animal he'd won for her at the fair. All of them remnants of a life lived together. A life she had finally summoned the courage to leave behind.

"Oh, that," she finally answered. "That's all junk for the dumpster."

Lena nodded, her eyes on her niece's face. After a moment, she said, "You can do this, you know. Don't be afraid. You got this, kid."

Giana nodded vigorously, blinking against the sting in her eyes. She was no longer a kid, far from it. But Lena's use of the old endearment suddenly made her want to weep.

"Come on." Lena gave her shoulder a final squeeze. "Your brother is on his way over here. If you want anything at all to eat, you'd better get in there now."

The women abandoned the gloom of the garage for Lena's sun-filled kitchen, where Giana settled herself in her customary spot at the dinette by the window. Her aunt mounded steaming piles of food onto her plate, and Giana beamed her gratitude.

All of her favorites were represented. A fluffy egg frittata with pesto, olives, and roasted red peppers. Mini Italian sausages, succulent and sweet, tucked inside of rosemary-scented bread rolls. But what nearly brought her to tears for the second time that morning were the *cornetti al miele*—those classic homemade pastries only her auntie seemed to know how to properly bake.

Warm and flaky, the *cornetti* from Lena's oven were infused with honey and love. They were normally reserved for Christmas dinner or Easter Sunday or some other very special occasion as that. Giana supposed her last meal at her auntie's house—on her last day in the only city she'd ever known—certainly fit the category.

She could hardly believe it, but it was finally about to happen. Whether she was truly ready for it or not. She'd sold her car last week and handed in the keys to her apartment this morning. By this afternoon, she'd be on her way to the airport. Off to the West Coast to start a new career and a new life in a town where she knew exactly one person. It was either the bravest or the stupidest thing she'd ever done, and she never would have had the nerve to even try it without her aunt's support.

The screen door leading to the backyard opened and shut with a bang as a massive body in a dark blue uniform eclipsed the doorway. The grinning giant crossed the small kitchen in one stride, leaning down to give his aunt a peck on the cheek. In another stride, he'd reached the kitchen table.

"Anthony." Giana nodded a greeting.

"Squirt!" Tony grunted in reply. He reached out a huge paw to ruffle her hair, as if she were still six years old and in pigtails. Giana ducked her head in annoyance. She watched over the rim of her coffee cup, mildly impressed as her brother managed to seat his bulky frame at the cramped little table without upsetting any of the glassware on top.

With a sigh, he shifted his gun belt to a more comfortable position. "You still got time to change your mind, you know." He was about to say more, but his attention was quickly waylaid by the small mountain of food Lena set down in front of him. He grabbed a fork and began to attack it before the plate had fully come to rest.

Their aunt seated herself at the table with them and joined in on the meal. For several minutes, the only sound in the room was the scrape of forks against plates. Anthony finally paused to take a slurp from his coffee cup, his eyes homing in on Giana once again.

"So, Squirt," he said with a lazy drawl. "You come to your senses yet? It's not too late to save yourself the embarrassment, you know. Maybe you can get a refund on that plane ticket you bought. So this whole fiasco doesn't turn out to be a waste of time *and* money."

Giana took a sip of coffee and gave her brother a contemplative stare. Then she returned her attention to her breakfast plate. Tony was trying to bait her, but she wasn't going to bite. Not today. In the end, she supposed it must be difficult for him. Finally being forced to face the fact that, after so many years of blind devotion, his baby sister was now an adult and no longer subject to his influence. If he wanted to spend her last meal at home taking potshots, so be it. She wasn't going to participate.

Giana took another bite of her *cornetto* and released a small sigh. It was still warm. She gave a nod of acknowledgment to the cook, and Lena gave her an approving wink in return.

Anthony watched the two women ignoring him. He snorted and shook his head. "I can't believe Pop is really gonna let you do this," he grumbled. "He could've got you a job in two seconds flat. Right here in the department. You know that, right?"

Eyes flashing, Giana set her fork down with a clank. "I guess it still hasn't occurred to you that maybe I don't *want* a job right here in the department. And Daddy's not *letting* me do anything. I don't need his permission to decide where I'm going to live, Tony. And I certainly don't need yours."

So much for calm detachment.

The two of them stared each other down, neither wanting to be the first to look away. Giana knew what rankled her brother the most, even more than her moving away, was the fact that he'd been shut out of the decision-making process altogether. It rankled the Chief too, but at least her father was trying to make his peace with it now. The men in her family had grown far too accustomed to being in charge of things for far too long. It was one of the reasons she'd applied for a job on the opposite side of the country. Nor did it hurt that there'd be zero chance of running into her ex-fiancé if she were three thousand miles away.

Lena cleared her throat. This was their aunt's unsubtle directive to cease and desist. "So, Anthony," she said mildly. "How are Grace and the kids?"

Tony stubbornly eyed his sister for several seconds longer before he finally glanced at his aunt. He shoveled another forkful of food into his mouth and mumbled around it. "Good. Junior just made All-City for the second year running. And Petey is just killing it in Little League. That kid's a monster."

Of course, Giana thought. Always the boys. She would never doubt her brother's love for each one of his children, but she knew what it was like to grow up the only girl in a household full of males. Giana was therefore her niece's most committed champion, and it pained her to know she would now have to fill that role from afar. "What about Chloe?" she interrupted. "I heard she went out for soccer tryouts the other day."

"Soccer?" Judging by the look on his face, this was the first Tony had heard about it. And he clearly wasn't sure if he liked the idea or not.

Giana suppressed a smile. Tony's wife Grace had a way of simplifying the most complicated situations. She'd learned years ago how to manage her husband—and their entire family unit, for that matter—exactly the way she saw fit. The only one who didn't realize this was Tony.

The screen door opened and banged shut again, and Giana started, surprised to see her father standing in the doorway. The Chief was only a slightly smaller version of his son, with grayer hair and a dark blue suit in place of the uniform. Joseph P. Falco, chief inspector of the Philadelphia PD, hadn't been required to wear a badge in years, but Giana suspected he wouldn't have minded.

When it came to suits, the man's imagination was limited to navy blue or charcoal gray—invariably paired with a starched white shirt and understated tie. This was her dad's uniform of choice, and her myriad attempts over the years to liven his wardrobe with the bold splash of a printed tie or the whimsy of a paisley pocket square had done nothing to change that. She imagined there was a drawer somewhere crammed full of these rejects. Like an abandoned pirate's chest, with colorful bits of fabric for booty.

"What are you doing here, Daddy?" Giana was out of her chair and into her father's arms. "I thought you had to be downtown today."

"What, and miss my girl's big send-off?" he rumbled. "Not on your life." Chief Falco's reputation in the Philly police force was based less on his charm than on his formidable bearing—though he did possess the former in spades. These fine qualities, combined with an iron resolve, had all but guaranteed his meteoric rise in the department.

Giana stepped back and inspected her father now with atypical clarity. She noted his thinning hair and the slight paunch around his middle. The creases that had always sprung like starbursts from the corners of his eyes were deeper than she remembered. She reached up and hugged him again, her throat tightening as she tried to process the full weight of his looming absence.

The Chief returned Giana's embrace, holding on tight until she let go of him first, and this made her want to cry for the third time that morning. She watched as he removed his suit jacket and carefully picked his way around the crowded dinette, ultimately sandwiching himself in next to his son. The two large men looked like a pair of mischievous grownups raiding the children's table for make-believe tea. Lena produced a fourth plate, as amply apportioned as the others, and the Chief joined the feeding frenzy.

Conversation bubbled around the table, and she took a moment to sit and quietly observe. The picture was complete. Flawed or not, these were her people, and this was her home. And yet, she was choosing to leave it.

She reached for another *cornetto*. She resolved to silence the doubts that niggled at the back of her mind—at least for the duration of this meal. It was the last chance she'd have for a long while to simply enjoy her family's company, and she vowed to make the most of it. A few hours from now she'd be boarding a flight to San Francisco. There'd be plenty of time for angst, ambivalence, and everlasting regret once she got on the plane.

CHAPTER THREE

Remy tipped her head back and drained the last disappointing dregs of her latte. She took aim at the waste bin in the corner and sent the paper cup flying. It clipped the rim of the can and hit the floor with a hollow thud. Two extra shots of espresso, and the fog on her brain had barely lifted. Rising from her desk with a lazy stretch, she bent to scoop the cup off the floor, depositing it in the bin on her way out into the corridor. She paused in front of the open door labeled Insp. A.P. Cook and peered inside. Her partner's office was as cramped and cluttered as her own—and at the moment unoccupied.

Remy's bootsteps rang hollow through the barren corridors of Homicide Division, each one as starkly lit as the last. She reached the main floor and found Cookie waiting for her at the coffee station, propped against the counter, a steaming mug of java cradled in his beefy brown hands. He watched her approach, his examination brief but incisive as one eyebrow inched upward in his rounded face. "How's it hangin' there, boss?"

Remy nodded and gave the question some thought while she went for the coffeepot at his elbow. She hadn't heard a word from Erica in ten days—not that she was counting. She'd been eating right, for the most part. And getting plenty of exercise. And she'd managed to get herself to bed by eleven o'clock every night for a week straight. The dreams notwithstanding, she was in pretty good shape. She was exhausted, of course, but that was beside the point.

"I guess I can't complain," she answered. She filled her coffee mug and waited for Cookie's standard response.

"Wouldn't do you any good if you did," he muttered.

Remy gave him a tired smile and took a sip of the scalding, flavorless brew. This was the point where they would normally hash out their plan for the day. The various calls to be made, which interviews to pursue, what leads to run down. But neither of them was very eager to jump right into it.

There was still no break in the Willard case. Samantha had disappeared on the morning of January 23 during her routine jog in the suburban town of Pleasanton. Six days later, she was found in a dumpster behind a Chinese food restaurant in San Francisco. The body bore indications of sexual assault, with ligature marks about the neck, wrists, and ankles. Notably absent were fingerprints, bodily fluids, or DNA matter of any kind other than that of the victim. Cause of death: a complete severing of the external jugular veins.

The husband's alibi was airtight, and a thorough canvassing of the neighborhood had turned up nothing out of the ordinary. It was three months and three weeks now without a lead. As much as they hated to admit it, Remy and Cookie were nearly resigned to the fact that the case would go cold.

Remy shifted and leaned her tall frame against the counter. At five foot eleven, she was shoulder to shoulder with Cookie. She took another sip of the bland coffee and winced. "Did you make this?"

"Anything from your ballbreaker yet?" Cookie shot back.

Remy eyed him over the rim of her coffee mug. No sense of humor this morning, obviously. And starting right in on Erica like that. Things must be on the rocks again with the wife and kids.

Remy injected into her tone a confidence she didn't feel. "Nope, no. Not a peep. I think this time it's gonna stick." She paused and forced herself to hold his gaze. Cookie had a way of dissecting people with a placid stare. Right now, he was taking Remy apart, and she felt her shoulders rising under the scrutiny. "What? I told you, the breakup is amicable, all right?"

Partners for almost four years now, Remy and Cookie had initially accepted their assignment together with a guarded professionalism. Over time, that reserve had mellowed into a deep and abiding admiration for one another—one that was rooted in genuine affection.

But it had taken some time to get there. Remy was senior to Cookie in both age and experience, and his habit of calling her "boss" let her know he was conscious of that fact. Even now, he was reluctant to comment much about her personal life, including the women she dated. Apparently, however, when it came to the assistant DA, he was willing to make an exception. There Cookie had abandoned his code of silence with a single unambiguous recommendation: "Boss, don't shit where you eat."

It was the first rule of the homicide detective. Cases didn't get solved by running down leads and gathering evidence alone—you had to see the thing through to the end. That was the whole point, after all. Without a conviction, an investigator's sweat and pain and due diligence were so much piss in the wind, and the district attorney's office was the final, most vital element in that equation.

Everybody knew about the pugnacious ADA with the killer legs and even more impressive conviction rate. Erica Forsyte sank her teeth into a perp and didn't let go. Not until he'd given up his contacts, his associates, and his friends—plus *their* entire crews and anyone else who'd ever had the misfortune of meeting the guy. Forsyte was a rising star, and she had the pull to bring a case to a swift and lawful conclusion—or to send it to the bottom of the pile, never to see the light of day again. Suffice it to say, you didn't want to get on the lady's bad side.

Remy glanced at her partner's brooding face, struggling to come up with the right thing to say to put his mind at ease. She knew he worked just as hard and had just as much invested in the cases they handled together. It was unacceptable to think of any one of them withering on the vine because of something so mundane as a jilted ex-girlfriend.

Erica Forsyte might be a ballbuster, but she was a professional above all else. The woman couldn't have gotten where she was by indulging in petty bullshit. No. Erica would move on, and this thing would blow over. Devereux and Cook would get back to solving cases, and the DA's office would do its level best to convict them. Remy had faith. She just needed to convince her partner of that.

"Cookie, look—" she began, but he abruptly cut her off.

"I think it's worth taking another run at the Jenssen woman before we let go of that thread."

It was a deliberate subject change, and she paused to analyze Cookie's expression. She could see the Erica Forsyte discussion was far from over—he'd just decided to shelve it for now. Fine. She was more than happy to let the matter drop. Even if the alternative was broaching the dreaded Willard case. "You think so? I don't know. I'm beginning to think the woman's a ghost."

Said ghost was one Rhonda Jenssen. On the day the Willard body was discovered, Jenssen had appeared in the Tenderloin police station with a story to tell. She claimed she'd been present when the body was dumped—which, if true, made her the number one witness in the case.

The processing officer on shift at the time was some greenhorn just months out of the academy. He'd left the witness unattended while he attempted to track down Devereux or Cook. In the meantime, Jenssen had simply walked out of the station, never to be seen or heard from again.

The officer's all-illuminating recollection was as follows: female Caucasian, middle-aged, possibly homeless. Brown eyes. Brown hair. Medium height and weight. It was a description fitting roughly one fifth of the population of the Tenderloin.

"Ghost or not, it's all we got," Cookie pointed out. "I say we hit the pavement down there again. Maybe check out that soup kitchen on Turk and—"

He stopped and tightened his grip on his coffee mug, just in time to catch a mock punch to the gut from Nicholas Pierce. The man had appeared like a whack-a-mole at Cookie's side. Pierce continued his attack, feinting an uppercut to the jaw, even providing his own whooshing noises for effect. Remy stifled a yawn.

"Too slow, Cooks. You're still way too slow." Pierce's face was overly tanned, his teeth a polished neon white. He barely acknowledged Remy's presence, tossing her a curt nod before he turned his back to give Cookie his full attention. "You still holding out for them beloved Warriors? I got twenty bucks says they're gonna get spanked tonight."

"Man, please. You still owe me for that game last week."

The banter continued, and Remy sipped from her coffee mug, watching the pair of them with mild disinterest. Pierce's icy demeanor toward her was typical—although some years ago, when she was the newest female face at Homicide Division, he'd taken a decidedly different approach. The charm had been cranked up to full wattage then. And he'd kept at it with a kind of dogged determination she normally would've admired. If it hadn't given her the creeps.

The man simply could not take a hint. Finally—exasperated after one too many come-ons—she was forced to spell it out for him, explaining he might actually have a better shot at drawing her interest if he shaved his legs and put on a pair of heels. Pierce had failed to see the humor.

Remy studied him now, noting his expensive haircut and the slim, form-fitting trousers. Pierce reached out to goose Cookie in the armpit, and she shook her head at the irony of their homoerotic play. She reached around them for the coffeepot, intent on topping off her mug and returning to her office. She'd catch up with Cookie later—after juvenile hour was over.

"Look alive, people!" Captain Bronson's throaty bark echoed down the corridor. Remy had to fight the urge to snap to attention at the sound of it. Cookie and Pierce paused in their antics as well, and the three of them stood in silence as Bronson approached, their gazes fixed not on their boss, but on the beautiful stranger who strode alongside him.

Bombarded with multiple impressions at once, Remy struggled to take it all in. Massive, sparkling green eyes. Thick sable hair, curling loosely at the shoulders. Olive skin and a full, voluptuous mouth. Stunning was the only word that came to mind, and even that seemed woefully inadequate. Mesmerized, she watched as the woman drew closer, transfixed by her flaring hips and shapely, athletic thighs. She easily kept pace with the captain's loping strides, although the heels on her feet had to be four inches high, at least.

Bronson and his companion halted in front of them, and for a moment nobody spoke. The captain cleared his throat. "I'd like you all to meet our latest addition in Forensics next door. This is Dr. Giana Falco, from Philadelphia."

Remy pried her gaze away from the woman to briefly glance at the captain. The older man's watery blue eyes were more animated than usual. "Dr. Falco," he continued, "these three characters here are Inspectors Devereux, Cook, and Pierce. On a few rare occasions, you might actually find them conducting a little police work around the division."

The woman, Dr. Falco, stepped forward and looked directly at her, and the air emptied out of Remy's lungs. "Please, call me Giana."

Giana. The husk in her voice was like a warm blanket. Remy nodded stiffly and held out her hand, supplying her own forename in what she hoped was a normal voice. Giana's grip was warm and firm. Her smile was dazzling. The nerve endings danced in Remy's palm long after the contact was broken, and she realized with a sinking sensation that she was in trouble. Even as Pierce sidled forward and blasted his thousand-watt grin.

Remy watched Giana's gaze skim over his muscular torso, lingering briefly at the trim waistline, flitting back up to his face to lock eyes a millisecond longer than necessary. The exchange was discreet, but it didn't take a detective. Nick was a good-looking guy, and this woman was clearly straight, clearly not an option. At least not for Remy.

The realization should have come as a relief—the last thing she wanted or needed at this point was another romantic entanglement. And yet, she couldn't explain the profound sense of disappointment that settled over her like a pall.

Suddenly annoyed—and then confused by her annoyance— Remy could barely wait for the introductions to finish. "Well, I'm swamped," she said abruptly. "Better get to it." Giana's green eyes were on her again, like a tractor beam holding her in place. "Uh, it was nice meeting you, Giana. Welcome to San Francisco."

Without waiting for a reply, she spun on her heel and narrowly avoided a collision with Cookie. Smoothly recovering, she set a brisk pace in the direction of her office, focused entirely on the complex and challenging task of placing one foot safely in front of the other.

CHAPTER FOUR

Giana dropped her keys in the glass bowl by the front door and headed for her bedroom, kicking off her heels as she went. There was nothing she wanted more than a glass of red wine and some mellow jazz music on the stereo. And soft, stretchy yoga pants to curl up in. After a quick change in the bedroom, she padded in her stocking feet to the kitchen to open a bottle of cabernet. Moments later, she sank into the couch with a grateful sigh just as the sun was beginning to set outside the enormous bay windows.

The view from Liz's living room was simply not to be believed. Sea gulls dove and rose above the glassy water, and in the distance the white sails of pleasure boats littered the inlet like confetti.

When she'd accepted the invitation to move into her college roommate's spare bedroom, Giana never imagined the place would be as spectacular as this. She glanced around at the high ceilings and vast windows that inundated the space with natural light. The furnishings were tasteful and well designed. The art pieces were sparse but carefully chosen.

Giana was happy to see that she and Liz still shared a penchant for the vibrant works of Pollock and Chagall. Art history was the sole class they had taken together as undergrads. She'd ended up minoring in the subject, she'd loved it so much.

With a contented sigh, she nestled deeper into the couch, running her hand over the supple leather. Liz had been far too modest about her success. She'd just completed a residency at SF General Hospital, which was an incredible achievement in itself, but when they'd spoken on the phone a few months ago, she'd barely even mentioned the fact. And she'd sounded almost apologetic when she'd confessed that her new condo was actually located in Oakland, instead of San Francisco. The difference in cost of living between the two cities was too great to ignore, she'd explained. And Oakland was actually a hidden gem—the best kept secret in the Bay. If you didn't mind crossing the bridge to get to work every day.

Giana hadn't needed much convincing. She didn't know the first thing about the Bay Area, so she was hardly in a position to be choosey. More importantly, it had been years since she and Liz were truly close. This was a rare opportunity, maybe their only chance, to rekindle an old friendship that had once meant a lot to both of them.

That was the idea, anyway. In the six weeks since Giana had relocated to California, she'd seen Liz only a handful of times. The work schedule of an emergency room physician was preposterous. Weekends, graveyards, 24-hour shifts—any combination of the above was routine. Liz and she were like two ships passing in the night, rarely crossing paths at the apartment for longer than a few minutes at a time.

It was hardly Liz's fault, and Giana was careful not to take it personally. She'd harbored no illusions that they'd be able to just pick up where they left off. But being this close, literally sharing the same living space, and still seeing so little of each other made her miss her friend all the more.

She took a sip of cabernet and resisted the urge to go melancholy. All things considered, she was proud of herself. It was a pretty gutsy maneuver, coming out here the way that she'd done. And she was learning to live with the loneliness. Social media helped, of course. She didn't feel completely cut off from the family back home. Almost daily, it seemed, there was a new action shot posted of her little niece in her soccer uniform. Most surprising of all, the shutterbug had turned out to be none other than the girl's father. Giana chuckled softly. Maybe there was hope for Tony yet.

She glanced at the clock and wondered if it was too late to call the East Coast. Truth was, she knew her aunt would always pick up the phone, no matter what time it was. Giana reached for her cell phone but paused at the sound of a key turning in the lock. The front door swung open and in strode Elizabeth Talbot, as buoyant and crackling with energy as the day they'd first met twelve years ago.

Unable to tame the grin on her face, Giana gasped, "Oh, my God. I think I must be seeing a ghost!"

"Oh, my God. Look at this gorgeous, fantabulous apparition in my living room!" Flopping down on the couch, Liz gave Giana a kiss and a hug. In the next moment, she was on her feet again. "Where'd you stash the bottle?" She disappeared from the room before Giana could answer, returning in an instant with the wine bottle and a glass for herself. "Holy Christmas, what a day!"

Amused, and then in equal parts horrified and impressed, Giana sat back and listened to the trials and tribulations of life in the emergency room of SF General Hospital. As narrated by Dr. Elizabeth Talbot, it was a far more entertaining tale than anything she could have watched on television.

Little had changed about Liz since their undergraduate days. Back then, Giana had looked on in awe as her roommate juggled an impossible load of premed courses, sports, and extracurriculars. Not to mention a near-constant stream of romantic adventures. Liz's tastes in that department were far-ranging, and Giana had witnessed a startling array of lovers—both male and female—find their way in and out of her roomie's bed. The woman had always seemed to draw on a bottomless store of energy, packed somewhere deep within her diminutive frame. Whenever they were together Giana couldn't help but wish that just a little of that stardust might rub off on herself.

"What about you? How's it going over there in that big fancy crime lab of yours?" Liz was abruptly on to the next topic. "Please tell me there's a hunky science geek or two lying around to distract you from all of those boring beakers and slides."

Giana snorted. True, a forensics laboratory was about as far as one could get from the pandemonium of a hospital ER. An action junkie like Liz would calcify from boredom in an hour. For her, however, it was exactly the right speed. The gentle hum of perfectly calibrated equipment. The quiet, focused intensity of expert technicians going about their work. The forensics lab was a temple to her—an inner sanctum that Liz could never understand.

"Hmm, hunky science geeks, eh? Let me think…" Despite her initial anxieties, the cadre of new coworkers Giana had landed amongst had turned out to be lovely people. Socially awkward perhaps, but lovely people nonetheless. Not one of them, however, even approached the category of hunky. "Yeah, no," she admitted finally. "Apparently, it's 'no hunks allowed' in that particular establishment. But not to worry. My boss asked me out a few weeks ago." She grimaced.

"You're kidding." Liz's nose wrinkled.

"Sadly, I'm not. Well, he's actually the lab's lead analyst, so *technically*, he's only my supervisor. But still. He tried to make it sound all very casual and off-handed. I said no, obviously, and it's been a little awkward between us since."

"Well, you can't blame the poor man for trying. I mean, look at you." Liz put a hand on Giana's arm. "You've never looked better, by the way. What the hell have you been doing with yourself?"

She laughed, shrugging. "Well, I've been running a lot. But truthfully, I think it's all of this fine wine and California sunshine." They clinked their glasses together at that.

"Well, if you're ready to get out there, just say the word," Liz offered breezily. "There's plenty of strapping young interns at the hospital I can send your way. Of course, I can't guarantee that I haven't already sampled the goods myself. So there's that."

Giana groaned. "Um, gee thanks, but I think I'll pass. I do appreciate the offer, though. But speaking of strapping young men, I did meet a detective in the homicide department next door. He's quite the physical specimen, I have to say. I think you'd be impressed. Now, *he's* asked me out, like, four times."

"Oh, really!" Liz's big blue eyes grew even wider in her pretty face. "Do tell! Have you said yes? Is he really really hot? Tell me."

"Oh, I don't know." She waved a hand. "I mean, yes. To be honest, he's ridiculously hot. Chiseled jawline. Dark, brooding eyes. Muscles on top of his muscles. He has this cocky sideways grin that seems to be surgically attached to his face. You'd like him."

"Mmm, sounds like I would," Liz agreed. "Well, what's the holdup? Don't tell me—he's married, right?" Her shoulders dropped.

"No, no, he's single. Or at least he says he is." Giana cut her a sidelong glance, and they shared a knowing look. "I don't know why I haven't said yes. I just…I don't know."

"What don't you know?" Liz looked genuinely mystified. "How long has it been now since Fuckface, I mean David, was in the picture?"

Giana snorted into her wineglass.

"Seriously," Liz continued. "Don't you think it's time you had a little fun? A gorgeous sexy policeman wants to take you out to dinner. Tell me what's wrong with *that* picture."

Giana shook her head, smiling at her friend. In Liz's mind, some things really were just that uncomplicated.

Liz reached over and placed a hand on her knee. "I'm not even kidding, honey. Really, has there been anybody since David?" She paused in the face of Giana's silence. "Okay, I'm going to take that as a no. Seriously, sweetie, as a woman and a physician, I have to tell you—you're facing a real medical risk here. Serious complications have been known to result from a prolonged lack of sex. A girl has needs. And, well, you gotta keep those joints lubricated. So to speak. And…"

"Oh, will you stop it?" Giana stifled a laugh, trying not to encourage her. "I just got here, all right? I have this brand-new job. In this brand-new city. These are big, big life changes going on here. The last thing I need right now is to get wrapped up in something romantic."

"Who said anything about romance?"

Giana threw her head back and groaned. "Oh my God, *where* do you come from?"

"Outer space," Liz responded. "Quite naturally."

"Clearly. Besides, even if I *were* looking for someone—which I'm not—I doubt a guy like Nick Pierce would be my first choice."

"Yeah, you're right. A mindless romp with a gorgeous sexy bad boy is the last thing anybody would want. Especially you. I know how much you hate fun."

"Excuse me? What exactly is *that* supposed to mean?"

Liz's mouth dropped open. "Oh, come on, Gee. First, there was Saint Peter, whom you dated for three, almost four, interminable years at Penn. Nice guy, I'll give you that. But let's face it, Mr. Personality he was not. And then came fuckface David, who, apart from his illicit sex life, seemed about as interesting to me as dryer lint. No offense." She shook her head, reaching for the wine bottle. "Ugh. I still can't believe that sneaky little dweeb had the nerve to cheat on you."

Giana held out her glass for a refill. "You know what? When it comes to David, things really did work out for the best. He could've waited until after we were married to do what he did. I dodged a gigantic bullet there, and I'm grateful. Just think of all the money I've saved on divorce attorneys alone." They clinked glasses again.

"And it's true," she continued, "I do tend to go for the quiet type, but so what? It doesn't mean I hate fun. Jesus. Just because I'm not running out to find the next pain in the ass in my life. Frankly, Lizard, you wound me."

"I'm sorry, Gee." Liz looked anything but apologetic. "But I know you know what I mean."

"You know what? This might seem like a bizarre concept to you, but I don't think it's necessary to sleep with half the county to feel entertained. Sometimes it's nice to just hang out with a friend once in a while. You should try it."

Giana saw the hurt look flash across Liz's face. "Oh, sweetie, no. I didn't mean it to sound like that. I just miss you, that's all. Look, I know you're a busy girl, and I totally get it. We'll see each other when we can. All I'm trying to say is, at this point in my life, I'd rather focus my energy on meaningful connections. Platonic ones. And nothing more complicated than that."

Liz was easily mollified. "Yeah. I totally get that. I'd be happy to introduce you to some of my pals, but they're all doctors and nurses with insanely busy schedules like mine."

Giana chuckled. "Of course they are. Actually, I did meet a new friend a few weeks back. At the same time I met Mr. Hunk in Homicide. She's a detective too—or inspector, I guess. Whatever they call them here. Anyway, we seem to keep bumping into each other. I've been trying to get to know her a little better, but so far, she seems a bit shy. Or reluctant, maybe. I'm not sure which."

"And yet, you think she's worth the effort." Liz's eyebrows bobbed suggestively. "Well, is *she* hot, at least?"

Giana rolled her eyes at the insinuation. "Yes. I mean, not yes she's hot, but yes I think she's worth the effort. Not that she *isn't* hot, of course. I mean, I suppose I *would* find her attractive, if I were into women. She has these gray eyes. Like a wolf's eyes, you know? And it's like, they just look right through you. I've never met anyone with eyes like that before. They're really quite beautiful. Even if it is a little unnerving to have to stand there while she's staring at you and just, like, peeling away the layers."

Giana exhaled and propped her elbow on the back of the couch. "Anyway." She glanced at Liz. "What?"

Liz shrugged, a smirk playing at the corners of her mouth. "Nothing."

"No, seriously. What?"

"I don't know," Liz said with a laugh. "You seem sort of... infatuated, I guess."

"Infatuated? Not at all. I mean, she seems like an interesting person, if that's what you mean. It's, like, she's got this quiet, slightly intimidating exterior? But at the same time, you can sort of tell she's just a big pussycat. She's, um…"—Giana also believed Remy Devereux was a lesbian, but she was suddenly disinclined to mention that fact to Liz—"she's, um…she's very tall. I just think we could be friends, that's all."

Liz stared at her a moment longer, then shrugged. "Well, then. Maybe you should ask her out for drinks. What could go wrong?"

"Maybe I will," Giana answered. They both nodded firmly and held each other's gazes. Giana chuckled softly. It was obvious little had changed between them in the years they'd spent apart. And that was a very good thing indeed.

After a moment, she stretched and unfolded herself from the couch. "Are you hungry at all? I could whip us up something to eat."

"Oh my God, I thought you'd never ask. I'm absolutely famished." Liz sprang off the couch. "I'll do my part and open another bottle of wine."

CHAPTER FIVE

The high-pitched squeal of rubber tires against polished concrete floors echoed in the garage. Remy swung her Audi into a parking space near the elevators and climbed out of the car, balancing a carryout tray of coffee drinks in one hand. She slung her satchel across her chest and began a weaving journey through the rows of parked vehicles, heading away from the Justice Building's entrance to the far side of the garage. A single elevator stood there, servicing the South Annex and Forensics. Using it was a detour that took Remy easily ten minutes out of her way. She'd stopped asking herself weeks ago why she continued to do it.

The ancient lift groaned to life when she hit the call button, trundling upward from the bowels of the building. The doors rattled open, and she stepped inside and reflexively inhaled, sampling the air for clues like the ace detective she was.

On some mornings, the car was redolent with a balanced blend of spice and flowers and soft woody notes. That meant Dr. Giana Falco had already come and gone, and Remy would have to start her day without their brief but witty repartee to dwell on. This morning, however, she was greeted only with the faint must of machine oil and cigarettes. Which meant there was still a chance.

The relic of a transport carried her only one level up before it lurched to a halt again. The doors slid open, and Giana Falco bustled into the car.

"Oh! Well, good morning."

"Uh, hi." Remy quickly stepped to one side to make room, though the space was scarcely bigger than a phone booth.

"We have to stop meeting like this." Giana's smile was devastating.

Remy returned it briefly and then found something else to look at. Namely, the cracks in the linoleum flooring. "Yeah. I guess we've been keeping the same hours lately."

"I guess we have." Giana nodded at the coffee. "Ooh, I'm jealous. I was running late this morning and didn't have time to stop."

"Triple soy latte, no foam, extra hot." Remy lifted the tray. "Take that one. I'm sure my partner won't mind. He drinks too much coffee anyway."

Giana burst into laughter. "I couldn't possibly. But it's very sweet of you to offer."

"Suit yourself." She could feel the grin spreading across her own face. The woman's laugh was musical and totally contagious. And she smelled amazing.

In a brutally short amount of time, the elevator came to a final stop. Remy's hand shot out to hold the doors open as Giana exited. In the hallway they turned in opposite directions, though she was less than eager to begin the long and arduous trek down the tunnel toward Homicide. "Well, it was nice to see you again. Have a good day."

"You too," Giana answered brightly. "Um, hey. Hang on a second…"

Remy's stomach dropped. She halted and turned back to face the woman.

"I was wondering…" Giana continued slowly. The sudden blush suffusing her features was unmistakable—and totally irresistible. "You wouldn't want to meet me for a drink after work sometime, would you? I mean, I don't know that many people here, and I thought it might be nice to hang out and chat a little. If you wanted to."

Remy blinked twice, then gave a half shrug. "I'm free tonight, if that works for you." She smiled tightly, stunned by her own response. Her right hand betrayed her, moving of its own volition to fish around in the side pocket of her satchel. It pulled out a business card and handed it over. "My cell number's on there," she heard herself say. "Give me a buzz, and I'll text you back with the address of a place I know."

Judging by her mildly startled expression, Giana hadn't anticipated such a response either. "Great, uh, fabulous," she said. "Well, I guess I'll see you later today, then."

"Yeah. Great. I'll see you later today."

They both waved simultaneously and turned to part ways. Giana soon disappeared around a corner, but the click of her heels echoed in Remy's ears long afterward. She kept her mind carefully blank as she continued her winding trek to the division offices. She was having drinks with a colleague today after work. It was a perfectly common thing to do. Perfectly normal.

Cookie's head was bowed over a crisp new file folder when Remy finally set the lukewarm latte down on his desk. He placed his fingers against the side of the cup to test the temperature, then glanced up at her with an accusing frown.

Remy's shoulders came up in a shrug. "What do you want? I got held up."

Cookie snorted softly and returned his attention to the folder in front of him.

"Hey, is that the coroner on Everett?"

Cookie nodded, and Remy turned and left his office without another word. In a few quick strides she'd covered the distance to her own office, powering on the computer and typing in her password as she rounded the corner of her desk. She located the report in her inbox and hit the print button, which brought the machine in the corner whirring to life. In the meantime, she rooted through her satchel and pulled out a hard copy of the Everett case file.

Lisa Everett, a sixteen-year-old resident of Pinole, had been reported missing by her parents the previous Friday, the evening of June eighth. The body was discovered three days later at a construction site in the Mission Bay district of San Francisco. As of now, the working hypothesis was abduction, likely as the teen made her way to school that Friday morning in the relatively small community of Pinole.

Another Caucasian female, taken from an outlying suburb and dumped in the city—with no witnesses and little to no trace evidence recovered from the body. These broad similarities to the unsolved Willard case were hard to ignore, but both Remy and Cookie were trained to resist the temptation to jump to conclusions. The victims differed in age by almost twenty years. Their socioeconomic statuses were similar, but while the towns of Pinole and Pleasanton were roughly equidistant to San Francisco, they could hardly be considered in the same vicinity to each other.

She flipped through the pages of the file and located a photo, which was obviously the girl's class portrait. Lisa Everett was pretty. She looked older than her sixteen years, with clear skin and almond-shaped eyes. And long, dark hair like the Willard woman.

She crossed the room to collect the pages off the printer. The coroner placed time of death at somewhere between eight p.m. and midnight on Sunday, June tenth. Whoever had taken the girl had kept her alive through the weekend. She made a mental note to go back and check the time frame on the Willard woman. Similar to Willard, the Everett girl bore ligature marks about the neck, wrists, and ankles. There were indications of rape and a complete absence of unattributed bodily fluids—also consistent with Willard.

But there the similarities ended. The girl's body was left clothed, while the woman's was not. The teen's official cause of death was hypoxia—the hyoid bone being fractured, with non-specific bruising about the neck indicative of barehanded strangulation. Remy didn't need to pull out the Willard file to recall that the young teacher was nearly decapitated. These were two distinctly different modi operandi. But was that enough to preclude a connection?

"What do you think?" Cookie stood leaning against the doorframe, hands dug deep in his pockets.

She exhaled. "I don't know. Could be." They stared at each other, neither of them eager to embrace the idea. It was beyond unsettling to think that they might have a series on their hands. And linking the two cases wouldn't necessarily get them any closer to solving them. Worst of all, if it truly was a series, this was likely just the beginning.

"The parents are asking to set up a day to come in," Cookie said. "You wanna handle that, or you want me to do it?"

"I'll do it," Remy said.

Cookie nodded, clearly relieved.

"And I'll take the construction foreman, too," she added. "Thought I'd head out there this morning and have a word."

"I guess that means I'm on my way to Pinole."

"Afraid so." Remy watched him frown. "Or I could take Pinole and you can take the parents. If you want."

Cookie turned without a word and disappeared down the hallway.

* * *

Giana glanced at the clock on the laboratory wall for the third time in as many minutes. Almost time to go. She sealed the chamber on the chromatograph and programmed the last analysis of the day, reminding herself to concentrate on what she was doing. A bubble of excitement had formed in her belly hours ago and refused to go away. She shook her head, embarrassed by how revved up she'd become at the idea of a couple of drinks with a new friend. Clearly, she needed to get out more. Facebook and phone calls back home just weren't cutting it.

"See you tomorrow, Giana." Curtis Mason waved at her on his way out the door. "Don't stay too late. And can you kill the lights for me when you leave?"

"Sure thing, Curtis. And don't worry, I'm right behind you," she called back, relieved that they seemed to be putting the awkwardness behind them at last.

She punched the final sequence into the control panel and left the machine humming while she tidied up her workstation. It was flattering to know that Curtis had thought enough about her to ask her out. But accepting was simply out of the question. Apart from the dubious propriety of dating one's supervisor, she didn't find the man remotely attractive. She certainly hadn't given him any reason to think that she did.

She shook her head as she slipped out of her lab coat, marveling at the unwavering audacity of men. As if on cue, her phone rattled on the metal worktable. The incoming call was from Nick. Again. She rolled her eyes and let it go to voice mail.

When it came to conceit, Nicolas Pierce was in another league. She'd recently come to the realization that he was the kind of person who embraced rejection as a challenge. From the moment she'd turned him down the first time, his strategy had been to simply redouble his efforts. She kicked herself again for being idiotic enough to give the man her phone number in the first place. She'd done it in a pathetic moment of weakness. Brought on by flat abdominal muscles and a nice pair of pecs. Not to mention Liz's voice in her head, nattering on about lube jobs and hating fun and other such nonsense.

She grabbed her purse and switched off the overhead lights, eager to catch the last of the afternoon sun on the short walk to the bar. As she left through the building's main entrance, she spied her own reflection in the glass doors and felt satisfied with the woman looking back. As luck would have it, she'd worn her favorite Betsy Johnson that day. Short and chic, the dress always gave her a boost of confidence. And it paired so well with the fabulous shoes she'd splurged on the weekend before. She felt the bubble of excitement again, and her stride lengthened as she pushed out the doors and into the balmy seventy-two degrees of downtown San Francisco.

The sidewalks of Market Street teemed with after-work commuters, most of them professionals in rumpled business attire, crisscrossing the red brick pavement as they hurried toward buses and commuter trains or to the happy hour at their favorite local bar. Giana minced and dodged along with them, thrilled to be a part of the workaday throng.

After just a few blocks, she reached the address Remy had given her and abruptly halted, confused by the building's blank facade. There was a massive steel door with the words "bridge bar" punched into it, all in lowercase letters. Giana pulled on the long wooden handle, and the door glided open, beckoning her into a seductively dim interior.

She stepped in and paused to give her eyes time to adjust. The cocktail lounge was vast yet inviting, made to feel cozier through the liberal use of warm woods and soft, velvety textures. The entire back wall was a bank of floor-to-ceiling windows that boasted an unfettered view of the Bay Bridge in all of its industrial splendor.

An immense semi-circular bar dominated the center of the room, most of its seats already taken up by lively, chattering patrons. Scanning the crowd, Giana spotted the detective at once. She didn't know at what point she'd started to think of Remy as "the detective." It wasn't a particularly clever nickname, as far as nicknames went. But it felt oddly appropriate all the same.

She examined the detective's profile as she edged across the room to join her. Remy's skin was enviably smooth, warmed by gorgeous tones of red and bronze. Dark eyebrows arched above a proud, straight nose. Her lips were generous and well formed, balanced in perfect harmony with a strong jawline and long, sculpted neck. It was an elegant profile, she decided. Handsome even. And that was before you ever considered the eyes.

At that moment, Remy glanced up and trained her penetrating gaze on Giana, who felt the impact like a physical tap against her sternum. Disquieting, but not entirely unpleasant.

"Hello there." Giana projected her best, most casual smile as she slid onto the barstool next to Remy. "I'm not late, am I?"

"Not at all. You're right on time." Remy's voice was smooth and even. Her lupine eyes were still homed in on Giana's face.

Giana turned away and gestured at the panorama outside the windows. "My God, this is outrageous."

"Best view in town." Her smile was a beautiful row of perfectly white, perfectly even teeth. Flustered by a sudden case of the nerves, Giana pulled her eyes away again. She searched for the bartender, who magically appeared before her as if summoned.

"What can I get you, miss?" His face was open and boyish, and she liked him immediately.

"Can you make me an Aviation?"

"Coming right up."

He stepped away to the other end of the bar, and Giana took a calming breath. She focused on the rocks glass on the bar in front of Remy, opting to avoid eye contact a moment longer. "I could've guessed you'd be a scotch kinda girl."

"Bourbon," Remy corrected. She nudged the glass forward. "Would you like a taste?"

Giana hesitated, then picked up the glass and took a sip, coating her tongue with the liquid's icy burn before she swallowed. "Mmm, very nice. Thank you."

The whiskey hit her belly and spread outward in liquid fingers of warmth, soothing her nerves along the way. She exhaled again and finally met Remy's gaze. The gray eyes were warm and direct. Their focus on her never faltered.

"Busy day?" Remy asked. "How are you settling in over there in Forensics?"

"Oh." Giana paused to consider the question. "You know, actually, it's been really great. Most of my coworkers are men, of course, but they're that super nerdy, super sweet kind, you know? Easy to get along with. Oh, and I came across one of *your* cases the other day. My predecessor left me some notes about it. I think the name is Willard?"

Remy groaned and ran a hand through her straight black hair. "Yeah. I'm afraid we're really up against it on that one. Four months now, and all we've got is a lot of nothing."

Giana nodded. "I'm not surprised. Very little material there to work with. But we're still holding those hair and fiber samples in the active file, though. If you think you might want to revisit anything."

"Thanks, but so far we haven't had much reason to. Unfortunately. And now we just caught another case yesterday that's gonna take up some time. Teenaged female from Pinole. Found her strangled in the Mission Bay. We're just hoping there's no pattern here."

Giana could feel herself shifting into professional mode. "Were they able to pull anything promising off the body?"

"I hear not much. We just got the coroner's report this morning. The lab pack should be headed your way tomorrow or the next day at the latest. Although, I'm sure you've already got a hell of a backlog over there to deal with."

"Well, that's certainly true. Talk about hitting the ground running. Um, where was the body situated? I mean, was she in a vehicle or out in the open…?"

"She was dumped. Wrapped in a tarp. Some construction workers found her in an empty debris container at the back of the lot."

"Hmm. Well, it isn't great, but the tarp may have preserved something usable. Fibers or partials. What's the name?"

"Everett."

Giana nodded. "I'll see what I can do." She paused as the bartender returned with her cocktail and gently set the coupe glass down in front of her.

"You doing all right there, Rem?"

"Thanks, Jimmy, I'm good for now." Remy had yet to take her eyes off the brimming new concoction. Giana was pleased to note that the cocktail was the exact proper shade of dusky bluish-gray. It was a good sign.

Without a word, she slid the glass toward Remy, who beamed and carefully raised it to her lips. "Oh, wow. That's freaking delicious. What's in there? Vodka?"

"God, no. Gin and Luxardo. And crème de violette is what gives it that gorgeous color." Grinning, Giana stole the drink back and sampled it herself. She nodded with satisfaction. "Jimmy makes a good Aviation."

"I'm getting one of those next," Remy laughed.

Giana laughed too, and then they fell silent for a moment, though neither of them seemed to mind. The sun was beginning to set outside the windows, bathing the bridge's gargantuan steelwork in an amber glow. Evening traffic crawled along the double decks like lines of metallic army ants.

It was a stunning view, but she found herself focusing on her companion's profile once again, unconcerned now if it was obvious she was staring. Remy's trousers were sharp. The pinstripe pattern was subtle, the fabric a good quality wool that tapered nicely toward the ankle. And the fitted vest hugged her torso perfectly. She was shirtless underneath, and Giana ran her eyes up the length of one toned arm, from the large, sculpted hand to the cleft in her deltoid muscle. Remy gave her a sidelong glance but endured the appraisal without comment.

"Sorry," Giana finally said with a laugh. "I do that sometimes."

"What's that. Stare?" There was amusement in her eyes, mixed with something else Giana couldn't quite pinpoint.

"I like your outfit," she confessed. "I'm a little obsessed with fashion, you see. And also... I was thinking your arms might actually be longer than my legs."

Remy snorted. She leaned over to brazenly inspect Giana's bare legs as she obligingly crossed and recrossed them for her.

"Hmm. I don't know..." Remy speculated. "You might be right. But it's a little hard to tell in those heels."

Giana lifted one foot, flexing it at the ankle to show off her Manolo Blahniks. The soft sueded leather was a fabulous oxblood red. "Oh, these," she said breezily. "They're new. What do you think? Are they working for me?"

Remy's grin was enormous. She covered one cheek with the palm of her hand. "Oh, gosh. Well..."

"Hello, Remy. I hope I'm not interrupting anything."

Remy and Giana looked up simultaneously. The blond woman standing in front of them was unsmiling—and absolutely gorgeous. Giana couldn't help but notice her beautiful suit, which looked to be worsted silk. It was an expertly tailored piece, in a classic bone white that managed to make the wearer look professional and hyper-feminine at the same time. The woman's cool blue eyes fixed on Giana and scanned the length of her in turn, pausing for half a beat on the shoes before flicking back to Remy's face.

"Erica. Uh...Hi." Remy's warm complexion seemed to deepen a shade, though the bar's dim lighting made it impossible to be sure. Giana watched as the normally smooth brow furrowed, and the gray eyes lost their steadiness, skipping from the blonde to Giana and back again. "Uh...Erica Forsyte, meet Giana Falco." It was all but a stammer, and Giana was suddenly intrigued.

She stuck a hand out to the woman, who glanced at it with thinly veiled distaste. Grasping it limply, she let it drop a split second later, and Giana didn't know whether to laugh or feel offended.

"Giana is new over in Forensics." Remy's voice had regained its steadiness. She turned to look at Giana with a clear apology in her eyes. "Erica here works in the DA's office."

Giana lifted her eyebrows and smiled sweetly at the woman but offered no comment. She took a sip of her cocktail and waited, content to sit back and observe this fascinating exchange. The silence lengthened, and Remy shifted on her barstool.

"Well," Erica said abruptly. "You never were one to waste any time."

Remy held up a hand. "Erica, now...hold on. This isn't what you think."

"Of course it isn't, Remy." Erica raised her chin and plastered a bright smile on her face, looking past the both of them to wave at someone on the far side of the bar. "You'll excuse me." Without another glance, she turned and strode away.

Giana watched her go, waiting until she was well out of earshot to speak. "Wow," she said simply.

Remy watched the woman's retreating back in silence. Seemingly with great effort, she rotated on her stool until she faced the bar again. "Jimmy, can I get another one when you get a chance?"

Jimmy nodded. "Double Maker's on the rocks?"

"Actually, let's make it one of those." Remy pointed a thumb at Giana's drink. She met her eyes and gave her a weary smile. "Are you ready for another one? These are all on me, by the way."

Giana shrugged. "Well, in that case."

"Make it a round, Jimmy, thanks." Remy ran a hand through her hair and stared straight ahead. Giana watched her profile in silence, waiting patiently until the detective finally glanced at her again. They both broke into subdued laughter.

"Um. So that happened." Remy grimaced. "Wow. I really don't know what to say. I'm sorry she was so rude to you."

"She was rude? Hmm. I guess I missed that." They both chuckled again. Giana followed Remy's gaze to the far corner of the bar, where Erica stood shaking hands with a young man in a business suit. She seated herself with her back to the room. "So. I take it she's your ex?"

"Yes." Remy's head dropped. "Well, sort of. That was one of the things we could never really agree on." Her leg bobbed twice, then settled. "I, uh…I wasn't sure if you knew that about me."

"Oh. You mean that you date women?" Giana swallowed. "Well, yes. I sort of guessed. I mean, I wasn't sure. I certainly wouldn't say I'm an expert, or anything. I don't actually have that many friends who are. Gay, I mean."

"Queer," Remy corrected. "We prefer the word queer. It's actually kind of offensive to use the term 'gay' these days."

"Oh!" Giana felt her face reddening. "Really?"

Remy's eyes glittered with amusement. "No. I'm kidding, Giana."

Giana clucked her tongue and tossed a balled-up cocktail napkin at her. Remy blinked as it bounced off her forehead and landed on the bar.

"As I was *saying*," Giana continued, "my roommate is the only gay-queer-whatever friend I have. But she's a pretty atypical person all around, so…I don't know."

Remy's eyebrows quirked, and Giana chuckled. "I just mean she's, um, equal opportunity. We were roommates back in college, too, and Liz was like…*active*. I mean, she dated *a lot*. Boys, girls, you name it. Sometimes two at a time. She's always been very inclusive, which is one of the things I love about her. I would never try to put her into any kind of box."

"Well, she sounds interesting."

"She is," Giana agreed. "Sometimes I wish I were more like her. Just meaning that she's a lot of fun. And a brilliant doctor, to boot. Maybe you two will meet one day. I think you'd like her."

"Maybe so." Remy's nod was noncommittal. "And what about you?"

"Me?" Giana's pulse jumped.

"Did you date a lot in college?"

"Oh! No. I mean, not really. I just had the one boyfriend. Peter. He was very sweet. We were on the tennis team together."

"You play tennis? Wait, where did you go to school?"

"U Penn."

"Oh." Remy straightened on her stool. "So you mean, you *play tennis.*"

Giana laughed. "What—do you play?"

"Well, I don't know if *you* would call it that. But I was Division I at Tulane, yes. Which is like, I don't know… badminton compared to U Penn's program."

"Oh my God." Giana grabbed Remy's arm. "We have to play!"

Remy laughed, shaking her head. "Oh, no. No way. I haven't played in like, half a century. And I don't have a masochistic bone in my body, believe me."

Giana shook her head. "That is *so* not acceptable." She was distracted then by Jimmy reappearing with a fresh round of drinks. She drained the last sip from her first glass before she surrendered it. "You're a magician," she told him. A pleasant buzz was beginning to creep its way over her cheekbones and down the back of her neck. "One who makes very strong drinks," she added.

"Devereux!" The name was shouted from across the bar, and Remy straightened. She raised her glass and nodded at the bellower. Giana recognized him as her partner—Cook, the man who drank too many lattes. His smile was genial as he made his way toward a large circular booth near the windows. And trailing behind him was none other than Nicholas Pierce. Nick stopped to shake hands with someone at a nearby table, and Giana turned her head away, desperately hoping she hadn't been spotted.

"So," she said abruptly. "Remy Devereux. That sounds very French. And you mentioned Tulane, which is in Louisiana, right?"

Remy put a hand to her chest. "New Orleans, born and raised." She pronounced the city's name like *Nawlins.* "My people are Creole. My mother named me Remy Valentine, which is embarrassing enough, but my brother got it even worse. He's Constantine Maximilien, if you can believe that."

Giana laughed in delight. "That is so fantastic. Do you call him Connie? I have a big brother myself. Tony—who is basically this incredibly annoying pain in the ass most of the time. I can't believe I actually miss him."

Remy chuckled at that. "Mmm. I know what you mean. But no, Max is actually not that annoying. And he's my baby brother by twelve minutes. That's not a lot of time, I know, but it still counts."

"Twelve minutes. Oh, so you're twins!" Giana was delighted again. "Oh my! He must be a handsome devil then, if he looks anything like you." She watched Remy's complexion darken, certain this time that it was indeed a blush. Amused, she added, "Is he single?"

Remy's smile was wry. "Well, I'm sorry to disappoint you, but Max happens to be a gay person also. Twins, right? No, I mean, we're fraternal, obviously. But maybe there really is something behind that whole genetic thing." She waved a hand dismissively. "I don't know. At any rate, he's totally in love with his boyfriend, Jerome, so I guess you're just shit outta luck as far as that goes."

"Damn," Giana murmured. She was trying hard to hide her fascination. She suddenly wanted to know this woman. She wanted to learn everything there was to learn about her.

"Well, a girl can always hope." She raised her glass to take a sip. "People do change, Remy."

The detective's eyes snagged on hers, and Giana found herself staring right back, wondering why it was so damned entertaining to flirt with this woman. The cocktails had nothing to do with it, she was certain.

Another shout came from across the bar, and this time Giana heard her own name called. She tensed, turning to see Nick Pierce approaching with his arms spread wide. It had only been a matter of time.

"You got my message!" He stopped in front of them, the bright, lopsided grin fixed in place as he looked from Giana to Remy. "Devereux. Hey, how's it going. Good to see you."

Remy stared at him for a long, awkward moment. "Pierce," she finally muttered. She looked at Giana, her expression softening again. "I think I'm gonna go stretch my legs a bit. Make the rounds and whatnot." She slid off her stool, rising to nearly match Nick's height. Her eyes remained fixed on Giana's face. "Are you gonna be okay here?"

Giana nodded. "Sure, of course. I'll be fine."

"Okay. Be back in a few." Remy turned and strode away without acknowledging Nick again. Nick promptly slid onto her vacated stool.

"So you got my message." He was repeating himself.

"Ah, no, actually. I haven't checked my messages in a while. Sorry." She found her eyes skipping past his shoulder, tracking Remy's progress as she maneuvered through the crowded bar. She was moving toward the far corner, where that Erica person had joined her companion. Giana scanned ahead and located the back of the blonde's head and noted that she was sitting alone for the time being. She forced herself to focus on Nick again, but her eyes jumped back a second later as Remy paused in front of Erica's booth and leaned down to speak to her.

Nick, in the meantime, had not stopped talking. "...because me and Cookie and some of the other guys were coming down here, and I thought, hey, maybe the beautiful scientist will want to come along." The smile persisted. "Our favorite booth is right over there. Plenty of room."

"Oh, right. Well that's very sweet, but I think Remy and I are going to finish our drinks here at the bar, and then I'll probably call it a night. But you know what, we should try catching up a little later in the week." She glanced to the far corner of the room again, mildly perturbed to see that Remy was now seated in the booth with Erica. She made herself promise not to look there again.

"Oh, no. I'm not falling for that one again," Nick said. "I think I'm just gonna sit right here and pester you all night until you make a firm commitment to go out with me." He leaned back and folded his arms, his chest muscles straining against the fabric of his shirt.

Giana rolled her eyes. Her gaze inevitably landed on Remy once again, just as she broke into a broad smile and reached across the table to touch Erica's arm. She wrenched her eyes away and zeroed in on Nick.

"What's the matter, Nick? Don't tell me a suave, good-looking guy like yourself is having trouble getting laid."

Nick's eyes widened. His lips parted, but no sound came forth.

Giana snorted softly. "Frankly, I'm surprised you'd be willing to work this hard for it." She took a sip from her cocktail. It was gratifying to see the grin finally wiped off his face. "Okay." She set her glass down with a clink. "I'll go out with you. But I'm promising nothing. Got it?" She watched him nod, apparently still speechless. "How does Friday sound?"

Nick cleared his throat. "Uh, Friday sounds perfect. Great. All right…Well, I'll be giving you a call." The grin slid back into place, and Giana almost reconsidered her decision.

Another throat cleared, and they both turned to see Remy standing at Nick's elbow. "I think you're in my seat, Pierce."

Nick lifted his chin at her and slid off the stool, his shoulder blades widening even more than usual. He gave Giana a wink and sauntered away, and she resisted the urge to bury her face in her hands. She pressed her lips together and looked at Remy. "Please…don't say anything, okay?"

Remy held up her hands, chuckling. "I didn't... I'm not saying a word. Not one word."

"Good." Giana nodded. "Thank you."

Remy resumed her position on her stool, her gaze centering on Giana's face. Giana didn't want to analyze why it felt so good to have her back again. The warm gray eyes were focused exclusively on her, and she liked it that way.

Remy sucked in a deep breath. "So."

"So," Giana echoed.

The full lips curved into a smile. "Can I tempt you with another round?"

Giana was thrown by her choice of words, but she recovered quickly. "Definitely," she replied with a nod. "Consider me officially tempted."

CHAPTER SIX

The next morning, Remy woke before the alarm, feeling surprisingly rested after only a few hours of sleep. The night had been dreamless, and she felt a surge of energy as she quickly dressed for her morning run. Outside, the breaking dawn sent streaks of violet and magenta across the morning sky. Remy left the porch at an easy trot and set her course down the middle of the empty street. For once, she'd opted to leave her earbuds behind. There was nothing to distract her as she cruised past the darkened windows of her Noe Valley neighborhood, focused only on the light slap of her sneakers on the pavement and the cool rush of air in her lungs.

She was showered and on her way to work well ahead of schedule. At the Starbucks on Folsom, Remy ordered the usual for herself and Cookie, though she didn't expect him in for another hour. Parking spaces beneath the Justice Building were plentiful when she arrived, and Remy took the elevators straight up to Homicide. No stalker detours allowed.

Cookie glanced up from his desk as she opened his door and strode in. "Still working on that knocking thing, boss?"

Remy halted abruptly, surprised to see him. "Yeah. Well, I thought I'd leave a nice cold latte sitting on your desk to greet you when you got in." She set the hot drink down in front of him. "You're here early."

Cookie placed his fingers against the cup, a satisfied grin rounding out his already round cheeks. "Yeah. I'm heading out to Pinole again this morning. Fat lot of nothing yesterday with the neighbors. Thought I'd get an early jump and hit the high school today. Plus, uh…I had to get up early anyway to make breakfast for Marla and the kids, so…"

Remy's eyebrows went up. "You don't say. So the family's back home. That's great news, partner, glad to hear it. Try not to screw it up this time, okay?" She gave him a wink and turned to leave.

"Roger that, boss. Hey, what about you? Things were looking pretty warm and snuggly at the bar last night, if you don't mind me saying."

Remy froze, one hand against the doorjamb. She fixed her features in a neutral expression before she turned back to look at Cookie. "Who, Forsyte? I told you, it's done between us. I'm just trying to keep things on a friendly keel. I thought you'd be happy to hear that."

"Mm-hmm." Cookie examined her face as he took a cautious sip of latte. He swallowed with a satisfied sigh and turned back to his computer. "But I think we both know I wasn't talking about her."

Remy started to object but thought better of it. She turned and left his office without another word. She was in a great mood, and she wasn't going to let Cookie get into her head about Giana Falco. Yes, she'd had drinks with the green-eyed siren and lived to tell the tale. More than that, she'd had a blast hanging out with the lady, and she wasn't afraid to admit it. It was stupid to try to read any more into it than that.

The situation *had* made for a pretty awkward moment with Erica, though. Remy knew running into her was bound to happen sometime, but last night was just painful. A month without a word between them, and then of course their first face-to-face just has to go down like that. In a bar. With Remy cozied up to a total hottie, checking out her legs. Erica had gotten the wrong idea, understandably, and Remy had done her best to smooth things over. Not that it would've been a felony if she *had* been on a date, but still.

Remy stepped into her minuscule, white-walled office and shut the door. She had an entire hour to herself before she had to head back out to the construction site where the Everett girl was found. In the meantime, there was an ever-mounting pile of minor but neglected casework to dig into.

She set her latte on the desk and seated herself, just as her phone let off a muffled chime in her jacket pocket. Already annoyed, she retrieved it. She was further dismayed to see that the text was from Erica.

Plans this weekend? Cookout at Keisha and Devlin's on Saturday.

Remy groaned and tossed the phone on the desk. Of course she was going to the cookout. Keisha and Devlin were two of her closest friends—Erica only knew them because of her. The way she'd worded the text, it sounded like Erica was extending a personal invitation.

Remy drummed her fingers on the desk, wondering now if maybe she'd tried a little too hard to smooth things over last night. A cloud of unease settled over her as she considered the possibility that this past month of silence had actually been some elaborate ploy. Erica Forsyte was nothing if not a brilliant tactician. When it came to getting what she wanted, her skills were unparalleled.

Remy opted not to answer the text for now. She felt like she was suddenly standing in the middle of a minefield, and the best course of action at the moment was to simply stay put.

The phone chimed again, and she instinctively shied away from it. Leaning forward, she peered at the screen, then scooped it up when she realized the text was from Giana.

I had a great time last night getting to know you a little. Hope we can do it again sometime soon!

Remy's thumbs darted over the keypad.

Same here. Aviations anytime.

She sent the text and set the phone aside, her eyes still fixed on it as another thought sprang to mind. It might be playing with fire, but Giana was so easy to get along with. And Devlin and Keisha would love her, there was no question.

She shook the thought away and turned to open her satchel, pulling out a stack of file folders and dropping them on her desk. She paused again as the idea persisted. Erica already suspected there was something going on between them—why not just let her continue to think that? She'd be sure to back off then, with Giana in the picture. At least for the duration of the party. It wouldn't take Erica long to figure out it was all a hoax, of course, but at least it would buy her some time.

She hesitated, staring at the phone. It was basically using Giana like a human shield. But the woman had already met with the wrath of Erica once and rolled with it like a pro.

She grabbed the phone and started to type, ignoring the fact that the idea of spending an entire afternoon with Giana Falco made her heart race.

Hey, would you happen to be free this Saturday? Want to join me at a cookout in WC?

The reply was prompt.

As a matter of fact, I am free! And a cookout in a bathroom sounds intriguing.

Remy's eyebrows knitted together. A second later, she barked with laughter.

WC stands for Walnut Creek.

Ah. That's a little less intriguing, but I'll say yes anyway.

Great. I'll call you later with the deets. That's details, in case you were wondering.

Giana's final reply was an emoji of a smiley face blowing a kiss. Remy rubbed her cheek with her palm as she set the phone aside. Playing with fire indeed. The woman was a flirt, there was no doubt about that. But she could handle it. She'd proved as much to herself last night. Giana was fun, and she was smart, and Remy wanted to spend some more time with her. There was no crime in that.

She sighed and took a sip of her latte, grimacing as she realized the drink had gone cold. She took another swallow anyway and pulled a folder from the top of the stack. Before she could read the first line, her phone set to trilling again. Remy was determined to ignore it, until she spied the image of the silver-haired woman displayed on the screen. Smiling and beautiful. She picked up the phone and hit the talk button. "Is everything okay?"

The accent on the other end of the line was heavy and lilting—an unmistakable Creole patois. Its rhythmic cadence made her instantly homesick. "Is that the way you answer the phone, chére?"

"Only to you, Maman. What you doin' callin' me so early?" Remy heard her own voice slipping back into a lazy Louisiana drawl. Like pulling on a favorite pair of pajamas.

"Well, it ain't so early over here where we at, ya know. We been up for hours over here."

Remy chuckled, leaning back in her chair. "Well, you got a good point there, Maman. How you feelin' today?"

"Ah, you know." Sabine's shoulders were surely rising in a shrug. Remy could just picture it. "I'm not gonna be complainin' all the time. These days, it's a blessin' just to draw breath, now ya know that's true. And that's good enough for me, chére. Good enough for me."

"Maman. That's all fine and good, but how's Pappy spose to know what you need if you don't say nothin' to him?"

"Oh, he all right. Your Pappy bein' real sweet to me, don't you worry 'bout that. When you comin' home, chére? I wanna see your pretty face."

Remy's chest tightened. "I gotta work, Maman. You know I do."

"I know that, child. I know." There was a pause on the other end of the line. "And you been havin' them dreams again. Ain't ya, baby? They bad this time?"

Remy held her breath. "Mmm, no. Not really."

"Mm-hmm." Sabine clearly wasn't fooled. "And you met somebody, too? Now, when was you plannin' on tellin' me 'bout that?"

"Met somebody?" Remy tried to keep her tone even. She had ceased to question Sabine's clairvoyance years ago, but still. This was a little too much. "I don't know what you mean."

"The girl, Remy. Maximilien said you met a pretty girl. Is she as pretty as you? Tell me 'bout her. She ain't nothin' like that ol' lawyer girl, I hope."

"Sabine…" Remy stared up at the ceiling. She was going to strangle Max the very next time she saw him. "Look, um, I gotta go. I'm sorry, but I'm really busy today, and I gotta go."

"Okay, okay. You don't wanna talk about the girl right now, I can see that. We'll talk about her a little bit later on."

Remy sighed. "I love you, Maman."

"I love you too, chére. And, baby…" Sabine paused to make sure Remy was listening. "Don't be so afraid all the time. Not everybody the same. Not everybody gonna leave."

Remy exhaled. "Look, um…I'll talk to you soon, okay?"

"Okay, baby. I'll tell your Pappy you said hello."

"Thanks, Maman. I love you."

They clicked off, and Remy sat staring down at her desk. She was tempted to call her brother immediately and ask him what the hell he thought he'd heard her say about Giana Falco. As usual, the other members of the Devereux family seemed to think they knew her better than she knew herself. She'd spent most of her life attempting to disabuse them of that notion—to very little avail. Max had promised to check in on Sabine and Pappy daily. Apparently, in his mind that service also included providing them with wildly inaccurate speculations about Remy's personal life.

She glanced at the clock, muttering under her breath. She didn't know where all of that extra time had gone. She rose to stuff the folders back in her satchel. Max would have to get a piece of her mind later. Right now, she was almost late for her first appointment.

* * *

It was a perfect sixty-five degrees outside as Giana crossed the bridge into the city. The morning sun beamed in an azure sky, and her eyes were drawn repeatedly to the bay waters, where rays of light glittered like a handful of jewels strewn across the waves.

It was evident to her now that she'd stumbled onto some kind of secret Shangri-La. It was all she could do not to gush about it to the people back home—namely the Chief, with whom she was still mincing her words whenever they spoke. In turn, the Chief's inquiries remained supportive, if rather cursory. All the while laced with a prevailing undercurrent that forever begged the question: When was she coming home?

Her father's stubbornness was exasperating, but Giana held her tongue because she knew, at the root of it, he simply missed his little girl. The poor man had even bought her a car. He'd had it delivered and waiting for her the day she'd arrived. The gift was too much—even if it weren't some bizarre kind of bribe.

But she had refused to argue with him about it. She couldn't be sure what she'd say. She was terrified she'd blurt out something hurtful in the heat of the moment—like, she was absolutely convinced she'd made the right decision and there was no chance of her moving back. Not ever. So he might as well get used to the idea.

With every passing day here, she felt a little more at ease, a little more certain that this new home *was* her home. Only Lena seemed to understand. Unlike the Chief, her aunt wanted to know all the details. She'd been delighted to hear about her date coming up on Friday, insisting she tell her everything there was to know about Nick. Giana had done her best to oblige.

She'd had a lot more to say about Remy, however. She thought about their text exchange that morning and smiled, wondering if her joke about a cookout in a water closet had made the detective laugh. She liked Remy's laugh. It was unexpected and genuine, and Giana felt like she'd scored a point whenever she said something to draw it out.

No doubt, Nick would be vexed to know that she was far more excited about a cookout with Remy than she was about seeing him. There was certainly no love lost between those two. She wondered if there was some specific history behind it, or if

Nick simply couldn't handle the fact that there was an attractive woman out there who was so plainly immune to his charms. It didn't bode well for him if that was the case, but she was willing to keep an open mind.

Twenty minutes later, she strolled into the SFPD crime lab, apparently the first to arrive. Greeted by muted lighting and the tranquil hum of instrumentation, she stowed her purse in a cabinet and made her way through the large, open room, flipping on the overheads and powering up equipment as she went. She was shrugging into her lab coat when she heard the sound of a timid knock. Crossing the room, she opened the door to a slight individual in round spectacles and neatly pressed chinos.

"Evidence delivery from Homicide?" The young man's voice cracked as he shoved his glasses higher up the bridge of his nose.

"Oh, good morning, Brian." She held up her ID badge and suppressed a smile. As expected, Brian's complexion bloomed a vibrant shade of red. He gave the badge a cursory scan, then handed her a clipboard. Idly scribbling across the form it held, she kept her gaze trained on his face. He cleared his throat and jerkily handed over the package, and she murmured her thanks as he turned and scurried off down the hallway.

Chuckling softly, Giana shut the door and carried the box to her workstation. Once the bar code was scanned into the system, a data block appeared showing the associated case and file numbers. The victim was listed as Everett, and the lead investigator was R. Devereux.

She paused and glanced around the empty lab. Protocol dictated that she now deposit the package into the evidence locker, to be processed in order behind the others already waiting their turn. She knew the backlog consisted of at least a dozen submissions, all linked to active investigations. At the lab's current rate, five or six weeks might pass before Remy's case could be addressed.

With no one else in the lab to stop her, she broke open the seal and began to carefully unpack the box's contents. If Curtis questioned her about it later, she'd just have to claim ignorance or blame it on a temporary lapse in attention span. Hopefully, it would never come up.

She finished unloading the carton and sifted through the pile of evidence bags now mounded on her workstation. Larger bags contained articles of clothing, while smaller ones held various tubes and vials with trace samples inside. A stack of crime scene photos depicted the body *in situ*—first concealed beneath the tarp and then exposed in the harsh glare of daylight.

Giana paused on a close-up of the decedent. The girl's eyes were clouded over, staring blindly out of a blue-white face. She set the photos aside and rolled a cushioned stool over to her workstation. She pulled on a pair of latex gloves and scanned the bar code on the first bag before she broke it open.

For the next hour, she worked steadily, her head bowed in concentration as her coworkers trickled into the lab around her. Her supervisor Curtis arrived, immersed in conversation with another technician. Giana gave him a nod as he passed, then went back to work, methodically cataloguing each sample before initiating a preliminary analysis, documenting her findings with meticulous care in the notebook beside her.

All trace evidence had a story to tell. The information was there for the taking—it was simply a matter of uncovering the message and understanding how to read it. It was this sly process of discovery that she loved most about her work.

Time passed beyond her awareness, and the clock was nearing the noon hour when she suddenly sat up straight on her stool. She stared without seeing at the wall in front of her, struggling to grasp hold of the thread that teased at the back of her memory.

Abruptly, she stood up. Striding past several workstations, she halted at a wide metal storage cabinet that sat in one corner of the lab and hastily scanned down its column of labeled drawers. She found the one marked "Willard/Devereux" and yanked it open.

* * *

Remy's good mood had all but vanished. Not one of her interviews that morning with the various personnel at the construction site had panned out. She was coming away with no new information and very little guidance as to where to steer the investigation next.

The construction lot was located in a sparsely populated commercial district on the city's east side, where foot traffic was scarce even during the day. At night, the place was a veritable ghost town. No security guard was employed on the premises, and the few surveillance cameras that were installed were directed at the office trailer and surrounding parking area. The debris container where the body was abandoned was well outside their range of coverage.

On the morning in question, the foreman had arrived on site at six thirty a.m., having observed no unusual vehicles or suspicious activity. The CSI crew that later worked the scene found nothing in the way of tire tracks or distinctive footprints near the body. It was as if the girl had simply materialized out of thin air.

Frustrated, Remy blew out a breath and checked her watch. It was almost noon. Other than her cold latte several hours ago, she had yet to put anything in her stomach. She returned to the unmarked Dodge she'd left parked across the street. The Charger was the pick of the department's motor pool—she loved its powerful engine—but she didn't feel the usual boost of energy as she dropped into the driver's seat and contemplated her next move.

As a crime scene, the construction site was a dead end. She'd passed out a dozen business cards regardless, just to ensure she could be reached if anyone remembered anything useful. She didn't expect a call back. She could only pray that Cookie was having better luck at the school in Pinole. Remy tried to shake the nagging sensation that had begun to creep in on her midway through the morning. It looked like the Everett case was headed the way of the Willard investigation—which was absolutely nowhere. They had to get some kind of lead soon.

She checked her watch again and tried to estimate how quickly the traffic would allow her to get out to Pinole. But then the aggressive rumbling of hunger pangs made her shelve the idea for the moment. She turned the key in the ignition, and the Charger released a throaty growl. There was an excellent taqueria on Third and Mariposa. Things were bound to look a little better with a couple of tacos and an agua fresca in her belly.

Five minutes later, Remy wedged the car into the taqueria's cramped parking lot and hopped out again. Pancho Villa's was slammed with a noisy lunchtime crowd. Remy waded into the fray, her mouth watering at the aroma of warm tortillas and meats sizzling on the grill. An army of skilled servers kept the line moving at the counter, and Remy had her food in no time. She headed back out to the sunny parking lot to eat.

Leaning against her vehicle, she set to fairly inhaling the succulent bites, humming with pleasure over the dripping carnitas, licking her fingers as she contemplated placing another order before she'd even finished the first. Her phone rang in her pocket, and Remy gave a tortured groan, halting her gorging to hastily wipe her hands on a napkin.

Without a glance at the caller ID, she hit the talk button and curtly answered. "Devereux here."

Giana's husky timbre crooned back at her. "Remy, hi. It's Giana. Is this a bad time?"

"Er...no. I, uh...Hi. It's you." She paused, chagrined by her sudden inability to articulate.

"Uh, yes it is." Giana paused a beat. "Um. I'm actually calling because I have the Everett lab pack in front of me here. There are a couple of things I think you should take a look at."

Remy's focus went razor sharp. "You're kidding me. You're into the Everett pack? I can't believe you got on that already."

"Yes, I...well, I was able to get to it, yes. Anyway, it's kind of a lot to explain over the phone. Maybe you could come by the lab? Today or tomorrow would be fine. I'm usually here until six or—"

"I'm on my way now." Remy tossed the rest of her lunch into the waste bin. "Be there in twenty."

"Oh! All right. Yes, um, that'll be fine. Okay. I'll see you soon."

"Yep. See you in a few." Remy clicked off and stood unmoving for a moment. Then she was in the car and steering out of the parking lot, impatiently nudging her way into the afternoon congestion of Third Street.

The sudden charge she felt was strictly about the case. She and Cookie desperately needed a break, and this could be it. It had nothing to do with seeing Giana again so soon.

She stopped the car at a red light and flipped down the visor to check her teeth in the mirror. Rummaging through the glove box, she found a stick of chewing gum and popped it into her mouth. Her good mood was back. She didn't know how Giana had managed to get at the Everett evidence so quickly, but she was the last person to question a miracle like that. Not her remit. She needed to get this investigation moving forward, and she would take any and all assistance in order to make that happen.

Early next week, Linda and John Everett would be sitting down with her in the division offices, anxious to hear about their daughter's case. Remy wanted to be able to tell them something. She wanted to be able to look them in the eyes and promise them she was going to find out what happened to their little girl. And that she was going to put the man responsible for it behind bars.

She stared up at the red light, her fingers tapping out a staccato on the steering wheel. At last, the signal turned green, and she punched the Charger's engine, flipping on the siren and strobes to clear the path in front of her.

* * *

Giana sat in the empty crime lab and munched on an apple while she waited for Remy. She had begged off joining her coworkers as they filed out the door for lunch, claiming to be in the middle of an analysis that couldn't be interrupted. Curtis had offered to bring her back a chef's salad from the cafeteria, and she had gratefully accepted. She knew he was still sweet on her, and she really didn't want to encourage him. But propriety was one thing—sustenance was something else.

She devoured the remains of her apple in a few bites and tossed the core into the waste can. Surely the jitters gripping her stomach were hunger pangs and nothing else. Prolonged sessions of intense focus like the one she'd had this morning always gave her an appetite. She stood and paced the room, stopping to retrieve her compact from her purse. She checked her hair and makeup in the little mirror, then abruptly snapped the case shut. Who was she kidding? This bout of nerves had seized her the moment she'd heard Remy's voice on the phone.

Giana shook her head and forced herself to be seated. Nerves were perfectly understandable in a situation like this. There was a serious chance she had just discovered a critical element in a murder investigation. It was normal to feel exhilarated about the possibility of making a contribution like that.

A sharp rap sounded at the door, and she jumped. Smoothing out her lab coat, she strode purposefully across the room and swung the door open.

"Hi, there! Wow, you made it. That was fast." She blinked as Remy stepped through the doorway. The detective seemed taller than before. Or the lab had just gotten smaller, she wasn't sure which.

"Yeah. Hey, thanks for calling." Remy's voice was low, almost vibrating with a steady hum. It felt strangely intimate in the quietude of the lab. "God, I'm amazed you were able to get at this thing so fast."

"Right. Well…" Giana shut the door and strode toward her workstation. "Let's just get started, shall we?" She glanced back, startled to see Remy so close on her heels. Remy paused, and Giana continued to the other side of her station, placing the worktable between them.

Without preamble, she launched into an abbreviated rundown of the trace evidence from the file, feeling her body begin to relax as she delved into the specifics of hair and fiber analysis. Remy listened intently while she explained how she'd spent most of the morning engaged in a process of elimination, discounting every specimen that could be attributed to the victim. What remained were several viable samples of unknown origin, ones that could possibly be linked to a person or environment encountered by the decedent near the time of her death.

She opened the Everett file and pulled out an enlargement of a microscope scan, rotating the photo on the table so Remy could view it right side up. Then she pulled out a similar graphic and explained that it was from the Willard file. She placed the two photos side by side.

"Now look at this, these fibers here. First of all, they're very unusual. At this point, I can't even be sure if they're natural or synthetic."

Remy bent at the waist to peer more closely at the images. The scent of her leather jacket wafted upward, and Giana's concentration was momentarily broken. She eyed the quality of the supple lambskin, approving of the cut. It hit Remy's waist at exactly the right point, about an inch above the hip.

Forcing herself to refocus, she pointed at one of the photos on the table. "You see this triangular shape in the cross section here? Well, it's repeated over here. And the width and color of the strands appear to be identical." She paused and looked at Remy's lowered head, her eye drawn to the saturated color of her hair. The individual strands were thick, coalescing in a dense and glossy mane. She was struck with a peculiar urge to sink her fingers into it.

"So you're saying you think there's a link? Possibly the same source, even?" Remy looked up, and their eyes locked, and Giana felt the impact again. Like a jolt against her breastbone.

"I can't be certain, not at this point. But that is my belief, yes. A common source."

"Christ." Remy straightened to her full height. She stepped back and rested her hips against the counter, then flipped open a small notepad and began to scribble into it.

Giana waited quietly, and she found her gaze drifting to the holster fastened at Remy's waist. The fluorescent lighting cast a dull sheen on the oiled leather. The pistol grip was exposed, riding flush against an abdomen that looked taut enough to thump. Her gaze wandered lower as she noted the snug fit of the dark denim jeans, the fabric hugging nicely through the thighs, then easing again at the knee. Her appraisal continued down the length of Remy's long legs, until the view was annoyingly cut off by the worktable between them.

It was only then that she realized what she was doing. She stifled a cough, her face growing hot. She pawed at the scattered documents on the table and shuffled them into a pile. Remy made a comment, which she missed completely. "I'm sorry—what?"

Remy shot her a quizzical look. "Are you okay? You look a little…flushed or something."

"No. I mean, yes. I, uh…Is it hot in here? I'm feeling a little warm, aren't you?"

Remy slowly shook her head. She glanced down at her notepad. "I was wondering if we could go back and comb through the Willard and Everett packs again, specifically looking for similarities this time. Well, I say 'we,' but that would obviously fall to you."

"Of course," Giana said quickly. "Absolutely. That's the next step. Unfortunately, we don't have much in the way of fluids from either one of them. Blood, semen, saliva—any of those would be immeasurably valuable here. And by the way, the total absence of those particular elements is far from incidental. It seems your perp has some familiarity with forensic investigations."

"Which is significant in itself."

"Precisely," Giana agreed. "But nobody's perfect. There was a human hair in the Willard pack that was initially tagged as questionable. My predecessor's final analysis was that it most likely derived from the victim. I'm not so sure I agree with his conclusion."

"Really. Well, maybe we should submit it to CODIS, then. See if we get any hits."

Remy's eye contact was beyond persistent. Giana lost her train of thought again.

"Um…yes. Well, we certainly could…submit it to CODIS. Um. If enough of the DNA is intact, of course. Sometimes, it's not possible to extract a sufficient amount of material from a single strand of hair—unless it's been ripped out by the scalp, of course. In that case, you'd have a ton of skin cells to work with and maybe even some blood. Or an intact follicle. Boy, what a gold mine *that* would be."

Giana realized she was beginning to ramble, but Remy's eyes were boring into her like diamond drill bits. "But, um, no. No such luck here. This one appears to be the product of normal shedding, which is not ideal. We won't know if there's enough for the national database until we take a closer look. But, uh…Anyway. I digress."

She forced herself to stop talking. She hoped the detective might say something now or at least find something else to look at. The gray eyes continued to stare directly at her. Did the woman ever blink?

"My point here," she went on, "and mind you, this is just a rough analysis based on the comparison scope. But my point here, is that the hair from the Willard set *appears* to be extremely similar to one that I was able to isolate just this morning. From the Everett pack."

Giana paused for effect. There it was. A blink. Remy had just blinked.

"I'm going to submit them both to DNA tomorrow, and then…Well, wouldn't that be something? If we could determine they came from the same head of hair? I mean, it's a long shot, with so little material to work with, but—"

"How long will it take?" Remy asked.

"Oh. Well, that depends. Curtis is responsible for all of the DNA analysis in the lab, and I know he's swamped right now. So it's hard to say. I'll be sure to let you know, though. The minute we have anything at all, I'll let you know."

Remy nodded. She flipped the notepad closed and crossed her arms, her head bowed in concentration for a long minute. Then she glanced up and flashed a smile. "Giana, I can't tell you how much I appreciate your help on this. You're literally saving my life here."

Giana waved a hand. "Oh…no, don't be silly. It's my job. I'm happy to be of use." Remy's eyes were still on her, but for some reason they were less unnerving now, lingering in a way that made it impossible not to return her stare.

Hypnotic. That was the only word that came to mind.

The door opened, and several lab analysts walked in, their voices loud and animated. Giana cleared her throat. "I'll, uh... I'll walk you out."

Remy nodded and they headed together across the lab. They reached the door, and Giana opted to step out into the hallway with Remy. "So. Hopefully we'll come up with something promising in the next few days. Fingers crossed. Either way, I'll let you know."

"Great." Remy nodded. She tapped her thigh with the heel of her thumb. "Okay," she said, and gave a small shrug.

"Okay," Giana echoed.

Remy nodded again, finally turning to go. Then she stopped short. "Oh, hey. About the cookout…"

"Oh, right!" Giana said quickly. "Thanks so much for inviting me. I don't get out much, as you can probably tell, so I'm a little excited."

There was amusement in Remy's eyes. "Well, I'm excited too. The hosts of the party are two of my best friends, and they're absolutely stellar people. You'll see when you meet them. But, um, look. I just wanted to give you fair warning here. Erica Forsyte will be there, too."

Giana shook her head. "Remind me again…"

"The assistant DA from last night—"

"Oh! God, yes. How could I forget?"

Remy chuckled. "It's not really a big deal or anything. But you'll be there with *me*, obviously. And uh…well, Erica seems to have this crazy idea about the two of us. You and me, that is."

Giana swallowed hard but said nothing.

"I just thought I should mention it ahead of time, you know. Full disclosure. In case you'd prefer to skip the drama and sit this one out."

"Absolutely not. I'm excited to go," Giana assured her. "Really. I love drama."

Remy's laugh came from the chest. She bent her knees slightly. "Awesome. Okay. So I'll pick you up at three o'clock on Saturday. You're in Oakland, right?" Giana nodded. "Perfect. It's on the way. So text me the address, and, um…okay. It should be fun." She winked, and Giana's stomach dipped.

Remy took a step backward and spun on her heel. She headed off down the corridor, sidestepping several more of Giana's coworkers as they straggled back to the lab. Giana stood there and watched her go—until Curtis appeared in front of her to block the view, beaming broadly with a chef's salad in one hand and a Coca-Cola in the other.

CHAPTER SEVEN

Saturday morning, Giana rolled over and stretched, blinking against the morning light streaming into her bedroom. Those high transom windows were her favorite thing about Liz's condo. She could never bear to cover them up, even to draw the shades at night before she went to sleep.

She yawned and blew the hair out of her eyes, trying to cling to the dream even as it faded so quickly from memory. It was a cloudy blur at this point, but Remy had been there, she was sure of it. Something about the two of them planning to go on a trip. Or maybe they were actually in the middle of a trip, having already traveled together for a long time. And it was someplace exotic, like a transcontinental tour or an African safari. Just the two of them. She had awakened feeling contented, and oddly secure.

She groaned softly as the pleasant feeling evaporated, and the anxiety of her waking life crept in on her again. She was still so rattled by her own behavior in the lab on Tuesday. Days later, the scene was still replaying itself in her mind, stuck on a relentless loop that had no off switch.

Giana had never been attracted to another woman before in her life. Even with a roommate like Liz Talbot. In *college*. Where trying on a different persona for a week was as easy as changing your shoes. If she had had any leanings in that direction whatsoever, surely they would have presented themselves then, in an environment where it was practically encouraged. It was nonsensical to her that now, years later, a woman could come out of nowhere and completely turn her head.

And yet, she was drawn to Remy Devereux. Captivated by her. She had a physical response to the woman's very presence in a room. A response that was undeniably sexual. There was no point in lying to herself about it any longer. The real question was what was she going to do about it, if anything at all.

Her smart phone pinged on the bedside table, and Giana groped for it with a heavy sigh. She read the message and let the phone drop back on the table. Poor Nick. He had turned out to be the perfect gentleman last night, showing up for their date on time, sharply dressed, eager to show her a good night out. They'd dined at a charming little restaurant on the waterfront, then strolled along the promenade, with the bridge lights twinkling in the distance. It was a perfectly romantic scenario, and yet she had found it impossible to give the man her full attention. Remy had burrowed into her brain like a tick.

And this afternoon was the cookout, which was bound to be hours spent in the detective's company. A few days ago, she was excited by the prospect of that. But now, suddenly afflicted by an acute case of self-awareness, she felt close to panic.

She'd already considered canceling but had immediately discarded the option as far too cowardly. And it wasn't like she actually had anything to be afraid of if she did go. She knew it was all in her head. Remy had so much as confessed she'd only invited her in order to make that Erica woman jealous. And the absurd thing about it was, Giana didn't care. She was just ecstatic to spend an afternoon with Remy—the piddling little details of how that came about were irrelevant. She had evidently lost her mind.

She pressed a hand to her forehead and wondered if she might be hyperventilating. She didn't understand why she was reacting this way. It wasn't like she'd never had a crush on somebody before, for God's sake. Albeit, until now, her crushes had always been on guys. But when you got right down to it, should this situation really be any different? She knew how to keep things fun and light. She could do that. Surely there was no need to spiral into crisis mode around it.

Except, this wasn't just anybody. It was Remy Devereux.

Giana's cheeks flamed, and she covered her face with her pillow. She was being ridiculous. She thought about phoning her aunt for a distraction, just to get herself out of her own head. But Lena would know immediately that something was up, and Giana wasn't ready to go there yet. Not out loud. Talking about it out loud would only make it more of a reality.

She tossed the pillow aside and rubbed at the sand in her eyes. She'd go for a run on the boardwalk instead. Yes. And then she'd have a nice long soak in the tub. And a cup of tea. After that, she would sit and maybe read for a while or just relax and think about nothing at all. And then, when it was time, she would get up and get dressed—and make herself look amazing for her date with Remy.

* * *

Remy sped across the Bay Bridge toward Oakland, holding the Audi to a sedate 85 mph while she tried to relax. She was about to spend the afternoon with Giana Falco. They'd had little contact since that peculiar meeting in the crime lab on Tuesday. Remy still hadn't decided if she'd imagined the woman's jumpiness or whether there might actually be something behind it.

There were few instances in life where she didn't feel she could trust her own instincts, but this was definitely one of them. In a situation like this, it was too tempting to see what you wanted to see. Too easy to project and misinterpret the signs. And then you'd find yourself stumbling into a situation that was cringeworthy at best. Or, at worst, too damaging to recover from. Remy enjoyed Giana's company too much to allow that to happen. It was a lesson she'd been forced to learn the hard way, but learn it she had: emotional involvement with a straight woman was a quagmire best avoided.

But then, there had been that one particular moment in the lab. Remy had gotten the distinct impression Giana was checking her out. She could practically feel the woman's eyes roving her body. And then that four-alarm blaze that had broken out on her face—there was no imagining something like that. Yes, the signals the lady was sending were hard to ignore. It made spending time with her all the more ill advised. And yet, Remy couldn't seem to help herself.

Bright sunlight exploded around the car as she shot out of the Yerba Buena Tunnel. The sweeping white trusses of the eastern span sailed upward against a cobalt sky, and she took a moment to appreciate the view. It was another spectacular day in the Bay. The temperatures were sure to be a good twenty degrees warmer in Walnut Creek, and she couldn't wait to get out and enjoy it.

Compared to all of the titillation on Tuesday, the rest of the week had turned out rather glum. She and Cookie had redoubled their efforts in Pinole, but by Friday they had little to show for it, save a very tentative, very general vehicular description. Several individuals had mentioned sighting a white delivery van in the area—an older model with tinted windows, absent of any identifying markings. They had no license plate number, of course, and not even a guess at the specific make or model. It wasn't nothing, but it wasn't far from it.

So far, the only real light in the case had come out of the crime lab, thanks to the amazing and talented Dr. Falco. Remy shook her head. It wasn't enough that the lady was kind, and funny and obscenely gorgeous. She had to be a brilliant scientist on top of all that.

Remy shifted in her seat as the tension in her shoulder blades reasserted itself. She was excited to see Giana, but she'd also spent the morning second-guessing her decision to bring her to the cookout. Apart from her family, these were the people who knew Remy the best—away from the job, sans the badge and armor. It was a kind of exposure, inviting Giana into her world like this, and suddenly she wasn't so sure she was comfortable with that.

It wasn't a date, but two people attending a party together could be a strangely intimate thing. Giana wouldn't know anyone there, of course, so for the next several hours she'd be Remy's guest. They'd be a couple, in effect. Even if it was only for a little while.

As for the hosts of the party, Remy had deliberately neglected to tell them she'd be bringing along a friend. Keisha and Devlin were nothing if not mischievous. And Giana was so beautiful. The ribbing they were about to deliver would be bad enough—no need to give them extra time to sharpen the barbs.

And then, on top of all of that, there was Erica. Remy didn't even want to contemplate how that was about to go.

At three p.m. sharp, she slipped the roadster into a parking spot on Water Street in Jack London Square. She cut the engine and dialed Giana's number. The husky purr answered on the first ring.

"Hi, Remy, are you here?"

"Yep, I'm parked right out front. Should I wait here, or—?"

"Oh, I'm so sorry, but I need a couple of minutes. Can you come up?"

"Uh, sure."

"Perfect. I'm in eight twenty-five. I'll buzz you in downstairs."

Giana hung up, and Remy sat and stared at the phone for a beat. She got out of the car and crossed the sidewalk in two long strides, reaching the building's entrance just as the door began to vibrate with a muted mechanical hum. The lobby inside was spacious and light-filled, with sleek leather seating and large modern paintings on the walls. Remy found the elevator and studied her reflection in the polished interior as she rode smoothly to the eighth floor. Her heart was thumping in her ears, and she leaned back against the handrail, wondering how long it was going to take her to stop reacting to the sound of Giana's voice.

The elevator doors opened onto a long, carpeted hallway. Halfway down the corridor she found the apartment marked 825. The door stood ajar, and she pushed it open and stepped inside.

"Giana?"

"Come on in! I'll be out in a second."

The call came from somewhere in the back of the apartment. Remy glanced around at the impressive interior and let out a low whistle. The condo was designed to the height of industrial chic, with open kitchen and living areas that flowed together into one harmonious space. Dramatic concrete pillars provided definition, and the light was simply outstanding.

Remy crossed the living room to the giant picture window and peered out at the sparkling marina and estuary below. She stood there and waited and tried to relax, tracking the progress of a small white sloop as it motored slowly westward, heading up the channel and eventually out to the blue waters of the San Francisco Bay.

She could feel Giana's presence before she heard her. When she turned, she saw her entering from a hallway off to the right, her green eyes flashing, a radiant smile on her face, fairly gliding as she crossed the room.

"Hey, you." She reached out and grasped both of Remy's forearms. Then she leaned up and brushed a kiss against her cheek.

Remy's breath caught in her chest. "Uh…Hello! Wow, you look amazing." She briefly scanned the short summer dress, her eyes skimming over bare arms and shapely thighs. Strappy platform wedges brought the center of Giana's forehead even with Remy's lips. Perfect for planting a kiss. Slow and soft, just exactly there. She shook the thought from her mind.

"Ridiculous place you have here, are you kidding me?"

Giana waved a hand as she turned and strode toward the kitchen. "Oh, I wish I could take some of the credit, but I'm just a squatter here."

Remy stared at her rear end as she walked away, mesmerized by the bounce of her hips and the delightful way their movement caused the fabric of the skirt to sway.

"It's my roommate's place, and these are all of her lovely things."

Giana glanced back, and Remy's eyes redirected to the nearest painting on the wall. "This one here is nice. I see she's a Pollock fan."

"That's right! *Blue Poles.*" Giana walked over and stood next to Remy, her arms crossed as she studied the print. "It was unusual for Pollock to title his work. Some say it's a disservice to this particular piece." Remy tried to focus on the words, but the scent of the woman was scrambling her thoughts. "Supposedly, it limits your field of comprehension. All you do is look for the poles."

Giana turned to Remy, her eyes like crystalline drops of jade. "What do you think?"

Remy scrutinized the painting again. "Yeah. I see poles."

Giana chortled with laughter. "Exactly." She strode away again, heading back to the kitchen to retrieve a bottle of wine from the counter. She tucked her purse under one arm and blew out a breath. "All right, Detective. I'm yours for the afternoon. Do with me what you will."

* * *

Remy's car was a beautiful little two-seater, painted a gleaming pearl gray. How appropriate, Giana thought, as the gray-eyed detective opened the door for her and waved her inside. She settled into the low bucket seat and slowly exhaled, watching as Remy's long strides carried her around to the driver's side.

Seconds later, they were in motion, pulling smoothly away from the curb, hitting all the green lights on the way to the freeway. They reached the on-ramp, and the car rocketed forward, pressing Giana deeper into her seat. She glanced at Remy fluidly working the gearshift, a look of total serenity on her face as the car darted through multiple lanes of traffic. Giana leaned over to make a point of peering at the speedometer, and Remy shied away.

"Hey, what are you doing?" A smile twitched at her lips.

"Nothing." Giana straightened in her seat. "So. You like to drive?"

Remy's grin broadened. "No, I hate it." She gave Giana a sidelong glance. "Thanks for coming, by the way."

"Thanks for asking," Giana answered. The silence lengthened in the car, and she pointed at the stereo. "May I?" Remy gave a shrugging nod, and Giana leaned forward to examine the sleek console. "This should be interesting," she mumbled.

Remy chuckled but offered no assistance as Giana began to poke at the screen—carefully at first and then at random. Music finally filled the car, and she adjusted the volume and sat back in her seat, satisfied.

Traffic abruptly slowed around them as the lanes divided into two tunnels ahead—narrow bores drilled into the base of a steep hillside. Remy chose the one on the left, and the soot-lined tube engulfed them, curving away into darkness. Giana felt like a time traveler on an expedition to the planet's core. The tunnel ended abruptly, and they burst out on the other side in a wash of sunlight and green rolling hills. A feeling of anticipation took hold of her then, crowding out the last of her nerves. She was on an adventure, and she resolved to embrace the experience, whatever the day might bring.

She turned to Remy. "So tell me about your friends. What are their names again?"

"Devlin and Keisha. They've been together for some insane amount of time. Fifteen years, or something like that. We all met in college."

"At Tulane."

"At Tulane," Remy nodded. "Devlin was this beer-swilling, softball-playing madwoman. We were instant friends, of course. And Keisha lived in my dormitory. She was this total bookworm. Super straitlaced, no nonsense. Her dad is a Baptist preacher from Selma, Alabama."

Giana raised her eyebrows, and Remy snorted softly. "Yeah, I know. She's come out of her shell a *lot* since then. You'll see what I mean when you meet her. Back then, though, I never would've put the two of them together. Not in a million years. But man, they just fit, you know? It was like, love at first sight. Still is. It's actually kind of nauseating, to tell you the truth."

"And what about you?" Giana asked. "When did you first…I mean, was it something you just decided one day, or…"

Remy glanced at her briefly and turned her eyes back on the road. Giana was afraid she'd asked the wrong question, but then Remy began to talk.

"I guess you could say I always knew. When we were kids, my brother's friends were always my friends, too. I didn't really like hanging out with the girls or doing any of the stuff they were into. I hated dolls, and makeup, and dresses. All of that. I just wanted to climb trees and crawl up underneath things, like porches and parked cars, and basically just stay filthy, like, all of the time. And then…"

Remy stopped, and Giana saw a flash of something cross her features, but it was gone so quickly she began to doubt she'd seen it at all.

"By the time high school rolled around," Remy went on, "things started to get a little more complicated. Because now, see, I *wanted* to hang out with the girls. Just for a different reason." She glanced at Giana with a wry smile. "Playing sports helped. Just being one of the jocks. It gave me an identity. A place where I felt like I actually fit in."

Remy stopped talking then. Giana wished she would say a little more, but she didn't want to push. "And what about your brother, when did he come out?"

"Oh, Max? Not until well after college. Yeah, he was a late bloomer. Jerome is his first and only boyfriend, and they've been together for, like, six years."

"Really." Giana couldn't hide her surprise.

"Yeah. What, does that seem strange or some—" She stopped abruptly as the music muted on the car stereo, replaced by a loud, gurgling trill. The name "Max" appeared on the center console screen. "Jesus. Well, speak of the devil." Remy glanced at Giana. "I'm sorry, but do you mind? I should take this." She waited for Giana's nod before she pressed a button on the steering wheel.

"What's up there, bud. Your ears must be burning. Everything all right?" Remy's tone was casual on the surface, but Giana could detect an edge, like concern, just underneath. She kept her eyes on the scenery passing outside the window.

"Yeah, take it easy there, sis. Everything's fine." Max's voice was a soothing baritone. "You know, you're gonna have to stop freaking out every time I call you."

Remy cleared her throat. "Yeah. Well, you're on speaker there, Max. I've got somebody in the car with me now, so…"

"Oh, yeah? Who is it? Yoo-hoooo!" Max called in a singsong voice. "Hello there…"

Laughing, Giana had no choice but to respond. "Hello there, Max, I'm Giana. We were just talking about you. It's nice to meet you officially. Or unofficially." From the corner of her eye, she could see Remy shift in her seat.

"Well, what do you know?" Max said thoughtfully. "How about that? It's Giana." He seemed to recognize the name. Giana renewed her interest in the landscape outside the window.

"Okay, Max," Remy cut in. "If it's not important, I'll catch up with you a little later, all right?"

"Sure thing, Rem. No problem." He paused. "It was really nice to meet you, Giana."

Swallowing a laugh, Giana answered. "It was nice meeting you, too, Max."

"Yeah. And I hope we get to chat again sometime real—"

"Okay, Max," Remy said quickly, "I'll talk to you soon, all right? Bye, now." She clicked off, and music swelled from the stereo speakers again.

Giana pressed her lips together and waited, her eyes still out the window. "Your brother seems nice," she said after a moment.

"Actually, he's not. He's a pain in the ass."

Giana laughed heartily, and Remy looked at her, shaking her head.

"But is everything okay with him? You sounded a little worried at first when—"

"No, not at all. Everything's fine." Remy's eyes remained on her driving. Giana decided to let the subject drop, though the silence after that was noticeable.

"Hey, speaking of pains in the ass," Remy said. "How was your date last night with Pierce?"

Giana inwardly groaned. "Oh that. You remembered."

"I did." Remy paused. "So how did it go?"

She didn't want to talk about Nick. "It was fine," she murmured, refusing to elaborate.

Their eyes met briefly before Remy glanced away. Giana found herself continuing to study the detective's profile, lingering on the curve of her lips. She forced herself to look elsewhere, but her eyes only made it as far as Remy's right hand. It rested on the gearshift between them, inches from Giana's thigh. The skin was bronzed and stretched taut, a network of plump veins roping their way underneath. She wanted to trace one with the tip of her finger, to see if the skin felt as smooth as it looked.

She glanced up, unsurprised to find the detective's eyes fixed on her again. She turned in her seat to face Remy more directly. "I have a question. You're bringing me to this cookout thing because you want your ex to think we're hot for each other. So…what does that look like to you?"

Remy's mouth dropped open. Her eyes darted back to the road. "That's, uh…Well, that's not exactly what I—"

"Look, I'm totally fine with it," Giana went on. "I'd just like to know what's expected of me. I mean, should I sit on your lap? Or maybe we should just make out in a corner somewhere. What do you think, tongue or no tongue?"

Remy's mouth finally closed, and Giana couldn't suppress the chuckle that bubbled up in her chest. It was fun to see the detective off-balance. Even better to be the one who put her there.

The car swerved as Remy swore and dove across several lanes of traffic, narrowly making the off-ramp. They exited the freeway, and Giana faced forward in her seat again. "Well. No need to overplan it, I guess. I'm sure we can just figure it out when we get there."

Walnut Creek was the picture of tree-lined suburbia, a bastion of large homes and well-tended lawns. Giana suspected they'd arrived at their destination when they turned down a shady lane, densely populated with parked vehicles on both sides of the street. They paused in front of a driveway packed with cars, and Remy pulled into it anyway, tucking the nose of her roadster practically underneath the bumper of a giant SUV.

She cut the engine and looked at her passenger. "You ready?"

"Why, yes I am." Giana was excited. "Let's do this."

She stepped out of the car, and the heat of the day and the music and the hubbub of voices all hit her at once. The party appeared to be in full swing. They strolled together up the driveway, her stomach grumbling at the tantalizing aroma of burgers searing on the grill. At the top of the drive, a wooden gate stood open. They stepped through it into a beautifully landscaped yard, plush with flowers and green grass and manicured trees. People were everywhere, milling about on the flagstone patio or clustered in groupings of lawn furniture scattered about the sizable yard.

An enormous shaggy brown dog spotted them and came trotting over, nails clicking on the pavers. "Here comes Murphy," Remy announced. "They think he might be part Dane, or wolfhound, or something like that. But mainly he's just a big, lovable mutt."

Giana didn't know much about dogs, but this one seemed harmless enough. Apart from the size of him. Remy squatted face-to-snout with the shaggy beast, scratching at his ears and ruffling the tuft of fur that sprouted from the top of his head. When the animal turned its attention on Giana, she was determined to hold her ground. He stretched his long neck upward, pointing his snuffling nose at her face, and she leaned forward a bit to give him a better whiff—until he lapped out a tongue the size of a flank steak. She swiftly ducked out of reach, and Remy gave a startled laugh.

"Whoa!" she exclaimed, grabbing Murphy by the collar. "He never licks anybody. Hmm. I guess he must've smelled something he liked." Her smile was mischievous as her gray eyes openly roamed Giana's face. After a moment, she refocused on the dog. "That's a smart boy, aren't you, Murphy?" She rubbed his massive head. "Isn't that right? Such a big, brilliant, beautiful boy." Giana raised an eyebrow at her fawning tone, wondering if this was the same woman she'd come here with.

A shout from across the yard drew their attention to a stout woman in a bright red apron. She set her grilling tongs aside and came marching toward them, the spikes of her strawberry blond hair translucent in the sunlight. Remy's face broke into a wide grin, and the two of them embraced in a bear hug until the burly woman wrestled herself free, shoving Remy aside to get a better look at Giana. "Hey now, wow," she said, her freckled face shining. "So who do we have here?" She loudly cleared her throat as she straightened her spine and made a show of smoothing out her apron. Giana had to laugh.

Remy stepped nimbly around her friend to return to Giana's side. "Giana, meet Devlin O'Reilly. She and her wife Keisha are our generous hosts for the afternoon. Devlin, this is Giana Falco. She's a forensic scientist at the crime lab in the city."

Smiling, Giana held out her hand. "It's so nice to meet you, Devlin. You have a beautiful home."

Devlin stood with her fists on her hips, her pink cheeks round as she gave Giana another once-over. "Well, hell. Come on over here, woman!" She clasped Giana's outstretched hand and yanked her into a bone-crunching embrace. Giana decided she adored her.

"Come on, let's go find Keisha."

Devlin waved them into the yard, and as they ventured forward, Giana gave in to an impulse. She reached for Remy's hand. There was the briefest stutter in the detective's step, but she recovered a split-second later. She gripped Giana's hand and interlaced their fingers, tugging her along as they moved together into the boisterous crowd.

What followed was a colorful blur of new faces and conversations. Giana gamely allowed herself to be ushered from one group to the next, introduced to one engaging individual after another. She sipped from her wineglass, content to mainly observe the animated exchanges. Remy seemed to shed an outer layer, her eyes dancing, the pitch of her voice rising in laughter. It was fascinating to watch, not to mention endearing. It felt like a special treat to be present to see it happen.

From the instant they'd first touched, it was as if some unseen barrier between them had shattered. Remy was never out of contact after that, either clasping Giana by the hand or resting a palm at the small of her back, leaning in close to listen more intently when she spoke. Their movements became synchronized. Her senses cleaved to the warmth of Remy's body next to hers—and her wonderful scent, which Giana could recognize now in her sleep. Like soap and juniper and sandalwood.

Eventually, they stopped at the beverage table, and Remy stepped away to replenish their drinks. Giana felt suddenly naked in the absence of her touch. Within seconds, however, the detective had returned, with fresh glasses of chilled wine for both of them. Giana murmured her thanks, and for one interminable moment they stood openly contemplating one another. Oddly, she no longer found it difficult to meet Remy's gaze. She stared into the silvery irises and noted that they were rimmed in black, striated throughout with flecks of charcoal and ash.

She watched the thick eyelashes lower and the full lips curve into a provocative smile, and she wanted to know what it would feel like to kiss them. The thought lodged itself in her brain, and she lightly cleared her throat, convinced that Remy had just read her mind. But then it seemed something else had caught the detective's attention, and it was like a shutter closing over her features. Giana turned to see what had happened. She stiffened when she recognized Erica Forsyte standing directly behind her.

"Remy." Erica's eyes were riveted on Remy's face. It was as if Giana did not exist.

"Erica," Remy answered. "You remember Giana Falco from the other night at the bar."

At last, Giana was favored with a glacial smile. "Of course," Erica sniffed.

Of its own volition, Giana's body moved a step closer to Remy's, at the same moment that Remy moved toward her. She felt the warmth of a steady palm in the hollow between her shoulder blades, brushing lightly downward until it came to rest at the base of her spine. She exhaled and met Erica's icy stare. "It's nice to see you again. That's a beautiful dress you're wearing. The color suits you perfectly."

Erica's blue eyes flickered in surprise. They flitted down to Giana's dress and then back up again to her face. "Thank you," she said. "I was actually thinking the same thing about yours."

Giana smiled and nodded, and Erica nodded stiffly in return. She looked at Remy again. "Well. I was actually just on my way out. I didn't want to leave without saying hello."

"It's good to see you, Erica," Remy said.

"You too." Erica glanced at Giana and gave her another quick nod. Then she turned and strode away.

They watched her departure, both of them silent until she'd disappeared into the crowd. Remy leaned over then and whispered in Giana's ear. "Thank you."

The intimacy of that gesture sent a shiver skipping down Giana's spine. She kept her eyes trained forward. "Mmm, I don't have a problem telling the truth. Luckily, it was something she wanted to hear."

The show was over now, presumably. Since their audience of one had left the premises. And yet she was acutely aware of Remy's hand lingering at the small of her back. She wanted it to stay there, and it wasn't a difficult thing to admit. At least not to herself. Neither of them spoke, and for a long while they remained where they were standing, content to watch the party as it streamed around them.

* * *

The car was quiet on the drive back to Oakland. Remy stole a glance at Giana as she sat relaxing in the bucket seat beside her, head back, eyelids half-lowered. She'd removed her shoes on their way out of the party, pausing to grab hold of Remy's shoulder as she balanced on one foot and then the other. She'd padded barefoot down the driveway to the car with the shoes dangling from one hand, and Remy had stood and watched, thinking it was the sexiest thing she'd ever seen a woman do.

Remy turned the car stereo on low and scanned through the stations until the sultry voice of Adele filled the space.

"Mmm, good song," Giana murmured as she stretched out her legs, her smooth thighs flexing below the hemline of her dress.

Remy allowed herself the briefest glimpse before she trained her eyes back on the road. It was time to come back to reality now, she knew. Her rational mind could accept the necessity of that fact. But as the sun dropped below the ridgeline and the witching light of dusk turned the hills a lusty emerald green, another more primal part of her willed the fantasy to go on.

"That was such a fun time, Remy. Thank you again for inviting me."

"Oh, it was absolutely my pleasure," Remy answered quickly. "I had a lot of fun. And honestly, you did me a huge favor back there."

"Ah, yes. Erica." Giana chuckled softly. "She's a very attractive woman, by the way. Once you get her to stop snarling." She paused, and Remy waited, sensing there was more coming. "So is that your type then? High-powered, semi-feral blondes. What the hell did you do to her, anyway?"

Remy glanced at Giana to see if she was kidding. The green eyes were inscrutable in the failing light.

"Don't answer that," Giana said after a moment. "It's really none of my business." She turned to look out the window. "Anyway. I had a wonderful time. Devlin and Keisha were lovely."

In what felt like an instant, they were exiting the freeway back in Oakland. A moment after that, they had arrived in front of Giana's building. Remy pulled into a parking spot and cut the engine, struggling with a pressing desire to remain in this woman's company. The thought of simply waving goodbye and going home now was completely unpalatable. But this was obviously the point where she should take her leave. Surely, it was better for the both of them that she did.

"Would you like to come up for a glass of wine? I have a nice cabernet if you—"

"I'd love to," Remy answered.

Giana smiled and looked down at her lap. "Well, okay then."

They exited the vehicle and entered the building together. She held the door for Giana, careful not to touch her. They were silent again on the elevator ride to the eighth floor.

* * *

Giana instructed her guest to sit and make herself comfortable while she bustled about the living room, turning on lamps and cuing her favorite playlist on the stereo. Remy's eyes seemed to follow her wherever she went. She did her best to ignore the case of jitters that seized her stomach now with a vengeance. But in an odd way, she was grateful for the sensation, too—it felt like a return to a state of normalcy, after so many hours spent in an alternate universe.

She pulled a bottle of wine off the rack and was on her way with it to the kitchen when her roommate appeared in the hallway. Liz was dressed for work in hot pink hospital scrubs, her hair still damp from the shower. She spotted Giana and gasped.

"Oh my God, you *do* still live here! I was beginning to think you'd left me for another woman." Liz strolled into the living room with an impish gleam in her eye. She halted abruptly when she spied Remy lounging on the couch. "Oh! Well, hello to you, fine stranger."

Giana watched in horror as Liz's eyes strafed the length of Remy's tall frame, from her head to her torso to every inch of her long lean legs. She pursed her lips and twirled a blond ringlet around her finger. "Let me guess. You're the detective."

"Remy." Remy rose halfway from the sofa and stretched out a hand. "Nice to meet you, Liz."

"Mmm. Likewise, I'm sure." Liz batted her eyes as she grasped Remy's hand and held on to it for way too long.

Remy flashed her an indulgent grin while she patiently waited to be released. Liz finally let go, and Remy masked her chuckle behind a cough as she dropped back on the couch. She picked up a magazine and suddenly became engrossed in reading it.

"Um. Excuse me, Remy. I'll be with you in just one second." Giana grabbed her roomie by the wrist and dragged her toward the kitchen. Liz trailed reluctantly behind, craning her neck to get another look at the woman on the couch. There was no wall for privacy, so Giana halted behind a concrete column and muttered through clenched teeth. "Lizard! What the hell was that?"

Liz's eyes were wide and brimming with laughter. She fluttered her hands in excitement. "Shhh! I have something to tell you!" She leaned forward and rasped at Giana in a stage whisper. "I don't know if you know this, but that woman in there is totally gay. And you never told me how smoking *hot* she is! How could you forget to mention a thing like that?"

"Oh my God, Liz, will you please lower your voice?"

"I will not." Liz turned to peek around the column. "She's single, right? Did you tell me she was single?"

"Back off, Lizzie!" Giana's voice had dropped to a hiss. "Don't even think about it."

Liz's shoulders slumped. "Oh, for God's sake, Gee, will you grow a sense of humor? I'm kidding!" She held Giana's gaze, a wicked little smile playing at her lips. "And just what the heck has crawled up *your* backside and died, anyway?"

Giana folded her arms and concentrated on the floor. She knew she had overreacted. And to deny it now would only make matters worse. She adopted a calmer tone. "Nothing. As it so happens, Remy is the only friend I have in the Bay Area. Besides *you*, I'm sorry to say. And I'd like to keep it that way, if you don't mind. So, please. Cut it out with the flirting."

Liz threw up her hands, the picture of innocence. "Fine, fine. I said I was kidding." She folded her arms and heaved a sigh. "It seems like a terrible waste, if you ask me. But if that's the way you want to play it, fine." She continued to scrutinize Giana's face, clearly working to suppress a smile.

Giana reached the end of her patience. "My God, Elizabeth, why are you still here? Aren't you late for work or something?"

Liz held up her hands again and left the kitchen. Giana followed close on her heels, watching as she gathered her purse and plucked her keys from the bowl by the door. She turned to Remy and smiled like a curly-haired pixie. "It was so lovely to meet you, Officer. But I'm afraid I've just been ordered to leave." Opening the door with a flourish, she whirled to give Giana a wink before she closed it behind her and was gone.

Giana stood for a moment and let the embarrassment wash over her. She finally looked up at Remy, who sat with one long arm thrown across the back of the couch. She was openly grinning at her now, the magazine forgotten on the coffee table. Giana put a hand on one hip and narrowed her eyes. "You didn't hear a word of that in there, did you?"

"No, I did not. Not one word."

"Good. That's what I thought."

She nodded firmly and returned to the kitchen, fighting off a smile of her own. Elizabeth Talbot was an absolute monster and always would be. And she adored her completely. She pulled two wineglasses from the cabinet and took her time working the corkscrew into the bottle. As she poured the wine, she was surprised to realize her butterflies had evaporated—thanks in no small part to the antics of her roommate. She gave her absent friend another silent nod of acknowledgment before she took the glasses with her and returned to the living room.

Remy had abandoned the sofa in the meantime and now stood investigating a collection of picture frames on a nearby shelf. She accepted the glass Giana handed her and pointed at a small faded photo in a silver frame. "That's gotta be your mom, right?"

Giana nodded, peering at the photograph. The pretty brunette posed in an 80s-style tennis dress, a racket thrown over one shoulder. "I don't really see it, but everyone says I look like her. She died in a car accident when I was three. Apparently, I was thrown from the vehicle without a scratch on me." Remy glanced sharply at her, and Giana took a moment to return her gaze.

"Jesus. I'm so sorry to hear that."

Giana nodded. "I don't remember a lot about her. I used to stare at that photo all the time, trying to imagine her voice or her laugh. Or what she smelled like. I can't remember any of those things. I think it's probably why I took up tennis. At least in the beginning. So I could pretend that I was just like her."

Remy watched her quietly for a moment, then reached for a different frame and picked it up. Giana groaned at the image of her younger self, skinny and awkward in a U Penn T-shirt, beaming out at the camera with a giant trophy cup raised above her head. Remy studied the photo for a long moment, then set it back in its place. "That settles it. I am *never* playing tennis with you. Ever."

"Now, Remy, that's not fair. That trophy was a fake. And it really has been ages since I played. And, I don't know if you're aware of this, but you happen to possess the wingspan of, of..."— she cast about for the right word—"a whooping crane. To put it mildly." Remy snorted softly, and she continued. "Whereas I, on the other hand, I'm more like a swallow. Or a falcon, at best. It should be a fairly even match. Besides, you owe me."

Remy cut her a glance. "Oh, I see how it is. You truly do get nothing for free in this world."

Giana nodded soberly. "Sad but true. Shall we say, next weekend?"

Remy's eyes glittered. Her mouth twitched in amusement, and Giana's gaze was drawn there once again. Suddenly aware of her proximity to the detective, she took a step backward, and then another, until she had retreated to the safety of a sitting chair opposite the couch. She sank into it sideways, her legs dangling over one cushioned arm. Remy resumed her lounging position on the couch, and Giana was at once relieved and disappointed, wishing she had the nerve to get up and go sit next to her.

She scoured her mind for a neutral topic. "Tell me more about Keisha and Devlin. Do they want to have kids?"

Remy eyed her quietly and took a sip of wine, the expression on her face unreadable. She gave a half shrug and began to talk. Giana sipped from her own glass and listened, lulled by the music on the stereo and the rhythm of Remy's voice. At one point the detective got up to retrieve the bottle from the kitchen, refilling Giana's glass and then her own. Giana continued to prompt her with more questions, just to keep her talking.

Time passed unnoticed, until Remy finally glanced at the clock on the wall and grimaced. It was past midnight. Disappointed, Giana watched as her guest rose from the couch and reached over to pluck the empty glass from her hand. Remy carried the stemware into the kitchen and rinsed the glasses in the sink, and Giana stayed where she was, gazing out the window at the twinkling lights in the marina. She didn't move until she heard the jingle of car keys scooped from the countertop and dropped into a jacket pocket. Reluctantly, she climbed out of her chair and joined her guest at the front door.

"Well." Remy turned to face her, inhaling deeply.

"Well," Giana echoed. She smiled and hesitated only a moment before she stepped forward and pulled Remy close, arms wrapping around her waist, cheek pressing against her collarbone.

Remy enfolded her in a loose embrace, and Giana inhaled, breathing in the scent of her, basking in the warmth that emanated through her thin cotton shirt. She felt a hand run lightly down her back—a touch that had grown familiar over the course of the day, until it was so ruthlessly taken away the instant they'd left the party. She welcomed it back now, sighing as her body relaxed into it. Strong fingers kneaded the muscles on either side of her spine, and a hand came up to lift the hair away from her nape, fingers brushing lightly along the side of her neck.

Remy's thumb began a lazy caress, circling the sensitive skin below her left ear, and Giana's pulse jumped. She stilled, her eyes fixed on the hollow at the base of Remy's throat. The exploration continued, tracing the line of her jaw, gliding forward to find her mouth, then grazing against the thickest part of her lower lip. The sensation left a trail of burning synapses in its wake, and her breathing all but stopped.

Remy's voice was barely audible when she spoke. "I wonder if you even realize the effect you have on me. Do you do it on purpose?"

Startled, Giana looked up to meet her gaze, and what she saw there robbed her of the last bit of air in her lungs. The gray eyes had darkened to a smoldering slate, and the hunger in them was undeniable. There was no effort to hide it, her nostrils flaring as her eyes raked Giana's face. She buried a hand in her hair, gripping her tightly at the nape, and Giana knew she was about to be kissed.

She closed her eyes, bracing and eager and panicked, gasping at the first touch of Remy's lips on hers. Lips that were smooth and full and incredibly soft. Softer than she could have ever imagined. Teasing and light. Maddening in their velvet caress. She held herself rigid, barely breathing as Remy's mouth pleasured hers, sparking an ember in the pit of her stomach, fanning it into a flame, until her fingers tightened around Remy's waist, and her lips began to move of their own accord, tentative at first, then urgent and plying and searching for more.

She opened her mouth, moaning when Remy's tongue found hers. Probing, insistent, tasting faintly of wine. They taunted and prodded one another, the kiss growing deeper with every aggressive stroke, and a nagging tension began to envelop Giana's groin.

She rose up on the balls of her feet, driving her hips forward, relishing the answering thrust of Remy's body against hers, reveling in the pressure of their heated straining until one of them emitted a tortured groan. She was unsure which one of them had made the sound, but then the contact was abruptly broken.

Remy gripped her by the hips, arms rigid as she stepped back, holding their bodies apart. Dazed, Giana struggled to focus, her breathing ragged, clasping at Remy's forearms for balance.

"I'm sorry, I...Jesus Christ," Remy breathed. She closed her eyes and let Giana go, taking another step backward until the distance between them felt like a mile. She raked a hand through her hair. "Giana, I..." Her face was flushed. Her lips were parted and swollen. She met Giana's gaze, but only briefly. "I'm, uh...I should go."

Remy paused to look at her again, then she opened the door and was out of the apartment in one swift motion, disappearing down the corridor before Giana could comprehend what was happening. The door swung slowly closed behind her, and Giana continued to stand there, staring at it in blind confusion, her heart pounding like a jackhammer in her chest.

CHAPTER EIGHT

Giana woke early Sunday morning in a fog, exhausted after a fitful night of sleep, her dreams muddled and vaguely disquieting—a series of bizarre tableaus that made no sense in the bright light of the morning. She retrieved her phone from the bedside table, and the glowing screen stared blankly back at her. No messages yet. Nothing from Remy.

Giana set the phone down and closed her eyes, and the scene from last night instantly began to replay itself, for the thousandth time. The heat of that kiss was nothing she could have ever prepared herself for. She was still reeling from the feel of Remy pressed against her. From the taste of her and the thrust of her tongue.

Giana's cheeks warmed as she felt her body begin to quicken again, and she buried her face in her hands, shocked by the hunger that clamored inside of her. It was nothing she recognized, nothing she had ever seen in herself before. It had declared itself last night like a genie out of a bottle, and it was so demanding. So…wanton.

She felt as though she'd had no fair warning. She'd never had a reason to believe she could react like that to a woman's touch. Not like that. But then it was Remy's mouth on hers, and Remy's thighs and belly pressed against hers. At the same time firm and yet exquisitely soft. And it was like...

Swept away. That was a term she had heard too many times before, but she'd never fully understood the meaning of it until now. Remy Devereux had kissed her, and it was as if a rolling tide of need had risen up and engulfed her within it, overtaking caution and reason and everything else in its path.

She didn't want to think what would've happened if Remy hadn't pulled away when she had. She hadn't wanted the kiss to end. And she hadn't wanted Remy to leave—certainly not the way that she did. The woman had literally bolted from the room. It was hard not to take something like that personally. Like maybe Remy had suddenly found the whole situation revolting and couldn't get away fast enough.

But Giana knew that wasn't true. Everything leading up to that point told her there was nothing further from the truth. Her stomach muscles clenched as she remembered Remy's hand in her hair the moment before she'd kissed her. That delicious tugging sensation as she'd tightened her grip, holding Giana immobilized. Claiming her.

She threw off the covers and sat up on the edge of the bed. She was embarrassed by the sheer intensity of her reaction, and then annoyed by her embarrassment. A gorgeous woman had kissed her, and she had responded to that. Was it really something to be ashamed of? And what did it mean, anyway? She was the same person she'd always been—nothing about her had actually changed, had it?

She raised her head at the muffled sound of the apartment's front door. She heard it open and close, and then the jangle of keys hitting the bowl. Liz was home. She felt the reflexive urge to call out to her friend but held herself in check. Liz would definitely have something to say about all of this—Giana just wasn't sure she was ready to hear it yet.

She needed to talk to Remy. She didn't expect the detective to have all the answers, or any, for that matter. Mainly, she just wanted to hear her voice. She picked up the phone but only stared at it resting in her palm. It wasn't that she was suddenly feeling shy, exactly. She simply had no idea what she wanted to say.

She knew what she felt for Remy was more than an idle attraction, more than a crush. The truth of that fact became more obvious to her every time they were together. And then the kiss last night, or rather the way she had answered it. Well, that certainly drove the point home, didn't it?

She wryly shook her head, wondering how long it would've taken her to come to this realization on her own, if Remy hadn't taken the first step and made it physical. But then she decided it didn't matter. Truly, all of these personal revelations were academic if Remy had no interest in pursuing things. And there was no guarantee that she did. So far, the detective's silence said it all.

At that moment, the phone pinged in her hand, and Giana almost dropped it. Her heart began to pound before she'd even read the message. Her shoulders slumped as she realized the text was from Nick. She'd forgotten to get back to him yesterday. The day had been so full.

Truthfully, Giana had been too consumed with Remy, from sunrise to sunset, to think of anyone else. Nick had never entered her mind. And the date they'd had two nights ago— well, that might as well have happened in another century. It wasn't fair to him, she knew. If she was seeing someone else, she should at least tell him so. Except, she didn't actually know if she *was* seeing someone else. She couldn't honestly say what it was that she and Remy were doing.

She groaned and fell back on the bed. Nick had been clear about his intentions, and they'd had a good time together on Friday. It was straightforward and uncomplicated—unlike whatever this was with Remy. She just wished she felt more enthusiasm for the man than she did. She'd probably be doing him a favor if she were to cut things off with him now. But then he would want to know why, of course. And she didn't have a ready answer for that, at least not one that she was willing to share.

She heard the muted sound of her roommate's voice in the hallway, humming a tune as she passed by. The door to Liz's room shut, and silence descended over the apartment again. It was still early, and she considered crawling back under the covers to try to fall asleep again. She discarded the idea immediately. There was too much tension in her body to sleep, and even if she were able to drift off, the dreams that likely awaited her were nothing she wanted to revisit.

She lifted her phone, compulsively checking again for any word from Remy. Then she heaved a sigh and dialed her aunt's number. Lena answered promptly, and it was the sound of her voice that finally did it. Giana released the sob that had been straining to break free from her throat, then she sat up and crossed her legs on the bed and proceeded to tell her aunt everything.

* * *

Traffic in downtown San Francisco was at a standstill. The congestion in the area was always bad, but for some reason, this Monday morning's commute was heavier than usual. Compounded by extensive and mystifyingly timed road construction, it was more than enough to paralyze the streets in gridlock.

Remy sat in her Audi and fumed, convinced the gods were colluding against her. She'd left the house absurdly late to begin with, somehow managing to sleep straight through the alarm. It was nearly eight a.m. before her eyes finally opened. Half delirious, she'd stumbled into the shower and out the door without the benefit of a morning run.

She'd even skipped her beloved Starbucks to make up for lost time. And it might have even worked, until she made the left turn on Harrison Street, and everything came to a shuddering halt. The Everetts were due in at nine a.m., and unless they were caught in the same miserable ball-up, Remy was about to commit the mortal sin of making the grieving couple wait.

She swore under her breath, her head pounding from a lack of caffeine, and scrolled through the contacts on her car phone.

She jabbed at the screen, and a tone buzzed loudly over the stereo speakers. Cookie answered, his voice raised above the chatter of a police radio in the background.

Remy skipped the small talk. "Hey, how soon can you get back to the barn? I'm totally jammed up here, and I've got the Everetts in at nine."

"Oh, man. No can do, boss. I'm already on the bridge."

Remy released a muttered string of expletives. "Okay. Ah… I'll check in with you later."

She clicked off without waiting for a reply, fixated now on the taxi creeping up on the left side of her vehicle. The car edged steadily over, its driver obviously intent on wedging into the half meter of space between her and the box truck ahead. Remy lurched the Audi forward and laid on the horn for much longer than she needed to. Her satisfaction in this was quickly eclipsed by a renewed throbbing in her skull. She should've stopped for the damned coffee.

Dialing again, Remy rang the Homicide Division's main office number. Mona Gladwell's harried, no-nonsense voice came on the line. "Homicide. How may I direct your call?"

"Mona. Remy Devereux here. Look, I need a favor—"

"Ohhh. Inspector Devereux." Mona's voice lowered to a gravelly purr. "It's good to talk to you, too. And how are we doing this morning?"

Remy smiled in spite of herself. "Uh, I'm fine, Mona, thanks. How about yourself?"

"Oh, wonderful, wonderful. Thank you so much for asking. Now, what can I do for you, sugar?"

"Well, I have an interview with Mr. and Mrs. Everett this morning, and I'm running a little late. Do you think you can set them up in the small conference room for me? And give them some coffee or whatever else they need? That's their daughter who turned up in the Mission Bay last week."

"I know who the Everetts are, baby. Don't you worry about it. I'll take care of them for you."

Remy exhaled. "Thank you, Mona, thank you. You are the bee's knees."

"Mmm-hmm. I know."

Remy chuckled as the call disconnected, relaxing a little in her seat. That was the most she could do for now. Apart from being horribly late, she was as prepared for the Everett interview as she could be. The good news was, the case wasn't dead yet. With the results of the fiber and hair analyses pending and the tentative vehicle description in Pinole, there was still some hope of movement in the case. She just wished she had more to tell them.

She'd spent most of the day on Sunday reviewing the file, though she could've recited the thing from memory before that. Going over the material again was just good due diligence. And it boded well for her sanity if she could keep her mind focused on something else besides Giana.

Remy glanced at the clock in the dash and congratulated herself. She'd gone almost an hour without thinking about the woman. She blew out a breath, drumming her fingers on the steering wheel. She knew she couldn't avoid it forever. She was going to have to grow a backbone and talk to her eventually. Remy could admit she'd fled the scene on Saturday like a twelve-year-old. She owed Giana an explanation for that, at least. And for the kiss. That incredible, mind-blowing kiss. A shiver rippled down the length of her spine, and she closed her eyes as the hunger gripped her again. She'd wanted Giana. It was frightening how much she'd wanted her. And the way Giana had responded...

It was beyond anything Remy could've anticipated. And at the same time, it wasn't a surprise at all. None of it was a surprise. They'd been driving toward it from the moment Giana grabbed Remy's hand at the party. The entire day after that had turned into one prolonged seduction. Foreplay. Leading to a very predictable conclusion. The question was, who had seduced whom?

Remy knew she was in over her head. Giana Falco was the perfect woman. Smart and funny and affectionate. Generous. Achingly beautiful. She was the kind of woman you fell in love with. The head-over-heels, howl at the moon, break your heart into a thousand pieces kind of love. Except for the minor complication of her heterosexuality.

That was more than an inconvenience, more than a technicality. Remy knew better, and yet she'd allowed herself to forget. For an entire afternoon and well into the evening, she'd simply blocked the truth of the situation from her mind.

But if she were being completely honest, this thing between them had started well before Saturday. She'd felt this ungodly attraction practically from the moment they'd first met. And it wasn't one-sided, though she'd tried to convince herself that it was. Giana was open-minded and obviously curious, and Remy had been deluding herself to think they could spend any amount of time together without something like this happening. It was irresponsible, and damned short-sighted of her, to allow it. Not to mention a tad suicidal.

The box truck's brake lights dimmed, and Remy quickly shifted into gear. They rolled nearly half a block before coming to a halt again. She was going to have to break things off with Giana. A wave of depression washed over her as she realized it was the only sensible thing to do. She was too attracted to the woman, and Giana was too curious about that attraction.

Remy inhaled deeply, her nerve endings springing to life again. She could almost feel the weight of those supple breasts pushing up against hers. Hear the arousal in that soft moan, rising from deep in Giana's throat, vibrating like a taut wire between them. She had wanted that kiss, as much as Remy had wanted it. And a combination like that was lethal.

She shook her head at the irony of her predicament. After the stress of the breakup with Erica, something like this ought to be exactly what she wanted. A beautiful woman, eager to experiment, no strings attached. It could've been a fun distraction for them both.

But there was a certain kind of woman—like Giana—that you just didn't go there with. It was too easy to overcommit. Like a grappler who lunges at the wrong moment, you could lose your balance and go sprawling. She had done it before, and she had no interest in repeating the performance. Better to cut bait and run. It wasn't the bravest thing to do, but it was damn sure the safest. Maybe a better individual could walk that line, but Remy knew herself. And she just wasn't that evolved.

It was 9:35 a.m. by the time Remy pulled into the garage below the Justice Building. She was parked and across the smooth concrete floor in seconds, slapping the elevator button to bring the car plodding downward from the fifth floor. The scarred metal doors had barely opened before she was inside the car and stabbing at the button again, pacing in a tight circle as the elevator began its glacial journey upward. At last she was released onto the fourth floor, and she hastened down the empty hallway to the division offices.

Mona manned the desk at reception, the silver in her hair shining under the fluorescent lights. She peered at Remy over the half-moons of her reading glasses. "They just got here ten minutes ago, sugar. Relax."

Remy exhaled and whispered her thanks. She never broke her stride as she rounded the corner and headed directly to the conference room.

"Mr. and Mrs. Everett, I'm so sorry to keep you waiting. I'm Inspector Devereux. Thank you for making the trip in this morning."

A florid, middle-aged man stood up to shake Remy's hand while his wife remained seated, a handkerchief tightly balled in one fist. The woman's dark hair was neat. Her large brown eyes were puffy and red-rimmed from crying. Remy had studied the photo of Lisa Everett many times, and now she could see the echoes of the dead girl in her mother's face. Remy offered a tentative smile, and the woman stared vacantly up at her, seemingly without comprehension, until her husband laid a gentle hand on her shoulder. Startled, she glanced at him, then quickly rose to shake Remy's hand.

Remy set her bag down in one of the chairs that ringed the oval conference table. "Can I get you anything else? More coffee. Or water, perhaps?"

They shook their heads in unison, eyes fixed on Remy as she pulled out the case file and a notebook, then took a seat facing the couple. Her cell phone buzzed, and she quickly reached into her pocket to silence it.

For the next ninety minutes she went over the case, providing the couple with as many details as possible while leaving out the most heinous. She gently plied them with questions about the girl's behavior in the weeks and days leading up to her disappearance—questions she knew had already been asked and answered multiple times. But it was crucial to be as thorough as possible. Memory sometimes worked in unexpected ways. A small detail dismissed as trivial one day could suddenly resurface with great significance the next.

Mrs. Everett did most of the talking, her voice low and wavering as she repeatedly referred to her daughter in the present tense, then corrected herself a moment later. Her husband remained silent beside her.

"It seems your daughter was very active in school," Remy commented.

"Oh, yes." Mrs. Everett nodded. "Lisa is just…well, she's just a ball of energy. And she's so good with people. Er… she was. Good with people." She looked down at her hands. "Anything social, and Lisa was the first one to sign up for it. Before anybody else could get a chance to. But the grades came first. We always made sure of that."

She glanced at her husband, whose eyes remained on his coffee cup. It sat untouched on the table in front of him. "She was captain of the cheerleading squad," Mrs. Everett continued. "She was really proud of that. And she was on the debate team. And she played volleyball in the winter. She was always doing some sort of volunteer work too. With the 4-H club. Collecting toys and clothing, food drives. All kinds of community activities. I swear, I don't know how she found the time for all of it."

Mrs. Everett's lips quavered in a tremulous smile. She smoothed her handkerchief out on the table, then began to fold it over on itself, again and again, into ever smaller squares. "But the 4-H club, that was probably her greatest joy. She just loved everything about it. And she made so many wonderful friendships there." Mrs. Everett unfolded the handkerchief and smoothed it out again. A large teardrop splashed on her wrist, which she didn't seem to notice.

"And there was nothing strange or out of the ordinary?" Remy prodded. "She hadn't mentioned meeting anyone new recently? Anybody who may have seemed overly friendly. Or unfriendly. Or just unusual in some way?" Lisa's boyfriend had competed in a wrestling tournament in Sacramento the weekend of the girl's disappearance. He'd been eliminated as a suspect.

"No, no. She never mentioned anything like that." Mrs. Everett's voice was a hoarse whisper. She shrugged, studying the hankie. "There was nothing wrong." She shook her head and looked up at Remy. "There was nothing wrong."

Remy felt the interview was drawing to a close. She checked her notes a final time to make sure she'd covered all the areas she'd originally intended. A corner of a photograph peeked out of the file in front of her—Lisa's school portrait. The autopsy photos were stashed carefully away in Remy's bag. Mrs. Everett reached for Lisa's picture, her fingers trembling, and Remy pulled out the photo and placed it on the table between them.

"She was a beautiful young lady, Mrs. Everett."

The woman nodded and brought the hankie to her lips. Remy laid a finger on the photograph, pointing at the gold necklace around the girl's neck. "Did she wear this often?" The pendant was the shape of a four-leafed clover, with tiny H's stamped into the center of each leaf.

"Yes," Mrs. Everett sniffled. "She never took it off. 'Learn to do by doing.' That's the 4-H motto. I think she really believed that."

Remy made a note in the file. The necklace had not been recovered from the body. She shuffled the materials into a neat stack, then rose from the table.

They walked as a group out past reception, and Remy paused with the couple while they waited for the elevator. "Thank you both again for coming in to see me today. This couldn't have been easy for you. Please know that we're doing everything we can to find the person responsible. I'll keep you informed of any significant developments in the case."

She waited until the elevator doors closed behind them, then heaved an exhausted sigh of relief. She turned on her heel and walked back through reception. "I'm going for coffee, Mona, and lots of it. Get you anything?"

"Milk and two sugars, sugar."

"Coming right up."

Remy stopped in the conference room to stow the case materials back in her satchel. Remembering her cell phone, she pulled it out to check her messages. There was only one, and it was from Giana.

Hi. I was hoping we could meet and talk about what happened the other night. I'm wondering how you're feeling about it.

Shit. Remy felt a stab of shame for having forced the woman to reach out to her first—followed by a surge of excitement at the thought of seeing her again. Excitement that she immediately tried to quash. It hadn't been two days, and already she missed her. A few hours ago, she'd convinced herself she should never see her again. Now, that suddenly seemed like a terrible idea. At best, it was rash. Immature and self-defeating, at worst.

It wasn't every day you met somebody like Giana Falco. Cutting her out of her life would be Remy's loss and nobody else's. There had to be a way they could coexist, without either one of them (namely Remy) coming away damaged.

She slipped the phone back into her pocket and slung her bag across her chest. She wasn't stalling. Not exactly. She needed to get some caffeine into her body first. And then she needed to transcribe her notes from the Everett interview, while her thoughts on the matter were still fresh in her mind. And then, after all of that, she vowed to handle the Giana situation. In the most mature and responsible way that she could.

CHAPTER NINE

He sat in the parked van and waited. He knew which way she was going to come. The route never varied. This was the best place, the most secluded place, to do it. He rocked back and forth, excited now that they were finally going to meet. A pair of teenagers with backpacks approached within a few feet of the vehicle, and he placed his hand on the key in the ignition and waited. If they looked over at him, he would start the engine and leave. But they took no notice as they passed by, and he settled back in his seat, his excitement growing. The minutes passed, and he checked his watch again. She should be here by now. Maybe she had gotten a ride today. That would mean he'd have to wait until Monday. He'd have to wait the whole weekend and come back on Monday. His hand balled into a fist, his fingernails digging into his palm as the rage surged up inside of him. Then he saw her. She was wearing the green coat and the white headphones, and her head was buried in her phone like it always was. Better now. He checked up and down the street one more time to make sure they were alone. Then he stepped out of the van to say hello.

Remy's eyes sprang open. She stared blindly up at the ceiling, listening to the empty room while she waited for her breathing to slow. The bedside clock read 3:07 a.m. Christ. She threw off the covers and stood up, shivering as the cool air struck her damp skin. Grabbing her robe from a peg on the back of the door, she slipped it on and strode barefoot down the dark hallway to the kitchen. At the sink, she filled a glass with water and drank it down in a few greedy gulps.

The dream was evolving now. The Willard woman had been replaced with the Everett girl, while the man remained the same, his malignant thoughts invading and intertwining with Remy's own. The glass slipped from her fingers and clattered loudly in the stainless steel sink. She needed to get some sleep. And she needed to get that sick fuck out of her head.

She picked up the glass and refilled it with water, then carried it with her to the French doors that looked out on the backyard. She stood gazing into the darkness for a moment before she flipped the latch and stepped out on the deck. The chill in the air was brisk. The wooden deck boards were dry and cold beneath her feet. Pulling her robe more snugly around her, she lowered herself into an Adirondack and leaned back, staring up at the clouded black sky.

Without any significant proof, she was convinced now that the murders were the work of one man. And she didn't know that they were ever going to catch him. Given the paltry amount of evidence and the total absence of a suspect, the likeliest outcome was that they would not. And if they didn't catch him, he'd be free to do it again. She knew with a chilling certainty that he *would* do it again. It would go on, and the bodies would continue to come in, and she would conduct more interviews like the one she had today. It would go on. Until he made a mistake or moved on to a different hunting ground.

She held the water glass against her forehead and breathed, listening to the night sounds in the yard. Insects whirred, and a small animal rustled somewhere in the brush. Toward the front of the house, she heard the tires of a lone car passing by on the street and then a return to silence.

Remy stood and walked back into the house, locking the doors behind her. It would be light outside in a few hours, and the day would begin again. Whether she was ready for it or not. She returned to the bedroom and climbed under the covers, keeping to one side of the bed to avoid the sweat-dampened spot.

She lay still and tried to empty her mind of the pain and the death and the suffering. She tried to go to a place of comfort, and a picture of Giana's face appeared. With that smile and the sheen of her hair and the laughter in her sea-green eyes. Remy felt her body begin to relax. She conjured Giana's voice, imagined she was breathing in her scent, and she sank even deeper still. She was going to see her later today after work, and that was a good thing. She had nothing to fear from that. It was only good things when it came to Giana. Only good things. Remy reminded herself of this as she drifted away into sleep, repeating the thought again and again, like a mantra.

* * *

Early Tuesday evening, Giana walked into bridge bar and scanned the room. The place was still quiet, nearly empty at this early hour, and there was no sign of the detective yet. She blew out a breath, grateful for a few extra minutes to gather her thoughts. She'd had days now to think about what she wanted to say to Remy. And yet, here they were about to meet—at Giana's behest, no less—and she had no more clarity on the matter than she'd had before.

She opted for one of the more secluded booths toward the back, nodding at Jimmy as she passed by the bar.

"Aviation for the lady tonight?"

She broke into a grin. "You remembered! Well, in that case, yes. And please call me Giana."

Jimmy nodded, his boyish face turning a deeper shade of pink. "Giana. Sure thing. Have a seat, and I'll bring it right over."

She settled into the cushioned booth and tried to relax. The day had been a draining one already, with thoughts of Remy crowding in on every task. Like a plague on her brain. And now, at last, she was about to face the woman, and she had no idea what to say.

She pulled out her phone and set it on the table in front of her, a part of her hoping the detective would call to cancel at the last minute. She was convinced now that Remy regretted the kiss. These last few days of silence from her were a clear indication of that. She was stalling, while she figured out a way to backpedal. Or to end the friendship altogether.

Giana didn't know what she could do about that or whether she even wanted to try. It had been a relief to talk things over with her aunt on Sunday, even if she'd ended the conversation as confused as ever. Lena had listened to her ramblings without judgment—or even surprise, for that matter. And that was now yet another thing Giana had to mull over.

And then there was lunch today with Nick, which had been a frustrating experience on multiple levels. Giana would've preferred to wait to see him, until after she'd had a chance to talk to Remy first, but he'd refused to be put off. So she'd sat across the table from him at Del Monaco's, smiling and nodding, at the same time she found herself conducting a critical examination. Had anyone ever been that happy to be alive? It was hard to imagine such unrelenting ebullience could really be genuine. And if it was, why did Remy seem to harbor such a visceral dislike of the man? There had to be something to that.

Giana had spent the rest of the meal feeling ashamed because she knew it wasn't fair. When it came to Nick, she'd allowed Remy's opinion to color her own. It was the height of hypocrisy to question the man's sincerity when she herself had been anything but honest with him.

In the end, she had chickened out and told him nothing. They'd strolled together back to the Justice Building, and as they'd stood waiting to cross the street, he'd reached down to hold her hand. And she had let him.

Jimmy stopped at the booth and set a chilled glass down in front of her. He strained her cocktail fresh from the shaker, and she glanced up to murmur her thanks, but the words lodged in her throat as Remy appeared beside him.

"I'll take one of those too, Jimmy, thanks." Her teeth were a brilliant flash of white. Her gray eyes were clear and filled with light, and when they turned on Giana, she felt that kick in her midsection again. Just as she had the first time they'd met. And every time since.

The detective leaned down and grazed her lips against Giana's cheek. "It's good to see you." The warm timbre of her voice was like a secret shared between them. She slid into the booth across from her, and Giana sat very still, waiting for her senses to clear.

"So." Remy placed her hands flat on the table.

"So," Giana echoed.

"Thanks for reaching out yesterday. That should've been me texting you, by the way. Not the other way around." Remy's eyes dropped to the table for a moment, and then her gaze was direct once again. "What happened at your place. After the party. I owe you an apology for that."

Giana felt her shoulder muscles tighten. She wasn't sure if Remy was referring to the kiss or the hasty departure afterward.

"I never intended to go there with you," Remy continued. "I know you're straight, and it was irresponsible of me to let things get out of hand."

Ah. She was referring to the kiss. The heat of embarrassment began to seep into Giana's cheeks. She prayed it didn't show. "So it was that bad, was it?"

Remy's eyes widened, scanning her face. "You're kidding me right now, right?"

"Of course," she answered quickly, though she wasn't sure if she was. "Look, I'm a big girl, Remy. Nothing happened that you need to apologize for."

"Um. Well…" Remy's shoulders inched closer to her ears. "I'm not sure I agree with you there. But there's something I need you to understand." She leaned forward slightly as her mouth opened and closed again. "Wow. This is hard." Her eyes dropped back to the table. "Look…I really like spending time with you. I think we work really well together. As friends. And I would really hate to lose that."

"Of course," Giana said again. She was being let down easy. She knew how it went. It's not you, it's me. In truth, it was nothing more than what she'd expected. She didn't understand why her stomach had just turned inside out.

"Are you all right?"

Remy wouldn't stop looking at her.

"Of co—" Giana paused and licked her lips. For the first time since they'd met, she wished she were somewhere else. Anywhere other than in the presence of Remy Devereux. Jimmy returned to the table with another drink, and she focused her gaze on him, hoping she might mimic his calm demeanor. He set the glass down and poured. When he turned and walked away, she didn't know where to look.

"Giana."

Her eyes snapped back to Remy, who looked as if she wanted to throw up now, too. Giana was perplexed as to why that should be.

"I guess I'm not explaining myself very well here," Remy said.

"No, no. I think you've done a fine job of that." The haze was beginning to clear. Giana adjusted herself in her seat, crossing her legs under the table. "You want to be friends. That's a simple enough concept to grasp. I'm not looking for any complications in my life right now, either. So actually, this works out perfectly." She lifted her glass to take a much-needed sip.

"And what about Nick?"

"Excuse me?" She set the drink down untasted. "What about him?"

"Are you sleeping with him?"

She stared at Remy for several seconds, flabbergasted. "You cannot be serious."

Remy simply watched her in silence, the curve of her generous lips flattening into a hard line.

Giana snorted bitterly. "Um. In light of our recent conversation, I can't see how that's any of your business." She was nowhere close to sleeping with Nick, but she'd be damned if she was going to tell Remy that now. The detective's gaze did not waver, and Giana returned her stare, refusing to be the one to blink.

"You seem angry," Remy finally said.

"Do I?" she countered. "I guess I'm just a little confused as to why you get to behave like a jealous girlfriend in this scenario." Remy straightened in her seat. "Wow." She crossed her arms, forcing a chuckle. "Wow."

Giana finally took a sip of her drink, savoring the tang of the cocktail almost as much as the consternated look on Remy's face. "What? A little too frank for you? Sorry. I've never been much for the bullshit."

"I'll say," Remy agreed. She brought her hands to her face, her fingers forming a steeple as she massaged the bridge of her nose. "Okay. All right. I guess I deserved that one." She laid her palms flat on the table again. "Um...You and Nick. Obviously, that's none of my business. You're absolutely right about that. I don't even know why I brought it up..."

Incredibly, at that moment Giana's cell phone buzzed on the table, with Nick Pierce's name displayed in bold relief. Giana made no move to reach for it, opting to watch Remy's reaction instead. The detective's eyes remained fixed on the glowing screen, long after it faded to black.

Giana folded her arms and sat back in her seat. "Just what exactly is it between you and Nick?" she asked quietly. "Can you explain that to me?"

Remy didn't respond for a moment, her eyes still on the phone. Then she shrugged. "I don't have a problem with the guy." She glanced up at Giana. "I just think you could do better."

Giana said nothing, opting to let the irony of that remark hang in the air between them. The sting of rejection was still quite acute, but the anger she'd been using to deflect it had already begun to wane. In the end, she just wanted to know why. Unfortunately, she suffered from too much pride to ever allow a question like that to cross her lips.

"And what happened between us," she began after a moment. "I guess you think I do that all the time." Remy's expression clouded in confusion, and Giana clarified. "That I just go around looking for poor, unsuspecting lesbians to seduce. For kicks, or whatever."

Remy snorted. "Come on, Giana. That's not what I said."

"But that's what you think."

"Well, no. Not exactly. But…yeah." Giana's mouth dropped open, and Remy rushed on to explain. "Not *you* specifically. Jesus. And I'm not implying it's some kind of predatory practice or anything either. But yeah, I do think you've got some curiosity about it, sure. And that's totally fine. I just can't be the one who explores those things with you."

"I never asked you to," Giana pointed out.

"I know," Remy answered. "I know you didn't. And I apologize again for what happened. Look, I've been down that road before. With straight women. And it was, uh…Well, let's just say I'm not looking to do it again."

"Why? Did something happen with one person specifically, or—?"

"There doesn't need to be somebody specific. My point here is that it's not a good idea in general. For me, anyway."

Giana had just been lumped into a category and summarily dismissed. It was insulting. And it was against her character to let something like that go unchallenged, but she didn't have the energy to pursue it. All of the fight had gone out of her. Remy's explanation was not entirely convincing—there was more to it than she was admitting. But the point was moot. Giana was the last person who was going to force herself on someone who didn't want her.

She leaned back in her seat and took another sip from her cocktail, disappointed to see that the glass was nearly drained. "So where does that leave you and me then?" Remy had said she wanted to be friends, but maybe that wasn't the truth either. She kept her eyes on the table and braced for more disappointment.

"Well, um…Actually, there's this farmers market near your place in Oakland. On Saturdays. It's pretty good, I was wondering if you'd had a chance to check it out yet." Giana looked up, and Remy was watching her closely. "I thought, if you wanted to, we could go by there this weekend. Maybe have a hike beforehand? There's some awesome running trails up in—"

"Fantastic." Giana was shocked by the intensity of her relief. She hoped it wasn't as obvious on her face. "Um, yes. That sounds fantastic."

"All right, then. Good." Remy released a short puff of air and sat back in her seat. That smile reappeared at the corners of her mouth, the one that was slow and teasing, and Giana felt a physical pull in her direction. She wished now that it were otherwise, but it was still there. Just like before. Persistent and unfailing. Like gravity. Or the weight of her own limbs. Funny how you didn't know what you wanted until someone told you you couldn't have it.

"Well, look at that," Remy remarked. "I'm almost empty over here. And so are you." She made a show of peering into Giana's glass. "What do you think, should we order another round?"

Giana heaved an exaggerated sigh, wanting to smile, but feeling like it was still too soon. "Well, all right," she answered in a measured tone. "But only because you're so desperate for company. And I'm buying, this time, Detective. No arguments."

CHAPTER TEN

Late Thursday afternoon, Remy parked the Dodge Charger in a red zone on Hyde Street. She tossed the police placard on the dash and sat in the car, staring at the alley across the street. It was the location where Samantha Willard's body was found. Over a month had passed since she had last visited the site, but little appeared to have changed. Like so many others in the Tenderloin, this alleyway was nondescript in its neglect, its pavement urine-stained and strewn with garbage. The crime scene tape had long ago been removed, but the dumpster still sat in its original position: about halfway down the passageway, situated beneath the grated platform of a fire escape.

Remy didn't expect to discover anything new here that she hadn't noticed before. Mainly it was an exercise, to keep the elements of the Willard case fresh in her mind. She got out of the car and crossed the street.

The slanted rays of the afternoon sun failed to clear the surrounding building tops, submerging the alley in gloom. The stench of urine was overwhelming. Remy locked eyes with a man seated on the ground with his back propped against the grimy brick wall. His clothing was multi-layered and soiled, and the shelter he sat beneath was jerry-rigged out of cardboard and tattered blankets. Shopping carts anchored the structure on either side, and overflowing from the carts were all manner of paraphernalia, from unmatched shoes to yellowing stacks of newspaper. An obsolete boom box sat on top of the heap and looked to be in surprisingly good condition. Remy nodded at the man as she passed, continuing deeper into the alleyway.

She could recite the details of the crime scene from memory. The service doors of two separate establishments provided access—a dry cleaner, which was situated directly across from the dumpster, and a Chinese takeout located at the end. The employees of both businesses had been thoroughly vetted, producing no viable witnesses or suspects.

Remy stared up at the fire escape, which scaled the side of a six-story hotel. It was unlikely the assailant had used this structure as a means to enter or leave the alley. At the time the body was discovered, the apparatus that lowered the stairs to the ground was nonfunctioning, cutting off access below the second story.

No, the method of delivery had to have been a vehicle. And if a vehicle was used, there was a good probability it was seen—by someone. Possibly even this Rhonda Jenssen, wherever in the world she might be.

"You here 'cause of that white lady they found in that dumpster."

Remy turned and walked back to the alley's entrance. She stopped in front of the man, who peered out at her from beneath his soiled canopy. "Have you heard much about that?" she asked.

Remy guessed him to be in his mid-sixties, though it was sometimes difficult to tell with people who lived on the street. His eyes were bulbous and tinged with yellow. At the moment, they were in the process of conducting a counter-examination of Remy. The man seemed in no hurry to answer her question.

"I've been here a few times," she continued, "but I haven't seen you around here before." The man scoffed, then hawked loudly and spit. Remy was careful not to react as the foamy globule landed an inch from her boot. "I'm looking for somebody named Rhonda Jenssen." The man's eyes shifted when she said the name, and her focus went razor sharp. She kept her tone matter-of-fact. "You know who she is?"

The man scoffed again. She said nothing and waited.

"You talkin bout Tick," he finally said.

Remy's mouth went dry. "Maybe. Is that the name she goes by?"

The man looked her up and down and muttered something under his breath. He crossed his arms over his chest. "She ain't been round here for a minute."

Remy nodded. "You know where I can find her?"

His laughter was a hoarse bark. "Ha! Now, how I spose to know that? She ain't *my* bitch!" The man doubled over in a bout of phlegmy hysterics. She waited quietly for the spasm to subside.

"How about a description?" she said finally. "Can you tell me what she looks like?" Remy held her breath as she waited for his answer. She already had a reliable description from the officer at the Tenderloin station. If the two didn't jibe, she'd be no closer to finding Jenssen now than she had been ten minutes ago.

"It ain't like she fine or nothin'." The man shrugged. "Skinny white girl. Scraggly brown hair."

Remy nodded and waited for him to elaborate, but he only watched her with a doleful stare. "All right," she finally said, her shoulders relaxing. It didn't paint a picture, but it was enough. Rhonda Jenssen did exist, and she went by the street name of Tick. It wasn't going to break the case, but it was more than they'd had before.

She dug into her pocket for her business card and pulled it out along with some loose bills. She let the man watch as she neatly folded the bills twice over, with the business card tucked in the middle. She held the money between her first two fingers and extended her hand. "What's your name?"

The man's eyes brightened as he reached up and snatched the little bundle from her fingers. It disappeared into the folds of his clothing. "Everybody call me Peabo. 'Cause I be singin' all the time." Remy quirked an eyebrow at him. "Like Peabo Bryson," he clarified. She gave him a small shrug, and the man threw up his palms. "Aww, come on, girlie! You don't know who Peabo Bryson is?"

Remy stared at him blankly, and the man shoved the blankets aside as he struggled to his feet. She stepped back to give him room while he rifled through one of the shopping carts and located a cassette tape. He dropped it into the boom box's tape deck and hit the play button as Remy turned to leave.

The familiar tune projected clearly from the alleyway, amplified by the surrounding brick walls. Remy crossed the street and turned to glance back at Peabo before she slid into the driver's seat. His arms were outstretched, and his voice had lost its gravel as he belted out the lyrics to "Can You Stop the Rain." It was a good choice, one of her favorites, and Peabo—the one who lived in the alley—didn't sound half bad singing it.

She started the engine but paused before she shifted the car into gear. Glide Memorial was just a few blocks away. The church provided more than two thousand meals a day, free of charge, to all comers. A large percentage of that number were members of the homeless community. She glanced at her watch. Dinner service wouldn't start for another hour, but plenty of staff would be there now. The soup kitchen was ground that she and Cookie had already covered, but maybe this time the name Tick would ring a bell where that of Rhonda Jenssen had not.

She cut the engine and hopped out of the car again, nodding at Peabo. He was in the middle of the chorus now, and Remy hummed along with him as she headed off down the block.

Her cell phone buzzed as she rounded the corner onto Ellis Street. Remy pulled it out of her pocket and didn't bother to tame the grin on her face as she hit the talk button. "Hey there, how's it going?"

"Hi, Remy. How are you?" Giana's husky voice tickled the base of her spine.

"Uh, great. I'm doing great. How about yourself?"

"I'm good..." There was a pause. "Um, look. Curtis just handed me the test results on the hair samples from Willard and Everett. I thought you'd want to know right away."

Remy slowed to a stop in the middle of the sidewalk. "And?"

"Inconclusive. There just isn't enough material here to confirm a match."

"Shit."

"I know," Giana agreed. "We were only able to build a partial profile from each of the samples, and unfortunately, the genetic markers are not corresponding. We can't make a proper comparison to determine one way or the other."

Remy blew out a frustrated breath. "What does that mean as far as CODIS goes? Can we still submit it to the database?"

"I'm afraid not. You'd need a complete profile for that, and we just don't have it here."

"Well, fuck," Remy grumbled. "What's the good news?"

Giana's voice was subdued. "Yeah. I know it's disappointing. But, Remy, there isn't anything here that *precludes* a match, either. I know it's not exactly compelling evidence, but the theory is still viable. These hairs are the same color, the same structure...I mean, I wouldn't swear to it in court, obviously, but my instinct tells me they came from the same head. Dark-haired male, Caucasian, mid-thirties. If it helps."

Oh, sure. That narrowed it down to only about a tenth of the population of the United States. But hey, it was a start. "Yes," Remy said aloud. "Of course it helps." She was struggling to rein in her disappointment. This case was driving her mad, but she didn't need to take it out on Giana. "Hey, sorry I got short a second ago there. I understand you're trying to help, and I want you to know I appreciate it. Thanks for getting back so quick on this."

"Of course. Anything I can do."

Giana's voice had mellowed again, and Remy decided she could listen to those velvet tones all day, every day. Good news or bad.

"Oh, and those other fibers," Giana continued, "the oddly shaped ones? It turns out they're definitely synthetic. My guess is carpeting or some similar application. Possibly automotive—although they do seem a bit long for that. And the color is quite saturated. We might be able to match the dye lot and track down the manufacturer that way. If we're lucky."

"Well, we could use a little luck with this thing right now, that's for sure."

"Fingers crossed." Giana paused. "So, um, are we still on for Saturday?"

"Absolutely. You bet." Remy realized she was grinning again. "I'm thinking a little on the early side, like ten o'clock? That way we can get out there before it gets too hot up in the hills. I'll come and pick you up, all right?"

"Yes, that sounds great. Well, I'm looking forward to it," Giana murmured. "Okay. I'll see you later, Remy."

The call ended, and Remy stood a moment longer with the phone pressed to her ear. Someone brushed past her, and she set herself in motion again, depositing the phone in her pocket as she continued absently down the sidewalk.

She and Giana had come to an understanding, it seemed, without either of them stating it out loud. She had thought their talk in the bar that afternoon was a total disaster, but then it was like neither one of them wanted to leave. They'd lingered there in the booth as the bar filled up around them, chatting about everything and nothing, until eventually it became obvious they should go somewhere to eat. Either that or drink themselves under the table.

They'd gone for dinner at a nearby restaurant, and the mood between them was cordial, if maybe a little guarded. Spending time with Giana that night—sitting directly across from her, with that smile and those warm eyes, close enough to touch—Remy had realized she was in fact capable of the balancing act. It took some effort, of course. Maintaining the right asexual tone, keeping the appropriate amount of physical distance. Remembering not to stare.

It was exhausting, frankly, but she had made her peace with it right then. She'd rather grin and bear it than not see Giana at all. Not seeing her at all was simply not an option anymore. Besides, it was bound to get easier with practice. This infatuation—or whatever it was—would surely fade over time, and it would get easier. It had to.

The polished stone slabs of Glide Memorial glinted in the failing sunlight. Architecturally nondescript, the building hunkered on the corner of Ellis and Taylor streets, built flush against the littered sidewalks that flanked it on two sides. A set of locked iron gates barred the nave's main entrance on Taylor, while a row of bright orange awnings shaded the sidewalk on Ellis Street. It was easy to walk by the building and never realize it was a church at all.

Remy reached the orange awnings and veered around a young man curled up on the pavement underneath. His head rested on a skateboard, a wadded-up sweatshirt serving as a pillow. "Spare change?" He looked up at her expectantly, and Remy noted his washed hair and relatively clean clothing.

"Sorry," she muttered and continued past him to the meal service entrance. She entered the vestibule and nearly collided with an individual backing his way out.

"Whoops!" The man's hand shot up to steady a tall stack of blue crates on a dolly. He turned his head to glance back at Remy. "Sorry about that, darlin'. Be outta your way in a second."

Remy nodded, offering her own apology as she stepped aside to let him pass. She continued into the building and down a short staircase to the level below.

Glide's main dining room was bright and inviting, with round tables arranged in communal groupings within the large space. A row of high windows on the west wall took advantage of the last of the afternoon light. Steam rose from an L-shaped chow line in one corner, which, like the rest of the room, was currently devoid of people or food. The sound of clanging pots and voices could be heard from the kitchen at the rear. Remy turned to head in that direction, spurred on by the delicious aroma of garlic and roasted tomatoes.

"Can I help you with something there, darlin'?"

Remy paused and looked back at the man she'd nearly run into on her way in. The blue crates and dolly were no longer present. He stood with one forearm propped up against the doorjamb, exposing a large sweat stain that covered the breadth of his armpit. His chin lifted toward her in a folksy grin, but the warmth failed to reach his eyes. They were shining beads of latent hostility that made the hair rise on the back of her neck.

She squared her shoulders to face him, pulling out her badge and watching closely for his reaction. "I'm Inspector Devereux. You have a minute?"

The man barely glanced at the badge, and his face registered no surprise. The grin remained fixed in place. "Pleasure. How can I help you, Officer?"

"Do you work here?"

"I guess you could call it that. I mean, they don't pay me or nothing, but yeah."

"So you volunteer then."

The man nodded. "A few days out of the week." He cleared his throat. "I've always believed it's important to give back to the community."

Remy raised her chin at that but said nothing. She watched him quietly as he shifted his weight in the doorway, leaning a shoulder against the opposite jamb.

"So, you, uh...Are you looking for anybody in particular or...?"

His voice trailed off, and Remy kept her silence. She allowed his discomfort to simmer while she took the time to memorize his features. A constellation of pockmarks riddled his face. Above that, a shock of thick black hair sprang like a fountain from a pronounced widow's peak. He was slim, but powerfully built. The muscles on his forearms stood out in cords.

"Do you ever work the chow line?" Remy finally asked. "I'm looking for somebody named Tick. Or Rhonda, maybe. She may have come here a few times to eat."

The man pursed his lips and looked down at the floor, but Remy caught the slight shading of emotion on his face. He was relieved.

"Hmm. Afraid I can't help you there, Officer. I mostly do the collections." Remy stared at him. "I go out and get the donations and things. Bring them back here."

"Food donations?"

"Sure. Food, clothes, you name it. Furniture sometimes."

"And is that mostly in the city here?"

"Oh, we go all over the place, ma'am. South Bay, East Bay. Wherever. I just got back from a run up to Pinole, matter of fact." The wariness crept back into his eyes, and Remy abruptly ceased her examination, glancing at her watch.

"Okay. I still need to talk to some people in the back." She took a step toward the kitchen. "Thanks for your help. Oh, and your name is…?"

"Oh, beg your pardon there, ma'am. I'm Franklin." He rubbed his palm against his shirt and offered Remy his hand. "Franklin Swaggett. With two G's and two T's." His grip was damp.

"Well, thank you for your time, Franklin." Remy nodded and turned away, resisting the urge to follow him out to the parking lot. She was curious to see what kind of vehicle he drove. A delivery van, no doubt. Probably white, with tinted windows.

She let him go and didn't look back, cautioning herself against the lure of red herrings. There was a reason behind his skittishness, to be sure. But that and the fact that he'd once visited the town of Pinole didn't make the man a killer. Plenty of people hated cops on principle alone—Remy had been forced to accept that reality a long time ago. She would find out about the vehicle soon enough. That, and everything else there was to know about Franklin Swaggett.

CHAPTER ELEVEN

Giana walked out of her apartment building into a bright but overcast morning. Her legs were immediately covered in goosebumps. She had dressed according to the weather report, which predicted the marine layer would burn off by noon. She wrapped her arms around herself and prayed the forecast was accurate. Spotting Remy's car across the street, she trotted over and quickly hopped into the cozy interior.

"Brrr! Good morning, you!" She resisted the urge to lean over and brush her lips against Remy's cheek. It would've been the natural thing to do, but things were anything but natural between them now.

"Good morning." Remy's smile was heart-stopping, as usual. The car was filled with the delicious and aggravating scent of her. She handed Giana a piping hot latte.

"Oh, God bless you." Giana allowed herself a few brief seconds to look into those silvery-gray eyes, then she wrapped her hands around the cup and faced forward in her seat. "I'm so excited! I've been wanting to explore some of these trails since I got here."

"Well, okay then. I'm about to show you some."

Remy put the car in gear, and they were away. In just a few minutes, they had left the hardscape of downtown Oakland for the wooded serenity of a two-lane highway. The road stretched out ahead of them in a smooth black ribbon, and Giana was on an adventure again—like the first time she'd gone for a ride in Remy's car. That had been the day of the cookout, a day that had ended in such an unexpected and dramatic way.

She had resolved not to allow her mind to dwell on it any longer. Or at least she'd been putting up a valiant effort. Of late, Remy had begun to visit her in her dreams, and against that she had little defense. She would awaken in the mornings feeling aroused and unfulfilled, reliving the kiss and wanting more. Shamelessly craving the touch of Remy's hands. And her tongue, and her lips.

Her mind refused to let it go, and she was at a loss to explain the obsession. It had only been a short period of time, but in a way, the last few weeks felt like months, and she had to constantly remind herself that she barely knew this person. It was as if they had undergone some sort of a trial together and had come out intact on the other side. Unfortunately, their new dynamic was self-conscious and frustratingly platonic. They'd shared a kiss, and she had caught a glimpse of something in Remy that was now inaccessible to her. Remy had drawn that line fairly starkly. The problem was, knowing there was a thing hidden away from her only tended to make Giana want to drag it out in the open.

"So then. Where are we headed this morning?"

"Redwood Regional," Remy explained. "There's miles of trails up there. Lots of hiking, of course. And mountain biking and horse trails, if you're so inclined. I'll show you one that's good for running. You said you run, right?"

Giana nodded. "Only around Jack London, so far. It's convenient. But I'd love to be able to get out among the trees every once in a while."

Remy nodded. "I think you're going to like this."

They exited the highway in no time, and already the clouds were beginning to break into broad patches of blue. The Audi cruised up a wide, curving boulevard, and in the next minute Remy turned onto a side road and parked on the gravel shoulder behind several other cars.

Giana got out of the vehicle and walked down the slope to a grassy clearing. Her mouth opened as she stared up at the soaring limbs of the redwood trees. She couldn't believe she was less than twenty minutes from her apartment.

She looked back at Remy emerging from the car. A pair of running shorts exposed the length of her long legs, from the midpoint of her thighs to the ankle socks on her feet. Giana gave herself just a few seconds to absorb it. Flexing calf muscles and smooth, bronzed skin. The bunch and release of well-defined quads as Remy trotted down the slope to join her. She turned her eyes away and refused to look again.

A wooden sign posted at the trailhead pointed arrows in several directions. Remy took a trail that snaked off to the left, and soon they were immersed in another time. Delicate ferns flourished in the underbrush, competing for growing space with plush hostas and stout-trunked palms. The silence was pierced by the trill of a bird calling high in the trees. The redwoods towered above, jostling against one another and crowding in on the trail, whittling the sun's energy to a muted trickle. It was still quite cool in the shade, and Giana briskly rubbed her palms over her arms for heat. Remy could not have looked happier.

"Do you want to run a little, just to warm up a bit?"

"You bet," Giana agreed.

They set off at a trot. Remy checked her long strides to match Giana's shorter ones, and they quickly fell into an easy rhythm. Giana couldn't remember the last time she'd run alongside someone else. Perhaps in college, when she'd trained routinely with the tennis team. Since then, running had become a solitary endeavor, almost meditative. It would've felt strange to have anyone beside her again. The fact that it was Remy made the experience preternatural.

She kept her eyes forward and directed her thoughts inward, concentrating on the sensations in her own body. Soon her muscles began to demand more oxygen, and she welcomed the familiar tightening in her lungs. A short time later, the tension began to ease again as she gained her second wind. Her quads and calf muscles loosened as they warmed, and she increased the pace, focused mainly on the terrain at her feet. She had no concerns about her companion's ability to keep up.

Remy was right—the trail was perfect for running. Wide in most sections, the dirt had long been pounded flat, with only the occasional embedded rock or tree root to step over. They entered a small clearing, where the branches opened up overhead. A blast of sunlight bleached the ground white. Then they were under the dappled canopy again, running amongst the trees.

The path gradually narrowed as it sloped downward toward a gurgling stream, and Remy dropped back a length to follow in tandem. They rounded a bend and crossed a small footbridge, and their feet pounded the boards in unison. Then the terrain was climbing once again.

Giana felt the strain in her quad muscles as she dug in, attacking the incline with her arms in full swing until the ground began to level near the top. There the path widened out, and Remy easily pulled up beside her, effortless in her stride, her breathing far from labored. Giana glanced at her and finally gave in with a laugh. Their pace slowed to a trot, which then became a stroll as the quiet settled in around them.

Giana's skin was blessedly warm at last. Breathing deeply, she reveled in the dull ache suffusing her limbs. She stole a glance at Remy, who looked as if her pulse rate had barely budged. "How often do you run?"

"Pretty much every morning. Or I try to, anyway. The whole day feels off if I don't." Remy's gait was now a loose-jointed amble. Her arms hung slack at her sides. Giana had never seen her look more relaxed.

"It suits you."

Remy glanced at her with a laugh. "What? Well, what about you, I could hardly keep up with you back there."

"Oh, please." Giana bumped into her shoulder. "You were toying with me, I could tell."

"I would never." Remy reached out to pull a leaf from a passing branch, twirling it between her fingers. She brought it up to her nose and inhaled. "Mmm. I forget how much I love it up here."

Giana looked around them. They were surrounded by dense shrubbery and all manner of trees. She recognized eucalyptus and sycamore and pine. The redwoods soared above it all, their trunks like the legs of giants standing knee-high in a grassy pasture.

"Have you heard of the Avenue of the Giants?" Remy had read her mind. "It's a couple of hours north of here, up in Humboldt County. Some of the redwoods up there are two *thousand* years old. Can you believe that?"

Giana shook her head. "Yes, I can, but not really. I mean, it's hard to imagine anything alive today that could actually be that old."

"Oh my God, I know. But the way it feels up there…It really is beyond amazing. I can't even describe it—you just have to see it for yourself. We should go there sometime."

"Mmm. Maybe we should," Giana murmured. "I'd love that."

Remy's eyes caught and held on to hers for a moment before she looked away. "So," she said lightly, "Giana Falco. That sounds very Italian."

Giana chuckled, instantly recalling the conversation they'd had about Remy's name, the very first time they'd met for drinks. "That's right. My grandparents are from Sicily, in fact. Wow, you really *are* a detective."

"Inspector," Remy corrected.

"Right. Yes, of course. I should know better—my father is actually chief inspector of the Philly PD. Did I tell you that already? And my brother just came up for lieutenant a few weeks ago. It looks like he's going to get it, too. *And*…we have two cousins who are patrolmen on the force, as well."

Remy laughed. "My God, your family is literally crawling with cops. No wonder you have a thing for LEOs. It makes perfect sense now."

Giana glanced at her in confusion. "What? No. Actually, I'm not into astrology at all... Oh, wait. You mean law enforcement officers. Right, very funny. But who says I have a thing for cops?"

Remy gave her a pointed look, and Giana cocked her head. "Did you just bring up Nick Pierce again?"

Remy's shoulders hunched as she held up her hands. "Okay. Easy there, tiger. I forgot that topic was off limits. So sorry."

Giana's aggravation was instant and profound. Nick was clearly a topic that Remy couldn't let go of. Yet, when asked about it directly, she skirted the issue. It was a sore spot with her, for whatever reason, and her use of sarcasm to try to cover that up was galling.

"I'm not the one who refuses to talk about Nick," Giana said evenly. "And it's none of your business, anyway. Remember? And why do you even *care* who I'm dating?"

Remy declined to meet her gaze. No answer was forthcoming, of course.

Giana faced forward. "I go where I'm wanted. You can't blame a girl for that."

Remy turned sharply to look at her. "I never said I didn't—" She stopped in mid-sentence.

"You never said you didn't what?" Giana prompted. She folded her arms, watching as a muscle in Remy's jaw began to twitch. "What, Remy?"

Once again, the detective refused to answer. After a minute Giana dropped her arms in frustration. "Do you find avoidance to be a very effective communication tool? Because I think it sucks."

Remy barked in surprise. "Whoa. That's aiming a little low, don't you think?"

"Is it?" Giana shot back. "You never answer my questions."

"That's not true. When have I not answered your questions?"

Giana didn't bother to respond to that. They walked on in silence, well past the point of comfort. She finally looked at Remy and said, "It doesn't feel very good, does it?"

Remy pressed her lips together, shaking her head. "All right. Fine. I'll tell you whatever you want to know. Go ahead. Ask me."

Giana paused to look at her, uncertain now in the face of the detective's sudden acquiescence. Remy raised her eyebrows at her and stared back.

"All right," she began slowly. "I'd like to know what happened with that woman."

"Who, Erica?"

"No, not Erica," Giana scoffed. "It's obvious why you wouldn't want to be with her." Remy started to protest, but she cut her off. "I'm talking about the other one."

"Who said there was another one?"

"You did. In so many words. The other day at the bar, when you were in the middle of your rant about predatory straight women."

"If you'll remember, I clarified that they *weren't* predatory. And I'm pretty sure it wasn't a rant."

"Whatever." She refused to be distracted. "Seriously. I'd like to hear what happened."

Remy strode on, her eyes on the trail at her feet, and Giana assumed she had clammed up again. But then she started to talk.

"Lexi," she said, clasping her hands behind her back. She stretched her arms out behind her, somewhat painfully, it seemed. "Her name was Alexis, and...well, what can I say? She was married." Remy dropped her arms to her sides. "Or separated. At least, that's what she told me. This was a few years ago and, uh, I don't know. We met through some mutual friends. We got together pretty quickly, and...I fell in love with her."

Giana glanced at Remy's profile. Remy found another leaf to pluck from a branch. Exhaling slowly, she went on. "She said she loved me too, but... I don't know. Anyway. We were getting ready to move in together, and then she decided to go back to her husband. End of story." Remy's throat worked as she swallowed. She glanced at Giana. "Honestly, it's my own fault. I should've known better. Lesson learned."

She fell silent after that, and Giana walked on quietly beside her. She wanted to know more. And she wanted to throttle this Lexi person. For more reasons than one. She glanced at Remy and decided not to press her. At least not for now. She knew the brief account she'd just given had not come easily. It didn't begin to solve the puzzle of who she was, but it explained a little. She chalked it up as a win.

"I'm sorry that happened to you," Giana said quietly. "I'm familiar with what it feels like to be betrayed by someone you love. My ex-fiancé cheated on me, and then he lied about it repeatedly until I caught him virtually in the act. Ugh." She shuddered.

Remy's eyes were glued to her now. "Wait. You were engaged? How long ago was this?"

"It was...oh, I don't know..." Giana was momentarily confused. "We broke up almost a year ago, I guess. Why?"

Remy blew out a short puff of air. "Nothing. I'm just surprised you didn't mention something like that before."

Giana shrugged. "Well, I would have. I mean, it didn't come up until now."

"Are you still in contact with him?"

"No, Remy, I'm not." She crossed her arms. "Why are you getting so worked up about this?"

"I'm not, Giana. I'm not." Remy ran a hand through her hair, inhaling deeply. After a moment, she said, "So. I guess it's safe to assume that's why you came out here then? To get away from him?"

"Partially, yes. Him. And my overbearing father. And my obnoxious brother..."

"All of the horrible men in your life."

"Well, it sounds horrible when you say it like that." She chuckled. "Honestly, I just needed a change. I love them to pieces, I do. Well, not David. But the other two. I just...I just needed a change. I knew Liz had a place out here, and then the job opening came up. And I thought, you know what, I'm going to spread my wings."

Remy nodded, quiet for a moment. "That's brave. I think that's really brave. Not everybody has the guts to do something like that."

"Thank you." Giana hadn't realized until now how much she wanted to hear someone say that.

"Well, are you okay?" Remy asked. "I mean with the breakup and everything. A year isn't that much time. How do you feel about what happened?"

Giana hunched her shoulders and grimaced. "Oh, that. You know, in some ways, David feels like a lifetime ago. Honestly, he hardly ever comes to mind. But when I *do* think about what happened between us, it's not the fact that he was with somebody else. It's the lying and the deceit that hurts the most.

"And then I think about who I was in that relationship and why I couldn't see what was going on right in front of me." She shook her head. "I don't know. Maybe I just didn't want to see it. I was lying to myself at the same time that he was lying to me."

She glanced at Remy. "That in no way excuses his behavior, of course. I just think it's important to look at my own stuff too."

"Well, the one true thing is this. The guy has got to be a total fuckhead to do something like that to someone like you."

Giana chuckled softly. "Thanks. Liz likes to refer to him as Fuck*face*."

"Mmm. Fuckface is better. You did say she was a smart lady."

They moved on to lighter topics after that, chatting amiably until they'd finished the loop and arrived back at the car. The sun was high in the sky, and Giana's stomach was beginning to rumble. "So they do have real food at this Farmer John thingy, right? More than just carrots and turnips or whatever?"

Remy's lips twitched. "Gee, I dunno. I guess we'd better go find out."

Gravel crunched and popped beneath the Audi's tires as the car swung around in a tight U-turn. Then they were heading back the way they'd come, down the curving boulevard and onto the black ribbon highway.

Remy pressed a button, and the sunroof whirred open, blasting sunlight and warm air into the car. Giana raised her hand through the opening and let the wind rush through her fingers. She felt good. They were having a good day. She reached for the center console, comfortable now with the stereo's controls, and quickly flipped to the station she wanted. She bobbed her head in time to the music, watching as a smile reappeared at the corner of Remy's mouth.

Remy kept her eyes on the road, and Giana kept her eyes on Remy. She took a moment to absorb the lines of her profile, recording the dip and rise of her features, memorizing the curve of her lips. The car came to a stop at a red light, and the detective finally turned to meet her gaze.

In a spark of defiance Giana refused to look away. She'd just spent the bulk of the morning avoiding those eyes, and now she wanted to see them. They were clear and unguarded, and they seemed to harbor neither a question nor an ounce of alarm.

"Hey," Remy said quietly.

"Hey, yourself," Giana replied. Satisfied, she turned and faced forward in her seat.

* * *

The Lakeshore Farmers Market lay in the heart of Oakland, situated on a grassy wedge-shaped acre a block from Lake Merritt. Once a week, an eclectic band of growers, vendors, and artisans gathered to hawk their wares. The food was delicious and the energy was high, and Remy couldn't think of a better way to spend a Saturday afternoon.

They both inhaled heaping plates of food as soon as they arrived. Giana chose Burmese, and Remy opted for Thai. Sated, they strolled side by side, close but not touching as they weaved their way through the crowd. Giana stopped at a jewelry stand festooned with colorful beads and baubles. She lowered her head to take a closer look, and her glossy hair shone in the sunlight, as brilliant as any of the trinkets on the table.

Remy hung back and observed, much as she had done earlier that morning during their run. Giana had taken to the trail with a feline grace, exactly as expected. Her stride was smooth and unhurried, her shoulders relaxed, her footsteps sure as they pounded the earth. She had lost herself in the run, the look on her face something akin to nirvana. Remy knew it when she saw it because she went there so often herself. It was a rare pleasure to get to see it in someone else.

The day was turning out to be spectacular, and Remy could admit her good mood had little to do with the run, or the farmers market, or the weather. It was all about Giana. Though this unrelenting physical proximity to her was no less of a strain.

That was Remy's excuse, anyway. She had no other explanation for why she continued to bring up the topic of Nicolas Pierce. And this time she'd done it in the snarkiest, most childish fashion possible. The thought of him even touching Giana drove her insane. She didn't have a leg to stand on—she knew it, and Giana didn't hesitate to let her know it, too. The woman's tongue was sharp enough to begin with, but when she was annoyed, it was positively lacerating. Remy didn't want to be the one on the receiving end the day the lady ever truly became pissed off.

Giana had a candor about her that seemed absolute. It was disconcerting to be in the crosshairs, but Remy couldn't deny that it was also deadly attractive. Like that strange moment in the car right after the hike. For some reason, Giana had decided to stare her down, to basically dissect her like a specimen under a microscope, and she had simply sat there and let it happen.

And it wasn't the fact that she was staring—Giana did that a lot, and oddly enough, Remy was starting to get used to it. It was the quality of the stare this time. Like she'd taken a flashlight and shined it directly into Remy's soul, casually sifting through everything there was to find.

Remy had felt powerless to stop it, but even stranger than that, she hadn't felt the need to. She realized now she should be more alarmed about the incident than she was. The fact that she wasn't troubled by it at all was something she would have to contemplate at a later time.

Giana left the jewelry stand and returned to her side, and once again Remy suppressed the urge to take her hand. They resumed their strolling, until Giana abruptly halted again, seizing Remy by the arm.

"Oh my God." She was staring at a bakery stand, where the table was stacked high with clear cases of pastries and baskets overflowing with rolls. An older woman in a red apron smiled at them and nodded.

"Do you have any *cornetti*?" Giana asked eagerly.

"Oh, sì, signorina," the woman replied.

Giana's grip tightened on Remy's arm as she spoke in a hoarse whisper. "My auntie makes those!"

Laughter bubbled up in Remy's chest. She'd never seen Giana quite that excited before. The baker lady pointed to several different cases and rattled off some names in Italian. Giana asked for a sample of one and was barely able to stand still as the woman cut her a piece. She took a bite, her eyelids fluttering shut as her lips closed around the pastry. Remy was too mesmerized to look away. Giana's tongue came out to lick at the crumbs, and Remy wanted to lean over and do that for her.

Inhaling, she forced her eyes back on the woman behind the table. "How many of those do you have left? Great, we'll take all of them." She glanced at Giana again, only briefly. "Anything else here strike your fancy?"

They left the stand a few minutes later, their arms laden with pastry boxes. Giana's green eyes were dancing. "Who's supposed to eat all of these?"

Remy shrugged. "Don't look at me. I don't even know what any of this stuff is."

Giana laughed, until she was distracted yet again. "Ooh, let's get some of that lemonade."

They juggled the boxes as Remy paid for the beverages, careful to ask for lids to go on top of the plastic cups. Awkwardly, she stacked one drink on top of the other, then tried to reclaim the load of boxes.

"No, here," Giana directed. "You take these two, and I'll take one of these…" She traded two boxes for a lemonade, balancing the beverage on top of her stack.

"Wait," Remy said, "that's going to—"

The cup slid toward Giana, who adroitly caught it with her chin—before the lid popped off and sent crushed ice and lemonade washing down the front side of her. She gasped and jerked the boxes away from her body, miraculously saving the pastries.

Speechless, the two women froze. Unavoidably, Remy's eyes dropped to Giana's shirt. The fabric was sopping wet and translucent and glued to her skin. The lobes of her breasts were clearly delineated, the nipples standing upright in bold relief.

Giana looked down at herself and gasped again. She shoved the boxes into Remy's arms, which quite naturally caused her to drop her own drink. A geyser of liquid shot upward as the cup struck the ground, sending both of them hopping out of its path. Giana clutched the hem of her shirt and yanked the fabric taut like a tent.

"Okay. Um...we're going." Remy was in motion. Her hands full, she mumbled an apology to the man at the stand, who was already stooping to clean up the wreckage. She nodded at a stack of napkins as they passed it. Giana grabbed a handful and wadded it underneath her shirt, trotting to catch up. The look of disbelief on her face was comical.

"Did you want any more of that lemonade?" Remy asked. "I think there was still some left in the cup."

"Oh, fuck you, Remy."

Remy burst into full-throated laughter. "Well, I hope you don't think you're getting into my car like that."

Giana was laughing now, too. "What do you want me to do, catch the bus?"

"No, no. You can ride with me. You'll just have to take off that shirt first."

"Oh, you would just love that, wouldn't you?" There was amusement in Giana's eyes, mixed with a glint of something like a challenge. Remy opted not to reply.

They reached the car, and Remy set the load of boxes on the roof while she fished for her keys. She opened the door for Giana and gallantly waved her inside. A few seconds later, the pastry boxes were stored in the rear and she was dropping into the driver's seat.

Already, the car was filled with the pleasing aroma of fresh lemons. Giana sat with her shirt pulled away from her body. Remy felt a chuckle rising up again. She pressed her lips together and pulled the car away from the curb and soon they were cruising amidst the slow-moving traffic of Grand Avenue, the rippling waters of Lake Merritt a study in tranquility.

Remy glanced at her passenger, whose head was still lowered, contemplating the Rorschach stain that eclipsed her shirt. "You smell kind of...fruity," Remy said thoughtfully. "Tangy, you know? Maybe a little sweet."

Giana answered without looking up. "Yes. I thought I'd try out a new fragrance this afternoon. What do you think, is it working for me?"

"Mmm, not so much. I prefer the one you normally wear."

Giana looked up at her then. "Do you?"

"I do." Remy glanced away. "You always smell amazing."

She heard no response to that, and she didn't look at her again. They rode on in silence until they reached the building on Water Street, Remy wondering what had possessed her to say what she had.

She parked the car and got out to gather up the pastries. It would be best to say their goodbyes at the curb. The tension pulsating in the air between them was not her imagination. And she couldn't get the sight of Giana's soaking wet bosom out of her head. The last place she should be right now was inside the woman's apartment. But dumping her on the sidewalk with a stack of boxes would only make an awkward situation worse.

Giana swiped her access card at the building's entrance and held the glass door open. Remy proceeded mutely inside. They were in the elevator on the way to the eighth floor before either of them spoke.

"Stay for a glass of wine?" Giana's voice was casual. "I have a nice savvy blanc chilling in the fridge."

Remy stared at their blurred reflections in the elevator doors. "I should probably get going."

Giana's likeness looked back at her, then down at the floor. "Remy, just...please stay for a glass of wine."

Remy moistened her lips and lifted a shoulder. "Sure. Of course. I can do that."

The elevator doors opened, and she followed Giana down the carpeted hallway, unprepared for the deluge of images that bombarded her then. Fragments of the last time she'd been there. On the night they'd kissed. She tried to channel her thoughts, but then it was the taste and the feel of Giana pressing in on her again, the weight of her breasts pushing up against her. She had a new mental image now to go along with that sensation, gorgeous and sopping wet in the bright light of day. An image that was now seared like a brand on her brain.

Giana paused to unlock the door to her apartment, and Remy found herself hoping there'd be no roommate on the other side to greet them. She chastised herself a second later. It didn't matter whether they were alone or not, because nothing was going to happen. Inside, Giana dropped her keys in a bowl and pried off her sneakers as she called out to her roommate. Remy walked to the kitchen counter and unloaded the pastry boxes, listening hard for a reply. There was nothing.

"Help yourself to whatever you'd like." Giana was already halfway across the living room. "Ugh, I need to get cleaned up. I won't be a second."

She rounded the corner to the hallway, lifting the shirt over her head as she went. Remy caught a glimpse of the flat planes of her shoulder blades and the shallow dip in her lower back. The white straps of her bra were stark against smooth, olive skin.

Remy stood rooted to the spot for a long moment after Giana had disappeared. She was in dangerous territory now. She knew it was time to leave. She pulled open a cabinet door and found the glassware instead.

Setting the glasses down on the countertop, she paused again, her ears keenly tuned to the muffled sounds coming from the hallway. A running shower, most likely. Water coursing over Giana's skin. The floral scent of soap or shampoo drifted into the room, and then the sound of the water abruptly stopped.

She left the glasses on the counter and abandoned the kitchen to go stand at the picture window. She scoured her mind for anything to think of—anything besides Giana naked on the other side of that wall. It was useless to even try. She'd been kidding herself to imagine she had any control over this situation at all.

Remy remained at the window until Giana's bedroom door finally opened. She listened to the soft pad of bare feet as they entered the room behind her.

"Oh my God, that was so good. Did you pour us some wine?" Giana's voice was breezy and completely relaxed. Remy felt anything but. She forced herself to turn around.

Dressed now in a wrap-around skirt and a plain V-neck blouse, Giana had never looked more beautiful. Her hair was damp and combed straight back from her brow, and her face was stripped bare of any trace of makeup. The color began to rise now in Giana's cheeks, and Remy realized she was taking much too long with her inspection. In the meantime, a look of wariness had crept into her subject's eyes.

"What?" Giana asked.

"You're stunning," Remy replied.

She knew she had to learn to think before speaking, particularly when it came to Giana, but she didn't care. "Do you have any idea how stunning you are?" Remy held her breath and waited for a response.

The eyelids lowered, and the blush deepened to completely saturate her face. It shattered the last of Remy's resolve. She took a step forward, dropping her gaze to examine Giana's bare feet. The toenails were painted a surprising indigo blue. She studied the shining half-moons of the nail beds and contemplated the perfect length of the toes.

And then she allowed her eyes to embark on a languid journey upward. Over the slender ankles and up the contours of one shapely leg. They lingered at the flaring hips, then continued onward to the dip in the low-cut blouse, hovering finally at the swell of those exquisite breasts. The gorgeous mounds began to rise and fall as she watched, their movement betraying Giana's accelerated breaths.

"Remy, what are you doing?"

Remy's eyes snapped to Giana's face. "I think it's called ogling," she admitted.

"Yes, I believe that is what it's called. Why are you doing it?" Giana's voice had deepened in register, its natural husk becoming more pronounced. Remy studied the luminous eyes. They stared back at her with a burning directness, and the accusation in them was plain to see.

Remy was unapologetic. "Well, you're very attractive," she explained. "And…I think you wouldn't mind it very much if I kissed you right now." She waited for the flare of defiance that was sure to come next.

"Is that what you think?" Giana countered, her full lips setting in a pugnacious line. Her green eyes narrowed, but then there was the slightest waver in her gaze. "Well, the last time we talked, you said you didn't want me. So which is it?"

"Is that what you took away from that conversation?" Remy felt a stab of regret. "Giana. I never said I didn't want you." She watched Giana's eyes drop to the floor, and she swallowed hard. She took another step toward her, barely breathing now. "Don't you know how hard this is for me? To be this close to you and keep my hands to myself? You have no idea how much I want to touch you. All of the time."

Giana didn't move or speak, and the tension built inside of Remy's body until she thought she would split in two. She closed the last of the distance between them. Until she was close enough to feel the heat emanating through Giana's clothes. Close enough to feel the maddening graze of her breasts as the air moved in and out of her lungs. "Tell me what you want me to do, Giana. Should I leave? Tell me now. Because, in about another second, I'm going to be all over you."

Giana's shudder was violent against her, and Remy descended, starving for the taste of her, licking and sucking at the fullness of her lips, hungrily probing at the firmness of her tongue. Giana met her at every stroke, her mouth opening wide, her hands coming up to grip at the flesh of her back. The kiss went on, dragging her in deeper, driving away any semblance of thought or reason, until she abruptly broke it off.

She stood there reeling, holding Giana's face in her hands, trying to regain her equilibrium as she dragged the air into her lungs. Giana's eyes were clear as she stared back, her complexion flushed, her mouth swollen and waiting.

"What are you doing to me?" Remy whispered. She rubbed a thumb roughly across the plump lower lip, pressing inward against the ridge of bottom teeth. Giana closed her lips around it and began to work at it with her tongue, scraping it with her teeth, sucking hard to draw it into the warmth of her mouth.

Remy gasped as the sensation shot straight to her groin. It fissioned into a pulsating throb, and she pulled her hand away, clasping Giana around the waist and partially lifting and walking her backward until she was pressed tightly against the wall. She cupped her breast, greedily testing the weight of it, first through the fabric of her blouse, and then impatiently pushing the cloth aside, pulling down on the lacy bra until the heavy lobe was exposed. The nipple was a dark rosy bud, firm and protruding in the middle of a pebbled areola.

"So fucking gorgeous," Remy murmured. She stared down, mesmerized, savoring the sight of it until the pull became too strong. She lowered her head and took the nipple into her mouth, and Giana's gasp was a sudden, hissing intake of air. She increased the pressure, applying the same forceful suction Giana had used on her thumb. Giana groaned loudly and sagged against her, and she gripped her by the backs of her thighs, dragging her hands upward, bunching up the skirt as she went, exposing the rounded flesh of the buttocks underneath.

Giana's panties were meager swatches of lace, offering little more coverage than a thong. Remy's hands traced the edges of the skimpy garment until her finger found the middle seam at the back. She rode it downward until it disappeared into the valley between Giana's cheeks, doggedly pursuing it even deeper into that heated crevice. A feral growl vibrated in Giana's throat and resonated at the base of Remy's spine. She could see herself dropping to her knees, spreading those cheeks wide apart, working her tongue into that sweet, puckered opening. Oh, the sounds she would draw out of her then. There was no part of this woman she didn't want to explore.

Remy inhaled and marshaled her self-control, only to test the limits of it again as she hooked a finger into the panties' waistband. Teasingly at first, then resolutely, she tugged them downward, feeling Giana's grip on her back tighten as the garment was inched to the midpoint of her thighs.

"Remy…"

The word was both a warning and a plea, and it sent another spasm of craving to the center of Remy's groin. "You can tell me to stop." She held herself rigid, locking them both in a tight embrace. "Just tell me you want me to stop, Giana, and I will." She waited, dreading and praying for the moment when one of them would come to her senses.

Giana leaned her head back and met Remy's eyes. Her voice was barely above a whisper. "I don't want you to stop. I want you to touch me."

Remy exhaled a shuddering breath. She leaned her forehead against Giana's, holding it there while they breathed together, sharing the air as it passed in and out of their lungs. Then she dropped a hand to run her fingertips up the inside of Giana's thigh. She shifted her weight, using her knee to coax the trembling legs apart, stretching the fabric of the panties tight. Slowly, she brought her hand up to cup the warm mound, massaging the soft curling hair, pressing in with the heel of her palm. She slipped a finger in between the folds, and Giana bit back a moan.

"You're so fucking wet," Remy groaned. "Is this what I do to you?" She felt Giana's fingernails dig into her back, and she shivered from the pain and the pleasure of it. "Is it, Giana?"

Giana's answer was a whispered hitch. "Yes."

Slowly, she dragged the pad of her finger through the molten slick. "Tell me you think about me when you're alone."

Giana's eyes were glazing over, her breaths coming in labored pants. "You know that I do."

"Tell me. I want to hear you to say it."

"I think about you, Remy." Giana's head fell back, her eyes closing. She licked her lips, her throat working as she swallowed. "All I do is think about you."

Remy descended on her again, kissing her hard and deep, forcing her legs wider apart as she found the swollen nub at her center. Giana gasped at the contact, and Remy retreated slightly, brushing her finger lightly past the nub, only to return and repeat the motion again. Giana's body began to coil up against her, hips and thighs rising up to meet hers, and she began to stroke her at a deliberate pace, timing the motion to the hitches in her breathing. Wickedly, she teased her, keeping the pressure light, delaying full contact as the rhythm gradually increased.

Giana's voice rose in pitch, and her gasping pants began to coalesce in a moan. "Mmmm...God, Remy, please..." Her hips began to move with the rhythm, rocking forward to capture every stroke. Her hands climbed up Remy's arms, gripping her at the shoulders, clamping onto the base of her neck.

Remy's vision had lost its focus, her pulse slamming in her ears. "You're so fucking sweet," she groaned. "How did you get to be so sweet?" She felt drugged, lost in the grip of Giana's rising need. She gritted her teeth, fighting to maintain control, desperately wanting to lock her legs around the top of her thigh. To grind herself against those feverishly thrusting hips. But she needed more time, and Giana was too close. There was no holding back this tide—she would never have dreamed of trying to. She wanted to see this woman depart from reason. To go to that place where there was no thought. Only lust, and need, and the fulfillment of that need. And Remy wanted to be the one to send her there.

"Please...Remy..." She was openly begging now. "Oh, God. That feels so good. Baby...You're gonna make me come."

The endearment was almost Remy's undoing. Crazed with desire, she drove her tongue into Giana's ear, simultaneously claiming her clit, using her finger to press in quick and ever-tightening circles, thickly swirling her tongue to mimic the motion at her ear, leaning in with her full body weight to hold her in place as the orgasm began to rip its way loose.

"Mmm...fuck..." Giana threw her head back. "Fuck, yes. Right there. Oh, God. Remy...Fuuuck!" Her pelvis thrust forward and locked in place. Her abdomen shuddered as her thighs clamped hard around Remy's hand, holding it imprisoned, bearing down on it as her muscles began to pulse in irregular spasms. Remy held on tight, riding it out, shutting her mind to the hunger that still raged inside of her, holding herself motionless until the last of the tremors subsided.

Giana's grip on her finally loosened, freeing Remy's hand as her body began to relax. Remy began to gently rearrange her clothing, sliding the panties up and around her hips, smoothing the skirt down over her thighs. She shifted the brassiere back into place and righted the blouse. And all the while, she rained her with feathery light kisses. Over her eyelids and across her cheekbones and down the bridge of her nose. The green eyes opened, lucid again, and Remy looked into them and felt herself falling. Deep into their depths, into the well, where she wanted to give this woman everything. Whatever she wanted. Anything she could possibly need.

She swallowed hard, a broad band of tension cinching like a vise around her rib cage. It slowly began to tighten, while her pulse—which had barely had time to slow—now spiked anew. It hammered away at a crazy staccato. Her vision blurred as a fine mist of perspiration broke out on her brow. She wondered vaguely if this was what people referred to as a panic attack. She'd never had one before, so it was impossible to be sure. Either that or she was having a stroke.

She took a step backward, and Giana's face slowly came into focus. It was filled with a look of alarm. "Remy…Are you okay?"

"I'm fine," she answered, taking another step back. Yes, she was perfectly fine. All she needed was a little air. And some distance, maybe. And then she'd be perfectly fine.

"Remy. Where are you going?" There was a clear warning in Giana's tone now. One that Remy could hear but was helpless to heed. "Remy, don't. Don't you dare leave here right now."

Remy glanced around herself, realizing she was already halfway across the living room, with no clear memory of how she'd gotten there. "I'm…I'm sorry," she heard herself say. "I, uh…"

In the next moment, she was out the door and down the hallway, slapping at the elevator call button, then opting for the stairwell instead. Bounding in a downward spiral as she took the stairs two and three at a time. She struggled to keep her mind blank on the long way down, but the image of Giana's face hovered above her like a wraith—a kaleidoscope of emotions as Remy had backed out of the room, each one of them naked and painfully easy to read. There was lingering passion, followed by humiliation, and then disbelief. The final stage had been unmitigated, overarching rage.

Remy hit the ground floor and stumbled out into the blazing sunlight, sucking in great drafts of air as she found her way to her car. She knew she needed to go back and explain. She knew she should have never left in the first place. But how could she explain what she didn't understand? She started the engine and set the car in motion, refusing to look back as she punched the lights all the way to the bridge.

CHAPTER TWELVE

"Would it kill you to return a guy's telephone calls?"

Giana looked up from her menu and tried to gauge the level of Nick's irritation. She couldn't tell a lot from his eyes, which were obscured behind dark Wayfarer sunglasses. But the grim set of his mouth was a good indication. "I'm sorry, Nick. I got a little busy over the weekend and, ah...I don't know. Time just got away from me. I apologize."

Nick rubbed at the stubble on his jaw. He slouched back in his seat, his muscular frame straining the bolts of the aluminum patio chair. "I was kinda hoping we could get up to Sebastopol. I told you my folks have a cabin up there, right? I was thinking it'd be good to spend a little quality time together, you know. Just the two of us. Hang out. Maybe do some fishing. The place ain't much, but it's quiet. And private."

Giana refocused on her menu. Quality time indeed. Nick had begun to press her lately about going away for the weekend, and she was running out of excuses. Going away for the weekend meant having sex—she harbored no illusions about that. To the man's credit, he'd been surprisingly patient on the subject until now, but it was obvious that his patience was wearing thin.

Unfortunately, there was nothing Giana could do to help the situation. She just didn't feel it. Regardless of whatever insanity was going on with Remy, sleeping with Nick Pierce was simply out of the question.

The waitress approached the table, and Giana looked up, happy for the interruption. The woman was young and pretty, and the bright smile on her face was all for the handsome man in the dark sunglasses. Nick barely acknowledged the poor girl's presence. He folded his arms over his chest and continued to stare across the table at Giana. She was distinctly reminded of her brother Tony, during one of his more puerile sulks.

Giana smiled warmly at the waitress. "I'll have the Cobb salad. But can we swap out the blue cheese dressing for something a little lighter?"

"We have an Italian that's made in house, and it's totally delicious. I can have them put that on the side for you, just in case?"

"That sounds perfect. And I'll have an iced tea as well. Thanks so much." Giana looked at Nick, who had yet to even touch his menu. The blushing girl smiled at him expectantly, and he tersely ordered a steak and fries, handing the menu over without a glance.

He was spiraling into churlishness right before her eyes, and Giana had to admit she was intrigued by the display. The shine on that high-polished veneer of his was looking a little tarnished. She wondered if this was a glimpse of what Remy seemed to find so objectionable in the man.

She chased the thought from her mind. Remy was not about to occupy one more second of her headspace today—she simply wouldn't allow it. Without her permission, her hand reached for her cell phone and compulsively lifted it to check for messages. Nothing from the detective, of course. She set the phone down again and calmly exhaled. It didn't matter. Two days without a word from her, and it did not matter. Giana refused to care.

"You expecting a call?"

She looked up at Nick. His voice had taken on a snide, slightly taunting undertone she didn't care for. She ignored the question and took a sip from her water glass. "Look, Nick, you're obviously in some kind of a mood today. Why don't we just talk about what's bothering you?"

"Who were you with last weekend?"

Giana stared at her own twin reflections in the lenses of his sunglasses. She couldn't see Nick's eyes, which made the last question feel like an interrogation. She had no intention of telling him the first thing about what had happened between Remy and herself. But she wasn't ashamed of it either. "I saw Remy on Saturday. Why?"

Nick snorted and shifted in his chair, banging his knee against the underside of the table. Water sloshed out of their drinking glasses, but he seemed untroubled by that as he spread his arms out wide and locked his hands behind his head. "I've been wasting my time here, haven't I?"

Giana wasn't sure if the question was rhetorical. "Nick, I told you from the beginning that I wasn't making any promises. Now, if you feel like I've misled you in some way—"

"Like, maybe you should've told me you were a fucking dyke?" He fairly spat out the word. "Too bad you didn't. It would've saved us both a lot of time."

The waitress had reappeared at the table with Giana's iced tea. The pink blush on her face deepened to flaming scarlet. Without a word, she set the glass down and turned to leave, but Giana placed a hand on her arm to stop her. "I'm so sorry. But would you mind packing up that salad to go?"

The girl nodded and gave her a tentative smile. Then her eyes drained of warmth as she cut a glance at Nick. "Can I pack that up for you as well, sir?"

Nick cocked his head to one side. As Giana watched, the features on his face rearranged themselves, eerily shifting like a chameleon's. The sneer disappeared, the lopsided grin reemerged, and in an instant he was charming, fun-loving Nick again. "Well, I guess it's just your lucky day, sweetheart. I'm gonna sit right here and enjoy your lovely company. And I think I'll have a beer while I'm at it."

The girl seemed less than charmed as she nodded tersely and strode away. Giana reached under the table and gathered up her purse, dropping her cell phone inside.

"So that's it?" Nick looked genuinely surprised. "No hysterics? No arguments? You're just gonna get up and walk away. Just like that."

"I don't associate with homophobes, Nick. Too bad you didn't show your stripes a little sooner. It would've saved us both a lot of time."

"Oh, come on, Giana, don't get your panties in a twist. I wasn't serious, all right? You're too goddamned gorgeous to be a lezzie, that much is obvious."

She bit back a response as she stood up from the table. She wasn't going to waste her breath on an inbred. "I'll pay for my lunch on the way out. Goodbye, Nick."

"Giana, come on," he cajoled. "You know you love me." His voice rose as she left the patio and strode into the restaurant. "Hey! I'll call you later, honey!"

CHAPTER THIRTEEN

Remy was glad Cookie had insisted on driving. It was the one thing they invariably fought about whenever they were working a case together in the field, but today she was content to let him have at it. Her mind tended to drift too much when she was driving, and lately there was only one place it wanted to go.

What happened the other day in Giana's apartment had sent Remy into a tailspin. The only way to stop the churning was to concentrate on something else. Conveniently enough, this investigation required her undivided attention, and she was more than happy to give it.

"So you really think it's worth a trip all the way out here, huh?" Cookie had frowned at her earlier that morning when she'd announced they were heading out to Pleasanton for the day. It was the hometown of Samantha Willard—the last place the woman had been seen alive, jogging in a lakeside park a few miles from her house. That had been months ago, and Cookie and Remy had covered the territory thoroughly in the early days of the investigation.

"We weren't looking for a link back then, Cooks. We thought it was a one-off. If we look at it again, with the Everett girl in the picture this time, maybe things will present a little differently."

Remy scrolled through the contacts on her phone until she located the number of Winnie Greer, who worked in ID Section. She dialed, hoping to catch the woman live instead of on voice mail. Remy had a special request, and it was going to take a little coaxing to get it done.

Winnie's voice was cheerful when she picked up. "Devereux! What's shaking, hon? Long time."

"Hey, Winn. Yeah, I know. It's been a little while. How's Sally and the kids?"

"Oh, well, you know. The kids are alive, and the wife still comes home at night, so who's complaining? We should grab a beer sometime and catch up."

"Definitely. But hey, Winn, the reason I'm calling…"

"Yeah sure, what's up?"

"I need you to take a peek at somebody for me. I haven't pulled any paperwork on him yet…I mean, don't worry, all right? I'll make sure to do it all official, if it ever comes down to that. But right now, I just need to know if this guy is worth my time."

Winnie hesitated on the other end.

"It would really be a big help, Winn. And this won't come back on you, I swear. You don't even have to write anything down. I just want to know if he pops up in any of the databases. Priors, arrests, parole. Anything at all."

The silence continued for a beat, and then Winnie relented. "What's the name?"

"Franklin Swaggett," Remy said quickly. "Swaggett, with two G's and two T's." She glanced at Cookie, who kept his eyes on the road.

"All right, Rem," Winnie said. "I'll get back to you when I can."

"Thank you." Remy exhaled. "You're the best."

The line disconnected, and Remy went back to her notes, refusing to look at Cookie.

After a moment he asked, "Is that the cat you ran into at Glide the other day?"

Remy nodded, glancing at him as she dialed the phone again. "Uh, hello, yes. Detective Finley, please." Cookie was still watching her, and she turned to look out the car window instead. They were entering the sun-dried flats of the Tri-Valley Area now, having left the cooler climes of the inner Bay behind. It looked like it was going to be a warm one.

She heard Finley's gravelly voice come on the line. "Bob. Hi, it's Remy Devereux here...Yeah, I was hoping I'd catch you at the station. Listen, my partner and I are in the area today and...That's right, yeah, still on the Willard case...No, no, pretty routine. Just going over the basics again. Hey, any chance we could stop by and have a quick chat?"

The Pleasanton Police Station was situated squarely in the bosom of slow-paced suburbia. Fronted by a neat lawn and garden planters full of pretty annuals, the adobe-style building looked more like the town library than a station house. Cookie pulled into the parking lot and parked the Charger beneath the fronds of a giant palm tree.

It was ninety-six degrees outside, and neither of them wasted any time crossing the baking asphalt to the building's main entrance. Inside, the lobby was quiet and blessedly cool. The door had barely swung shut behind them before Finley came lumbering down a hallway to their right.

"Saw you pull up." He was smiling, as usual, though the bushy gray mustache made it difficult to tell. His grip was just as bruising as Remy remembered. "Hot enough for you yet? Just you wait, it gets better."

He clasped Cookie's hand next and rattled his arm, then turned to lead the two of them back down the short corridor to his office in the corner of the building. The room was small but bright, with large windows looking out on the parking lot. Finley waved them into a pair of seats, then squeezed himself into the battered leather chair behind his desk.

"All right now. Let's see what we got here." He pulled open a file drawer at his knee and began to rifle through its contents.

"Bob, we really appreciate you taking the time," Remy said. "This is really just a review. Keeping it fresh in our heads, you know. Making sure we haven't missed an angle."

Finley found the file he was searching for and pulled it out. "No problem whatsoever." He glanced up and met Remy's eyes. "I'm sure the lady's family appreciates your diligence."

He laid the file open and proceeded to go through the local end of the investigation line by line. Cookie took several notes, while Remy listened quietly. None of the information had faded from her memory bank.

Finley narrated a brief recap of the husband's involvement. "So, according to Mr. Willard the missus leaves the house at the usual time to go for her morning jog. That was at, uh… approximately seven thirty a.m. Okay. He feeds the kids their breakfast, drops them off at school, then goes directly to work. The kids and the folks at the school all corroborate that timeline. He's at work at eight twenty-seven a.m.—that's according to company records—and, let's see here…is not made aware of Mrs. Willard's absence until approximately three fifteen p.m. That's when the school called on his work number to tell him nobody came to pick up the kids."

"Cell phone?" It was the first time Cookie had spoken since they sat down.

"Phone company records show no calls. He leaves the thing turned off in his locker when he's at work. Says it wasn't unusual for him and the wife to go that amount of time without talking. The wife's phone was never found." Finley shook his head. "The guy is rock solid for the entire day."

"And what about her run that morning?" Remy asked. "Her usual circuit was about a four-mile loop. Any reason to think she might've done something different that morning?"

Finley shrugged. "No reason to. The husband says she was pretty consistent about that. The loop at Shadow Cliffs was her normal route. We combed that area multiple times and didn't come up with anything. Even dragged the lake looking for her. Before the body turned up in the city, of course."

"Any chance she wasn't taken at the lake? It could've happened before she ever got there or on her way home afterward."

"Yeah, I suppose there's always that possibility. But the lake is the most secluded spot anywhere along that route, see. If I was looking to make an abduction, that'd be the place I'd do it at." He leaned back in his seat and ran his meaty fingers down the length of his tie. "She was supposed to volunteer at the food drive later that morning. Never showed up to that, of course. My gut says it happened at the lake."

"You said food drive?" Remy asked.

Finley nodded. "It's a regular community thing over at the church. Folks over there said she never missed it."

The hairs were standing up on Remy's arms. She flipped open her notebook, skipping past the Willard section to scan through her notes on her interview with the Everetts. There it was. The girl was in the 4-H club. Community outreach. Toys and clothing. Food drives.

Remy looked up at Finley. "Mrs. Willard's church. I'd love to talk to somebody over there if I could. You wouldn't happen to have the name of a contact handy?"

Finley's eyebrows inched upward in his face, like fuzzy gray caterpillars. "Well, yeah. Matter of fact, I know the pastor." He glanced at his watch. "I can run you over there right now, if you want to."

It was past six p.m. when Cookie finally dropped Remy at her car in San Francisco. He wasted no time heading back out of the parking garage, and she felt glad for him as she watched him go. Apparently, things were still working out with Marla and the kids. She hopped into her own car and pulled out close behind him. She was due for dinner at seven p.m. at Keisha and Devlin's house in Walnut Creek. With traffic the way it was, she was going to be late, but there was nothing she could do about that now.

The backup on the bridge approach was heavy when she got there, but at least it was moving. She settled back in her seat, her mind still racing from the major advances they'd made in the case that day. First thing in the morning, she and Cookie were heading back out to the Everett girl's school in Pinole. They needed to compile a comprehensive list of every establishment associated with the food drive efforts out there. Remy knew in her gut they were going to find Glide Memorial on that list. Just as they had at the church in Pleasanton.

All she could see now was Franklin Swaggett's face, with that widow's peak like a black stake in the middle of his forehead. And the genial grin that couldn't mask the coldness in his eyes.

She knew it was a mistake to zero in on him too soon. First, they needed to get their hands on a roster of every employee and volunteer at Glide. In particular, the ones who did any driving for the church. Then out of that group, they needed to identify the ones with routes that took them anywhere near Pleasanton or Pinole. At that point, assuming Swaggett was still in the pool (and Remy was all but certain that he would be), they could bring him in along with a few of the others for questioning. Deciding when to do it was the tricky part. And coming up with a plausible explanation that wasn't going to tip their hand. Hopefully, by then they'd have enough to obtain a search warrant. Hopefully. But they would deal with that hurdle when they came to it. One step at a time.

She leaned her head back against the headrest and blew out a long breath. She was attacking the case with a degree of clarity she wished she could muster all the time. It was the one upside of resorting to denial and avoidance to cope with one's personal life. She closed her eyes, shaking her head. She couldn't imagine what Giana must think of her now. The whole scenario was still too mortifying to contemplate for longer than a few seconds at a time.

She glanced at the clock in the dash, then picked up her phone and texted one-handed, informing Devlin she was running late. She set the phone aside and exhaled. She was relieved she was seeing her friends tonight. She needed to talk to somebody about this. She clearly had no idea what she was doing with Giana—maybe a frank chat with the people who knew her well would help her get her head on straight around it.

She had no excuse for her recent behavior, and this holding pattern she and Giana had tacitly entered into wasn't going to last forever. It was the silence that scared her the most. Giana was usually so forthcoming. The fact that three days had passed now without a word from her was a very bad sign indeed. The woman was furious with her, that much she could assume.

Remy pulled into the driveway in Walnut Creek thirty minutes late for dinner. She was hungry and cross from having sat in traffic for too long. As she climbed stiffly out of the car, she felt every one of her thirty-two years. The adrenaline from the earlier part of the day had long worn off, leaving a pall of anxiety and fatigue in its wake. She grabbed the bottle of wine she'd brought along and strode up the walkway of the rambling home.

The front door was unlocked, as usual. Shaking her head, Remy silently entered the foyer and paused there to let the sounds and the smells of the house embrace her. Bustling could be heard in the kitchen. From the smell of it, dinner was on the stove, and her stomach gave a rumbling acknowledgment. But Murphy had yet to detect her presence, so she waited. In the next instant, she heard the frenetic scrape of claws against the hardwoods and a fierce low growl as the hound came scrambling around the corner, barreling down upon the hapless intruder.

"That's my Murphy boy!" Remy squatted to catch him as he slid to a halt in front of her, his vicious growls dissolving into an apologetic whine. The tail set to furiously wagging, and she scratched at his scruffy mane. "Isn't that right, boy? We're gonna make a police dog out of you yet."

"Is that you, Rem?"

The call came from the kitchen, and she rose to head toward the rear of the house, with Murphy close on her heels. "When are you guys gonna start locking that front door?"

"My parents never lock their doors, either." Keisha looked up from her chopping board. "The one time they did, somebody broke in and robbed the place."

"Oh, I didn't realize. Well, that makes perfect sense then." Remy set the wine bottle down on the counter. "Hey, sorry I'm so late."

"Yes, we're both outraged. No dinner for you." Keisha's long, ropy braids swung about her pretty face as she stepped around the island to give Remy a hug. "Please. Devlin got home ten minutes ago, okay? She probably did it on purpose to get out of cooking tonight."

"I heard that." Devlin strode in from the hallway. She squeezed Remy's shoulders with two powerful hands as she passed by. "And I wasn't late. I was pacing myself."

Keisha rolled her eyes, then smiled sweetly at her wife. "Sweetheart, why don't you pour us some wine. Since dinner is almost finished."

Remy snorted softly, refraining from comment as she climbed onto a counter stool. She plucked a carrot from Keisha's cutting board and munched on it while Devlin opened the wine. The impatient nudge of a canine nose prodded her thigh, and she reached down to idly scratch at Murphy's ears, feeling the tension slowly begin to ebb from her body. The wine was poured, and the three women raised their glasses, clinking them together in a silent toast.

Devlin took a sip before setting her glass down. She eyed Remy quietly and nodded. Remy nodded in return, waiting. "Well?" Devlin finally prompted.

"Well, what?"

"Well, who the hell is this Giana woman? Are you kidding me?"

Remy dragged a palm roughly down the front of her face. "I know. Oh my God. I know."

For the next several minutes, she talked. The words fell out of her mouth in one continuous stream, retelling the events of the past few months, clear back to the day she'd first laid eyes on Giana Falco. Devlin and Keisha listened without interruption, moving around each other in a synchronized rhythm as they finished preparing the meal. When she got to the part about her and Giana's first kiss, her friends paused in their respective tasks, staring at her with rapt attention. Remy skimmed over the details. She omitted any mention at all of their most recent encounter.

"So the problem here," she said in summation, "is that I really like this woman. I mean…I *really* like her. It's suicide, I know this. And I keep trying to put the brakes on. But every time I see her, it's, like, all of that just goes out the window."

"Well, maybe you shouldn't be seeing her then." Keisha's stare was brutally direct. Remy took a deep breath and held it. This was going to hurt. "I really don't know what it is with you and these straight girls. It's like you just *want* to get beat down." Devlin looked at her sharply, and Keisha put a hand on her hip. "Hey. That's the truth, okay? Remy, you were destroyed after Alexis. *Destroyed.* Do I really need to remind you of that?"

"Uh. No, you don't…" Remy muttered.

"And I seriously don't think anybody in this room wants to see *that* shit again."

"Whoa," Devlin interrupted. "Honey…"

Keisha crossed her arms. Her skin was a rich chocolate brown that glowed with a healthy sheen under the overhead light. Her eyes were light brown and fixed on Remy. "You were better off with Erica. I don't know why you couldn't just try to work that out."

"Pfft! You don't even *like* Erica," Remy scoffed. "What are you even talking about?"

"Well, at least she's gay. That's a good place to start, don't you think?"

Devlin interjected again. "Is it beyond the realm of possibility here to think that Giana might be coming out?" She glanced at her wife. "I mean, *you* were straight at one time, sweetheart. Until you weren't."

"That was *freshman year*, Devlin. Please." Keisha turned her back on the conversation, searching the cabinets for a salad bowl.

Devlin lowered her voice as she spoke to Remy. "Well, what does the sexy scientist have to say about all this?" Keisha sucked her teeth behind her, and Devlin ignored it, her eyes still on Remy. "Does she think she might be gay?"

Remy's shoulders inched toward her ears. "I…It's not like… Well, I haven't actually asked her that. I mean, not exactly. Okay—I haven't asked her that. But I *know* that she's not."

"But *how* do you know, if you haven't asked her?"

Remy raked a hand through her hair.

"Why haven't you asked her?" Devlin pressed.

"Because she's afraid of the answer." Keisha plopped the salad bowl down on the counter. "Never ask a question you don't wanna hear the answer to, honey. Look, Remy,"—she put a hand on Remy's shoulder—"Giana is a beautiful girl, nobody's denying that. And she actually seems really sweet. Hell, *I* even liked her when I first met her, and that's saying something." Devlin and Remy shared a glance of agreement. "But that don't change the facts," Keisha went on. "You need to get some perspective, girl, and if I'm the only one who's willing to give it to you, then so be it."

Devlin looked like she was about to object again, and Remy abruptly stood up, the legs of her stool scraping against the tiled floor. "You know what? It doesn't even matter, because I'm breaking it off. It's over, all right? So we can all just stop talking about it now."

She yanked open a drawer and grabbed a handful of silverware. Murphy raised his head to stare up at her as she gathered a stack of plates and stepped over his body sprawled on the floor. "This is all just so fucking ridiculous," she muttered. She dropped the plates one by one on the dining table and left the silverware in a pile.

"So anyway," she said abruptly. "Are you guys free this Saturday? You should come over. I'll fire up the grill, and we can throw on some steaks and corn or whatever."

The two women watched her in silence. She stared back at them expectantly, refusing to acknowledge the subject change.

"Sure," Devlin finally answered. "We're free this Saturday. Aren't we, babe?"

Keisha's lips pursed, her eyes still on Remy. "Mm-hmm. But we ain't nearly done talking about this shit, honey. Uhn-uhn. Not by a long shot."

CHAPTER FOURTEEN

Giana shut the lid on the coffeemaker and hit the start button just as Liz walked into the kitchen.

"Did you make enough for me, too?"

"Oh, hey, you. I didn't realize you were home." Giana switched the machine off and reached for the bag of coffee beans. She glanced at her roomie's jeans and faded T-shirt. "Looks like somebody has the day off. I'm jealous."

"Don't hate me because I'm beautiful." Liz heaved a breezy sigh as she pulled out a chair and sat down. "My God, I hardly know what to do with myself. Call in sick, Gigi." She poked her lips out in an exaggerated pout. "Stay home and play hooky with me instead."

Giana set the grinder to whirring and seriously considered the idea. The workweek felt interminable, and it was far from over. Her spirits had not improved—indeed, her mood seemed to be growing steadily grimmer as the days trudged on. But she doubted even the unsinkable Elizabeth Talbot was enough to lift the malaise. "I'll have to take a rain check on that, hon. It's still a little soon for me to become an unreliable employee."

"As if you ever could. Come on, sit down for a minute. I feel like I haven't seen you in forever."

Giana added more water to the reservoir and started the coffeemaker brewing again. She joined Liz at the little table, praying the conversation was not about to turn into an inquisition.

"So. How are things with the hottie?" Liz's eyes were bright with anticipation.

Giana rubbed at her temples, convinced she felt a headache coming on. She didn't know which hottie Liz was referring to—Remy or Nick—but at this point she wasn't inclined to discuss either one of them. Her roommate continued to stare at her expectantly, and she sighed. "I'm afraid you'll have to be more specific."

"Hmm, good point." Liz chuckled. "I'm talking about that tall drink of deliciousness I saw sitting on our living room couch the other day. Of *course*! How did *that* go? I swear, there was something cooking in the air between you two. My God. Talk about smoky bedroom eyes. I hate to break it to you, hon, but that police lady has the hots for you. No doubt about it."

Giana lightly cleared her throat, and Liz's nostrils flared like a bloodhound's. "Wait. You already knew that, didn't you?" Her eyes raked Giana's face. "Did something—?"

"All right, yes," Giana admitted. "We kissed, okay?"

Elizabeth gasped. "Oh...my God. I *knew* it!" Her mouth fell open and stayed there. It was almost enough to make Giana laugh. Almost. "Well, hell's bells. Tell me! How was it? I mean, did you like it? Who made the first move? Remy did, of course. Big, beautiful daddy that she is."

"Christ." Giana stood up from the table. She grabbed two mugs from a cabinet and set them heavily down on the countertop. She stood at the coffeemaker and waited, watching the steaming trickle fill the pot. Her roommate had fallen blessedly silent behind her, and she took a moment to breathe. The gurgles and hiss of the brewer were the only sounds in the room.

"It's all these labels I can't stand," she finally said. "Gay, straight, lesbian. Whatever. And what the hell is a 'daddy' supposed to be, anyway? Honestly." She filled the two mugs and set them down on the table.

"So you're really not going to tell me what happened?"

She stared at her roommate. Liz had a one-track mind. "You're certifiable, you know that?" She expelled a breath and seated herself at the table again. Liz was still waiting, and Giana took her time formulating a response.

What exactly *had* happened? She would love to know the answer to that herself. It was a pretty hot and heavy scene that had played out in the living room just a few feet away. Liz would love to hear all about it, there was no doubt. Not that she was any more inclined to discuss the details with her friend than she had been with Nick. She was barely able to reckon with it herself. The intensity of it. Or what it meant. Or how good it had felt. Her anger at Remy eclipsed everything. The detective had absconded once again—at the moment Giana felt her most vulnerable. Her most exposed. And four days now without a word.

"Remy doesn't think it's a good idea," she finally explained. "The two of us. Seeing each other. We're not even speaking at the moment."

"I see." Liz nodded slowly, her eyes enormous. "Did she say why?"

"She's prejudiced against heterosexuals."

Liz's brow puckered. "She *said* that?"

"Of course not." Giana took a slow sip from her mug, enjoying the heat as it wafted up to steam her cheeks. "She has trust issues. Like the rest of us, I suppose. The woman is about as forthcoming as the Sphinx, but that much at least is not very hard to figure out."

"But you still want to see her." Liz waited for her acknowledgment, which came as a barely perceptible nod. "And you kissed just that one time? Or was there more?"

Giana met her eyes but said nothing.

"Okay. So there was more." Liz slumped back in her chair. "Wow." She took a sip from her coffee cup. "Wow. I have to say, Gee. I'm a little impressed here. I didn't think you had it in you."

"Had what in me?"

"The stones, you know. To stray off the reservation."

Giana rolled her eyes. "I haven't strayed anywhere. Remy and I...we have a connection. It's a fact—whether she wants to admit it or not. I've just never had much interest in lying. Least of all to myself. And not about something that's so painfully obvious as this."

"Amen to that." Liz set her mug down on the table. "Holy shit. I really can't get over this. It's just so mind-blowing. Giana Falco, with another woman. You know, I would've killed to have known this about you back in college. I mean, if you wanted to experiment, sweetie, I would've been more than willing—"

"Lizard, no. Just stop it." Giana looked at her, exasperated. "That's really kind of gross."

"I know," Liz agreed, laughing. "It is, isn't it?"

A chuckle percolated in Giana's chest. It was the first time she'd felt any semblance of levity in days.

"So what are you going to do?" Liz asked after a moment. "If she doesn't want to see you?"

"Mmm. But I know that she does. It's why she's been behaving like such a freak show."

Liz laughed, then narrowed her eyes at her. "Who *are* you right now?"

Giana drew in a deep breath. "I feel like I'm more myself than I've ever been."

Her roommate stared at her, nodding. "So...You're really not going to tell me *any*thing about what happened? Come on! I'm dying to know the details here. I mean, at least tell me how far it went. You must've been losing your mind! Did she just grab you by the hair and—"

"Liz..." Giana stood up and retrieved her travel mug from the dish drain. She poured in the remaining coffee from her cup, then topped it off with more from the pot. "Look, I know what you're driving at. And the answer is no, we did not have sex. Not exactly."

Liz perked up, straightening in her chair, and Giana snorted at her. "That's all the detail you're going to get. But I have to tell you, I really don't think having sex with a woman is some great big scary deal. I don't know if you've noticed, but I happen to *be* a woman. I have all the parts, and I know how they work. There ought to be some advantage to that, don't you think?"

"Hey. You're preaching to the choir with this one, sister."

Giana did laugh at that, and it felt good. "I have to go to work, Alien. I love you." She dropped a kiss on Liz's forehead and headed out of the kitchen.

CHAPTER FIFTEEN

Remy shrugged her satchel off her shoulder and let the bag drop to the floor. She sank heavily into her desk chair and sat still for a moment, trying to resign herself to the fact that the day had only just begun. Her head was splitting in two, and she felt as if she hadn't slept in a month.

Focusing exclusively on casework in the early part of the week had served to keep her functioning, but even then, it was only during the day. When the evening hours descended, all bets were off. The dreams had recently kicked into overdrive, making her dread the moment her eyes would inevitably close. But if she wasn't waking in a cold sweat in the middle of the night, she was wrestling with bouts of insomnia, inundated by thoughts of Giana.

Instead of fading over time, the memory of what had happened between them had only grown more acute—magnifying in detail, dogging her with an unrelenting clarity. Giana had met her with a willing frankness, trusting her enough to show herself in the raw. She had touched something in

Remy's core, and it was overwhelming and too intense. It was simply more than she could handle.

She was still hiding from the sad truth of that fact even now, mortified she had ever let things get this far. It wasn't like she hadn't seen it coming. A part of her had known from the very beginning she would wind up here. And yet, she hadn't been able to stay away. Inevitably, inexorably, they had gravitated toward one another. And the chemistry between them was staggering.

Remy found herself on the brink, ready to give herself over, to lay it all at Giana's feet. In precisely the way she had feared she could. It was terrifying and paralyzing, and there was no way to explain any part of that without revealing the whole of it. She had panicked. There was no other way to put it. The only thing she could think to do was turn tail and run.

And now she had spent five days avoiding the woman, too embarrassed to articulate the depth of her own cowardice. The longer she delayed, the worse it got. She'd dug herself into a hole, and by the time she finally worked up the courage to face her, there was a real possibility Giana wouldn't be there waiting anymore.

Remy's stomach twisted at the thought of that. It shouldn't matter, she knew, since she had resolved to end things anyway. But in all honesty, she had no confidence in her ability to do that either. It wasn't what she wanted. And yet, the alternative was nothing she could afford. She was more than off-balance—she had lost her moorings altogether and she had no idea what to do about it. In the meantime, her brilliant solution was to do nothing at all.

She yanked open a desk drawer and pawed through its contents in search of ibuprofen. Her cell phone rang, and she sighed as she pulled it out of her pocket and answered.

"Hey, little brother."

"Hey, sis. Bad timing?"

"No, no." She gave up on her search for the pills and slammed the drawer shut. "I'm just a little off my game this morning, that's all. How's it going over there? How's Maman?"

There was a pause on the other end of the line, and she slowly sat up in her chair.

"Okay, Rem. Now, I don't want you to freak out about this, but Pappy and I decided to call in a nurse to be with her full time. She starts on Monday."

Remy held the phone, trying to absorb the information.

"Rem?"

"Yeah. I'm listening."

"It's just getting to be too much for Paps to handle on his own. I'm getting over here as much as I can, and Jerome is helping out, too. But we both have to work, and—"

"Hey, look," Remy cut in, "I've been saving up my hours. I could take an extended leave of absence. I'd just need to wrap up some things here at work, and then I could probably be home in a couple of days."

"No, no, we don't need you to do that now. Not yet."

She rested her forehead in her hand, focusing on her brother's breathing on the other end of the line. Even and true. "I didn't think it was going to happen this fast," she said quietly.

"I know. I didn't either." After a pause, he said, "I'm going to tell you when I think it's time for you to get back here, sis. You trust me on that, right?"

Remy nodded, forgetting for a moment that he couldn't see her. She cleared her throat. "Yeah. Yeah, I do, Max." Her exhalation was heavy. "All right. I'm going to hang up with you and give Maman a call."

"Actually, I'm at the house now. She's sleeping."

Remy nodded again, staring down at the desk blotter.

"You still there?"

"Hmm? Yeah, I'm here. So, uh, all right. Well, how are things with Jerome?"

"Oh, he's driving me nuts, as usual." Max's tone had softened. "He was just offered a position with the Chicago Ballet."

"You're kidding me. Really? That's amazing. As a choreographer?"

"Yes. And the idiot actually thinks he's going to turn it down."

She sighed. "Because you're stuck in New Orleans, and he doesn't want to leave you."

"I'm not stuck, Rem. This is my home. I'm glad I can be here for Maman. And for Paps, too."

"God, I feel terrible."

"Remy, stop. Jerome is taking that job—don't you worry about it. And I can sell real estate anywhere. I'll go up there and join him when I can, all right? When things, uh…When this is over down here."

She didn't respond.

"All right, Rem?" Max asked.

"Yeah. Okay. I'm really glad you're there for them, Max."

"There's no other place I could be. We're gonna get through this, sis. It's fucking awful. But we're gonna get through it. Look, I gotta run. I'll talk to you in a few days, okay?"

"Okay. Give Pappy a hug for me."

"I will."

The call ended, and Remy sat with the phone in her hand, staring blindly at the opposite wall. Then she scrolled to Giana's number and hit the call button. The line rang once and went directly to voice mail. Her heart suddenly pounding, she listened to the husky timbre on the recording. She felt her own throat begin to constrict as the greeting drew to a close. The beep sounded, and she disconnected the call.

She dropped her forehead to the desk and left it there for several moments, breathing in the dusty scent of the blotter. Then she reached for the phone again and typed out a text message, quickly sending it off before she could change her mind.

I'm sorry I've been so out of touch. I hope you're doing okay.

Remy moved to set the phone aside but jumped at the loud ping of the answering text.

Where are you now?

Swallowing hard, Remy typed:

In my office.

The response came a second later.

Stay there.

Remy set the phone down and seriously considered fleeing the room. The only thing that held her in place was the thought of running into Giana in the corridor. She forced herself to remain seated at her desk, shuffling file folders and staring without comprehension at her computer screen for the entire eleven minutes it took Giana to appear in the doorway.

She seemed utterly calm as she stepped in and closed the door behind her, leaning back against it with both hands on the knob. The small room grew smaller still as the two women eyed each other.

Remy leaned back in her chair and hungrily grazed the planes of Giana's face. God, she missed her. It was painful to realize how much she missed her. Giana's expression gave away nothing, though the green eyes glinted with a simmering anger that was hard to ignore. She looked tired. And beautiful. And like she needed to be kissed.

"I, uh…" Her throat was dry. "Do you want to sit down?"

Giana remained standing but slipped her bag off her shoulder and set it on the chair by the door. She was elegantly dressed, in a crisp white shirt with oversized cuffs and collar. The navy-blue pencil skirt hugged her curves in exactly the right way. She was stunning, and Remy wanted to tell her so, but now was clearly not the time.

"I thought of a hundred different things to say to you on the way over here." Giana's voice was quiet, controlled. Remy held her breath for what was about to come next, but nothing followed after that. Giana broke eye contact and studied the floor.

"Giana," Remy said after a moment. "I know I owe you an explanation. Leaving like that was pretty, um…lame." Giana's eyes pinned her to the chair. "Okay, it was shitty. It was a shitty thing to do. Running away like that."

"It seems to be a habit with you."

A rush of heat suffused Remy's cheeks. "It's not. Believe me, this kind of behavior is entirely new to me." The look on Giana's face was blatantly skeptical, and Remy felt her defenses kicking in. "Look, I tried to tell you before…" She paused, struggling to tamp down her frustration.

"You tried to tell me what, Remy? And I really don't want to hear any of that bullshit about straight women again."

"It's not bullshit! Don't you realize how fucking nuts this is? I mean, this whole thing is just…" Remy blew out an exasperated breath. "I can't do this, all right? I'm not…I just don't…"

"Right, I know," Giana interrupted. "You don't date straight women. And I don't date *women*. So tell me, how did we get here? We both know I'm not the one who started this."

Remy's temper flared at last, and she clutched onto it like a lifeline. "Oh," she scoffed, "forgive me, but I'd have to say that's a question up for debate."

Giana's eyebrows shot up. "And what the hell is that supposed to mean?"

"It means you're a flirt. You flirt, Giana. You flirt with me all the time."

"Oh…" Giana's voice dropped to a dangerous level, and Remy immediately regretted her words. "So you're saying this is my fault." Her eyes hardened into gemstones. Remy braced for impact.

"Yes, I see. Of course it's my fault. Despite the fact that I'm a heterosexual—as unappealing as that so clearly is to you. And the fact that I have zero experience with women. And the fact that, other than you, I've never even *looked* at another female that way in my entire life. Not ever. But in spite of all that, I somehow managed to seduce you anyway. Because I'm a flirt. With my wily ways and my wanton stares, and you just couldn't help yourself."

"Well, Remy, that sounds exactly like something a man would say. Congratulations. Thank you for making this all feel so familiar."

"That's not what I…" Remy trailed off, withering beneath the woman's imperious stare. Every possible response sounded absurd to her own ears. Giana was right, of course. Brutally so. In every respect. Any attempt to lay the burden at her feet was sheer lunacy.

Once again she found herself wanting to bolt from the room. She gripped the arms of her chair to hold herself in place. "I, uh…Look, that was a ridiculous thing to say. I'm claiming temporary insanity, all right? Please excuse."

Giana was far from appeased. "Don't you think it's time you got over this gay-straight obsession of yours? I mean, really, Remy. Why does it make one fucking bit of difference *what* I call myself if—"

"Because I'm not gonna be your fucking guinea pig, all right?" She was vaguely aware that she was shouting, but she had no control over that now. "Because I don't want to be the plaything you get to have your fun with and then drop a few weeks later when you realize you can't actually *be* with a woman. Because, believe me, that's exactly what's going to happen here."

Giana looked as if she'd been slapped, and Remy abruptly stopped. She raked both hands through her hair and held them at the back of her head.

"I'm sorry," she said after a moment. "I didn't intend to say any of that. Jesus, Giana. You look at me, and I don't even know what I'm *thinking* half the time."

She dropped her eyes to her desk and kept them there. "Look, um…Obviously, I'm a little out of my depth when it comes to you."

She stopped again, shaking her head. She'd already said far too much. The conversation was a step beyond her worst nightmare and becoming more lurid by the second. She glanced up, praying for an interruption, but Giana simply raised her eyebrows and waited for her to continue. She tore her eyes away and tried to gather her thoughts. "You're right," she began again. "This situation is my responsibility. I'm the one who sent us down this path in the first place. So it should fall to me to put an end to it."

"And how do you intend to do that?" Giana's tone was eerily calm again. "Just cut it off? Cut *me* off, and pretend like none of this ever happened—is that your solution?"

"That's not what I want. Look, Giana, it isn't. But I can't…I don't see where we go from here."

Giana crossed her arms and leaned back against the door. Remy watched and waited, half of her hoping that scientific brain would come up with a valid objection. The other half just wanted to lie down and give in to the wave of exhaustion now flushing through her body.

Giana unfolded her arms and reached into her bag on the chair. "I have a fiber analysis for you."

"What?"

"The synthetic fibers. From Everett and Willard."

Remy watched in a state of confusion as she produced a folder from her bag and stepped over to the desk. She laid it open so it faced Remy right side up.

"We matched the dye lot."

Giana's voice had lifted in tone, and Remy gazed up at her, struggling to comprehend what she was saying.

"Remy, did you hear what I said? The fibers are identical. We matched the dye lot, and we have the manufacturer." She tapped her finger on the file on the desk. "The company is Duratone Incorporated, out of Bakersfield. They manufacture carpeting for commercial and domestic applications. The color on our fibers is dye lot seven sixty-four-B, trade name Sunflower Dreams, and it was used exclusively on their line of indoor shag carpeting from 1978 to 1982. The plant production manager is expecting your call."

Remy had finally managed to focus again, and her mind was racing. If production ended in 1982, the carpet those fibers came from was something like forty years old. How much of the stuff could still be around? And what were the chances that the two victims had coincidentally come into contact with two different sources of it that *weren't* connected? The odds of something like that happening had to be a billion to one.

This was the first compelling evidence that placed both of the victims in the same location at or around the time of their deaths. It was huge. She looked up at Giana, speechless.

Giana nodded and took a deep breath. "I know. You've got some work to do."

She left the file on the desk and headed for the door. As she slipped the strap of her bag over her shoulder, she glanced back at Remy. "I've decided that I'd like you to cook dinner for me."

"What?"

"Dinner," Giana repeated. "I'd like you to cook it for me. At your house." Her expression was placid and totally unreadable.

"I want to see where you live. And quite frankly, it's the least you can do."

"Um..." Remy was once again struggling to catch up. Giana was speaking perfect English, but for some reason she was still having a hard time deciphering it. "So, ah...when you say 'dinner,' you're not meaning like, on a date or..."

"You don't date straight women, remember?"

She scanned Giana's face for the slightest sign of sarcasm or calculation. She found none.

"I'm free this weekend," Giana offered helpfully. "Saturday would be great."

"Uh. Well, I'm... I have Keisha and Devlin coming over on Saturday."

"Great, that sounds perfect. It'll be nice to see them again." Giana opened the door and paused. "Okay. Well, I'm glad we had a chance to talk. Just let me know what time, and what I can bring." She turned to go but stopped again. "Oh, and one other thing. You still owe me that tennis match. I haven't forgotten about that. Maybe we can play somewhere near your place on Saturday. In the afternoon. And then I'll help you cook dinner."

She waited with her hand on the doorknob while Remy stared at her. "Okay, then," Giana said. "I'm looking forward to it, too." She stepped into the hallway and closed the door behind her and was gone.

Reeling, Remy sat back in her chair and tried to digest what had just happened. She couldn't be certain, but she thought she'd seen a hint of a smile on Giana's lips a second before the door had shut behind her.

The door abruptly opened again, and Cookie poked his head into the office. "Hey, boss, you got a second?"

"Yep." Remy seized on the distraction. "Get in here. We just got another lead on the case."

CHAPTER SIXTEEN

Giana drove through the halcyon streets of Noe Valley and silently cursed her father's name. Instead of an automatic, the Chief had selected a car for her with a manual transmission—in total disregard of the unique characteristics of San Francisco's hilly terrain. As she was forced to stop at a red light, just below the crest of a very steep incline, Giana wondered if her father's oversight had actually been intentional. Some sadistic form of retribution for his daughter abandoning him and his beloved Philadelphia.

Every muscle in Giana's body tensed as she waited for the light to change—her foot jammed on the brake, her eyes fixated on the rearview mirror and the vehicle behind her that had obviously pulled up much too close. The signal turned green, and she groaned, clenching her teeth as she took her foot off the brake and stomped on the clutch. The car began a stomach-churning roll backward, and she hit the gas, trying to use restraint as first gear finally engaged. The tires squealed beneath her, and the car roared over the crest of the hill, her face warming as the smell of burnt rubber filled the air.

A few minutes later, her guidance system instructed her to make a right turn onto a quiet, tree-lined street (one that was blessedly flat), and she had arrived. She stopped the car and peered out at the pretty little Craftsman. The house was neatly painted, set back from a small yard bursting with green succulents and yucca plants. Remy's Audi took up all of the truncated driveway, so Giana improvised and parked her car on the street directly behind it, as there was no other available parking in sight.

Juggling her keys from palm to palm, she walked up the stone pathway to the front porch. She was jittery with a mixture of emotions—eager to see Remy, at the same time that she was still supremely irritated with her. For better or worse, she was learning to read the detective well, and it was clear now that Remy was just as thrown by what was happening between them as she was. Perhaps even more so. It was this knowledge that gave her confidence where she might not have had it otherwise.

The confrontation in Remy's office the other day had rapidly turned volatile, and in the midst of the detective's tirade, Giana had realized a better option might be to change course and de-escalate the situation. Remy's instinct was to cut and run—she had demonstrated that unambiguously. If she was pushed at the wrong moment, things could end between them before they'd really had a chance to begin. And that was an outcome Giana found unacceptable.

And so, she had resigned herself to exist within this nebulous gray area where nothing was decided. It was unsatisfactory, but she was willing to do it. For a time. And then she would have to see. She punched the doorbell and forced herself to stop fidgeting.

"Open!" The muffled shout came from somewhere deep within the house. Giana pressed the latch on the door handle and let herself in. The house's interior was filled with sunlight and the welcoming scent of fresh-brewed coffee. She immediately wanted a cup, though it was well past the middle of the day.

She glanced around at the cheerful space. The hardwood floors gleamed, with throw rugs scattered here and there to add a bright splash of color. A fireplace dominated the small living room, along with an overstuffed leather couch that made her want to lie down and stretch out full length on it.

She looked up and drew in a quick breath at the sight of Remy strolling toward her down the hallway. She was barefoot and scantily clad in tennis shorts and a sleeveless tank. It was an assault to the senses, so much skin. All warm and glowing like that. The detective's smile was radiant, and those long, muscled legs were downright scandalous.

"Hey, there. Welcome," she said.

Giana recognized genuine fondness in Remy's voice, and she embraced it like a caress, forgetting that five minutes ago she had still been annoyed. She reached up and gave her a hug, careful to break contact sooner than she would've liked. The smile on her face, however, was nothing she could control.

"Hey, yourself. My gosh, what a beautiful home."

Remy glanced down at the floor and nodded. "Well, thank you. Come on in. I'll give you the ten-cent tour."

Remy led her through the house, narrating briefly as they poked their heads into each of the small but inviting rooms. She kept moving past the bedroom. Giana caught a glimpse of some art prints on the wall and a king-sized bed that dwarfed everything else. She was glad they didn't stop to linger. At the rear of the house sat the kitchen, which was spotless and well-appointed. The U-shaped design of the counters maximized the limited space, and the walls were painted a saffron yellow that reminded Giana of her auntie's kitchen back home.

Remy reached for the coffeepot that had only just stopped gurgling. "Will you have some? I know it's a little late in the day, but…"

"Oh, definitely. Thank you." Giana's eyes fell on a set of French doors that looked out on the backyard. "Can we see what's out there?"

Remy silently handed her a mug, then filled another for herself. She motioned Giana to follow, and they stepped out the doors onto a spacious redwood deck.

"Oh my God," Giana breathed. The yard was lush and unexpectedly large, teeming with flowering plants and low-hanging trees. A flourishing bougainvillea scaled the backside of the house, its trellis long overrun in a shower of purple blooms. She could see there was order to the chaos, if only barely contained, and the overall effect was magic. In the breadth of two steps, they had left the city and escaped to the tropics. "Remy...this is absolutely gorgeous." Remy looked at her and chuckled warmly, obviously pleased.

They seated themselves in a pair of Adirondacks, propping their feet up on matching ottomans. Giana took a sip from her mug. "Mmm. And she can make a cup of coffee too. My, oh my."

Her host made no response to that, which was far from unusual. Giana laid her head back and closed her eyes, content to let the birdsong in the yard suffice for conversation. The muffled roar of an airliner passed high overhead. She listened until the sound faded into the distance, imagining that the people on board were headed to far away and exotic places. She didn't realize she was dropping off until Remy's voice startled her awake.

"So. You're sure you want to do this?"

Giana opened one eye to peer at her companion. "Do what?"

"Tennis, Giana. There's no shame in admitting defeat now. It's not like I'd lord it over you or anything like that."

Giana closed her eye again, chuckling softly. "No such luck, Detective."

"Inspector."

"Whatever." She stretched her arms above her head and slowly sat up. "You should put some shoes on. You're gonna need them."

Remy snorted softly and moved to get up. Giana watched her, admiring the flex of her triceps as she pushed herself out of the chair. She disappeared into the kitchen, and Giana gathered up their mugs and followed.

As they were leaving the house, Remy paused to lock the front door. "You okay to drive?"

"Sure, um..." Giana hesitated. "Are there any hills between here and there?"

Remy gave her a quizzical look. "No...I don't think so."

"Great." She trotted down the steps and popped the trunk. Remy followed and deposited her rackets inside. "Nice car."

"Thanks," Giana said with a grimace. She slid into the driver's seat and waited for Remy to join her. "It's actually a little embarrassing. My dad bought me this car."

"Really." Remy studied her pained expression, then busied herself with her seat belt. "You're right, that's a terrible thing to have happen to you. A Beemer for a present. God, what a bummer."

"Um," Giana scoffed. "It's a little more complicated than that."

"I'm sure it is. Maybe you should give it back."

Giana stared at her profile, then started the engine. "Where are we going?"

"That way." Remy pointed down the street. "Where there's no hills."

Giana drove as directed through the quiet streets of Remy's neighborhood. As promised, there were no hills—only speed bumps, and she managed those without incident. In just a few minutes, the rows of tightly spaced bungalows suddenly opened up to a sloping lawn. A series of high, chain-linked fences stood at the top of the rise.

"Public courts," Giana remarked with surprise.

"Yeah, and they're actually pretty good. We'll probably have to wait for one to free up, but maybe we'll get lucky."

Giana found parking, and the two women retrieved their gear bags from the trunk. Remy led the way up the slope, and as they approached the fences, Giana could hear the familiar thunk of ball against string. Her excitement began to grow. She couldn't remember the last time she'd been on a court. She studied the movement of the players as they passed each match, itching to feel a racket in her hand again. Miraculously, a lone empty court sat waiting for them at the end of the row. She felt like they'd won the lottery.

They deposited their bags by the fence line, and Giana was pleased to note that the court was clean and in good condition.

She had her favorite racket out in an instant, popping open a fresh can of tennis balls as she moved to the far end of the court. "You want to hit a few short to warm up?"

"Sounds good. Go easy on me, tiger."

Shaking her head, Giana dumped the balls out of the can, catching each one as it bounced. She stashed two in her pocket, balanced the third on her racket, and tossed the empty can aside. Remy's grin was enormous.

Giana dropped the ball at the service line and batted it over the net, watching as Remy answered with an easy abbreviated stroke. Her form was gorgeous. Giana sent the next shot to the opposite side, studying Remy's feet as they repositioned to meet the ball. They were quick and light, with no wasted movement. Remy popped a clean backhand return, and she smiled. She could hit to this woman all day.

The rally continued for several minutes, their shots gradually deepening until they were hitting groundstrokes from the baseline. Giana relaxed into the rhythm of the exchange, her breathing deep and even, her muscles warming as the familiar tension began to spread through her limbs.

They practiced a few serves, and then Giana caught the ball and paused. "You ready to play?"

"I guess so." Remy frowned. "But you're gonna give me first ball in, right? I need all the help I can get over here."

Giana sent three balls her way without complaint. It was all posturing, she knew. Remy was far better than she'd let on. "You've got some pretty fancy footwork there, Detective." She watched as Remy retrieved the balls and strolled to the baseline. The fit of her shorts was snug. A light sheen of perspiration highlighted the flex in her calf muscles. "Nice form," she added.

Remy glanced back at her. "Thanks," she muttered. She reached the baseline and turned, bouncing the ball unnecessarily. "You sure you don't wanna spot me a few right up front? Just to even things out?"

"No way." Giana bounced on her toes. "And quit stalling."

Remy caught the ball and poised for the serve, and Giana settled onto the balls of her feet. She tensed as Remy bent her knees and drew her racket back, tossing the ball high in the air. This was going to be fun.

* * *

By the time they called it quits the sun was clipping the tops of the trees, its yellow hue warming to amber. Remy was grateful the ordeal was over, though she had to admit she'd never had that much fun getting shellacked on a tennis court before.

Giana was even more skilled than she could've predicted, dominating each game they played, on serve or not, every shot placed with pinpoint accuracy. She was like a seductive lioness prowling the court, toying with Remy to lure her into extended rallies, then ruthlessly closing the point whenever she chose. It was abuse, pure and simple. And Remy loved it.

As they squatted to gather up their gear, two young men who'd been waiting on the other side of the fence entered the court. "Nice tennis," one of them commented. Remy glanced at Giana, who beamed a smile and nodded.

They zipped up their bags and left the court, Remy half a step behind. She used the opportunity to observe the fluid movement of Giana's hips—without the distraction of a tennis ball rocketing at her face. Giana bore the weight of the gear bag easily, her back straight, white polo shirt clinging damply to her spine. The downy hair at the nape of her neck was dark with perspiration. Remy felt the insane urge to lean over and taste it.

Giana glanced back at her. "That guy was right, you know. Very nice tennis."

"Uh-huh." Remy sniffed. "I'm pretty sure he was talking about you. But I did get in an excellent workout just now, so thanks for that."

"Oh, come on, you were an animal out there. I'm just happy to have a tennis partner again. But next time, I'm not going so easy on you. So be warned."

"Oh my God," Remy muttered. "You know, I'm not so sure how I feel about this new, somewhat sadistic aspect of your personality. It's pretty sexy, I have to admit, but I'm a little concerned for my well-being."

Giana's eyes latched onto hers, and Remy hesitated, then looked at the ground. Shit. She was talking without thinking again.

"Hmm. I have a feeling you can handle more than you think." Giana faced forward again. "Pity. I left my whip and stilettos at home. But maybe we can improvise."

Remy kept her mouth shut after that. Sexual banter with Giana Falco was not the route she wanted to take that afternoon. It was a slippery slope, and she felt like she was at a distinct disadvantage. Somewhere along the line, the dynamic between them had begun to shift—in a way she didn't fully understand. She still had several more hours to survive alone with the dominatrix before her chaperones would arrive from Walnut Creek to save her. She wondered if it was possible to simply not speak until then.

For the length of the short ride home, she managed to do exactly that. Giana drove unerringly back to the house, parking again in the snug spot across the end of the driveway. Remy retrieved her rackets from the trunk and pretended not to notice when Giana pulled out a smaller overnight bag and slung it over her shoulder. "I hope you have running water in there," she said.

"I do," Remy confirmed. She climbed the steps two at a time to unlock the front door and ushered her guest inside. "Clean towels too."

"Impressive."

"Yeah, it's pretty posh around here. But I don't like to brag."

She closed the front door, and the house fell painfully quiet around them. Giana stood in the middle of the room, her bag on her shoulder. She idly ran a hand along the back of the couch. "So it's okay if I hop in your shower then?"

"Of course." Remy sprang into motion. "Uh, you know where the bathroom is. Let me get you a towel." She strode to the linen closet in the hallway, supremely conscious of Giana's presence as she waited behind her at the bathroom door. She grabbed a stack of too many towels and brought them back, fully intending to walk away after that. Instead, she found herself standing there in front of Giana, inches apart in the narrow confines of the hallway. "Can I get you anything else?"

Giana's green eyes were wide and steady. Her skin was still flushed from the afternoon's exertion. The smell of her was maddening.

"I think I have everything I need," she murmured. She accepted the towels and backed into the bathroom, her eyes still on Remy. "I'll see you in a bit." She reached out with her foot and closed the door.

Remy stayed where she was in the hallway, staring at the whorls of the wood grain in the bathroom door. She stood there listening until she heard the sound of the shower turning on, which made her feel like a stalker. Turning abruptly, she headed into the kitchen, where she found herself standing again, with the refrigerator door open, staring dumbly into its interior.

This wasn't a problem. Giana Falco was naked in her shower, just a few feet away, and it wasn't a problem. Muttering to herself, she pulled a bundle of steaks wrapped in butcher paper out of the fridge and dropped it on the counter. She added several sacks of vegetables to the pile. There was plenty to do, and Devlin and Keisha would be here in a couple of hours. Remy could cope until then. She just needed to keep a clear head. And maintain a respectable distance from the lady. And keep her hands to herself, like any normal human being would.

* * *

Giana sighed as the hot water coursed over her back and shoulders. She leaned her forearm against the cool tiles and dipped her head under the spray, groaning as the pulsing stream massaged her scalp. The shower felt amazing, but it was doing nothing to ease the band of tension that gripped at her midsection.

The bathroom she stood in was small and intimate, and it belonged to Remy. She felt like an intruder peeking behind a very private curtain, about to be discovered in the act of spying at any moment. And it wasn't just the closeness of this bathroom.

She'd been aware of the sensation from the moment she'd stepped foot in Remy's house. The woman was everywhere, all at once. Surrounding her in a heady embrace without so much as a touch.

And that stare she'd given her in the hallway just now. Like a timber wolf stalking her prey. Desire had cinched around Giana's belly and refused to let go, pulling tighter even now as the water pelted her skin.

She had dreamt of Remy again last night and then spent most of the day successfully blocking it from her mind. She gave in to it now, and the images came rushing back in sharp detail. Remy creeping into her room, climbing into the bed on top of her. Pressing her down against the sheets. There'd been murmurs and kissing and restless hands roving. But no release. Giana had awakened acutely aroused, bitterly disappointed to find herself alone in the bed.

She felt the craving now as it traveled downward and slowly enveloped her groin. She cupped her breast and squeezed, her nipple a hardened pebble beneath the running water. The throbbing between her legs intensified, and she fought the temptation to reach down and stroke herself. It would be so easy to come right now. Just to ease the tension. So she could think.

She kept her head pressed against the tile and waited for the urge to pass, but soon enough her hand left her breast and began to make its way downward. Into the soft fur, and in between the folds. Just for a moment. She was slick and swollen, and she teased herself, swirling her finger in the slippery warmth.

Then she groaned and dragged her hand away. She needed an orgasm badly, but she didn't want it like this. She wanted Remy's hands on her when she came. Her hands and her mouth and her skin. Face-to-face, flesh against flesh. Free from barriers of any kind.

Giana raised her head abruptly and turned the water to cold. The bracing chill slammed against her chest, and she gasped. Soaping herself briskly, she ignored the sensations rioting across her skin, forcing herself to stand beneath the frigid blast until she started to shiver. She gave herself a final rinse and turned off the spray.

Clearheaded now, she stepped out of the stall and wrapped herself in a warm and fragrant towel. She wiped at the fog in the mirror and stared at the face that appeared in the murky porthole. The situation with Remy was becoming untenable. Giana was going to have to make a decision soon.

She'd been honest in Remy's office the other day, when she'd told her that she was the first woman she'd ever been attracted to. What she hadn't said was that she'd never felt this kind of magnetic pull to *any*one before. She was hopelessly infatuated with Remy Devereux, and for her, the attraction was as much in her mind as it was in her body.

She had to be open about her feelings—it was simply the way she was built. And if Remy couldn't meet her on that level, then she would have to take her leave. It was the last thing she wanted to do, but she simply couldn't continue with the charade any longer.

Some minutes later, she emerged from the bathroom looking her casual best. She felt strangely settled, too, with a renewed sense of resolve. She left her bag in the living room and went to join Remy in the kitchen.

"Whoa. Someone's been busy in here." Most of the limited counter space was now covered with food. There was a large wooden bowl mounded with crisp green salad, and platters of vegetables, cleaned and prepped for the grill. A quartet of beautiful steaks glistened in a marinade of chopped herbs and olive oil. "I was supposed to help you with all of this," she protested.

"True. Except you're my guest. How was your shower?" Remy glanced up and paused, and Giana braced herself for the onslaught. The gray eyes traveled the length of her body, and it was the same brazen undressing she'd been subjected to that fateful afternoon in her apartment. She had confronted Remy head-on about it then, and what had ensued between them was shocking and explosive and sublime. And then Remy had disappeared for five days.

Giana refused to go that route again. She trained her eyes back on the counter. "My shower was fantastic, thank you so much." She surveyed the spread in front of her and selected a wedge of red bell pepper to snack on. "There has to be something left here for me to do."

"Actually, there is. You can be the official taster." Remy reached to the far end of the counter and produced a glass tumbler containing a bluish-gray liquid that looked suspiciously familiar. She poured the contents along with several ice cubes into a steel shaker, capped it with the tumbler and began to shake.

"You didn't." Giana couldn't hide her excitement.

Remy's answering smile was huge. "Well, just hang on a minute, now. You might hate me after you try it." She pulled an appropriate coupe-shaped glass down from a shelf and expertly strained the cocktail into it. She even finished with the requisite maraschino cherry. Giana was impressed.

"Okay," Remy said as she carefully set the drink down in front of her. "Now...be honest."

Too excited for words, Giana took a cautious sip. She closed her eyes to get the full experience, free from Remy's distracting stare. The drink was perfect. "Oh my God. How did you do it?"

"I asked Jimmy." Remy's eyes were focused on Giana's lips. She glanced away, then took a step backward and leaned against the counter. "I, uh, I made him write down his personal recipe. He didn't want to at first, but then I told him it was for you."

"Oh, I just love him. He's such a sweetie."

Remy rolled her eyes. "Okay. Well, I think I've got all of this under control here." She waved a hand over the food on the counter. "You go relax on the deck, and I'm gonna jump in the shower."

Giana was more than happy to comply. Remy's deck had won her heart at first sight, but now, with an Aviation in her hand, it might just be her favorite place on the planet. She put her feet up on the ottoman and took a sip, nodding again at the perfect quality of the drink. It was extremely thoughtful of Remy to go to the trouble. The sweet side of the woman was showing itself again. The side she tried so hard to conceal for some reason, though it was obvious just the same. And damned hard to resist.

If it came to it, she didn't know how she was going to say goodbye. Remy plainly cared about her—a blind person could see that. But she also seemed hell-bent on keeping this emotional distance between them that didn't make any sense. Giana was certain fear played a primary role, but in the end, that was just an excuse. It was folly to sit around and wait for another person to change, and she refused to be that girl. At the same time, it was impossible not to hope.

She put her head back and closed her eyes. Nothing was going to get resolved today. Remy's friends would be here soon enough, and then they would all be relegated to safer, more prosaic topics. She could hold her tongue for one more evening.

After a short while, she heard the rattle of the bathroom doorknob from inside the house. Remy was finished with her shower—in a fraction of the time Giana had taken with hers. She smiled. There was true compatibility there, if they ever lived together and were forced to share a bathroom.

Giana's eyes popped open at that. Her thoughts had taken a perilous turn, and she strove—unsuccessfully—to head them off at the pass. She realized it was idiocy, but a part of her wondered what it would be like. Not just to make love to Remy, but to *have* her love as well. It would be incredible, she acknowledged. Almost certainly.

* * *

Fresh from the shower and dressed, Remy walked out on the deck to discover that her guest had apparently dozed off. She took a moment to quietly observe, unsure if Giana was asleep or merely resting. Her face was aglow in the light of the setting sun and utterly serene. Her eyelashes looked about an inch long, fanning out like thick sable brushes against her cheeks.

"What are you doing, Detective, some sort of investigation?"

Remy chuckled softly. "Yes. We've had some reports of miscreants in the area. Everything okay here, ma'am?"

"Miscreants?" Giana cracked one eye open. "Sounds like someone I know."

Remy reached down and plucked the empty cocktail glass from her hand. "It looks like one of them may have made off with your beverage."

"Scoundrel."

"Rapscallion," Remy agreed. "I'm going to make one for myself now. Would you like another?"

"Yes. But only because I won't have you drinking alone."

Remy returned to the kitchen, unaccountably pleased. She pulled out her phone and diligently referred back to her recipe notes. Jimmy was emphatic about the importance of exact measurements, and she knew she'd just scored multiple points on her first try. She wasn't going to screw it up now that she was ahead.

Giana was alert and gazing out at the yard when she returned with a new batch of cocktails.

"Feeling refreshed after your siesta?"

Giana chuckled. "I don't know what it is about this yard of yours. It's the cure for insomnia."

How Remy wished that were true. She couldn't count the number of times she'd sat in that same chair, in the smallest hours of the morning, longing for sleep. "Well, it's nice to see you enjoying it."

She took a seat next to Giana, stealing another glance at her tranquil expression as her eyes closed again. She seemed so at home in her own skin. "How *are* you enjoying it out here? In the Bay Area, I mean. So far away from your family and everything else that you know. Any regrets?"

"No." Giana's eyes opened, and she turned to look at Remy, holding her gaze in that way that she could. Making it hard to think. "No. I'm glad that I came."

Remy swallowed and turned to look out at the yard. "I'm glad you came too."

"Are you?"

Remy could still feel the weight of Giana's eyes on her, but she couldn't turn to look at her again.

"Why are you glad?" Giana prompted quietly.

Remy drew in a deep breath and held it. She still felt like she was starving for air. She blew it out again. Too cowardly to look Giana in the face, she quipped, "Because the only thing I've been lacking in my life is someone to whip my ass at tennis."

Giana was silent beside her after that, and she suddenly wished she'd been born a different person. Someone who wasn't such a chicken shit. She racked her brain for something else to say, but then the sound of car doors slamming drifted to them from the front of the house. Murphy's deep-throated bark announced his presence to the neighborhood.

"Well, that'll be them," Remy muttered. She waited for the wave of relief she'd been expecting to feel. As she climbed out of her chair, however, it was only disappointment that clung to her like a leaden veil. Disappointment directed squarely at herself. Giana rose from her chair as well. Remy tried to gauge her expression, but her face remained obscured behind a dark curtain of hair. Then she turned without a word to head into the kitchen.

Impulsively, Remy grabbed her by the wrist, yanking her back and catching her as she spun, kissing her fast and deep. Giana's weight rocked against hers, and she absorbed it, swaying with her in a sultry slow dance as she eased off and suckled at her lower lip, then deepened the kiss again. Giana emitted a quiet moan, and Remy released her. "I'd better go let them in."

She left Giana standing on the deck. As she strode through the house, she kept her mind carefully blank. Once the front door was open, the place became a maelstrom of noise and activity. Murphy tore through every room, his nails clicking, tail wagging furiously, investigating everywhere at once. Devlin and Keisha were in the midst of a heated debate, the topic of which remained unclear.

Giana looked composed when they all bustled into the kitchen. Her laughter was easy, and her humor was quick, but she wouldn't hold Remy's gaze for longer than a second at a time. Remy knew she was going to have to answer for that kiss, though she couldn't say, even in her own mind, why she'd done it. She'd felt like she was about to lose something and had no other choice. It was hardly an adequate explanation, she knew—certainly not one that was going to satisfy Giana.

She tried again, unsuccessfully, to catch her eye. She was huddled in deep conversation with Keisha and refused to even look Remy's way.

Fighting a growing sense of unease, Remy abandoned the kitchen to go warm up the grill. Devlin followed her out on the deck and stood there watching as Remy attacked the grates, furiously scrubbing away with a wire brush.

"Nice to see you've put the kibosh on things with the sexy scientist. How's that working out for you?"

Remy grabbed the beer from Devlin's hand and took a long swallow.

"That well, huh?"

They both turned to observe the two women in the kitchen, who were still immersed in intimate conversation. Keisha threw her head back with a throaty peal of laughter, and Remy and Devlin snorted at each but said nothing. Remy knew the strident objections Keisha had voiced the other night about Giana were born of a fiercely protective instinct. But like it or not, Giana had a way of inserting herself into people's hearts. Remy had no doubt that she and Keisha were destined to be fast friends.

As they watched, Giana lifted one sandaled foot and modeled it for Keisha, and Remy and Devlin glanced at each other again. "Better hide the credit cards," Remy advised.

"Mmm," Devlin agreed.

"Hey, would you mind grabbing those steaks off the counter for me?" Remy wasn't ready to go back into the kitchen with Giana. It was too painful to be in the same room with her and be totally ignored.

Remy stood and watched as Devlin stepped inside and was immediately waylaid into the discussion, Keisha grabbing her by the arm to emphasize a point. At last, Giana looked out the open French doors at Remy, and their gazes locked and held for a long moment. Giana gave her the slightest of nods before returning her attention to their guests, and Remy's heart lifted.

It was only a truce, but she would take it. She'd take anything over that cool indifference of a minute ago. She'd endured five miserable days without her and had only just got her back. She couldn't stomach the thought of going through that again.

* * *

Giana stood on the porch next to Remy and watched as their dinner companions straggled down the steps to pile into their SUV. Murphy didn't want to go. The gigantic dog stood motionless, head lowered, as Devlin opened the rear of the vehicle and attempted to order him inside. Eventually, she was forced to lift his front paws and place them on the bumper, then she shoved at his hindquarters until the beast finally acquiesced. Devlin looked back at them with an embarrassed shrug. She climbed in behind the wheel, and Keisha blew them a kiss from the passenger's side. With a honk and a wave, they were off, disappearing down the tree-lined street.

Giana stood motionless as the silence descended around them. After a few moments, Remy shifted beside her and glanced at her watch. "Wow. It's late."

Giana didn't bother to comment. It was irrelevant to her what time it was. "I'm going to use your restroom, and then I'll help you finish up in the kitchen." She turned and left without waiting for a reply.

In the bathroom, she studied her reflection in the mirror for a long time. She felt acutely alert, considering the lateness of the hour. She wasn't angry with Remy. Not exactly. She simply realized now that she had allowed the detective to steer the course of their relationship for too long. And that was about to change.

Most of the cleanup was already completed by the time she returned to the kitchen. Unnoticed at first, she crossed her arms and leaned one hip against the counter, watching as Remy finished loading the dishwasher.

Remy turned to reach for a water glass and started when she saw Giana standing there. "Jesus. There you are. You're like a stealthy ninja or something. We should tie a bell around your neck."

Giana said nothing, and Remy paused to briefly examine her face. "Well, that was fun." She went back to her task, dropping the last of the silverware into the basket one at a time. "You and Kee sure hit it off, although I kind of expected you would. Did I hear you two make a date to go to some museum exhibit without me?" She didn't wait for a reply. "And I think Devlin has a really bad crush on you, it pains me to tell you. At any rate, my friends seem to like you better than they like me, and I'm not sure how I feel about that."

Giana waited patiently for Remy to stop her rambling.

"Why don't we talk about what happened before they got here?"

Remy shut the dishwasher door and wiped her hands on a towel. "What do you mean?" It took her several moments to turn around.

"The kiss," Giana clarified. "You kissed me. Again. After being so incredibly adamant about not wanting that to happen. So. Remy. I'd like to know why you did that." She watched the detective's gaze skirt away.

"Look," Remy said after a moment. "I don't know, all right? I just...It happened before I could think about it. But you're right. Of course. I shouldn't have done that, and I'm sorry, okay?"

"No, it's not okay. And I don't think you're sorry about it at all." Giana advanced into the cramped space of the U-shaped counter, blocking Remy's exit. "I think you knew exactly what you were doing. Waiting until the last second like that. So I wouldn't have a chance to react. You did it because you thought you could get away with it."

Remy took a step backward and bumped into the counter behind her, and this gave Giana a small thrill. The detective's flight instincts were kicking in, but she was cornered. There was nowhere to run. Remy looked at the floor, and then at some distant point past Giana's left shoulder. Anywhere but at her face. Giana was content to watch her fidget. She was a little alarmed by how enjoyable it was to watch her fidget.

She moved in a few steps closer, only stopping when they were inches apart. "You love being the one who gets to call all the shots," she observed. "Remy says when, and for how long. Like in my apartment the other day."

That got Remy's attention. She looked up at her sharply, and Giana leaned in and spoke in a lowered voice. "Let me ask you something. What makes you think you can finger me against the wall like a teenager and then just turn around and walk away?"

Remy's intake of breath was audible, and Giana watched with great satisfaction as the color rushed to her cheeks. At the same time, a look of raw hunger eclipsed her features, the gray eyes turning almost feral in their intensity.

Remy's head dipped, and Giana quickly stepped back out of reach. "Did I say you could kiss me?"

Remy slowly straightened, her nostrils flaring. She leaned back and placed her hands against the counter, and Giana advanced on her again.

"You like to be in control, I get that about you. But tonight, that's not what's going to happen."

She reached out and lifted the hem of Remy's shirt. She toyed with the bottom button for a moment before she popped it free of its hole. As her fingers moved to the next button up, she glanced up to inspect Remy's face. The eyelids were lowered to half-mast. A fine sheen of perspiration had broken out across her brow. The next button popped loose, and the eyelids fluttered shut.

"Look at me," Giana said. She waited until the gray irises were focused on her again. "I'm going to do what I want to do to you tonight. And you're going to let me. Now don't move."

Remy's eyes widened, but she held herself rigidly still. Giana tugged at the remaining buttons until the shirt fell open in front of her. She took a step backward, conscious that her own breathing had gone shallow.

There was no bra to spoil the view—only the warm planes of Remy's skin. Her breasts were slight, rounded mounds, with nipples as brown as chestnuts. They were thick and pronounced, and they stood defiantly erect, daring her to touch them. She reached out, but her hand began to shake, and she laid her palm against Remy's abdomen instead.

Her heart rate jumped at the contact. Remy's stomach muscles tensed, and Giana flattened her hand against the warm flesh, pressing in on it, splaying her fingers as she studied the contrast between their skin tones—Remy's reddish bronze, hers a little more golden.

She ran her hand boldly upward then, her breath catching in her throat as she covered one breast. The flesh was silken beneath her fingers, softly giving under the pressure of her grip, the nipple firm and coarse as it pushed back against the center of her palm.

Suddenly overcome with the need to taste, she dropped her mouth to the other breast and lapped at its hardened bud. Remy's body shuddered against her. Hungrily, she closed her lips around the nipple, sucking and licking at it aggressively, then opening her mouth wider, feasting on Remy's flesh as the throbbing between her own legs began to grow.

Remy's breathing devolved into a tortured rasp, and her hands came up, her fingers sinking deep into Giana's hair. Abruptly, Giana straightened and stepped back. "I told you not to touch."

Breathing heavily, they eyed one another, their chests rising and falling in unison. She stepped forward again and ran her hands up Remy's torso, from her belly to her breasts to her throat. She gripped her by the back of the neck and brought her mouth down closer, holding it there, an inch above her own, tempting herself as the craving in her own body grew until she was unable to contain it. She kissed Remy then, forcing her lips apart, pushing past her teeth, invading the depths of her mouth until she thought they'd both die from lack of oxygen.

When she'd had enough, Giana broke off the kiss and released her. "Meet me in the bedroom," she commanded. Then she turned and walked out of the kitchen without another glance, pulling her blouse over her head as she went.

By the time Remy appeared in the doorway, Giana was almost nude. She continued to disrobe in the moonlight streaming through the window, draping each article of clothing over the back of the sitting chair beside her. She watched the detective watching her. "I'm taking off my clothes because I want to feel your skin against mine. But you're still not allowed to touch. Do you understand?"

Remy nodded once, and Giana slipped off her panties and dropped them on the chair. "Now get undressed and lie down on the bed."

Remy stood unmoving for a beat, then she shrugged the shirt off her shoulders and let it fall to the floor. She unbuttoned her jeans and stepped out of them as she moved to the center of the room. Giana's stomach clenched at the sight of it. This wordless compliance was more arousing than anything she could have imagined.

She waited for Remy to lie back in the middle of the bed, then she climbed slowly on top of her, straddling her hips, tensing as she lowered herself onto the smooth, muscular thighs. Remy's eyes fluttered shut again, and she ordered them back open. She held Remy's gaze as she leaned forward and flattened herself against her. Belly to belly, breast to breast.

The shock of the sensation made her gasp. Remy's skin against hers was intensely erotic, unbearably soft. She lifted herself slightly and undulated her body, lightly grazing the surface of Remy's skin, her jaws clenching at the excruciating sensuality of it, unable to stop the moan that escaped her throat.

Remy's mouth opened, silently straining as her hands reached up and seized Giana's buttocks, gripping and kneading them, her fingers working deep into the flesh. Giana shuddered from the pleasure of it. She allowed the fondling to continue for several delicious seconds longer, groaning as the strong hands squeezed and separated her cheeks. Then she reached back and pulled them away. She brought Remy's arms up above her head and held them there by the wrists. "Don't make me tell you again," she warned.

Remy went still, and Giana watched the rapid play of emotions cross her face. Frustration and lust. Aggression barely restrained. Giana released her wrists and sat upright, deliberately adjusting herself until their pelvises were pressed directly together. Her eyes fastened on Remy's face, and she subtly shifted her hips, working the folds of her labia apart. She reached a hand down to do the same to Remy. Sliding her fingers between their bodies, she found the spot she wanted and gently pulled Remy's lips apart, exposing her slick and molten center.

Carefully, she guided her own clit on top of Remy's. A spasm of pleasure shot through her, and she bit back a whimper. Slowly, ever so slowly, she rocked her pelvis, intent on maintaining that single exquisite point of contact. Their clits began a silken, liquid slide together, and Remy's expression grew agonized. Giana savored it, reveled in the low, animal growl that rose up from her throat.

She teased her like that, with several slow and languid strokes, then brutally lifted herself away. There would be no release for either one of them yet. Not right now. Not nearly so soon.

Leaning forward, she laid a hand against Remy's cheek. The detective's eyes were glazed over, her breathing coming in labored, uneven rasps. "Look at me, Remy." She watched as the gray eyes grew lucid again, rapidly scanning Giana's face. "Do you know how beautiful you are?" Remy's breathing hitched, and Giana leaned in closer, lightly grazing her lips. "Do you know how I feel about you?" Remy lay frozen in place, and she sat upright again. "No, of course you don't. You couldn't possibly. I'll just have to show you what I mean."

"Sweet mother of God."

They were the first words Remy had uttered in what seemed like hours, and Giana chuckled softly as she slid lower on the bed. "No, my darling. My name is Giana."

Remy lifted her head off the bed to watch her, and she stared back as her knees touched the floor. She wedged her body between Remy's knees, pushing impatiently against them until they parted wider to let her in. She saw Remy's hand come up to cover her forehead, and Giana scolded her again. "Your instructions remain the same." The hand dropped obediently back to the bed, and Giana focused her attention on the dark triangle between Remy's thighs.

Hunger gnawed at the pit of her groin, and she didn't hesitate as she lowered her lips to the tempting mound. She buried her nostrils in the soft fur of it, inhaled the heady scent of it, exhaling hotly through her mouth, basking in the sultry heat as it rose up and fanned against her cheeks.

"Giana…"

Remy's voice was a pleading moan, and her pussy clenched at the sound of her own name, quickening to hear it uttered in a woman's voice—in Remy's distinctive tone, grown husky now with need. She opened her mouth wide and took her first taste, working her tongue into the gap between the folds.

She found the hard nub immediately—and gasped in surprise as Remy yelped and shot straight up on the bed!

"Oh my God, I'm so sorry!" Giana put a hand against Remy's heaving chest. "Was that too much?"

Remy nodded vigorously, and Giana nodded too, holding back a chuckle.

"Oh, baby. Okay. I'll go slower now. I promise."

Gently, she pushed Remy back down against the bed. Then she promptly went back to task, applying less pressure this time, counseling herself to move slowly. She began a leisurely exploration of this most secret of places, and it was intoxicating. The musk and the salt and the sweet tang of it. The silken folds that resisted, then gave beneath the pressure of her tongue, springing back against it, growing more engorged the longer she persisted.

She was acutely aware of Remy's movements on the bed. Her flat stomach muscles beginning to tighten, hips flexing and relaxing, then flexing again against the mattress. Giana worked her way around Remy's clit, avoiding it initially, then cautiously circling in closer, homing in on the prize that slowly began to dominate her focus. She could feel her own center throbbing now in concert, and she imagined that this clit, Remy's clit, was her own. That it belonged to her, was actually a part of her own body, and hers to do with as she pleased.

Remy's moans grew deeper, thickening with lust, and she reveled in the power of it, thrilled in the knowledge that she was the cause of it and she alone would bring her release. At last, she wrapped her lips around the swollen pebble and began a gentle suckling, then lapping at it with her tongue, over and across and around it, until Remy's hips began to lift off the bed. Her hands moved to grasp at Giana's hair, sinking her fingers deep into the strands, gripping it by the roots, and this time Giana did not object, the tension inside her own body building in pace with Remy's.

"Oh, God. Baby...fuck. Just like that." Remy's voice was strained, barely recognizable. "Fuck, Giana. Yesss...Oh God, don't stop."

Giana knew that she would not, could not stop. They were linked now, she and Remy. They had become one, and as the moans from the bed increased in pitch, she felt her own pussy begin to contract in answer.

She was already past her breaking point, and with a groan she squeezed her thighs tightly together, sending the orgasm rocketing through her, crying out at the instant Remy's body went rigid, their voices blending together, Remy's hips freezing in space, then collapsing back on the bed as she pulled Giana's head in tight against her, the walls of her canal clenching and opening again as Giana buried her tongue deep inside of her, content to lose herself in that holy place, never to resurface again.

Minutes passed, or perhaps it was only seconds, before Giana struggled back up on the bed. The two women lay facing one another, each quietly regarding the other, waiting for their breathing to slow. Remy finally stirred and began to weakly tug at the covers, and then the two of them summoned the effort together. They became a naked, climbing tangle of limbs until they settled once again, facing each other amid the coolness of the sheets, eyelids drooping in unison.

"I feel like I should tie you to that chair over there." Giana stifled a yawn. "Otherwise, I'll wake up in a little while, and you'll be gone."

Remy eyed her drowsily. "Mmm, that sounds like it could be fun. The tying me up part, I mean. I'm not going anywhere, Giana. I live here, remember?"

"Right," she murmured. She wasn't convinced, but she was far too exhausted to argue. "I guess we'll find out in the morning."

She nestled in closer, shifting and burrowing into Remy's side, until they were both settled in comfort again. She kissed Remy's flesh, whatever part lay closest to her lips, then she heaved a deep sigh of contentment. Sleep's heavy tentacles rose up to close in around her, and she offered no resistance. There'd be plenty of time in the morning to worry about what was going to happen next. Right now, she was exactly where she wanted to be.

CHAPTER SEVENTEEN

Giana opened her eyes and stared at the unfamiliar ceiling above her head. A thick curtain was drawn across the window, even as the morning light managed to seep in around its edges, revealing a large painting on the wall opposite the bed. She recognized the Rothko print. It was one of her favorites—she'd seen the original at the MOMA last summer in Manhattan.

Turning her head to inspect the rest of the room, she froze as her gaze collided with Remy's. The detective lay propped up on one elbow, naked in the bed beside her. Images of the night before came flooding back, and Giana felt a wash of heat suffuse the surface of her skin.

"Oh, shit," she murmured, "you're still here."

Remy's eyes were calm and alert. She didn't speak as she reached up and grasped the edge of the sheet with two fingers, pulling it steadily downward until the cool air touched Giana's thighs. Giana lay still as the gray eyes began a lazy survey, inevitably halting at her bare breasts. Remy had a thing for her breasts, she thought, even as her nipples began to shrink and harden in response. Remy's eyes flicked up to meet hers, the smoke in them darkening to near black. "Where do you want me to touch you?"

Giana's stomach muscles contracted at the husk in Remy's voice, softened with sleep and arousal. She felt herself grow instantly wet. Remy leaned forward, her lips hovering above one turgid nipple. "Would you like it if I touched you here?" Her breath was warm against Giana's skin.

"Yes," Giana breathed. She sank her fingers into Remy's hair and pulled her head closer, holding it against her breast until she felt the hot, moist probing of her tongue. She groaned and pressed her head back against the pillow, then reached for Remy's hand and dragged it downward to her swollen center, gasping as the fingers complied and quickly grew slick. "And there." Her own voice was a hoarse rasp.

Remy raised her head to watch Giana's face, languidly stroking her silky dampness, coaxing and teasing in delicious, maddening circles until Giana felt her abdomen grow taut.

"Do you want me to fuck you?" Remy's eyes were locked on hers, her fingers continuing to pleasure her clit. Giana opened her mouth in a silent gasp. "Spread your legs," Remy ordered.

Licking her lips, she obeyed. She opened her thighs, her hips beginning to flex, grinding her buttocks against the mattress, her hands gripping the sheet in her fists. Remy slid lower on the bed and propped herself on one arm, her knees straddling Giana's leg. Then she pushed her fingers firmly inside. The fit was achingly tight, and Giana moaned, arching her back off the mattress, her hands clamping onto Remy's shoulders.

"Yes?" Remy eased yet another finger inside of her, stretching her wide as she slowly began to fuck her.

"Yes." Giana's answer was a demand. Guttural, insistent, laced with impatience as her need began to grow. She tightened her grip on Remy's shoulders, arms straightening, pushing back against her at the same time that her hips rose up to meet her deepening thrusts.

"Oh, God…Yes. Just like that. Harder." Gasping, Giana held herself rigid, opening herself wider, digging her fingers into

Remy's flesh. The greed was taking over now, surging beyond her control. "Baby...Fuck me." Her teeth were clenched. Her lungs were heaving, her heart seeming to seize in her chest. Her eyes fixed on Remy's as her mind sank into delirium, caring only that the pleasure continue, convinced she would never get enough.

The next time Giana awoke, she was alone in the bed, and the room was flooded with bright sunlight. She gave a languorous stretch, inhaling the scent of fresh-brewed coffee. A terry cloth robe was laid out at the foot of the bed, and she slipped it on as she stepped out in the hallway. The sound of the running shower filtered through the bathroom door. She continued drowsily past it, beckoned by the nutty aroma of dark Italian roast. In the kitchen, she poured herself a steaming mugful and paused to take a grateful swallow.

The loud buzz of her cell phone on the granite countertop made her wince. She glanced at the bright screen and tried not to let the irritation sink in. It was Nick again. Giana had lost count of the number of messages he'd sent since that horrible lunch on Wednesday—each one of which she had flatly ignored. Perhaps she'd been too naive to think he would go away that easily. She placed her finger on the screen and swiped the message away unread. Taking her mug with her, she strode across the kitchen to the French doors and stepped out on the deck.

Outside, the rays of the morning sun had only reached the far end of the yard, leaving the deck still shrouded in the shadow of the house. Giana welcomed the bracing chill in the air. She hoped it might bring her mind some clarity. She stood perfectly still, breathing deeply, her hands cupped around the warm mug of coffee.

A hummingbird appeared in the yard, darting from bush to tree to flower. She followed its jagged path with her eyes, while her mind tried to digest the events of the past twenty-four hours. She was still sore from their lovemaking. Sore from Remy. Inside of her, and above her, and beneath her. Her center throbbed achingly to life again at the mere thought of it. She had never wanted anyone so badly. And she wanted her still, even now, standing barefoot on the deck in the cold.

She knew she was the same person she'd always been, and so was Remy. And yet, everything between them had changed. Remy had met her last night. She'd come to her completely unguarded, voracious in her appetite, exposing herself entirely. And Giana had thought she would die from the wanting.

From inside the house, she heard the rattle of the knob on the bathroom door, and a sudden spasm of anxiety seized her. She had no doubts about her own feelings, but that was only half of the equation. She was suddenly terrified that the magic of the night they'd just shared would wither in the cold light of day. She was terrified she was about to look into Remy's eyes and see the shadow of regret.

Minutes passed before she heard the sound of footsteps in the kitchen. She stood immobilized, unable to turn around as the steps drew closer, moving out on the deck and ultimately halting behind her. For long seconds, Remy didn't touch her, or speak. Giana waited, stalling as long as she could, until at last she was compelled to turn around and face her.

She was tall and so stunningly beautiful, and her eyes were loving as they scanned Giana's face. She reached out to tug at the bathrobe's collar, pulling Giana a step closer as she adjusted the fabric more snugly around her neck. "You must be freezing." The skin at the corners of her eyes creased in amusement. She waited, but Giana had yet to find her voice.

"Are you hungry?" Remy asked. "I know a great little place." Still, Giana could not answer, and Remy abruptly lowered her head, kissing her slowly and deeply before she straightened. "Come on, beautiful. I'm freaking starving. Let's go get you dressed."

CHAPTER EIGHTEEN

The elevator doors whispered open on the eighth floor, and Remy strode down the carpeted hallway, noting the increase in her heart rate as she approached Giana's door. She shook her head, marveling at her own body's unflagging response. She had just spent the weekend engulfed in the woman's arms, but apparently one day apart from her was still too many.

Remy rapped the knocker twice, and the door instantly swung open. Giana's enormous green eyes dropped to the flowers in Remy's hand. She pushed them aside, stepping forward to wrap her arms around Remy's neck, rising up on her toes, her full breasts pressing in. She pulled Remy's head down to meet hers, and her kiss was long and deep and searching.

Giana stepped back and took the bouquet from her hand. "These are gorgeous, Remy. Thank you." She left her standing in the doorway.

Remy snapped out of her trance a moment later and stepped into the apartment. She found Giana in the kitchen, arranging the flowers in a vase. "I'm sorry to tell you that dinner won't be ready for another half hour. The Ferry Building was an absolute madhouse, and then the bridge was a horror show, as usual. I'm sure you got a taste of that on your way over..."

Giana's voice trailed off as Remy stepped up behind her and gently lifted the hair away from her neck. She lowered her head to nuzzle at the sensitive skin behind her ear.

"Remy, don't." Giana's protest was unconvincing. "I have to cook now."

"Mmm, I know." She trapped an earlobe between her teeth, nipping and tugging at it lightly before she let it go. "But you can't imagine how much I've missed you today." She buried her nose in the glossy hair, inhaling the intoxicating scent. She reached her hands around to caress her breasts.

"Remy..." Giana breathed.

Remy squeezed them in her palms, circling the nipples with the tips of her fingers, pinching the hardening buds.

"Goddamn it." Giana gripped the edge of the counter and drove her buttocks back hard against Remy's thighs.

The glowing clock on the nightstand read 9:32 p.m. Remy stared at it in disbelief, until Giana sat up naked in the bed and leaned across her to switch on a bedside lamp. Mesmerized, she watched her stand and cross the room to the closet, her bare buttocks rising and falling with a tantalizing bounce.

"I suppose you're expecting me to feed you now. I hope you realize, I can't actually cook. I only promised you dinner to get you to come over here and ravish me."

"Mmm. So the truth comes out." Remy propped herself up on one elbow, enjoying the show as Giana stood in front of the closet, hands on her hips, completely unselfconscious while she perused the neat stacks of clothing. She selected a pair of worn sweats and stepped into them, tying the drawstring low on her waist. Then she chose a form-fitting tank and wrestled her way into it, reaching a hand underneath the snug fabric to adjust the swell of her breasts. Remy's eyes tracked her every movement, utterly enthralled by the spectacle.

Giana turned around to face her, and their gazes held as she gathered her tousled mane in both hands. She wound it in a loose knot at the top of her head, her hands coming to rest on her hips again when she was finished. "See something you like?"

Remy wasn't sure if her voice still functioned. "I just...I wonder if you know how amazing you are. I think you're amazing, Giana." The words had come out perfectly clear.

Giana's eyebrows lifted as a mild blush colored her cheeks. She strode back to the bed and leaned down to plant a kiss firmly on Remy's lips. "Flattery will get you everywhere, Detective." She stared into her eyes for a moment, then straightened and left the room.

Remy flopped back on the mattress and brought her hands up to her face. She needed a moment to collect herself, though she knew it was fruitless to even try. She'd been hit by a freight train and left without a will of her own. Gobsmacked and steamrolled, stripped of all ability to reason.

Giana made love the same way she did everything else—with conviction and unrelenting candor. And in the span of a very short period of time, she'd managed to wrap herself around the deepest recesses of Remy's heart. She was defenseless against her. She was completely at the woman's mercy, and she did not care.

Already missing the glow of her company, Remy climbed out of the bed and scanned the floor for something to wear. She spotted her jeans and shirt in a heap by the door. Unable to locate her underpants, she went commando-style and stepped naked into her jeans. She hastily shrugged into her shirt as she strode down the hallway and into the kitchen. "God, that smells good."

Giana glanced up from the stove, her gaze seeming to devour every inch of Remy's face in a second. Then the green eyes dropped lower, taking the time to linger on her unbuttoned shirt, and Remy felt the heat like a firebrand on her skin. She took a step toward her, but Giana menaced her with a spatula, brandishing it at her like a weapon. "Don't come near me. I'm serious."

Remy halted, a smile playing at her lips, and Giana shook her head, returning her attention to the salmon steaks sizzling in the pan. "I have to do this now, or we're both going to starve."

She glanced at Remy again. "Go away. Go open a bottle of wine or something. Go."

With a sniff, Remy turned and left the kitchen. The wine rack in the corner of the living room was a modest size, but it was crammed to capacity. "Which one?" she called out.

"How about a pinot?" Giana called back.

She grabbed a bottle and carried it to the kitchen, where she begrudgingly took a seat across the island from the cook. Without looking, Giana opened a drawer and slid a corkscrew at her across the countertop. Remy broke into a grin. Uncorking the wine, she watched the meal unfold in avid silence.

Giana had lied about not knowing how to cook. The salmon steaks were given an aggressive sear before they went into the broiler, replaced in the pan by a mound of colorful vegetables. Her arm lifted high in the air as she added a drizzle of olive oil. She shuffled the hot pan on the stove, tossing the veggies up and back into the skillet. After a few minutes, she turned with a graceful pirouette to retrieve the salmon from the broiler. The sizzling steaks were scooped onto two dinner plates, with the veggies heaped in glistening piles alongside them. The finale was a sprinkle of herbs and a squeeze of fresh lemon juice. Remy let out a low whistle.

They sat at the dining table and ate, glancing at each other repeatedly, their knees grazing beneath the table. Giana paused to take a sip of pinot, her eyes landing on Remy once again. "I want you to know how worthless I was at work today. I couldn't focus on anything. I kept looking at the clock, counting the hours until I could see you again."

"Is that right?" Remy bit into a crisp sprig of broccolini. She hummed with pleasure at the flood of lemon and olive oil and sea salt that hit her tongue. "Well, I'm sorry to hear about that, I really am."

"Mmm. I don't think you are."

"No?" Remy took a bite of the fish, which was excellent too. She closed her eyes, blissfully chewing. When she opened them again, Giana was staring at her intently. Remy leaned over and kissed her hard on the mouth, then hungrily returned to her plate.

"I'm actually serious, Remy." A subtle tremor had crept into Giana's voice. Remy looked up and stopped chewing. "I mean, what exactly is happening here between us? Do you know?" Giana's brow was creased. "I literally cannot think about anything but you—about any*one* but you. I've never…This is nothing I've ever experienced before. Not even remotely." Her eyes had turned into huge, glistening marbles, and Remy was speechless. They stared at each other for a moment.

"Well." Giana forced a laugh. "I suppose this all must feel a little more familiar to you. But, frankly, it scares the shit out of me." She moved to get up from the table, and Remy's hand shot out to stop her.

"Whoa, whoa, hey. Just…hang on a second here."

Giana sat down heavily in her chair.

"I'm scared too, you know," Remy said quietly. Giana's eyes would not lift from the table, and she reached out to push a strand of hair back behind her ear. "Giana, you *terrify* me. You have to know that." Giana looked at her then, and Remy's ribcage contracted. The sensation was almost painful.

Pushing back from the table, she gripped Giana by the wrist and gave a powerful tug, bringing her up out of her seat and landing her squarely in Remy's lap. She wrapped her in a tight embrace, and they gently rocked together, back and forth, until she felt Giana's body begin to relax against hers.

"We don't have to have all the answers right away. It's okay to just…*be* in this for now." She placed her mouth against Giana's ear. "Is that okay? Can you just be here with me for now?"

Giana shifted then, standing briefly so she could turn and straddle both of Remy's legs. She resettled on her lap, face-to-face, her bosom rising to the level of Remy's chin. "I can do that if you can," she said.

She held Remy's gaze, in that way that she could, and Remy felt herself falling again. She tightened her grip and held on, and Giana rocked her hips forward, her thighs tensing as she pressed their bodies closer together. Remy brushed her cheek against the swell of her breasts, buried her face in their fragrant softness. Her mouth sought out one taut nipple, beginning to work at it through the fabric of the tank top, soaking the thin cotton until Giana groaned and arched her back.

Remy gripped her by the hips then. Tensing her core muscles, she stood up from the chair. Giana gasped and reflexively wrapped her legs around Remy's waist, one hand grasping her by the jaw, pulling her mouth open to plummet her tongue inside. Remy staggered across the living room floor, rounding the corner to the bedrooms, blindly bumping into a wall as Giana began to giggle uncontrollably. Panting, she careened them into Giana's room and unceremoniously dropped her on the bed, where she climbed immediately on top and silenced the giggling with her tongue.

The morning came quickly. Remy opened her eyes and blinked several times to bring the room into focus. She had slept. More soundly than she could remember ever sleeping. The sky outside the tall window was a dull pale gray. It reminded Remy of a cold winter's morning—the kind that made you want to stay in bed until late, reading the paper next to your lover and sipping on coffee or tea.

She glanced at Giana, who lay tucked up against her, one naked thigh thrown across Remy's pelvis, embracing her in her sleep. Remy yawned and stretched, and Giana murmured in protest, tightening her grip as her thigh slid firmly down between Remy's. On cue, a throbbing pulse ignited in her groin, and she steeled herself against it. She was determined to exert her own free will—at least for this morning—and make it to work on time.

She wrapped her arms around Giana and rolled them both over in the bed. Landing on top, she stared down at her lover's face, her features still softened in sleep. The eyelids opened, fluttering against the light, as Giana began to awaken. Remy watched in total fascination as the green irises focused in on her, and recognition quickly warmed to affection, which slowly sharpened to desire.

Unbelievable, Remy thought, her own heartbeat quickening in response. "I have to go," she said out loud.

Giana gazed up at her for a moment longer, then nodded. "Okay." Subtly, she shifted her body beneath Remy's weight, the flex of her hips nearly imperceptible.

"Giana, don't."

"Don't what?" The wide eyes were innocent. "I'm not doing anything." She yawned and stretched then, her body tensing, arching upward as her pelvis lifted them both off the bed.

Remy let out a low growl and pressed back hard against her, forcing her down against the mattress. Giana resisted but gave up quickly, chuckling in her husky morning voice as Remy rained kisses over her nose and cheeks. Inevitably, their lips came together, and Remy decided that free will was overrated.

Something emitted a jarring buzz on the nightstand, and Remy glanced up in annoyance. It was Giana's phone. The screen was a garish glow in the soft light of the bedroom, and the name Nick Pierce screamed out in bold letters on the display.

Remy's body went rigid, doused with a cold bucket of sobriety. Carefully, she lifted herself away from Giana, then rolled and sat up on the edge of the bed.

She didn't understand how she could've been so stupid. To forget such a critical element, one that was obviously not going away. But she had. For days now, the thought of Giana with Nick Pierce—or anyone else for that matter—had never entered her brain. Not once. It was unconscionable to be so foolhardy.

Remy stood up and began a search for her clothing. She was vaguely aware of Giana still in the bed, picking up the phone, letting it clatter back on the nightstand. "Remy, will you just wait one second and let me explain?"

Remy found her jeans and stepped into them, pulling them roughly up over her bare hips. She hadn't seen her underwear since last night before dinner. "It's fine, Giana." She was surprised by the placid tone of her own voice. "You don't owe me anything. You never made any promises." She shoved her arms into her shirtsleeves, then quickly dropped to the floor to pull her socks onto her feet.

"My God, you are absolutely infuriating." Giana was sitting up in the bed now, in all of her naked glory, eyes flashing, her hair a wild mane. Remy felt a sharp pang of desire, wanting her even now, when it was so clearly against her interests to do so. "So what are you going to do now?" Giana's voice was rising. "Bolt from the room? Disappear again? And then I won't see or hear from you for another month?"

"What do you care?" Remy was on her feet, looking for her boots. "You should be relieved. Now you can stop juggling the two of us. You can give Pierce your undivided attention. I'm sure he'll like that very much."

Giana was out of the bed and flying at her almost before Remy could react. She managed to catch the fist before it connected with her face, but the rushing weight of the attack took them both to the floor.

"What the…" Remy rolled over and pinned Giana beneath her, clamping her legs between her own in a vise, holding her struggling wrists against the carpet. "Are you fucking insane?"

"Get…the fuck…*off* of me." Giana spoke through gritted teeth, her eyes blazing.

Remy released her immediately. Panting, they both sat up on the floor. Giana turned her back and drew her knees up to her chest. She put a hand to her head, raking her fingers like a claw through her tangled hair.

Her voice was barely audible when she spoke again. "I'm not sure I like who I am when I'm with you."

Remy's breath froze in her chest. It would have been painful to hear that sentiment from anyone. Coming from Giana, it was the most cutting thing she could imagine. Stunned, she remained where she sat on the floor as Giana rose and crossed the room to the closet.

Seeming to move in slow motion, she pulled on a robe and cinched the belt at her waist. Finally, she turned around to face Remy. "I stopped seeing Nick a week ago. We never slept together. We never really did anything. He's a pig. You were right about that. He continues to text me anyway because he can't take no for an answer. I meant to tell you sooner, but we weren't speaking for a little while, and then after that, it never seemed like the right time."

Remy sat still, staring at Giana as she tried to absorb the information. It was like wading through a pool of sand in search of something that resembled a feeling.

Giana watched her for a moment, and then her gaze dropped to the floor. "I think you should leave now."

Remy's gaze dropped to the floor then, too. She finally spotted her briefs in a crumpled heap beneath the sitting chair. She reached for them and stuffed them into her back pocket, then stood up to jam her feet into her boots. She glanced once at Giana, and the green eyes were cool with detachment. Remy recognized the look, but her heart had already cocooned itself in a thick sheath of ice. She felt nothing. The pain would come soon enough, she was certain of that. She just wanted to leave Giana's presence before it did.

Remy walked to the bedroom door and opened it, pausing there as her feet seemed to mire in place. Against her better judgment, she turned to look at Giana again. She refused to even meet her gaze this time.

"I know it must not seem like it," Remy said, "but you really do bring out the best in me. The best, and the worst, I guess. It kills me to think I don't do the same for you."

Giana gave no indication that she'd heard. Remy closed the door behind her and left the apartment.

CHAPTER NINETEEN

The bridge traffic heading into the city was a nightmare. Remy kept scanning the sea of cars in her rearview mirror—in the irrational hope that she might catch a glimpse of Giana's blue BMW somewhere behind her. She picked up her phone yet again, and the dark screen glowered back at her, mocking her for the fool that she was. Giana wasn't calling. And she wasn't somewhere back there, chasing after her, begging her to come back.

Remy had really screwed it this time, and she knew it. Flying off the handle like that, assuming the worst, allowing herself to spiral into jealous idiocy. As if she didn't know the woman at all. She'd let her own pathetic insecurities get the better of her again. She'd allowed them to come in and violate this perfect bubble of nirvana they'd created together and smash the thing to smithereens. It was unforgivable.

Giana had come at her like a demon from the underworld, and Remy should've just let her have at it. She should've fallen to her knees and begged for forgiveness—even after she'd been ordered to leave. But that look of cold indifference in Giana's eyes. It was worse than frothing anger. And her ears were still ringing from the words. Giana had said she wasn't sure she liked herself when they were together.

All this time, from the moment they'd first met, Remy had been so frightened, so fixated on the need to protect her own heart. She'd never once stopped to think that it might actually be Giana who needed protecting from her. She didn't want to believe that. It was too devastating to think of. But what if it were true? Giana was this remarkable, incredibly special individual—it was a privilege to even know her. What had she ever done to deserve her?

She let the phone drop on the seat next to her and laid her forehead against the steering wheel. The angry blast of a car horn jerked her upright again. Swearing, she eased the Audi forward in the slow-moving traffic. She had to make this right. She needed to look Giana in the face, whether those beautiful green eyes of hers were furious or not, and tell her the truth of how she felt about her.

Remy swallowed hard, rubbing her palm against her thigh. It was the most terrifying thing she could imagine, but she had to do it. For whatever difference it would make. Giana may have already decided she wasn't worth the effort, and she wouldn't blame her if she had.

* * *

Giana stepped out of the shower stall and stood on the bath mat dripping wet, her face buried in a towel. She felt like she was still in shock. She had never physically attacked another person in her entire life. Except for maybe her brother. But they had been children at the time, and he undoubtedly must've deserved it. But what had happened a few minutes ago with Remy—Giana had no words.

It was the woman's mulish obstinance. Her abject refusal to see the truth that was staring her right in the face. And after everything they had shared in the last few days. After Giana had laid herself bare. Remy was still so quick to jump to conclusions. To actually believe there could be someone else. Without even pausing for an explanation. It was more than galling—it had sent Giana into a paroxysm of rage. Her fury had been instant and blinding and quite beyond her control. And it scared her.

Her phone buzzed on the vanity, and she grabbed for it, suddenly desperate to hear Remy's voice. The text message was from Nick.

"Goddamn it!" She barely suppressed the urge to hurl the contraption at the wall. The situation was utterly ridiculous. The asshole she couldn't stand wouldn't leave her alone, and the woman she loved could not get away from her fast enough. Giana stared at her reflection in the mirror, inhaling deeply through her nostrils.

There, she'd said it. The woman she loved. That wasn't so hard.

Calm again, Giana picked up the phone and read Nick's message.

You can avoid me all you want, but you know that just makes me try harder.

Giana pressed the button to call him back. She checked her nails as she waited for the line to connect.

Nick answered promptly, his voice slightly winded. "Well, holy hell, what do you know. She's alive." Giana heard the unmistakable clank of gym weights hitting the floor.

"Nick, I'd like to come by your office today to see you. When would be a good time?"

Nick's voice was strained. "Uh...anytime would be great, you know that. Uh...you tell me." He was clearly working out as they spoke.

Giana rolled her eyes and glanced at the clock on the wall. "I'll see you in an hour."

"Hey, great! Great. I'm looking forward—"

Giana disconnected the call and tossed the phone in the sink.

* * *

The parking garage below the Justice Building was still half empty when Remy pulled into it. She cut the engine and reached for the latte that wasn't there, realizing only then that she'd completely forgotten to stop for coffee on her way in. Swearing softly, she climbed out of the vehicle and yanked her overnight bag from the rear compartment. There were showers and a dingy little gym in the basement of the building. Remy wasn't excited about using the facility, but it beat fighting the city traffic to drive all the way home and back again.

For once, the elevator car was there waiting for her, and she stepped in and made the lonely descent into the belly of the building. The doors rumbled open, and she moved to exit the car, but halted in front of the brawny figure blocking her path.

The flat features of Pierce's face registered no surprise as he stared back at her. Oddly, they seemed to register nothing at all—until that cocksure grin of his slid into place. His eyes dropped to examine her rumpled clothing, then rose slowly to settle on her face again. "Looking a little rough around the edges this morning, Devereux. Late night?" He leaned forward and blatantly sniffed at her shirt.

Remy shouldered past him, clearing the cramped space of the car before she whirled around to face him in the breadth of the hallway. "Back the fuck off, Pierce. I'm warning you."

Pierce stared back at her, the hostility in his eyes wholly unguarded now. A pronounced vein stood out on the side of his neck. He didn't move or speak, and neither did Remy. A door swung open somewhere down the hallway, and Pierce blinked once, then stepped backward into the elevator. "Lighten up, Devereux. You need to get a sense of humor."

"Yeah. And you need to get a fucking clue. Leave her alone."

Pierce jabbed the elevator button and leaned back against the handrail. "Hm. I got no idea who the hell you could be talking about." His lips curled in a parting smirk as the doors closed on his face.

"Remy! Fancy meeting you down here."

Reluctantly, Remy turned to see Winnie Greer from ID Section striding down the hallway toward her. The short, buxom brunette had just left the women's locker room. She paused grinning in front of Remy, a damp towel draped around her neck.

"Yeah. I, uh…" Remy was struggling to shake off the rage that had consumed her mere seconds ago. "Yeah. Wow, I had no idea this place was so popular."

Winnie laughed. "Oh, I know. It's kind of a dump, right? But who has time for anything else? You know, it's funny running into you, though. I was going to call you when I got back to my desk." Winnie lowered her voice. "I finally got that info you were looking for."

Remy stared at her blankly.

"Swaggett?" Winnie prompted.

"Oh, Jesus, yes!" Remy said quickly. "Were you able to dig anything up?"

"As a matter of fact, I was." Winnie's dark curls bounced on her head as she turned to check the empty hallway. "Two arrests in Texas on suspicion of rape. Both times he was held and arraigned, and both times the cases were dropped on a technicality. And that name 'Swaggett' he's using? That's a fake. That's why it took me so long to run him down. He's actually one Franklin Hubert Wallace, originally out of Odessa, Texas. Not sure why he took the other name—he was never convicted of anything, so he wouldn't be listed anywhere as a sex offender. Anyway, that's all I could find on him. I hope it helps."

Remy's mind was racing. She and Cookie could haul him in today for questioning, but that would almost certainly end in disaster. With two arrests under his belt, Swaggett (or Wallace) had some experience with the process. It was doubtful he'd spill anything in an interview that would be enough to hold him. They'd have to let him go, and then he'd be free to make himself scarce. And who wouldn't, under the circumstances?

No, they needed a search warrant to get into his house first. Before he figured out they were onto him and started destroying evidence. Animals like him were fond of stashing away little tokens of their victims. Like jewelry or locks of hair. If Swaggett had held onto anything like that, it would be the first thing he got rid of.

But in the end, the entire case might hinge on those sunflower yellow fibers in the lab. And a roomful of carpeting was a little harder to make disappear. Remy practically salivated at the possibility of finding something in Swaggett's house that matched. They'd have his ass then. Dead to rights.

She suddenly remembered Winnie standing in front of her. "I owe you one, Winn, I mean it." Remy reached out and squeezed her arm. She turned and headed down the hallway, calling back over her shoulder. "You are the very best at what you do. You know that, right?"

Winnie watched her go. "You mind calling my wife and telling *her* that?"

Remy laughed and winked before she disappeared into the locker room.

* * *

Giana stepped out of the elevator on the fourth floor of the Justice Building and took the long way around to Nick's office. The direct route would've taken her past Remy's, and she wanted this thing with Nick put to bed before she saw her detective again. He was nothing more than a nuisance now, a nagging loose end that she should've tied off some time ago.

She'd let it go too far. Far enough to become this convenient trigger for Remy to fall back on whenever things were getting a little too intimate. Giana was learning to read the detective like a map, and she realized that was exactly what had happened here. Things were getting real between them now, and it was scary. Left to her own devices, Remy was predisposed to use every available roadblock to slow or completely sabotage the process.

Giana knew she was partially to blame for giving her the ammunition. She'd allowed Remy to believe there was more between Nick and herself than there was. Initially, it was a defensive reflex, a lame attempt to dull the sting of Remy's rejection. But then, after that, perhaps she'd meant to punish her?

Whatever her reasoning at the time, she regretted it now. It was just another needless delay, a pointless distraction working to keep them apart, when in fact there was nothing standing in their way. And nothing to fear. Giana understood that now, and she was determined to make Remy understand it too.

Her cell phone buzzed as she rounded the final corner to Nick's office. Giana stopped in the middle of the hallway and pulled the phone out of her purse. The message was from Remy, thank God.

I'm so sorry about this morning. I really need to talk to you—there's something I'd like to say. Can we please meet later on today?

Giana wasted no time with her response.

I'm really sorry too. I have a terrible temper. It's just awful. You seem to bring it out in me.

Remy's reply was equally quick.

One of my myriad talents.

Sighing with relief, Giana sent a final message.

I really want to see you too. I'll call you a little bit later.

Her mood immensely lighter now, she stowed the phone back in her purse. Communication was everything. When it came to Remy and herself, it was vital. If they could just remember to *talk* to each other, everything would be okay, she was sure of it.

The door to Nick's office stood open. Giana inhaled and strode toward it with renewed determination.

* * *

Remy read Giana's message and felt a wave of relief wash over her. The nerves came shortly after that, as she thought about what she was going to say later that day when they saw each other again. But it was a good kind of nervous, she decided. And there would be no chickening out this time—she was going to woman up and walk the walk if it killed her.

Energized, she hit her office at a brisk pace. It was time to work. She yanked open the file cabinet and began to rifle through it, gathering the forms she would need to set the search warrant on Swaggett in motion.

They had to present a cohesive argument in order to win a judge's approval, and the way she saw it, there were three main factors they needed to emphasize. First, they had the carpet fibers, which linked the two victims and pointed to a single perpetrator. Second, they had the volunteer work and the subsequent connection to Glide Memorial, which linked Swaggett to the victims. And finally, they had his history of arrest.

True, he had never actually been convicted of rape, but falling under suspicion of that particular crime on two separate occasions was enough to lean toward probable cause. Remy paused to jot down another note—she needed to conduct that background check through official channels now before they took this to a judge.

She stopped to think, folding her arms as she leaned against her desk. Which judge they should take it to, now that was the million-dollar question. The meager amount of evidence they'd gathered so far could only be described as circumstantial—and that by the most generous of magistrates. A real hardliner would call it conjecture and toss them out on their asses.

She definitely wanted Cookie's input on this decision. She pushed off the desk, intent on heading to his office. The trill of her cell phone stopped her short. Hoping it was Giana, she whipped it out of her pocket, only to see Max's handsome face grinning back at her.

Remy stared at his image as the room turned in a slow revolution around her. She leaned heavily against the desk and watched as her thumb hit the talk button.

"Remy? Hey, sis…Are you there?"

She had forgotten to say hello. "Hey, bud," she answered quietly. She couldn't explain how she knew what he was about to tell her, but she did.

Max held the phone, and she waited, listening to the even rhythm of his breathing. "I think you need to get back here now, sis."

"Is she...?" Remy's voice broke.

"No," Max said quickly. "No, no, she's still here. But she's taken a turn. The nurse is saying that she might only have a few weeks left...or, or days. I'm sorry, Rem, I should've called you sooner. But it happened so quick, and I wanted to be sure before I—"

"It's okay." She blew out a wavering breath. Her throat was full of sand. "I'll catch a flight out tonight. Um...I'll get a ticket as soon as I hang up with you, and I'll catch a flight out tonight." She couldn't believe this was happening, but it was. "I, uh...I'll text you the info as soon as I have it."

She paused and tried to swallow, and it was painful. "Tell her I'm coming home, all right? Tell her I'll be there when she wakes up in the morning."

"I'll tell her, Rem. Just get here as soon as you can, all right? Safe flight."

He clicked off, and Remy didn't know what to do next. She looked at her phone and found herself clicking to photos, then scrolling through her favorites until she landed on an older picture of Sabine. She remembered the day it was taken clearly. It was some years ago, on a sweltering hot afternoon in August, at the Devereux family reunion on the shores of Lake Pontchartrain. More than a hundred relatives had been in attendance that day, all of them a Devereux by birth or relation. And Sabine had been among them, laughing and vibrant and full of life.

Remy put the phone away and raked a hand through her hair. The scope of everything she had to do now was overwhelming. And she had to get it all done today.

The plane ticket was first, and then she needed to talk to Captain Bronson about a leave of absence. She didn't think it would be a problem, but you never knew with the captain sometimes. And then she had to bring Cookie up to speed on the latest development with the Swaggett situation. The case was about to break wide open, and Remy was leaving him in the lurch to deal with it by himself. He could handle it. He would have to, because she had to go. There was no other choice in the matter.

But worst of all, above everything else, there was Giana. Remy felt a sharp pang in her chest at the thought of leaving her now—for multiple weeks, perhaps. Selfishly, she couldn't stand the idea of being without her, certainly not with the pain of what she had to face back home. But this was the worst possible timing for *them*. Whatever they were together, they were only just beginning. There was still so much that needed to be said. So much they needed to learn about each other. It was fragile and new, and Remy was terrified she would go away, and *this*, whatever it was, would simply evaporate. Like it had never existed at all.

Giana would wait for her, wouldn't she? Remy didn't know if she had a right to hope, or believe, or even ask her to do that. But she wanted to. She desperately wanted to ask her to do just that.

* * *

Giana stepped into Nick's office and shut the door behind her. He looked up from his desk, and that stupid grin appeared on cue, his eyes dropping to take in her body. "Wow, honey, you look great. It's good to see you."

The endearment was glaringly inappropriate. Either Nick was trying to bait her right out of the gate, or the man was staggeringly obtuse. Whatever the root of his dysfunction, she didn't care.

"Nick, I want you to stop texting me. And I want you to stop calling. I'm here because I need you to look me in the face and understand that I'm completely serious. It's over between us. I can't put it any more plainly than that. I wish it could've ended under friendlier circumstances, but that's it. There's nothing else to say." She placed her hand on the doorknob, and Nick was out of his chair.

"Well, Jesus! Hang on a minute, will you? Don't I get to say something here?" He stepped around the desk and leaned his hips on the front edge of it. His overdeveloped quad muscles threatened to burst the seams of his pants. "I just…I wanted to apologize."

She slowly exhaled, counseling herself to be patient. "Sure, Nick," she said, her hand dropping heavily against her thigh. "Go ahead. Apologize."

Nick crossed his arms over his chest. She watched his face as the grin slowly melted away, dissolving into a hardened mask. He was Real Nick again, the one who had shown himself so vividly at the restaurant last week. "You're not here to listen to a goddamned thing I have to say, are you?"

Giana shrugged. "Actually, you're right about that, Nick. What would be the point?"

She turned to open the door, and Nick came across the room with the quickness of a cat. His palm slammed the door shut as his body collided with hers, crushing her against the doorframe, the metal knob digging painfully into her hip. She gasped from the shock of it. The wind was knocked out of her lungs, and she couldn't speak as he gripped her by the hair, forcing her to turn and face him.

"Did you really think you were just going to waltz out of here like that? We're not done talking yet, princess."

In paralyzed disbelief, Giana watched as he slowly leaned his head down. With a bruising intensity, he clamped his mouth onto hers, his heavy tongue forcing her lips apart, sliding thickly against her teeth. With a muffled protest, Giana pushed back against his chest and swung hard at his face.

The stinging slap reverberated in the room. She turned for the door, barely grasping the knob before he caught hold of her again, pulling her away and shoving her face first into the wall. He used his hips and thighs to hold her in place, the weight of his muscle mass pinning her against the cold sheetrock as he reached down and clicked the lock on the doorknob.

"Nick..." Giana injected as much withering contempt into her voice as she could muster. "Don't be an asshole." She was trying to project a calm that she did not feel.

His hot breath fanned against her ear. "Don't try to turn this around on me, bitch. I cared about you. Couldn't you see that? I could have loved you."

Panting, he began to work his hips against hers. Giana felt his penis through their clothing, hot and fully erect, pressing hard as he wedged himself between the cheeks of her buttocks. "I bet I know what you really want. Hmm?"

Giana swore an oath and reared savagely back against him, but his powerful arms only encircled her waist. He lifted and dragged her backward, legs kicking, until he was leaning against the desk with Giana in his lap. Her struggling intensified, and Nick gave a lurid groan as he held her body locked tight against his.

"That's it. You fight. That's gonna make it better for the both of us." His legs were like iron as they clamped on either side of hers. He wrapped one arm around her stomach, squeezing the breath out of her until she was immobilized, his other hand pawing at her breast, roughly groping her flesh. His tongue slathered at her ear and down the side of her neck, and his fingers moved to the buttons of her blouse, working with unrelenting dexterity until the fabric gaped open.

When the cool air hit her skin, a shockwave of adrenaline bolted through her. She reared back against him again, and this time her skull connected with his chin. He grunted in pain, and his grip on her loosened but only slightly. Giana did not hesitate. She twisted her body around to face him, her fist clenching as she swung. Her knuckles smashed painfully into the corner of his mouth, and it felt like she'd punched a cinder block.

Nick uttered a grunt of surprise, but she did not stop. She took a step backward to regain her balance, then swiftly kneed him in the groin. Her kneecap sank squarely into the soft pouch of his scrotum, and Nick convulsed in pain.

"Fuck…" He groaned and doubled over with a wheezing cough. He looked up at her as his face turned a purplish shade of red, his hands clutching at his crotch. His complexion quickly drained of color then, racing from cardinal to pink to white, and Giana watched the progression with an overwhelming degree of satisfaction. Once he'd turned a ghastly shade of gray, she was sure he was about to vomit, and she reflexively stepped out of range. Nothing came out of his mouth, however, she was disappointed to note.

Nick sucked in several gasping gulps of air. "What the fuck?" he finally croaked. "What the hell was *that* for?"

She stood blinking at him, her chest heaving, her hands balled into fists at her sides. The blood was pumping so loudly in her ears, she wondered if she'd heard him correctly. "You *cannot* be serious."

Unbelievably, Nick's shoulders began to shake with laughter. He straightened slightly, still wincing in pain. "No, *you're* the one who's too goddamned serious." He sniffed, dabbing gingerly at his mouth where she'd struck him. "You fucking broads are all the same. No fucking sense of humor."

Giana turned to leave the room. She halted abruptly when she realized her state of undress. "You know, Nick," she said as she rapidly buttoned her blouse, "I don't know what kind of rock you crawled out from underneath, but I wish to hell you would go back there."

Nick was silent behind her as she stooped to collect her purse from where it had fallen on the floor. Half of its contents were scattered across the linoleum. She swore and proceeded to gather up the items as quickly as she could.

After a few moments, Nick stepped up behind her. He crouched to retrieve a tube of lipstick and handed it to her. "So I guess you're saying you don't want to be friends."

Rather than touch him, Giana held her purse open, and he dropped the lipstick inside. "You'll be lucky if I don't press charges." She stood up and walked to the door, releasing the lock with a click before she opened it.

Fake Nick was back, chuckling at her again, the lopsided grin firmly in place. "It's your word against mine, baby. There's not a scratch on you. And everybody knows we've been seeing each other. Why don't you come back real soon, and we can do this again." He gave her a wink before she shut the door on his face.

Outside in the hallway, she stood perfectly still and tried to breathe. Her mind refused to process what had just happened.

She absently glanced down and realized she had missed a button on her blouse. Horrified, she fastened it quickly and adjusted her skirt, then pulled out her compact to check her makeup. Her lipstick was lewdly smeared, as if she'd just survived the heaviest of high school petting sessions. She needed to find a restroom immediately.

Snapping the compact shut, Giana turned to head down the hallway. She drew up short when she spotted Remy. The detective stood gaping at her a few feet away, motionless, her complexion nearly as ashen as Nick's had been a few moments ago.

Giana stared dumbly back at her, the realization of what this looked like dawning with terrible clarity. Time seemed to slow, and she watched, as if from a great distance, as the emotions paraded across Remy's face. Shock turned to disbelief, which quickly became rage. Ultimately, her features settled into a cold look of disgust.

Giana dragged in a shallow breath, willing herself to speak. "Remy, now…now, just please wait one second. This is not what—"

"Don't, Giana." Remy held up a hand to silence her. "Just… don't."

Giana's voice froze in her throat. This wasn't happening. She watched as Remy closed her eyes and stood motionless for several seconds. When she opened them again, they were dead, stripped of any perceptible emotion. They fixed on a distant point down the hallway, and then Remy was in motion, veering to the right, striding past her.

"Don't do this." Giana reached out and caught her by the wrist, and Remy spun on her heel, wrenching her arm free, her eyes alive again and blazing.

"Don't touch me." Her voice was deadly calm. "You stay away."

Giana took an involuntary step backward, and Remy turned and continued down the hallway, her long strides compounding the distance between them at a sickening rate. She rounded the corner and disappeared from view, and the floor seemed to tilt beneath Giana's feet. A wave of nausea washed over her, and she braced a hand against the wall to steady herself.

The injustice of it all was breathtaking. She would not go after her. She would not. She had tried so hard. And yet the result was always the same. Remy was impossible. Insufferable. And the two of them together were cursed.

CHAPTER TWENTY

Remy set her suitcase down on the porch, just as the Lyft car pulled up in front of the house. She waved at the driver before she turned to insert her key in the lock. The tumbler rotated, and the bolt slid home with a depressing click. Remy refused to dwell on it as she slung her satchel across her chest. She lifted the suitcase and lugged it down the stairs, then dragged it bumping over the uneven paving stones to the street.

The driver stepped out of his car to assist, but Remy waved him off, hoisting the heavy bag and dropping it into the trunk with a thud. She had probably overpacked, but there was no telling what she'd need or how long she'd be away. She had crammed everything she could think of into the bag until it barely zipped shut. It was easier than having to choose. If she had to make one more decision or rearrange her life in any greater detail, she was certain she would break.

Her phone set to buzzing again as she opened the car door and slid into the backseat. Remy barely glanced at the screen before she declined the call. She greeted the driver, then slouched down in her seat, her head dropping back against the headrest, her eyelids threatening to close for good.

The only sound in the car was the thrum of the windshield wipers as they headed south through the dampened city streets. Remy glanced at her watch and exhaled. If luck was with her, the redeye tonight would be half empty. She could stretch out and try to get some sleep. The exhaustion she felt enveloped her. It permeated her tissues and flesh, more thoroughly than anything she could ever remember feeling.

Her phone started up again, and Remy answered without looking. "Giana, stop calling me."

She hung up and scrolled through her contacts until she found Giana's number. She selected Block This Caller, then powered the phone off and dropped it into her satchel. She closed her eyes then and slid further down in the seat and tried her best to think of nothing.

In what seemed like moments, Remy sat upright again, squinting against the harsh glare of white light streaming in through the car window. Disoriented, she stared out until she recognized the passenger terminal at SFO.

"You said you wanted Terminal 3, right? United?" The driver's eyes were kind as they peered at her through the rearview mirror.

"Right," Remy mumbled. She spurred herself to get out of the car. The driver beat her to the trunk this time, wrenching her suitcase out with a grunt before he gently set it on the ground. He was back in his car with a wave, and she waved back, still bleary-eyed as she turned to trudge through the wide sliding glass doors into the building.

She was blessedly relieved of her luggage at check-in, which was accomplished very quickly. Then she was one of a scant few travelers to straggle through security, efficiently released a few moments later into the vacant cavern of the concourse.

She dully traversed the gleaming floors, riding the moving walkways when she could, staring at the window displays as they glided past, stacked and artfully arranged in their dark and shuttered storefronts. She arrived at her gate and was quickly waved through, her bootsteps thumping hollow down the sloping jetway.

On board the plane, unoccupied rows were plentiful. She stowed her satchel in the overhead bin and gratefully dropped into her window seat, dutifully buckling her seat belt, struggling to hold her head upright as the plane lurched back from the gate. The taxi out to the runway was rapid. Green and blue lights streamed by on the ground outside. The plane turned sharply, and her body sank into the seat as they accelerated, barreling down the runway. The ground tilted outside the window and dropped away, and they floated upward into blackness.

Once the seat belt sign dimmed, Remy unbuckled and stretched her legs out across the seats. She bundled her jacket into a makeshift pillow and tried to make herself comfortable, staring through the small porthole of a window across the aisle. There was nothing to see. The night outside was as black and featureless as a void.

She had the same morbid thought she always had when she flew. Her body hurtling downward into the abyss. Freezing air collapsing her lungs. Frigid wind whipping at her clothing as the ground rushed up to meet her. She shook the image away and closed her eyes and begged the gods for mindless sleep.

Dawn was breaking on the horizon when the plane began its descent. Remy slowly sat up, her limbs painfully stiff, a dull throb beginning to pound at the base of her skull. She leaned her forehead against the cold window and peered out at the earth rising below. As she watched, miles of dark green swampland slowly gave way to low buildings and solitary houses. The structures were sparse at first, gradually becoming more frequent as the plane lowered in altitude. They would be on the ground soon, and Max would be waiting for her at the curb. She felt her throat constrict, and she swallowed hard, tamping the emotion back, refusing to give in to it yet.

The wheels of the plane hit the pavement with a violent jolt, and they rumbled down the tarmac, the loud roar of reverse thrusters engaging, damping their speed. They taxied into the gate, and the cabin filled with the clamor of seat belts unclicking and overhead bins unlocking. She rose to retrieve her bag and fell in line, one among the rest of the disheveled lot as they filed off the plane.

It was early, but the arrival terminal at Louis Armstrong already bustled with energy. Autopilot was the best Remy could muster as she weaved her way through the throngs of morning travelers, foggily waiting at baggage claim, almost disappointed to see her corpulent bag slide down the chute.

Outside the exit doors, the air was a thick wall of tepid humidity. Remy gasped from the shock of it—until her body remembered. It was New Orleans in the summer. She removed her jacket and draped it over her suitcase. Then she stood for a moment to breathe it in. She was home.

A familiar voice called her name from a short distance away, and Remy turned to see Maximilien striding across the pavement, tall and broad-shouldered and capable. Her delivering knight. He reached her and wordlessly pulled her into a tight embrace. She clung to him, unable to let go as the watershed finally broke. The tears came rushing forward, her sobs wracking and deep. Max simply tightened his grip on her and waited for the torrent to subside.

After a time, he released her, ducking his head to peer into her lowered face. "This is about more than Sabine." It was a statement that didn't require a response. Max used his shirtsleeve to dab at her cheeks. Then he held it up to her nose and said, "Blow."

She pushed his arm away. Chuckling, he reached for her suitcase and lifted it without effort.

"Come on, we gotta go. Jerome is about to get into a fight with airport security."

CHAPTER TWENTY-ONE

Giana sat in her parked car and stared across the street at Remy's house. The little Craftsman was unoccupied, a fact that grew only more bleakly evident as evening descended around it. The windows were dark and shut tight. The Audi sat in the driveway, a thin layer of dust and dried leaves coating its normally gleaming surfaces. The car hadn't been moved in days, and Giana had expected to find nothing to contradict that. Remy wasn't here. She knew it—had known it in her bones for days—and yet she had needed to come here anyway to see for herself.

The word around Homicide Division was Inspector Devereux had taken an extended leave of absence. Under what circumstances, Giana had been unable to determine. Remy's partner Cookie had managed to avoid speaking to her directly, in spite of her best efforts to corner him. He was clearly in on the conspiracy.

Remy had blocked Giana's number on her personal phone, and calls placed to her division phone immediately kicked over to voice mail. There seemed to be no breaching the stronghold the detective had constructed around herself.

Giana sat in her car and considered her options. A part of her couldn't believe she was even here, camped out in front of Remy's home like some lovesick teenager. After everything she had endured. After that...*incident* in Nick's office. Only to step outside and have Remy look at her the way that she had—misconstruing the situation in the most ungenerous of terms possible, piling insult upon injury. Really, it was too much to bear. She should be outraged. Outraged at Remy, and as for Nick...

Giana shifted in her seat, clearing her throat as she felt her airway begin to constrict, her pulse rate suddenly hammering. She dragged a breath of air into her lungs and forced her mind to empty. She wouldn't allow herself to think about that right now. She couldn't.

She gazed across the street at the house's darkened windows until she felt calm again. She had to make Remy listen. What was broken between them could be fixed, but she was convinced the passage of time was their enemy. The longer they went without speaking, the wider the rift between them would grow. And then at some point, there would be no crossing the gap.

She wasn't prepared to simply stand by and watch that happen. At least not until she'd forced Remy to hear the facts. If the detective still wanted to leave after that—if she couldn't get past her own pigheaded, risk-averse paranoia to see the value in what they had together—then she had no interest in stopping her.

She scrolled through her contacts and found Keisha's number. A note in her calendar informed her they were to meet at the museum tomorrow to view the new Chagall exhibition. They'd made the date last Saturday over dinner at Remy's house—a night that now felt like it happened a thousand years ago. In reality, it hadn't even been a week, which seemed impossible given everything that had transpired since then.

Keisha had not reached out, either to cancel or confirm, but Giana had next to zero expectations. If Remy's partner at work didn't want to talk to her, there was no way Devlin or Keisha ever would.

Yet she picked up the phone and texted anyway. At this point she had nothing to lose.

Hi, it's Giana. I'm looking forward to seeing you tomorrow at the museum. What time should we meet?

She set the phone aside, chuckling bitterly. Nothing like blind optimism in the face of total calamity. She put her head in her hands and exhaled. She supposed she should go now. There was nothing here for her in this place. Remy's house was a vacant shell, and sitting in front of it pining away wasn't going to change that fact. She told herself to start the engine and go, but it seemed impossible to move. She was sick with longing for Remy, and there was no relief from that. None at all.

Her phone dinged, and she looked down in disbelief at the text message from Keisha.

I'll meet you outside the main entrance of de Young at noon, if that works for you.

Her fingers sprang to life.

That works for me. See you tomorrow.

Finding the energy now to start the car, she left Remy's street and slowly drove north through the city, back toward the bridge and home. By this time tomorrow, she would have some answers. At the very least, she'd find out where Remy had gone. She suspected it had to do with whatever she'd been worried about that day on the car phone with Max. Some sort of crisis had been brewing then, and now it had come to fruition. She wanted to be with her to help, in whatever way that she could. She wanted to be the person who could do that for her.

But Remy was too walled up in her cave of self-protection to allow that to happen. Frustration and yearning closed in on her again, and Giana lowered all the windows in the car, convinced she was about to suffocate. This couldn't be the end of it. She had to see Remy again. To touch her and know that she was real. And that the time they'd spent together was real. The painful parts of it along with the sweet.

CHAPTER TWENTY-TWO

The woman shifted the weight of the grocery bag to the opposite hip and walked on, peering at her watch in the failing light. It was getting late. A single male figure approached from the opposite end of the block, and she briefly considered crossing to the other side of the street. But it would be too obvious if she did that. She shook her head and told herself not to be so suspicious. The man smiled and nodded as he passed. She gave him a tight smile in return and walked a little faster. After a moment, she glanced back and saw that the sidewalk was empty. She exhaled and faced forward. If she hurried, she could get the place tidied up a bit before she had to make dinner and get in the shower. She had spent a long time hoping for this, and now the date was finally about to happen. There were butterflies in her stomach. She looked up and stopped short as the man stepped out of the shadows ahead of her. But how did he get there, when a moment ago he had just been behind her? He was smiling and breathing hard. She took a step backward at the same instant that he lunged forward, grabbing her hard by the wrist and causing the grocery bag to fall.

The eggs broke open as they hit the sidewalk, their yolks oozing bright yellow against the pavement.

Remy woke and sat straight up in the bed, mildly panicked as she cast her eyes about the unfamiliar room. Then she remembered. She was back home in New Orleans, and this was the guest room of the house she'd grown up in. And Sabine was upstairs dying.

She scanned the room in vain for a clock before she quickly gave up and dropped back against the pillow. It was the middle of the night. She didn't need to know much beyond that. And neither did it matter how many days she'd been home, though at the moment, she honestly couldn't figure. More than a couple, less than a week.

She tossed the covers aside and sat up again, swinging her feet to the floor. It had been folly to hope that she might get a reprieve from the dreams while she was here. Simply because she was home and away from the investigation. Instead, they'd come to molest her every night, the tableau shifting once again, ushering in a macabre new sequence of events.

The Everett girl had been replaced with a third unknown woman. But as always, the man remained the same, his face still nothing more than a vague impression. Remy couldn't understand why her dreamer's mind didn't just fill in the blank. She could picture Franklin Swaggett so clearly when she was awake—pockmarks and widow's peak and all. But it didn't matter. She knew who he was, and she knew where he was. And as long as she and Cookie played it right, they were about to bring him down for good.

She stood up and crossed the room in the dark. Her T-shirt and boxers clung damply to her skin, but she knew she wouldn't require a robe. She left the room and traveled the length of the short hallway to the foyer. The wide mahogany door always creaked, and she tried to minimize the noise as she opened it. The screen door gave a small whine as she slipped out onto the porch.

Outside, the chatter of cicadas and crickets brought the warm night teeming to life. She took a seat in the old wooden swing, its worn slats groaning beneath her weight. She and Max ought to replace the thing while they were here. Pappy was getting too old to trouble with a job like that, and it was Sabine's favorite place to sit and think.

Remy caught herself there. The truth was, Maman was never going to sit in this swing again. In a few days, or maybe a week, she wouldn't be here at all.

She pressed a foot against the floorboards and pushed off, setting the swing in motion. It swayed gently on its chains while she stared out into the yard. The first fingers of dawn were beginning to creep across the morning sky, and she patiently watched as the mammoth live oak emerged from the gloom.

The tree was draped in thick beards of moss, its heavy canopy spreading wide across the yard. Remy stared up into its murky branches and tried to trace the path she'd climbed so many times as a child. Cheeks smeared with dirt, knees and elbows scraped raw, her brother clambering close behind her. They would race to see how high they could go, and the rest of the neighborhood kids were never invited to join. That tree belonged to Max and Remy alone. It was theirs, the source of their greatest pleasure. Their only place of refuge when the pain was too great to bear.

Muffled sounds of movement drifted to her from inside the house, soon followed by the scent of brewing coffee. Somebody was up and about. Either Max or Pappy or Jerome. Without ever discussing it aloud, the four of them had taken to working in shifts, so there was always at least one of them awake in the house. So Sabine would never be alone.

The screen door opened, and Max stepped out on the porch, dressed in sweatpants and a rumpled tee, his hair still mussed from sleep. He handed Remy one of two steaming mugs of coffee. She shifted over to make room for him in the swing.

Max lowered his bulk down next to her, and Remy stared warily up at the crossbeam where the chains were bolted into the ceiling. "We have to replace this thing," she said.

His eyes followed hers upward. "Yep, we do. But it'll hold for now."

They rocked together in silence, watching as the yard labored into the light of morning, most of the sun's rays hijacked by the branches of the huge oak tree.

"Have you checked in on her yet?"

Max nodded. "She seems alert. Jerome is making some oatmeal, in case she wants to eat something. I think we should let Pappy sleep in today. He's been looking pretty beat."

Remy nodded in silence.

After a while, Max spoke again. "Are you ready to talk about it yet?"

Remy considered pretending she didn't know what he meant, just to put it off a little while longer. She knew something like that would never work with him, but she tried it anyway. "Well, she's still with us for now. Why don't we just focus on that."

"No, Remy, I'm not talking about Maman. You've been home for days now, and you still haven't said a word about Giana. Are you going to tell me what happened with you two, or do I have to guess?"

She shifted in her seat, her agitation beginning to rise. She'd managed to keep that part of her mind locked down tight until now. There was no telling how long she could've kept it going, if he hadn't brought it up. But she knew he wasn't going to quit now. She was surprised he'd waited this long.

She took a deep breath and exhaled. "She lied to me, okay? I was just starting to think that maybe she was different. That I could actually trust her, but..." She shook her head. "And you know what the sad part about it is? I knew this was going to happen. I fucking *knew* it. And I walked right into it anyway." She snorted bitterly. "Giana's a liar, and I'm an idiot. I don't know which is worse."

Max continued rocking quietly beside her. "Well, I've known you to be an idiot before, that's certainly true. But that other part doesn't sound much like Giana."

Remy didn't react to that. Not for a long minute. When she spoke, her voice was low. "What the hell do you know about it, Max?"

He shrugged, his shoulder brushing against hers. "Only what you've told me. The way you've described her, Giana is this brutally honest kind of person. Even when she doesn't have to be. It doesn't make any sense that she would just start lying to you out of the blue."

Remy cleared her throat, feeling her temper begin to flare. She said nothing.

"Well, I don't know if *you* realize this," Max continued, "but you're in love with her. That's pretty obvious. You *could* try working it out. Don't you think maybe she's worth the risk? From what I can tell, she's nothing at all like Lexi."

"From what you can tell," Remy repeated bitterly. This was betrayal. Max was betraying his only sister for someone he'd never even met.

"Well, how does Giana feel about you?" he asked. "Does she love you? Has she said?"

"She's straight, Max. She doesn't *know* how she feels about me. And how am I supposed to trust a word she says?"

"Why don't you just tell me what happened, Rem."

"Well." Remy exhaled. "To put it bluntly, she's... she's fucking this fucking *guy*!"

"You mean the one she was already seeing? Did she make you a promise she wasn't gonna see him anymore?"

"Yes! I mean, no." Remy was sputtering. "Well, she *told* me she wasn't seeing him anymore! She told me...She said that, that they'd never even had sex, *period*."

"Okay," Max said calmly. "So then...did you *see* her fucking this guy?"

"Of course I didn't! Fuck. Don't be stupid."

Max looked at her, his expression annoyingly benign. "Well, what exactly did you see, Rem?"

"I don't *know* what I fucking saw, all right! Look, I'm not talking to you about this anymore. You've obviously got some weird kind of agenda when it comes to her."

Max chuckled softly, which incensed her even more. "How could I have an agenda? I've never even met the woman."

"That's exactly my point! So why are you taking her fucking side?"

"All I'm trying to do is stop you from doing something stupid, all right? Something I know you're gonna regret. That's taking *your* side, by the way. Just like I always do. Dummy."

The screen door swung open suddenly, and Jerome's lithe form glided onto the porch. He posed with the grace of a dancer, a carafe of coffee held aloft in his hand. "Who wants a refill?"

Max and Remy lifted their mugs in unison, and Jerome silently poured a splash of hot black coffee into each one in turn. Then he stood with a hand on his hip, observing the two of them as they rocked together in the swing. The twins tilted their heads at the exact same angle and stared impatiently back at him. Jerome scoffed and turned to leave.

"If the two of you are done squabbling out here," he said over his shoulder, "your grandmother would like to see you both upstairs."

CHAPTER TWENTY-THREE

The café inside de Young Museum was a zoo. Giana paid for her salad and turned to scan the sea of tables that crammed the light-filled atrium. She spotted an empty one toward the back and wasted no time carrying her tray over to claim it. She sat down gratefully, turning to search for Keisha, who was still paying for her lunch at the register. She looked up, and Giana waved her over, chuckling at the faces the other woman pulled as she cut a weaving path through the crowd.

Amazingly enough, Keisha still had a knack for making Giana laugh. She'd done it several times today already as they'd strolled together through the museum. Giana had thought she'd lost the ability to feel any kind of joy at all—the moment Remy had turned her back on her and left her standing in the hallway outside Nick's office.

Keisha reached the table and collapsed into the chair across from Giana. "Nice score!"

"Right? This place is a mob scene."

"God, I know. Whose idea was it to come out here on a Saturday?"

"Um, yours, I'm pretty sure."

"Hmph. You're probably right about that." Keisha took an enormous bite of turkey sandwich.

Giana made an effort to fiddle with her own salad, though she hadn't had an appetite in days. And that was hardly about to change now. Not with the seven-ton elephant in the room that neither of them wanted to address.

"I still can't believe you agreed to meet me," she said, attempting to sound casual. She watched as Keisha's eyes briefly landed on hers. They skipped away again, and she waited quietly while the other woman finished chewing her mouthful of food.

"Now that you mention it," Keisha finally said, "I am a little impressed you had the balls to text me."

Giana took a long swallow of iced tea. "I can't imagine what Remy must've told you. Well, I *can* imagine, actually, but it isn't true. She thinks I'm into this guy, and I'm not. I mean, I kind of let her *think* that I was at one point—which was stupid, I'll admit. But, um, anyway. This, uh…this *thing* happened, you see. And…" She paused to glance at Keisha's blank expression. "I'll spare you the details. But this guy…" She forced a laugh. "I mean…he is really just, *such* an asshole. You wouldn't believe me if I told you exactly how big of an asshole—"

Keisha held up her hand, shaking her head. "Look, that's between y'all, okay? Ain't none of this my business."

"Really?" Giana gave her a dubious stare.

Keisha broke into a smile. "What? You think you know me?"

Giana chuckled. "Not very well, I'll admit. But I know enough to call that last line what it is—a big sack of bullshit."

Keisha threw her head back and laughed. "Ooh, girl. You do know me."

"Seriously," Giana said. "I'm really glad to see you, I am. But I'm just so surprised you're even talking to me. I expected you to be thoroughly ensconced in the Remy camp."

"I *am* in Remy's camp," Keisha clarified. "One hundred percent. But, truthfully? Her brother called. Trying to find out what kind of person *you* were. And what the hell went down between you and Remy."

"What kind of person I am?" Giana was taken aback by that. "What did you tell him?"

Keisha took a sip of her soda and shrugged. "I told him you were all right. He said Remy wasn't thinking too clearly, and maybe somebody should talk to you about it. Try to get you to call her."

"I've been *trying* to call her, but she won't answer the goddamned phone!" Giana gripped the edge of the tabletop and told herself to breathe. "Is everything okay with Max? I honestly have no idea what's going on here."

Keisha eyed her steadily. "Max is fine. Sabine is the one who's dying of cancer."

Giana paused. "And Sabine is…?"

Keisha straightened in her chair. "Wow. Remy hasn't told you a damned thing, has she?"

"No," Giana admitted. "Not much at all." She wished Keisha would just spit it out. Either that or she would scream.

"Sabine is Remy's grandmother," Keisha explained. "Max and Remy were raised by their grandparents—after their mother died. She, um…I think she might've been bipolar or something? I'm not sure. Remy doesn't talk much about it. All I know is, she took a bunch of pills when Remy and Max were ten."

Giana stared at her, struggling to process what she'd just heard. How could she not know something like that about Remy? They hadn't had time to talk about any of these things. Or, maybe they had had time, but they'd wasted so much of it pretending not to care about each other.

"Their father is some deadbeat loser they haven't heard from in years," Keisha went on. "Nobody even knows if he's still alive. It's Sabine and Pappy, those are their folks. In every way that counts."

"So that's where she is right now? In New Orleans?"

Keisha nodded.

"Will you give me Max's number?" Giana understood now what she needed to do. She wished she could leave tonight, but she needed to talk to Curtis first to secure a few days off. She didn't know exactly what she was going to say, but somehow she'd make him understand it was imperative that she go.

Keisha had yet to answer her. Giana returned her even stare and waited while the other woman took a slow sip from her soda can and set it back on the table. "Let me tell you something. I want you to be careful with Remy, okay? She acts like she's tough, but she's really not. And she really likes you."

"I know she does," Giana answered, unblinking. "I really like her, too."

Keisha eyed her a moment longer. Then she nodded and pulled out her phone.

CHAPTER TWENTY-FOUR

Remy sat in the old porch swing and slowly rocked, waiting for Max to come out and join her. It had become their morning routine. Rain or shine, in the cold war of an argument or not, they would sit together and watch the yard as the night turned into day. Waiting.

A squirrel hopped through the tall grass a few feet away, cutting an erratic path that terminated at the base of the oak tree. Tail flicking, the critter paused and sat on its haunches. It chittered loudly at her, as if to assert she no longer held any claim on that tree. Remy was inclined to agree.

Max pushed out through the screen door, freshly showered and dressed for work. She acknowledged him with a nod then turned back to the yard, eager to continue her wildlife observation. The squirrel had already scrambled up the trunk of the tree and disappeared amid the branches.

She accepted the mug Max handed her, eyeing his slacks and blazer. "You're heading into the office today?"

"Not the office—I just have a couple of properties to show. Shouldn't take too long." Max eschewed his usual position in the swing beside her, opting to lean against the porch's banister instead.

The ease between them had yet to be restored. Max had tacitly agreed to leave the topic of Giana alone, although Remy knew it didn't necessarily mean the debate was over. At this point, she wasn't sure she wanted it to be. Giana had become a raider amidst her thoughts once again, and the assault was relentless. It was as if the scab had been ripped off a wound, and talking about it was perhaps the only way to stanch the bleeding.

Remy took a deep breath and looked up at Max. "So, um, about the other day…" She stopped when the cell phone in his pocket began to play a 70s' disco tune. "You have *got* to change that ringtone," she muttered.

"Not a chance." Max chuckled at her expression as he reached into his pocket. He frowned at the phone's screen before he answered it. "Hello?"

She watched him, mildly curious as her brother slowly leaned forward, his eyes fixed on his shoes. "Um…wow. Well, hello. Uh, were you trying to…?" He paused and glanced up at Remy briefly, then stared at the floor again. "Right. Uh, can I ask you to hold on for just a second?"

He pushed off the banister and raised his chin at Remy. "I should take this inside." His long strides had already carried him halfway across the porch. "It's a work thing," he added before he disappeared into the house.

* * *

Giana held the phone until Max's warm baritone came back on the line.

"Yeah, uh, sorry about that," he said in a lowered voice. "So, wow. Giana…Hello! I have to say, you're catching me a little off guard here."

Giana rushed in. "Oh, I can only imagine! Uh, Keisha gave me your number, by the way. I'm so sorry to be dragging you into this, Max, but Remy will just hang up the phone if she knows it's me." She heard Max's low chuckle, and the tension in her body eased just a little.

"Yeah. She can be pretty stubborn, that's for sure. But I guess I don't have to tell you that."

"No, you don't." Giana laughed nervously. "Is she…So, that was her you were talking to just now?" She felt her heart begin to pound in her chest.

"Uh, yeah. She's right out on the porch. Are you sure you don't want to—"

"No!" Giana said quickly. "Um, sorry. But I think it's best if maybe you don't mention you've spoken to me." Max fell silent, and Giana took a deep breath. "I was actually hoping I could come and see her. I thought maybe you'd be willing to give me the address where you are…"

"Wait, are you saying you're in New Orleans right now?" Max's voice had gone up an octave.

Giana swallowed. "Yes, I am. I got in early this morning." There was silence again on the other end of the line. "Max, please. I know you don't know me. And I can't imagine how difficult things must be for you and your family right now. But I'd really like to see her. I…I think I might be able to help. If she'd let me."

Max groaned quietly. "Giana, I've heard so much about you. And, I don't really know what's going on between you two, but…I'm inclined to believe you. But my *sister*…" He snorted softly. "She would kill me, she really would."

He was wavering, and Giana sensed that it was better now not to push him. She held her breath, waiting.

"Look," Max finally said, "where are you staying?"

"I'm at the Hotel Dauphine," she answered quickly. "It's on, um…oh…" She struggled to recall the name of the street.

"That's okay, I know it. It's in the Quarter. Look, uh…" He paused again. "Why don't I come and see you a little bit later today? We can talk. And then… I don't know. We'll see. That's the best I can do for now. Can you live with that?"

Giana hastily agreed. "Yes, I can. Thank you. Thank you so much, Max."

"Well, to be honest, I've been dying to meet you." He chuckled again. "Okay. I have to take care of a couple of things this morning, and then I can come by your hotel—hopefully around noon or so? I'll text you when I'm close by."

They hung up, and Giana set the phone down and exhaled. She'd made contact. Surely, that was the hardest part. Her stomach lurched as she remembered the look of undiluted fury on Remy's face the last time they'd seen each other. And then she imagined what her own face must have looked like the time before that—just as she was launching herself at Remy's throat.

She buried her head in her hands. They certainly did bring out the worst in each other. She wondered again if she'd been out of her mind to fly all the way down here uninvited.

Yes, she was certifiably insane. And Remy was an irretrievable myope. They were a perfect pair.

Giana rose from the sitting chair and crossed her hotel room to a set of narrow French doors. She swung them open and stepped out on the small balcony, peering down at the cobbled street one story below. The still morning air was remarkably warm. She leaned against the iron railing and watched as a middle-aged man strolled toward her on the sidewalk, his cane tapping out a cadence that matched his easy gait. He was elegantly dressed in a light summer suit, accented with a colorful vest and tie. He glanced up at her as he approached and tipped his hat. Charmed, she smiled and nodded a reply.

The man crossed the street and disappeared into the building opposite, and she took the time to examine its lovely old facade. White wooden shutters cut a sharp contrast against the rough-hewn building stones, which were rendered nearly smooth by now from untold layers of paint. This latest was a glossy forest green. Two tiers of balconies boasted ornate iron railings, and those in turn were festooned with lush hanging plants.

It was a view as picturesque as any postcard she'd ever seen. She was in New Orleans, a place she had always wanted to visit. It was tragically ironic that the trip should come now, under such woeful circumstances.

She left the balcony and stepped back inside the room. She had some time to kill before Max was due to arrive. Sadly, she was far too unsettled to wander out into the streets of the

French Quarter. She would take a calming shower instead and order something to eat—though she doubted she'd be able to force anything down. Her stomach was a ball of knots, tied even tighter now than it had been for the past week.

Her cell phone buzzed on the table. Giana started, then moved quickly to retrieve it. She swore loudly at the sight of a message from Nick.

I've decided I probably owe you an apology. We shouldn't let it end like this. Call me.

The man was unbelievable. Giana was seriously beginning to question his sanity, and she had no idea how to handle that. She'd never experienced this kind of harassment before. Or attempted rape.

She blew out an unsteady breath. In the beginning, she had refused to call it what it was. For days afterward, even to herself. Calling it that made the encounter too terrifying to contemplate. And if she couldn't contemplate it, she certainly couldn't discuss it—not with anyone, including Liz, though she regretted that decision now. Liz was a good listener, and she had a way of putting things (often quite bluntly) that usually brought clarity to almost any issue. She would have had some choice words to say about Nick. And about the right way to approach Remy around this. Somewhat perversely, Giana was actually relieved the detective had refused to give her a chance to explain in the hallway. In that moment, she would have told her everything, and a second later Remy would have gone tearing after Nick. And then…God knows what would've happened after that.

She tried to shake off the cold fear that gripped her now. The thought of Remy harmed in any way was…intolerable. Giana had not wanted to admit—neither in the midst of the struggle in Nick's office nor directly afterward—that she had been in real physical danger. But somehow, picturing Remy in the scenario brought the reality of the situation into stark focus.

She picked up the phone and swiped Nick's message away. Then she scrolled to her contacts and blocked the caller. She realized it was a feeble gesture that did nothing to truly address the problem. But one hurdle at a time. Right now, all she wanted to concentrate on was repairing the rift between herself and Remy. How she was going to tell her the truth, but not the whole truth, Giana didn't know.

She dropped the phone on the bed and stepped into the bathroom to turn on the shower. The water heated rapidly, and she stared at her anxious face in the fogging mirror and reminded herself to breathe.

The café in the courtyard of the Hotel Dauphine was small and lush like a garden. Giana sat at a bistro table for two and fixedly watched the entrance. A narrow stone archway led out to the street, and when Max strode in beneath it, she knew him instantly. His features and his hair and his coloring were all just a bigger, more masculine iteration of Remy.

She stood up from the table and gave him a small wave. Max nodded and crossed the courtyard toward her, extremely handsome in linen slacks and a light summer blazer. A wide grin spread across his face, and she could see his sister mirrored even more clearly in his smile. The stab of longing to see Remy was overwhelming.

Max reached the table, and Giana somewhat formally proffered her hand. Max grasped it without hesitation, pulling her into a close embrace. Hot tears sprang into her eyes, and she rapidly blinked them back, struggling to regain her composure as they took their seats.

Max adjusted his tall frame to the little table, extending his legs out to one side of it. He nodded pleasantly at the server, who set glasses of ice water down in front of them and strode away. Giana grabbed a glass and drank from it thirstily, aware that his eyes had not left her face. He was quietly observing, waiting for her to begin.

"First of all, I'd like to thank you again. For taking the time to come here and see me." She was relieved her voice sounded normal, at least. "I'm so sorry to hear that your grandmother is ill."

The sadness was evident in Max's eyes, and her heart ached for him. He murmured his thanks and fell silent, obviously waiting for her to continue. She was distinctly reminded again of Remy. Talkativeness apparently ran in the family. She snorted softly, and Max cocked his head, his expression inquisitive.

"This is a little unnerving," she confessed. "You look so much like Remy."

Max chuckled warmly. "Yes, we get that a lot." He leaned forward in his seat. "Why don't you try to tell me a little bit about what happened."

Giana nodded and took another sip of water. She stared down at the tablecloth, unsure of where to begin. "Oh boy, let's see. Well, we started out as friends. I'm new to the Bay Area, you see. When Remy and I met, I really only knew one other person there, who was my roommate. She's a doctor and works all the time, and I hardly ever get to see her."

Giana trailed off and looked at Max. He nodded encouragingly. "Well, I was just so happy to have Remy's friendship, in the beginning. I mean, I'm still grateful for her friendship, of course. She's an amazing person, as I'm sure you'll agree. Even when she's being impossible."

Max's lips quirked, in the exact same way that Remy's so often did. Giana smiled. "But…I mean, I don't really know how to put it. Something just clicked between us, right away. But it was so much more than that—well, it was for me, anyway. Remy definitely had some reservations about it. About *me*, I should say. Or *us*. She still does, unfortunately."

Max's expression was completely noncommittal. Completely not helpful. Giana told herself it was too late to back out now. She cleared her throat.

"So I was starting to see this guy at about the same time that I started seeing Remy. Well, precisely at the same time, actually. And then things started to change between us. Between Remy and me. And it happened so fast, and it didn't make any sense, and Remy was like, no. But then it happened again."

Giana felt her cheeks flush uncontrollably. She looked down at the table and gestured helplessly. "I don't know. I went crazy for her. I just…I went crazy." She took another sip of water. "So I broke it off with this guy, or at least I thought I did, but he wouldn't stop texting. And then Remy saw that he was still texting and didn't believe that I'd broken it off. So I went to see him to get him to stop."

Giana's throat constricted, and she paused, aware that her heart rate was suddenly elevated. She glanced up at Max, who was watching her intently. She lifted her water glass and drained it, and he silently took the empty from her hand and set his full one down in front of her. She nodded gratefully. She waited until she felt calm again, and Max waited patiently with her.

"Remy has this idea about what happened," she said, finally meeting his eyes. "And it's not accurate. I'd really like the opportunity to clarify things with her. Before she makes any final decisions about us. She thinks I lied, and I didn't. I've never been dishonest with her. Not ever. I just want her to know that she can trust me. And that the last thing I ever intend to do is hurt her."

Max's expression remained frustratingly neutral. Giana blew out a wavering breath, considering whether she should say more. She thought better of it and clutched the water glass instead, resigned to wait him out.

Max crossed his arms and rested his chin in his palm, his gaze still fixed on Giana. She hadn't noticed until now that his eyes weren't ash gray like Remy's, but a warm chestnut brown.

"I hope you can understand why I needed to come here and meet you first," he finally said. "Before I run the risk of being slaughtered by my own most beloved sister."

Giana held her breath as he unfolded his arms and rose from his chair. He offered his hand. "Well, come on then. Let's go see her and get this over with."

* * *

Remy leaned down to check the burner under the cast iron pot. She adjusted the flame just a hair, then straightened to resume her careful stirring. The roux was beginning to darken now, slowly turning from creamy white to a toasty caramel brown. She nodded with satisfaction. Gumbo started and ended with the roux. The roux was the most important part, and the browning of said roux was everything. The best technique was to keep it stirring almost constantly, lest you burn it and ruin the entire dish.

Remy could admit she was somewhat fanatical about the process, but she had Sabine to blame for that. The only time she ever cooked gumbo was right here in this kitchen. And she and Sabine had always cooked it together.

Jerome stepped up next to her and held a hunk of Andouille sausage about an inch from her nose. "Okay, now how's that?"

Remy had to lean her head back to focus. "Um. Maybe you could go just a skosh thinner?" She pinched her fingers together to indicate the width she wanted. Jerome scoffed and dramatically rolled his eyes. Remy laughed—for the first time in what seemed like ages. "Hey, you're the one who wanted to help."

Her cell phone buzzed in her pocket, and she pulled it out and answered with one hand, using the other to continue stirring her roux. "Cooks! What's happening, partner? It's good to hear from you." She was surprised to realize how much she missed him.

"How's it hanging there, boss?" Cookie's voice crooned in its familiar, unhurried tone. "How's, uh…how's the family and everything? It's not a bad thing to be calling you now, is it? I was gonna wait to hear from you first, but—"

"No, no. It's fine. It's, uh…" Remy paused, unwilling to get into the emotion of it. "It's hard, you know. But hey, I was actually planning to talk to you today anyway, Cooks. Just to check in. See if you had any luck with that search warrant on Swaggett." She heard Cookie's deep inhalation, and her stirring hand slowed.

"Uh, yeah. The warrant is still in the works there, boss. But, uh…" He paused, then spoke in a rush. "We brought Swaggett in for questioning."

"You did *what*?" The wooden spoon stopped its stirring. It hovered dripping over the pot.

"Yesterday." The steadiness in Cookie's voice was gone. "We…well, *I* didn't bring him in, but yeah, he was in here yesterday for questioning."

"I thought we agreed we weren't gonna do anything like that until we got inside the fucker's house, Cookie!"

"Yep, we did, boss. You're absolutely right about that." His voice was uncharacteristically apologetic. "But, what can I say? It wasn't my idea. It was my day off, for chrissakes. I didn't even get the call until they were already at the station, and I mean, I busted my ass getting down there, but it was too late at that point."

"What the hell are you talking about? Who the fuck brought him in, if it wasn't you?"

Cookie's voice lowered to a mutter. "Uh, that would be Pierce. He thought he could lend a hand."

Remy swore loudly and profusely. She turned and glanced at Jerome, whose eyes remained glued to his cutting board. She lowered her voice. "You tell me, Cookie…How the hell is Nick Pierce suddenly involved in this case?"

"Look, I know you two don't get along, okay, Rem? But we got to talking the other night over a couple of beers. I gave him a little background, you know—about the fiber evidence and your theory on Swaggett and all that. He got pretty interested when I told him Swaggett works at Glide. Nick had that detail in the Tenderloin a few months back, remember? Anyway, he's still got connections in the area, you know, so he went over there to Glide to poke around for himself. He ran into Swaggett, and, uh…"

"And what? Don't tell me Swaggett volunteered to come in."

"Uh, no. He took off, actually. Nick had to run him down. Brought him in for resisting arrest."

"Fucking Christ!" Remy slammed the spoon down on the stovetop, and Jerome dropped his knife on the floor. She turned around to check for blood, then held up her hand apologetically. "Resisting arrest," she said into the phone. "Tell me I didn't hear that right, Cooks."

His reply was reluctant. "No, you heard it right, boss."

"Without an arrest warrant."

Cookie paused again. "Right."

"You *are* familiar with the concept of probable cause, aren't you, Cooks? Or do we need to go over that one again? A grand jury is gonna laugh us right out of the fucking courtroom. If Swaggett doesn't sue us for police harassment first. Please tell me you let him go."

"Yeah, of course we did. We had to. But, I mean, technically speaking…the guy did flee the interview."

"I don't fucking *care* what he did! You've tipped our hand! We haven't got a shred of evidence on this guy, Cookie. Zero. We need time to build a goddamned case, you *know* that. You were supposed to watch him, see what he does. We lay it out in front of a judge, we get the warrant, and then we take his goddamned life apart! I can't believe you let *Pierce* in on this thing to fuck it all up."

"Like I said, Rem, I didn't know he was gonna go down there." Cookie's voice was regaining its usual soothing cadence. "What do you want me to do? The guy's a wild card. Always has been."

"Exactly. So maybe you should've thought of that before you opened your mouth to him. I left *you* in charge, Cookie." Remy stopped to take a breath. The extended silence on the other end of the line suggested she had made her point.

She suddenly remembered her roux, whirling around to face the pot as she released another string of expletives. She'd caught it just before it started to burn. Barely.

She grunted and resumed her diligent stirring, holding the phone to her ear while she tried to comprehend the extent of the damage done to the case. They'd been hanging on to this thing by the thinnest of threads from the very beginning. She couldn't help but feel that unknown forces were rising up to thwart them at every turn.

"Well, what happened in the interview?" she grumbled. "Did he say anything? Not that we could use it if he did."

"Yeah, not much, boss. We went at him pretty good for a couple of hours. Told him he was a person of interest in a murder investigation, said we had probable cause—even though we didn't. You know, the whole nine. But, I swear, the guy never flinched. Said he didn't know what the hell we were talking about, and why didn't we go there while we were at it." Cookie chuckled bitterly. "The balls on this guy. And get this—he gave us his fucking DNA."

"He did what?" Her stirring hand stopped again, and she gave up, reaching for the burner knob to turn off the flame.

"I'm not even kidding. He offered it right up, no resistance whatsoever. Can you believe it? We sent his sample into the lab pronto."

Cookie paused, and she couldn't think of a single thing to say.

"So, uh, how sure are you about this guy really, boss?"

Remy blew out a breath. That was an excellent question. Why the hell would anyone submit to DNA testing unless they were absolutely certain they had nothing to hide? Could Swaggett really be that confident he'd covered his tracks? Or was he simply too psychotic to know any better? Remy didn't believe he was psychotic.

The simplest explanation was the one she was most reluctant to admit: they had the wrong guy. Up until a few seconds ago, she was utterly convinced that Swaggett was their man. Now, she didn't know what to believe.

She exhaled into the phone. "Hell, Cookie, I mean…I've been wrong before." If she *was* wrong, they'd just spent several weeks chasing their asses trying to build a case against an innocent man. Which meant they were now back to square one. Which was positively nowhere.

"Look, uh," Remy said with a sigh, "just do your best to keep tabs on the guy for now. I mean, keep your distance, all right? But just try to keep aware of his activities. If that search warrant comes through, I want us to be ready to move on it right away. In the meantime, we'll wait to get the test results on that free sample of his."

"Sounds like a plan," Cookie agreed. "But I was thinking about that, boss. Those tests at the lab usually take a while. Unless, uh, maybe you still had a connection over there that we could tap into…"

Cookie trailed off, and Remy held the phone, refusing to fill in the gap.

"She's been asking about you, by the way," he said in a low voice. "Nonstop around the offices. The lady is persistent, you gotta give her that." He chuckled softly, then cleared his throat. "Just thought you should know."

Remy spoke up abruptly. "All right, Cooks. Um, thanks for checking in. I have to say, I wish you'd brought me some better news about the case, but we're just gonna have to roll with it now. I'll call you in a couple of days, all right?"

Cookie hesitated only briefly before he relented. "All right, boss, I'll let you go. You take care of yourself, okay? Talk to you soon."

Remy clicked off and slipped the phone back into her pocket. A wave of defeat washed over her as she leaned against the counter.

"Everything okay over there?"

She glanced up at Jerome. She'd forgotten he was even in the room. "Hmm? Yep, everything's fine. Sorry if I got a little loud for a second there."

Jerome mumbled something in reply, but she was already lost in thought again. The case had turned into a veritable train wreck in her absence. She doubted there'd be anything left to salvage by the time she got back. Never mind that it was starting to look like she may have been on the wrong track to begin with.

And *Pierce*, of all people, getting involved. The man was like a flaming urinary tract infection she couldn't get rid of. And he hated her just as much as she hated him, that much was clear. The last time they'd run into each other, he'd looked like he was seriously contemplating actual bodily harm. Remy snorted softly. Just let him fucking try it.

She couldn't help wondering now if Pierce had nosed his way into the investigation for the sole purpose of jamming her up.

It was chilling to think that anybody, especially a professional, would do something like that. But Pierce—the guy was a different animal. And now he had Giana all to himself.

Remy closed her eyes, and against her will it came to her again. The sight of Giana stepping out of his office. Her clothing disheveled, that gorgeous hair of hers all tousled from *his* hands being in it. Her lips swollen, from…

Remy shut the image down, before the rage could take hold of her again. She breathed in through her nostrils, gripping the edge of the counter. Giana was a grown woman. She had a right to see whomever she wanted to see. Remy desperately wished she could just find a way to accept that. She wished she didn't go apoplectic at the thought of her even touching someone else. She knew this kind of jealousy wasn't healthy. She knew it wasn't enlightened or evolved. And if it meant the difference between seeing her again or not, she could at least *try* to get a handle on it, couldn't she?

But Nick fucking *Pierce*. He was just a bridge too far. Giana was no fool, not by a long shot, but that prick had clearly figured out a way to game her. And Remy had stood by like an idiot and let it happen. She could've at least warned her about him. She could've just been honest, and told her flat out what he was really like. Instead of trying to pretend like she was unaffected and didn't care. When nothing could be further from the truth.

"How small do you want these onions chopped, Remy? Like this?"

Remy glanced up at Jerome holding a ragged chunk of onion in his hand. She sighed, stifling a chuckle in spite of herself. The man was a brilliantly gifted talent on the dance stage, but in the kitchen, he was a disaster.

The kitchen door swung open then, and they both turned to see Max enter the room. The look on his face was bizarre— cautiously guarded, yet openly apologetic at the same time. Remy stared at him, her body beginning to tense. "What's the matter with…" She stopped speaking and her mouth fell open as Giana Falco walked into the room behind him.

It was an apparition. She knew there was no conceivable way the real Giana Falco could be standing here, right now, in this kitchen. Just a few feet away.

"Hello, Remy," she said.

Remy felt light-headed. She was glad her weight was already propped against the counter. She couldn't control her eyes as they raked Giana's face, hungrily consuming every detail. She was suddenly starved for the sight of her. She stared for a long minute into those stunning green eyes, which were somehow even larger and more penetrating than she remembered. With vague irritation, she wondered how the woman could have possibly grown more beautiful in a week. But at the same time, she looked exhausted. And too thin. Like she hadn't been eating.

"What the hell are you doing here?" The question floated in a bubble, bobbing on a draft of air between them. Remy could only assume it had come from her.

Giana blinked, then she turned to glance around the kitchen, her gaze landing on Jerome. "Oh, hello. You must be Jerome. I'm Giana."

"Oh, it's so nice to *meet* you!" Jerome hurriedly stepped around the island. Unbelievably, he gave her a hug.

Remy narrowed her eyes at him. And then she leveled her gaze accusingly on Max. She was going to kill the both of them tonight in their sleep.

Max refused to meet her eyes. He put a hand on Jerome's shoulder, and the two men turned to leave. The swinging door rocked closed behind them, and Remy and Giana were left alone in the kitchen.

* * *

Giana stood in the cavernous old kitchen and waited for Remy to do something. To speak, or to shout, or to flee the room. But the detective only stood there, leaning against the counter, staring mutely back at her. At least the color had returned to her face. For a moment, she had looked as if she were about to pass out, which was exactly the way Giana had felt the second before she followed Max into the room. She was at a loss for what to do or say next. She had only planned ahead as far as this moment.

Her breathing shallow, she took a cautious step forward, halting when Remy shifted her feet and folded her arms across her chest. Giana cleared her throat and glanced around the room. "This house is incredible," she heard herself say. "Is this where you grew up?"

Remy stared back at her for another long moment. She gave a curt nod before her eyes dropped to the floor.

"Can I help you with some of this?" Giana gestured at the food covering the center island. "Whatever it is, it smells delicious."

She found herself moving toward the sink, taking the long way around the island to avoid coming into contact with Remy. She washed her hands and dried them on a dishtowel, then stepped to the cutting board Jerome had abandoned. She took up the chef's knife and commenced to chopping, aware of Remy's eyes tracking her every move.

"Jerome kinda massacred that onion," Remy said quietly. "I need a smaller dice than that. Maybe a quarter inch."

Giana nodded without looking up. "How many?"

"Everything in the bowl," Remy replied.

Giana nodded again, already finished with the first onion and moving on to the next. She stole a glance at Remy's back as she turned to face the stove and lit the burner beneath the pot.

They went to work together in the kitchen then, quickly falling into a familiar rhythm. The silence remained between them, but the tension slowly began to ease. Remy periodically turned from the stove to gather up the product of Giana's labor, dumping the chopped vegetables into the pot, pulling more whole ones from the fridge, systematically cleaning them in the sink before she set them in the bowl to be processed.

There were green and red bell peppers and celery and okra. Remy specified the size and shape of the chop, and Giana delivered. She was relieved to have something to do with her hands. She was more than relieved to be here with Remy, though things were far from mended between them. It was enough for now to be in the same room with her. To be able to glance up and see that she was there.

Suddenly, the kitchen door swung open, and an older gentleman strode into the room. He was a bit shorter than Max, and his skin was darker, but otherwise the resemblance between them was uncanny. Despite the ravages of age.

"Well, looka here! Who is dis pretty girl standin' in the kitchen here?" His face broke into a wide grin—that unmistakable Devereux grin—and Giana could not have stopped herself from grinning back at him.

Remy turned from the stove to glance at the man who was obviously her grandfather. Her expression remained stubbornly impassive. "Pappy, this is my, er…This is Giana."

Giana wiped her hands and stepped around the island. "It's so nice to meet you, Mr. Devereux." She held out her hand to him, and Mr. Devereux's white eyebrows lifted in his brown face. He glanced at Remy, who quickly turned back to the stove.

Grasping Giana's hand, he raised it to his lips and brushed a light kiss across her knuckles. "It's an absolute pleasure, young lady." His voice was suddenly formal and deeply resonant. "Welcome to our home. And I won't have you calling me anything other than Lucien. Or Pappy."

Giana felt her cheeks warm beneath his steady gaze. She suppressed a strange compulsion to curtsy. "Well, thank you, Lucien. It really is very nice to be here."

The Devereux charm appeared to extend to all generations. Giana resumed her position at the cutting board and pretended not to watch as Lucien walked to the stove and rested his hands on his granddaughter's shoulders. "Hello, baby girl. You makin' me some lunch?"

Remy shook her head, chuckling warmly, and Giana's chest tightened at the sound of it. "No, Pappy. I'm sorry to tell you, but you're on your own for lunch. This gumbo's for dinner tonight."

Lucien clucked his tongue. He stretched around her to reach into a large bowl of fruit that sat on the counter at her elbow. He pulled out a nectarine and took a hearty bite. Then he turned to exit the kitchen, inspecting Giana with another long glance as he went. With a wink and a nod, he backed his way through the wide swinging door and disappeared.

Silence descended over the kitchen again. Giana stared at the back of Remy's head, suddenly overwhelmed by the desire to touch her. She'd heard that chuckle low in Remy's chest, and it was like it broke the seal on everything she'd been holding bottled up inside of her own. She didn't think she could keep her distance much longer.

"Remy…we need to talk."

Giana watched Remy's shoulders rise as her chest filled with air. They lowered again, and her tone was calm, almost matter-of-fact, when she answered. "Okay. Let's finish up in here, and then we can go have some lemonade on the porch."

Before long, the last of the remaining ingredients were added to the gumbo. Remy lowered the flame and covered the pot with a heavy lid. She retrieved two tall glasses from a cabinet, wordlessly filling them with ice and then lemonade from a carafe in the fridge. She handed one to Giana, glancing briefly into her eyes. Then she turned and exited the kitchen, waiting with the door held open for Giana to follow.

They crossed the polished hardwood floors of the living room and foyer, and Remy held the screen door again as she stepped out onto the porch. A wooden swing hung in one corner, suspended on a set of steel chains. Remy motioned to it, and Giana took a seat and slowly began to sway. She sampled the sweet tang of the lemonade, and it took her back to that afternoon they'd spent at the farmers market. When she'd decided to drench herself in the beverage instead of drinking it. That was a good day. She yearned to get back to the feeling of that day.

Giana raised her eyes to openly study Remy. The detective was still avoiding her gaze, standing with her hips propped against the banister. Remy took a long swallow of her drink, then leaned over and set the glass down on a side table. "I can't believe you came all the way down here," she said. Her tone was low and absent of anger. She straightened and finally looked directly at Giana. "You're fucking nuts, do you know that?"

Giana heard it in her voice then. The strain riding just below the surface. The valiant and failing effort to hold back the emotion. She leaned over and set her own glass down on the table next to Remy's. Then she stood up and took a careful step toward her.

Remy didn't move. Her eyes had grown glassy, beginning to brim over, but she didn't turn away. "Why did you come down here?" she whispered. "Are you trying to kill me?"

Giana reached up and touched her face. She used the pad of her thumb to brush away the tear. Another one followed, racing fast down Remy's cheek, and then another came rushing after that. She stepped in closer, using both of her hands now, gently wiping with her palms and the backs of her fingers, dabbing until her hands came away soaked. She could feel the tremor running through Remy's body, as acutely as if it were her own. She pressed in closer, embracing her, holding on tight as the shudders only increased.

She leaned up and whispered in her ear. "I came here because I love you, you idiot. You know that it's true. And you know that you need me here with you right now. So, just...deal with it."

Remy brought her arms up around her then, clinging to her, crushing her with the strength of her embrace. The sob that tore from her throat was wrenching, piercing Giana's soul. Tears sprang into her own eyes, and she spoke into Remy's ear, urgent and low, her voice breaking. "Listen to me. What you think you saw between me and Nick—that's *not* what happened. I need you to believe that."

Remy went still in her arms, her breathing harsh and uneven. She lifted her head to look at Giana's face. "What are you saying?"

Giana swallowed hard and looked back at her.

"Did he hurt you?" Remy asked.

Giana could see it. The fury latent in Remy's eyes. A venomous snake in the black of her pupils, coiling and tensing, ready to burst out of control.

"Giana, did he hurt you?" Remy asked again.

"No," Giana answered, holding her gaze, girding herself to lie like both of their lives depended on it. "No. He got a little pushy. He kissed me, even though I didn't want him to. But that was it."

Remy closed her eyes, inhaling deeply. "Motherfucker," she whispered. "I am going to fucking kill him. I swear to God."

"No, you're not," Giana said. "Remy, look at me." She waited until Remy's eyes were focused on her again. "No, you are not. You're going to let it lie, because we don't care about him." Remy shook her head, and Giana laid a hand against her face. "Listen to me. We don't give a fuck. Our only concern right now is *us*. And this family. And taking care of your grandmother upstairs."

The screen door opened then, and Max poked his head out. "Um…I'm really sorry to interrupt." His eyes skated past Remy's and settled on the floor. "But Sabine is awake. And, uh…she says she wants to see you both."

* * *

Remy led the way up the narrow staircase to the second floor, Giana following close behind her. The day had gone from shocking to draining to surreal, and it was only halfway done. Truth be told, Remy had been living with this strange out-of-body detachment from the moment she'd returned home. She could only assume it was her way of coping—mentally standing back to analyze the activity around her, much in the way an impartial observer would do. The last time she'd allowed herself to fully experience a loss of this magnitude, she'd been ten years old. And the damage was irreparable.

A row of family portraits marched up the wall alongside the staircase. Remy regarded each with the passivity of a stranger as she climbed the steps. She came to the one in a large gilded frame, and her mind focused in on it with keen recognition.

Sepia-tinted and cracked with age, the photograph was of a teenaged Sabine, seated on a sofa in an elegant party dress. She stared soberly back at the camera from the center of the frame, and balanced on her lap was an enormous sheet cake, littered with birthday candles. The photo was warped and faded, taken decades before Remy was born. She could not remember a time in her life when it had not hung in that exact position on the wall, third from the left, almost at the top of the stairs.

They reached the second floor, where the door to Sabine's room stood open. Remy paused in the doorway and rapped her knuckles lightly against the frame. Maman lay propped up on several pillows, and as she turned her head to greet her visitors, Remy felt the shock of it wash over her again. She couldn't reconcile the image of the woman she'd carried in her mind's eye her entire life with the wasted form that now lay on the bed in front of her.

In the corner of the room, a nurse in a white tunic rose to her feet. She nodded and smiled at Remy and Giana, then quietly stepped out into the hallway.

Sabine held Remy's gaze for a moment, and Remy could see her features were drawn tight with pain. Sabine's eyes then shifted to take in Giana, and a weak smile spread across her lips. Her voice was hoarse when she spoke. "Come over here, girl. Let me get a good look at you."

Giana promptly stepped closer to the bed. As Remy watched, she reached down to touch Sabine's hand where it lay on the quilt. Remy stood motionless, watching as Sabine's grip tightened around Giana's fingers.

"You come a long way to see my Remy." Sabine's chest heaved as she began to cough.

Remy crossed the room quickly, grabbing the pitcher on the side table to pour a glass of water. She moved to the opposite side of the bed and gently slipped her arm underneath Sabine's back, raising her slightly so she could take a sip. She weighed nothing.

Sabine swallowed and nodded, gently clearing her throat. She lay back against the pillows, her eyes still fixed on Giana. "Remy, she been real upset. She upset about me, and she upset about you, too."

Giana nodded, looking at Remy. Their gazes held as she answered. "Yes, we've both been very upset. We misunderstand each other sometimes, but we're working on that."

Remy's chest tightened.

Sabine clucked her tongue. "Hmph. You talkin' 'bout *Remy* misunderstandin' things. Yeah, she can be ignorant sometimes. Mule-headed, too."

Remy coughed in surprise, and Sabine glanced up at her. "Child, you know that's true." Remy opened her mouth to object, but Sabine was speaking to Giana again. "She ain't never been as sweet as Maximilien. He the gentle one in the family, always has been. Remy, she ornery. Take after her Pappy Lucien in that way. I been puttin' up with the two of them for decades now."

"Sabine, I'm standing right here," Remy complained. "I can hear you."

"I know you can hear me, girl. I'm dyin', I ain't senile."

Remy blew out a puff of air. She watched as Sabine gave Giana a wink, and Giana's face broke into a broad grin.

Sabine closed her eyes for a long moment then. As if to gather her strength. She opened them and said, "You care about Remy." It wasn't a question.

Giana nodded. "Yes, ma'am, I do. Very much."

Sabine nodded and closed her eyes again, her chest slowly rising and falling. Remy looked down at their hands clasped together on the bed—Sabine's and Giana's, resting palm in palm—and she felt that out-of-body sensation again.

Sabine's eyes remained closed, and Remy reached down to lightly touch her shoulder. Her skin was like paper, the bones pushing out prominently. "Do you want to rest now, Maman?"

Sabine's eyes opened. "Mm-hmm. I think so, chére." She looked at Giana again. "I'm glad you came to visit us, child. I'm glad I got to meet you."

"It's really good to meet you too, Sabine." Giana's eyes were shining.

Sabine nodded. Her eyes closed, and Giana released her hand and stepped away from the bed, swiping at the tears on her cheeks. They both turned to quietly leave the room, but Remy halted at the doorway when Sabine called her name. She pivoted and crossed the distance to the bed in two quick strides.

Sabine gazed up at her, and her eyes were suddenly bright with a burning clarity. Remy sat on the edge of the bed and clasped her hand, surprised by the sudden strength in her grip.

"Baby, I want you to stop making everything so hard." Remy nodded, the tears burning at the back of her eyes. Sabine gripped her hand harder. "All I ever wanted was for you to let yourself be loved. You love a lot, child, Lord knows that's true. But sometimes the hardest thing in the world is to let somebody love you back. You wanna be strong, then be strong in that way. You do that for your maman. Okay, chére?"

Remy nodded her head several times, unable to speak. She leaned over and laid her cheek against Sabine's, her shoulders shaking uncontrollably as the tears began to stream, the choking sobs rising up yet again from deep within her chest, straining and burning her throat as they tore their way free.

CHAPTER TWENTY-FIVE

Sabine Brunet Devereux passed away on a Tuesday. Six of the living gathered around her bed, and Giana was among them, hanging back toward the rear of the room, alongside the nurse. The moment was painful and incredibly private, and she didn't want to intrude. Yet she wanted to be close enough to get to Remy's side—at the instant she was needed, as many times, and for however long that Remy needed her.

The days that followed were a dizzying blur. Funeral arrangements were made, and relatives were contacted. Within hours of Sabine's passing, a steady stream of people began to arrive, continuing nonstop throughout the rest of the week. They came from all over the state and beyond, friends and loved ones alike, descending on the beautiful Victorian in the Garden District.

Giana did her best to keep out of the way, though it was impossible to do with so many different groups of loving and lovely people constantly crowding in through the doorway. The kitchen was commandeered by a band of impromptu cooks—

stepsisters and great aunts and second cousins by marriage. Giana met dozens of Remy's relatives, their names and faces swirling together in a muddled soup. By the end of the second day, she'd stopped trying to keep them straight. They were family. That was the common thread that ran through them all, and nothing seemed to give them greater pleasure than to sit and "visit" for hours.

Remy and her brother rapidly became Giana's heroes. Stoic and high-functioning as a pair, they were pillars of strength for Lucien, working in sync to keep everything else running without a hitch.

It was only at night that Remy dissolved into a haze of raw emotion. Giana lay awake with her for hours, holding her head pressed against her chest, her own heart breaking as she listened to the agonizing sobs that would not stop coming. Remy had a well of tears inside of her that was boundless. There was nothing to do but let it flow.

On the morning of the funeral, Giana drove Max's car out to the airport. Keisha and Devlin's flight was delayed leaving San Francisco. They'd be arriving into Louis Armstrong with little room to spare for unforeseen hiccups. She had volunteered to scoop them up and run them safely to their hotel. After that, the three of them would head straight to the funeral services.

She was glad to have something useful to do, but in truth, she also needed a reprieve. Away from the constant press of inquisitive eyes and polite conversation. She felt as if she and Remy had barely had time to reckon with who they were to each other, and now their relationship was on public display. The exact nature of their connection was never openly addressed in Giana's presence, but Remy had no compunction about demonstrating her affection, regardless of whoever was in the room.

It was all very new and strange. Giana hated to be apart from Remy, but as for the rest of it—she needed to take a step back and exhale. Oddly, Keisha and Devlin felt like the closest thing to home to her now, and she couldn't wait to see them.

Passenger loading outside the airport terminal was mayhem scarcely controlled. Giana nosed Max's Saab bravely into the fray, edging persistently closer to the curb as she scanned the crowd for a familiar face. Devlin's spiky blond head stood out like a beacon. Giana honked and pulled over, a grin spreading across her face as she spotted Keisha's ropey braids next.

Popping the trunk, she hopped out of the car and met them halfway. Keisha reached her first, and the hug she gave was long and bruising, and badly needed. Her brown eyes were damp when she finally let go.

"I'm so glad you were here for Remy. How's she been doing?"

Before Giana could answer, Devlin's arms came around her in a bear hug that nearly lifted her off her feet. It was so good to see them both.

They were in the car and headed out of the airport when Keisha asked the question again. "What about Remy, how's she holding up?"

Giana looked at her, one hand lifting off the wheel in a helpless gesture. "She's shattered, you know? It's just…It kills me to see her so devastated, and not be able to do a single thing to help. And at the same time, she's handling all of this incredibly well." She shook her head. "Max too. The two of them together are…amazing. And, oh my God, at the house. It's just people and more people *every*where. And they just *keep* coming. This whole experience has been…" She stopped, inhaling deeply. "I'm really, really glad to see you guys."

Devlin's hand reached out from the backseat and squeezed her shoulder. Keisha put a hand on her leg. "I don't think you realize how important it is that you're here. You're helping her, Giana. Believe me, you really are."

In good time, they pulled into the semicircular drive of the Grand Marquis in Mid-City. Giana handed the car key to the valet and advised him they wouldn't be long.

"Wait, we do have time to shower and change, right?" Keisha was eyeing Giana's dress. "You look fantastic, by the way."

Giana glanced down at herself. She usually took so much pleasure in shopping, but this most recent foray had been accomplished in a mad rush. She'd chosen the dress because it was black, and it fit. "Oh, thanks. But yes, we have some time. The service doesn't start until three, and the church is only fifteen minutes from here. So you guys go get checked in and get yourselves settled, and I'm gonna find the lounge. I could use a cocktail—or four. Come find me when you're ready."

The bar inside the Marquis was large and nearly empty, with comfortable lounge chairs and picture windows that looked out on the teeming foot traffic of Canal Street. She chose a seat by the windows and sank into the generous cushions. Pulling out her cell phone, she sent a quick text to Remy.

At the hotel with the girls now. Thinking of you. I'll see you at the church.

The waiter approached, and Giana set the phone aside and ordered an Aviation. For once, she wasn't worried about the quality of the cocktail that might come back. She'd drink anything they gave her.

She blew out a breath and tried to relax, glancing around the lounge without really seeing it. The funeral loomed ahead like a specter. She didn't know what to expect, or how to behave, or what she could do to bring Remy any comfort.

She had been too young to remember her own mother's death or any of the events surrounding it. She suspected her toddler's mind had suppressed the ordeal out of self-protection. The memories were buried so deep now they were inaccessible to her as an adult. She couldn't say she regretted that. Watching Remy suffer like this was enough for the both of them.

Remy grieved for Sabine, but it was plain to see that she was also that ten-year-old girl experiencing the loss of her mother all over again. A mother who had chosen to take her leave. Giana couldn't imagine what that must feel like. Or the festering hole such a purposeful abandonment would leave behind.

As if conjured by her thoughts, Remy texted in with a ping.

Give your name to the parking attendant at the church and he'll have a spot for you. Hurry back. I'm missing you already.

Giana's stomach dipped. She felt exactly the same way. The morning's logistics had forced them to separate shortly after breakfast, but before that they had barely left each other's side in a week. And still she couldn't get back to her soon enough.

These were highly unusual circumstances, she realized. In a way, she and Remy were suspended in time while they were here, insulated from the mundane reality of everyday life. From the challenge of routine. But soon enough, they would have to fly home and resume their normal lives. It was by no means a given that the extraordinary bond they had formed here would survive the transition.

The waiter returned with Giana's Aviation, and she could see right away that the color was off. She took a sip and then a longer swallow. She'd had better, but it would do in a pinch.

She stopped the waiter before he could turn and leave. "I'll take another one, thanks." The man gave her a surprised look, and Giana glanced pointedly at her watch. She was self-sedating now, and she didn't care who knew it. The waiter nodded and strode quickly away.

By the time Devlin and Keisha appeared at the lounge's entrance, Giana had finished her second drink and paid the bill. She definitely felt more relaxed, and as she rose to go join her friends, she reminded herself that she had made it this far with her sanity intact. She would get back to Remy, and they would get through the next several hours together, whatever may come.

As they approached the church on St. Charles Avenue, the traffic grew increasingly more congested. It took Giana a moment to realize that the cars, and the dozens of people now streaming around them on foot, were all funneling toward St. Gregory's Cathedral. They were all here for Sabine.

A streetcar rumbled past on the center median, grinding to a halt a few yards away. She stopped the car and waited as a group of pedestrians, all sharply attired, disembarked and crossed the street in front of them. She had to admire the finery as they passed by, the men in dapper suits, escorting ladies in heels and fancy dresses, many of them accented with dramatic large-brimmed hats tilted jauntily to the side.

Devlin let out a low whistle from the backseat. "This is incredible," Keisha agreed.

A few of the pedestrians nodded and waved at Giana—Devereuxs she had met earlier in the week. She smiled and waved back before she set the car in motion, creeping steadily onward toward St. Gregory's elegant facade.

As Remy had promised, a handsome young man in a dark suit functioned in the role of parking lot attendant. He asked for her name, then directed them to a space near the church's side entrance. Moments later, they were parked and entering the building.

Once inside, the three women halted abruptly as a unit. The cathedral's central nave was spectacular. Giana gaped at the towering wooden arches, richly preserved under thick coats of varnish. They soared upward to meet in angular ribs at the vaulted ceiling, framing a single gathering space that was cavernous. Muted sunlight filtered down through stained glass windows, which were arranged in ornate rows along the side aisles and upper balconies. A cloying cloud of incense permeated the air, this vying for dominance with the mingled scents of perfume and cologne that wafted upward from a roving herd of humanity.

The hall was filled to near capacity. Many churchgoers had already seated themselves shoulder to shoulder in the long wooden pews. Others still milled about in the side aisles, their feet shuffling on the marble floors as they warmly greeted family members and acquaintances.

A line of mourners snaked down the broad center aisle, slowly inching toward the front of the church. Giana's eyes followed the queue to its endpoint in the light-filled apse, which housed the altar and a stunning altarpiece painted in shining gilt. The casket resided there. The mourners shuffled toward it in an unhurried stream, pausing one at a time to view the body. She stared, transfixed, as some individuals reached a hand inside the coffin and gently touched Sabine on her arm, or her hand, or her face.

A teenaged usher approached the three of them and politely inquired if they were Remy's friends from California. The girl smiled, and then she led them on a journey—back down the side aisle toward the church's main entrance, crossing to the opposite wall and then up the adjacent aisle toward the front of the church again.

Their young guide finally paused at the pew closest to the altar and motioned them forward. Giana spotted Max and Jerome, who were seated to Lucien's left. Remy stood talking nearby, and Giana couldn't get past the sight of her in that suit. It was black, of course, in a slim tailored cut. The white silk blouse had a flaring collar and was buttoned low on her chest. The effect was simple and classic—and unbelievably sexy.

Remy turned her head then and caught sight of Giana, and the look they exchanged set her pulse racing. Mortified, she glanced away, only to look again a second later. Remy's gaze persisted, and the heat in her stare was flagrant, and arousing, and incredibly inappropriate for the occasion.

In the next moment, Remy was standing in front of her, pulling her into a tight embrace. Cheeks flaming, Giana whispered fiercely in her ear, "Why, in God's name, are you *looking* at me like that!"

"Well, I didn't mean to!" Remy whispered back. "But you shouldn't have worn that *dress*."

Giana could hear the warm chuckle in her voice, could feel it vibrating in her chest, and she squeezed her harder. This was her Remy, coming back to life. Coming back to her.

Remy loosened her embrace but held on to both of Giana's hands, her gray eyes sobering as they took in her face. "I don't know how I can thank you for being here with me. Through all of this. Thank you." She paused. "You see? When I say it like that...it doesn't feel like it's enough."

"It's enough," Giana replied.

"Do you know that I love you?"

Giana inhaled and held Remy's gaze. She wished they could be alone. In a quiet room somewhere. Just the two of them. "Yes," she answered. "Yes, I do know that."

Remy stared at her a moment longer, and then she nodded and let go of her hands. She moved on to give her attention to Keisha and Devlin and then to the dozens of others who stood patiently waiting to greet her, all of them wanting to touch her, perhaps to feel that small piece of Sabine that lived on inside of her.

Before long, the priest approached the altar, his vestments surprisingly colorful. He was flanked by a pair of teens in similarly styled robes, and the three of them turned to silently face the congregation.

A general rustling could be heard as the churchgoers who were still standing moved to take the last of the remaining seats. Remy found Giana again and grasped her hand, and they claimed their place on Lucien's right.

A quiet fell over the building, accented only by the occasional cough and creaking of wood as someone shifted in a pew. And then a solitary voice rose up from the back of the church. Clear and strong, the gospel hymn projected through the cathedral, growing steadily louder until Giana turned and caught sight of the woman pacing slowly up the center aisle.

A dozen or more choir members marched in silent procession behind her. Male and female, they were identically dressed in lush purple gowns, trimmed at the cuffs and collars with shimmering gold lamé. The soloist was the only voice to be heard as they filed past and took their places in the choir box to the left of the altar.

It wasn't until the lead had reached the chorus of her song that at last the choir joined in. Their voices rose as one, in strident harmony, the sound of it bracing and melodious, swelling to fill the cathedral to its rafters. Giana gasped, and Remy's grip on her hand tightened, riding the wave of the symphony until the last notes had faded away.

Silence fell once again over the building, and the priest raised his arms, palms open and facing the ceiling. His voice was resonant as he said, "Let us pray."

The service that followed was beautiful and moving. The priest read from the Scripture, and more gospel hymns were sung by the choir, most of them songs Giana had never heard before. People rose to step up to the podium and speak. They talked about their love for Sabine and Sabine's love for her family and her church and her community.

Giana held Remy's hand in the center of her lap, cocooned between both of her own. The stress and the dread she had felt earlier that day had left her at the first note from the choir. She felt nothing other than gratitude now. It was an honor to be here to bear witness. To give tribute to someone who had clearly meant so much to so many people.

Well over an hour later, the last speaker stepped down from the podium. The priest and the altar boys rose to approach the coffin once again. One of the teens carried a folded cloth held forward in both of his hands, while the other carried a censer that swung gently on a long golden chain. The priest stood before the casket and raised his arms, his voice ringing out as he intoned a final prayer. He struck a match to light the censer, and wisps of smoke began to waft through the vents in the metal urn.

The priest turned and stepped up to the casket then, and Giana felt Remy's body go tense beside her. She tightened her grip on her hand and watched as the priest reached into the coffin and took hold of the silken lining. Remy's body began to tremble as he gently pulled the fabric up and over Sabine's face. Then he reached up and grasped the lid of the coffin and lowered it shut. The finality of that click was unbearable.

Remy's body sagged against hers, and Giana leaned into it, bearing the weight for the both of them. The priest took hold of the censer, and the two youths unfolded the pall, stretching it evenly between them before they lowered it over the casket. They stepped back as the priest began to swing the censer back and forth on its chain. He held it aloft and circled the coffin, the scented smoke billowing around him as he chanted a blessing in Latin.

He finished his circuit, and Giana saw his gaze come to rest on Lucien in the front pew. They exchanged a nod, and then the priest proceeded down the center aisle with the two altar boys in step behind him.

The voice of the choir's soloist rang out again, solitary and piercing, in a soulful dirge. Max and Lucien stood up and carefully climbed past Remy and Giana to exit the pew. They were joined in the center aisle by four other men. One of them

Giana recognized as Sabine's younger brother. Two of the others were cousins she'd met earlier in the week. And the last man, she couldn't remember.

Their faces somber, the pallbearers approached the casket and flanked it on either side. They each grasped a handle, and with a nod from Lucien, they hoisted the coffin off its stand, turning with it as a group. Max and Lucien led as they commenced a slow pace toward the main entrance of the church.

The usher who had greeted Giana and the others when they first arrived now reappeared in front of their pew. She bade them rise and follow the procession. Giana and Remy stood along with the rest of their party, and they all fell in step, escorts to the casket's final march down the aisle.

CHAPTER TWENTY-SIX

Remy opened the door to Cookie's office without knocking and set a latte down in the center of his desk. He turned from his computer screen and held his fingers against the side of the cup. Nodding his approval, he took a sip and swallowed, then stifled an enormous yawn.

"Whoa. Marla been keeping you up at night or what?"

Cookie glanced at her soberly, and then a slow, mischievous smile spread across his round cheeks.

"Well, all right," Remy said with a grin. "You still got it, Cooks. I don't care what anybody says."

She took a seat in the chair opposite his desk and stretched her legs out, crossing them at the ankles. Cookie locked his hands behind his head and leaned back in his chair to watch her. He remained that way for a few moments, openly assessing, until Remy finally lifted a shoulder and said, "What?"

"I don't know, boss. You've got this whole, sorta, relaxed vibe about you these days. Ever since you got back. I gotta say, it looks good on you."

Remy held his gaze for a moment, then snorted softly. She did feel good, she couldn't deny it. The pain of losing Sabine was no less severe—she was still welling up with tears at unpredictable moments throughout the day. When she talked to Pappy on the phone, it was damn near uncontrollable. But then, there was so much else to be thankful for, too.

She inhaled deeply and sat up abruptly in her chair. "Anyway. I need to take another look at Swaggett's interview tape this morning. I'm meeting with Erica Forsyte later on today to go over some options, and—"

"Wait. Don't tell me you're bringing *her* in on this."

"Look, Cookie. However, uh, *coarse* the lady's personality might be, you cannot deny she's one hell of a DA. And she's graciously carved out a sliver from her very busy schedule to help us try to salvage something out of this steaming shitpile of a case. I need to pick her brain from a legal standpoint—to see if there's anything at all to be done. Is that okay with you? Besides, do you really want to have a conversation about bringing other people in on the case?"

Cookie had already fallen all over himself apologizing for the debacle with Pierce and Swaggett. Nicolas Pierce was now the name never to be mentioned in Remy's presence. As luck would have it, Pierce had departed on vacation leave a few days before she'd returned to work. It was a good thing. She couldn't be sure what she would do the next time she saw him. The longer the cooling-off period before that happened, the better.

Cookie looked as if he were about to launch into another long-winded explanation, but Remy held up her hand. "Hey. What's done is done, Cooks. Water under the bridge." She inhaled deeply and stood up from her chair. "And don't worry. I'm not expecting you to sit in on the meeting with Forsyte, either."

The look of relief on his face was comical. Remy turned to leave. "Anyway, what's going on in the conference room today? I was gonna put us in there, but it looks like they're setting up for something major."

"Yeah, some kind of forensics symposium or something. The folks from next door are heading over."

"Oh, yeah? Everybody in the department, or…?"

Cookie eyed her with renewed interest. "So how are things working out with your scientist friend there, boss? You didn't happen to mention anything about the Swaggett sample by chance…"

Remy was halfway out the door, checking her cell phone for a message from Giana. It pinged in her hand, but the text was from Erica.

Something's come up in my schedule for later today. I can see you in five minutes, or not at all. Your choice.

Remy halted. "Shit. Forsyte is on her way over here. Uh, Cooks, the tape?"

"Well, I don't have it, boss. It's back in Evidence. You never said you wanted me to—"

"Yeah, okay, that's fine. I can run down and get it. Uh, would you be so kind…?"

Cookie wordlessly opened a drawer and proceeded to fill out the necessary form. Remy texted Erica while she waited.

No problem. I'll take what I can get. Text me when you're in the building.

Cookie handed over the form, and Remy was out the door in the next second, headed for the elevator. She punched the call button and waited, glancing up impatiently at the indicator light. The car seemed to be lodged on the first floor.

Swearing, she headed for the stairs. Her footfalls echoed in the musty hollow of the stairwell as she rapidly descended five flights to the basement. The lonely corridor that led to the evidence locker was a lengthy one. Remy covered the distance in seconds and slid to a halt in front of the gated cage, peering inside to see which hapless individual had drawn the short straw. It was Baker, of course. Fantastic.

Sgt. Baker's leg was the size of a hindquarter of beef. He'd somehow managed to prop it up on the corner of his desk, exposing the wiry hair that curled over the edge of his crew sock. A cigarette burned in an ashtray at his elbow. Remy stared at the thin line of white smoke as it drifted silkily upward to the ceiling. There was no smoking in the building. She held her tongue and waited in pained silence until Baker lowered his magazine and peered at her through Coke-bottle glasses. "Baker," she said with a nod.

Sgt. Baker stared blankly back at her. "You need something, Devereux, or are you just happy to see me?"

Remy slid the requisition slip through the opening in the window. "Take your time," she muttered, knowing full well that he would. She watched as the man heaved a beleaguered sigh.

He dropped his magazine on the desk and hoisted his tremendous bulk out of his chair. Slapping a paw at the requisition slip, he held it up to his face, squinting through his thick glasses at the small print on the form. Without a word, he turned and lumbered away, disappearing among the many rows of utility shelves that stretched deep into the building.

She tapped her foot and waited. Another message pinged in from Erica.

Pulling into the parking garage now. See you in your office.

Groaning, Remy peered into the evidence cage, relieved to see Baker already laboring back down the aisle toward her. He shoved a clipboard and a small plastic box of digital media through the opening in the window.

She grabbed the pen and scrawled her signature across the form. "You're a peach, Sgt. Baker, you know that? Don't ever change."

She didn't wait for his reply as she snatched up the box and headed back the way she'd come. Erica texted yet again as she reached the elevator and hit the call button.

This asshole won't let me through security.

"Christ," Remy muttered. She'd forgotten about the new security protocol. Glancing up, she noted the elevator car had finally reached the fourth floor now, apparently with no intention of leaving it. It was like a game of cat and mouse, only she had no idea which she was supposed to be.

She yanked open the door to the stairwell and took the steps two at a time. When she reached the building's main lobby entrance, there was a logjam of people trying to get through security. Erica was easy to spot as she paced off to one side, heels clacking against the marble floors, her thumbs busily pounding away at her smartphone.

She was dressed to the nines, as usual. Her makeup was flawless, her hair perfectly coifed. She paused with a hand on her hip, and the slit in her skirt opened just a tad wider, bringing one gorgeous gam enticingly into view. Remy had to give it to her—the lady was a knockout. But she still couldn't hold a candle to Giana Falco.

Erica glanced up at her then, her cool blue eyes flashing with irritation. Remy raised her chin in greeting, then leaned over to speak with Teddy behind the security console. He looked up at her with obvious relief.

In the next minute, Erica was waved through, oblivious to the aggravated glowers from the others still stuck in line. Remy handed her a plastic visitor's badge, and Erica recoiled from it as if it were an insect.

"New procedures," Remy said apologetically. She patiently held out the badge until Erica swiped it from her hand and dropped it into the side pocket of her attaché.

"Okay, then," Remy said brightly. "Uh, thanks again for making the time. I really do appreciate it." She watched Erica's face as the woman rolled her eyes and audibly inhaled. It mystified her now that they could have ever been a couple. For any amount of time.

"It's fine," Erica replied. "Let's just get on with it, shall we?"

They turned to head for the elevators, joining a small group of individuals already waiting there. Remy recognized Curtis Mason from Forensics, and she felt the impulse again to text Giana. One glance at Erica's pinched expression made her think better of it.

"What the hell is happening here, anyway?"

"Oh, I guess there's some sort of forensics conference going on upstairs."

The elevator doors opened, and the group of people began to crowd into the car. Remy held the doors and motioned for Erica to follow. Erica was clearly disinclined.

"Ah, perhaps we should wait for the next one?"

"Trust me," Remy said mildly, "it's only gonna get worse." She placed a hand on the small of Erica's back and firmly guided her forward.

The group of males in the elevator amiably shuffled together to make room for the two women. Remy noted with amusement that one of the young men—probably a lab technician—was openly gawking at Erica. Her face taut, Erica stepped into the car and inadvertently brushed up against him. The man's blush was violent behind his round spectacles. Remy felt a wave of inappropriate laughter rising in her chest, and she cupped a hand over her mouth, coughing as the doors slid closed and sealed them inside.

The air in the packed car was stale and uncomfortably warm. They made their painstaking ascent to the fourth floor in total silence, with the exception of a sneeze from someone in the back. The car dipped to a halt, and the doors slid open, and Remy and Erica were the first to exit.

But alas, the blushing lab technician moved forward too eagerly. His shoe caught the back of Erica's heel, causing her to stumble, and Remy seized her by the arm to prevent her from falling. The tech gasped in dismay, his complexion turning a new shade of crimson. "Oh, jeez! Miss, I'm so sorry!"

"Christ! Will you fucking watch where you're *going*?" Erica clamped a hand on Remy's shoulder as she struggled to regain her balance. She teetered on one foot, her shoe dangling from her toes.

Remy was overcome once again by the insane urge to giggle. She looked away, staring down the corridor as she tried to regain her composure. A group of people milled in the hallway outside the main conference room, and several of their heads turned to observe the commotion at the elevators.

A pair of stunning green eyes drew Remy's gaze like a magnet. Giana's expression was mild as she stared back, her eyebrows lifting slightly in her beautiful face. She glanced away, returning her attention to a colleague.

"Well, these are as good as ruined!"

Remy forced herself to focus on Erica again. She had jammed her foot back into her shoe. Still clinging to Remy's arm, she bent one leg and peered over her shoulder to inspect the large scuff mark that now coated the back of her cream-colored pump. Incensed, she looked up at Remy. "Well? Tell me we'll get to your office sometime today."

"Right. Of course. I mean, no." Remy peered down the hallway again, but the group of people had already begun to file into the conference room. Only stragglers remained in the hallway, and not one of them resembled Giana.

Erica made a sound in her throat, her annoyance clearly directed at Remy now.

"Right," Remy said again. "Uh, I'm gonna set us up someplace else. Where there's some room to spread out. Coffee?"

Remy wasted no time depositing Erica in the Interrogations room, with the Swaggett tape primed in the computer and ready for viewing. Then she made an excuse to leave. "I just need to grab my case notes and a hard copy of the file. I'll be back in two shakes. Coffee?"

"You already asked me that." Erica glanced at her watch.

Remy turned and promptly left the room, shutting the door behind her. She covered the distance to the conference room quickly. There was a small viewing window in the door, and she sidled up to it and peered inside. A quick scan of the backs of multiple heads told her Giana was not among them.

Remy turned on her heel and headed for the ladies' room. She rounded the corner into the small vestibule just as Giana was exiting.

"Oh." She halted abruptly. "So you found me."

Remy paused just a few inches away from her. "Are you surprised? I *am* a detective, after all."

"Inspector," Giana corrected.

"Whatever. How's your day going so far? You should've told me you were coming over here." She leaned forward to sample her intoxicating scent, but Giana quickly retreated a step. Her back met the wall behind her.

"I just came from your office," she said coolly. "Cookie told me you were busy. How's Erica?"

Remy hesitated a beat before she advanced again, closing the distance between them. "Oh, you know Erica. She's like a ray of sunshine."

"I see. Well, maybe you should hurry back to her then."

Remy snorted softly, then lowered her head to bury her nose in the silky hair, relishing the quiet sound Giana made as she slowly exhaled. Their bodies were very close now but not touching. The restraint required to maintain the distance was sweet agony.

"Oh, I'll get back to Erica, all right," Remy breathed. "As soon as I'm done here with you." Giana raised her head at that, her green eyes narrowing. Remy's pulse quickened in response. God, she was sexy.

"I don't know what you have in mind, Detective, but we're in public here. In case you've forgotten. You have colleagues all over the place, and so do I."

"I see. Well, maybe you should get back to them then."

Remy waited, praying Giana wouldn't turn and leave. She did not. Emboldened, she propped her hands against the wall on either side of Giana's head, carefully preserving the sliver of space between them. When Giana's eyes dropped to her mouth, the urge to kiss her was almost overwhelming. She held off, stoking the tension between them, until Giana released a quiet, frustrated sigh.

Her hands came up and grasped Remy firmly by the backs of her thighs, and still Remy did her best to show no reaction. Her hands continued upward, caressing and insistent, gripping her hard by the buttocks. Remy barely managed to stifle a groan.

"What are you doing?" she whispered, holding herself immobile, watching as Giana's pupils began to dilate and her nostrils widened in a flare.

Giana didn't answer. She slid her hands around to Remy's belly, traveling up and over her chest, flattening her palms against her breasts, circling the nipples with her thumbs and fingers, teasing, and then pinching hard. The sensations were running riot through Remy's body. Stubbornly, she held Giana's gaze, refusing to give in, even as she felt her resistance beginning to slip.

Then Giana dropped a hand to Remy's crotch. She inserted her fingers between Remy's thighs, her eyebrows lifting slightly as Remy's mouth gaped opened. Her touch was light and caressing at first, growing steadily firmer as she began a rhythmic kneading through the fabric of Remy's jeans.

"Oh, shit." Remy released a shuddering breath. "Giana…" She was paralyzed now, her hands glued to the wall. She couldn't move if she'd wanted to, and she was convinced they were about to be discovered at any second.

"Is this what you were looking for?" Giana's voice was all husk. Her eyes never left Remy's face. "I can keep going, if you want. Or maybe I should stop."

Remy bit back a moan, her muscles gone painfully rigid, her vision beginning to blur.

"You're right," Giana exhaled. "This really isn't the time or the place." Abruptly, she removed her hand from Remy's crotch and dipped out beneath her arm, leaving her standing there with her palms flat against the wall. Like a perp about to be frisked.

Giana glanced back as she stepped into the main hallway. "Dinner at your place tonight or mine?" Remy was still speechless, so Giana made the call. "Let's make it yours. Your headboard works better for a few of the things I have in mind."

When Remy returned to the interrogation room, Erica was well into the interview footage. Remy set the case summary down in front of her, along with a steaming mug of coffee. "Uh, sorry for the delay. I got hung up for a second there."

"How's Giana?" Erica didn't look up.

"What?"

Erica glanced at her and released a mild scoff, then went back to viewing the tape. Remy mutely took a seat at the table beside her.

After a few minutes, Erica paused the tape. "If the whole interview is like this, you're wasting your time." She picked up the document Remy had brought and began a rapid scan through the case notes. Remy watched, quietly amazed at the speed at which she could process information.

"So the search warrant was denied?" Erica glanced up, and Remy nodded. "Not surprising. Which judge did you use?" "Keriakas," Remy replied.

Erica snorted softly, shaking her head. "Resubmit it, and this time take it to Monroe. And make the request for an anticipatory warrant, pending the DNA results from the lab. That way you can move on both search and arrest simultaneously, should the opportunity arise."

"So you think we still have a shot at this?" Remy was incredulous.

"No, I don't," Erica said. She tossed the document on the table. "Whose bright idea was it to bring him in without an arrest warrant?" Remy drew in a breath. Erica didn't wait for the explanation. "Even if the DNA does match, you realize that particular sample will likely be suppressed at trial. Even if we could manage to get it in, you've given the defense plenty of ammunition here on the grounds of harassment alone."

Remy slumped back in her chair. "Well, obviously you know way more about the legal end of this than I do. But it seems to me, matching DNA ought to be a slam dunk, however we happened to come by it."

Erica shook her head impatiently. "It's complicated, Remy. And this discussion is purely academic unless you actually get something concrete back from the lab. What's taking so long on that, anyway? I would've assumed you'd be able to exert *some* degree of influence over there."

Remy held Erica's gaze for a moment, expecting to see a veiled hostility in her eyes. There was none. "Right. Well, sadly, the reports of my influence are greatly exaggerated."

The truth of the matter was, Remy had decided not to even mention it to Giana. It would've been a big ask, and she was beginning to question whether any of this Swaggett business was worth the effort. A seed of doubt about the man's guilt had been planted in her brain when she was still in New Orleans, and that suspicion had only continued to grow. As far as she was concerned, the Swaggett angle of the case was essentially a cleanup operation now. It was just good due diligence to completely eliminate the man as a suspect. She wasn't about to put Giana in an awkward position at work for something as underwhelming as that.

Erica was eyeing her now with open curiosity. "What's this? Trouble in paradise? Devereux, don't tell me you're losing your touch."

Remy scrutinized the cool blue eyes. To her surprise, there was a glint of actual humor in them, completely absent of malice. Remy raised her chin and chuckled lightly but made no reply. It was more than a little strange to be sitting here with Erica like this. Talking, but not really talking—about Remy's new girlfriend, of all people.

When she had asked to pick that big attorney's brain of hers about the case, it had been a way of extending an olive branch. She had no illusions that she and Erica would ever be great friends, but she did hope to reestablish a good professional rapport. A crack district attorney was a vital asset to have in her line of work, and she was fully aware that she had more to gain from their association than Erica did. It was all the more surprising then, that Erica had agreed to come here today. Yet, here she sat, and the mood between them was almost…affable.

Erica stood up and began to gather her belongings. Remy remained seated, quietly watching. "It was kind of you to send the arrangement, Erica. Thank you. The flowers were lovely."

Erica paused, feigning interest in the contents of her attaché case. "Yes. Well, I know how close you were to Sabine." She looked up and held Remy's gaze. "I was terribly sorry to hear about it, Remy."

"Thank you." Remy nodded briskly. She swallowed hard as the emotion surged up again. Erica didn't try to touch her, and Remy was grateful as she stared down at the table and waited for the swell to pass. "Okay," she said after a long moment. "It looks like you're all set. Let me walk you out."

CHAPTER TWENTY-SEVEN

Giana strode into the crime lab and set about flipping on lights and powering up equipment. She was alone at this early hour of the morning and therefore made no effort to stifle her gaping yawn. Finally left to her own devices last night, she'd been able to catch nearly seven hours of sleep. She was still operating at a deficit, however, and she didn't hesitate to blame it on Remy.

Their passion for each other showed no signs of cooling. Last night, in fact, was the first night they'd slept apart since before New Orleans. They had both agreed a small amount of distance would serve to their mutual benefit, but less than twenty-four hours into it, Giana was embarrassed to admit she already missed her detective terribly. She had it bad for Remy Devereux, there was no denying it.

She brought her attention back to the task at hand, determined to use her time in the empty lab wisely. Curtis would be absent for the first part of the week. He was serving at trial as an expert witness, which meant—as the lab's sole DNA analyst—everything he was working on would have to be put on hold in the meantime.

The system was horribly inefficient. Giana saw no reason why the world should grind to a halt due to one person's absence. She was perfectly skilled in the technique of polymerase chain reaction, a breakthrough lab technique developed in the 80s that made it possible to generate a near-complete DNA profile from the tiniest sample. Any forensic scientist worth her salt would be well studied in the PCR process, and Giana was no exception. This was a great opportunity to gain some hands-on experience, and truthfully, there was only one case she was interested in moving along. In the end, she was certain Curtis wouldn't mind.

She felt like a marauder as she invaded his workstation and scanned through his active files. Franklin Swaggett's submission was not among them. Clucking her tongue, she redirected her search to the storage locker at the back of the lab where the pending cases were kept and quickly found what she was looking for there. Pilfering the kit, she took it back to her workstation and promptly got to work.

* * *

Remy parked the Charger in the red zone across the street from the alley on Hyde. Weeks had passed since the day she'd first met Peabo here. Much had happened in the interim, but locating Rhonda Jenssen had never been far from her mind. With Swaggett all but out of the picture now, a potential eyewitness like Jenssen was the last best hope in the case. And Peabo was the only link to Jenssen she had. The chances she'd find the charming crooner here today were slim—it was more likely he'd packed up his carts and tent and moved to another location long ago. But it was worth a shot.

Exiting her vehicle, she peered across the street at the alley's entrance and was more than a little surprised by what she saw. The shopping cart shelter was still in place, with the boombox teetering on top of the pile. The soiled blanket had been upgraded to a waterproof tarp, and Peabo sat on the sidewalk a few feet outside his domicile, the rays of the morning sun warming his dark brown face.

But more interesting than Peabo was the person seated beside him. The individual appeared to be a female Caucasian, dark hair, of medium stature and weight. Or, as Peabo would put it, a skinny white girl with scraggly brown hair.

Checking for cars, Remy started across the street—at the same moment that Peabo seemed to catch sight of her. He leaned over and said something to his companion, and the woman's head turned sharply in her direction. Remy's hands came up in a harmless gesture. She slowed her pace as she quickly assessed the possible escape routes, angling her approach to cut off at least one of them. If it came down to a foot race, she was confident she would win. But that was an adversarial kind of introduction she'd prefer to avoid.

"Ms. Jenssen?" The woman didn't respond, and Remy halted her advance when she was about ten feet away. "I'd like to talk to you for a minute, if I could."

The woman's gaze shifted, glancing away and down the street.

"You're not in any kind of trouble," she said quickly. "I'd just like to ask you a few questions, if that's all right."

Rhonda's age could have been anywhere from her mid-twenties to her mid-forties—it was impossible to tell. Her face was acned, with scaly patches of red. She sucked her teeth in a gesture of annoyance but made no effort to flee.

"I'm Inspector Devereux," Remy said. "You came into the police station a few months back, isn't that right? After they found the woman in the dumpster. I was disappointed I didn't get a chance to talk to you that day. I'm the detective in charge of the case."

Rhonda turned to look at Peabo, who sat observing the exchange with keen interest. Remy raised her chin at him, and he nodded in return. "How you doin', girlie?"

"Hoping to get another serenade, if I'm lucky."

Peabo grinned. His teeth looked surprisingly strong and clean. And he seemed to be coughing less than before.

Remy turned her attention back to Rhonda, raising her eyebrows in a question. The woman exhaled and slapped her palms against the ground. She pushed herself to a standing position and wordlessly strolled into the alley past Peabo's tent. Remy followed.

Rhonda paused a few feet before they reached the dumpster. She pointed to a spot against the wall. "I was over there, up under some blankets and stuff. The car backed in, and this dude pulled something heavy off the back and threw it in the dumpster."

"Something heavy?" Remy pulled her notepad out of her back pocket. "You didn't see what it was?"

Rhonda crossed her arms over her chest. "No. But you could hear it was somethin' heavy."

"Did you look into the dumpster after the car drove off?"

Rhonda sucked her teeth. "Now why the hell would I do something like that?"

Remy didn't react. "And this was in the evening, Ms. Jenssen, or was it still daylight out? Do you remember the exact time and date?"

"I don't know." Rhonda shrugged, crossing her arms. "This was like, a day, maybe two days before they found her, I guess. I remember it was nighttime, though, 'cause I fell asleep right after."

Remy paused in her scribbling. "Had you been drinking that night, Ms. Jenssen? Or were you under the influence of any substance whatsoever?"

Rhonda refused to answer. Her chin came forward in a jut.

Remy exhaled, trying to hide her exasperation. "Okay. Let me see if I have this straight so far. You didn't actually see what went into the dumpster. You don't remember the time. And it was one or two or possibly three days before the body was discovered, but you're not sure which."

Rhonda stared at her defiantly.

"What kind of car was it, Ms. Jenssen? Do you recall?"

"It was a black truck. You know, like a pickup truck."

"Did you happen to notice the make and model? Or the license plate number?"

"I wasn't lookin for all of that." Rhonda's eyebrows puckered in irritation. "It was big. One of them monster-truck lookin' thangs. Looked brand new almost."

"Okay," Remy said mildly. "Was there anyone else besides the driver?"

Rhonda shook her head no.

"What did he look like? Can you describe him for me?"

Rhonda's gaze shifted away from her then, flicking down the alleyway and then back at Remy in a split second. "I couldn't really see him. It was too dark."

"Do you remember anything about him at all? Race, age, height?"

Rhonda used the toe of one grimy sneaker to work at a glob of chewing gum stuck to the ground. "He was white. That's all I could really tell." She was no longer interested in meeting Remy's gaze.

Remy waited, watching her closely. Rhonda had been truthful up until this point. What she'd had to offer had not been very helpful, but she had been telling the truth. Her sudden hedging was curious, to say the least. She decided to shift gears. "So what made you decide to come into the station that day?"

Rhonda glared at her. "Well, excuse me for being a concerned citizen. It ain't like I don't got better shit to do."

"Yes, ma'am. I absolutely appreciate your being a concerned citizen. I'm just disappointed I didn't get a chance to talk to you back then, when some of these details might've been fresher in your mind. Why did you leave the station house so fast that day?"

Rhonda's tell showed itself again. Her gaze shifted away for a millisecond before returning. "Like I said," she grumbled, "I got better things to do with my time. Hey, are we finished here yet? 'Cause they're about to start servin' lunch at Glide…"

"Of course," Remy said agreeably. "Thank you for taking the time to talk to me, Ms. Jenssen. Uh, is there any way I can follow up with you later? In case I need to ask any more questions?"

Rhonda was already backing toward the front of the alley. "I be around," she said. "Here and there."

Remy nodded and thoughtfully watched her go. She was surprised she didn't feel more disappointed. She'd spent months trying to track this woman down, and as it turned out, Rhonda Jenssen as a witness was a big fat zero. Nothing she'd said was of any value. The sound of something heavy going into a dumpster was far from compelling courtroom testimony. What she'd heard that night could have easily been an old tire or a roll of carpeting. The possibilities were endless.

That is, if she in fact had heard anything at all. Remy didn't work Vice—the hallucinations of a tweaked-out junkie were nothing she was familiar with. Rhonda had as much as admitted to being under the influence of something that night, which rendered anything she had to say about the incident worthless.

But still...

She'd been weirdly dodgy about getting a look at the driver. And then again on the topic of her visit to the station. There was obviously something about those two particulars she didn't want to discuss. Like maybe she'd seen something at the station that day. Or someone.

A feeling of unease began to settle over Remy's shoulders. Something didn't smell right here. Was it possible Rhonda had recognized somebody at the station house and gotten spooked?

Remy peered down the vacated alley. Terrible witness or not, maybe it wasn't such a good idea to let her walk away so easily. Remy knew where Rhonda was headed—she considered hoofing it over to Glide right now but then thought better of it. The woman was already reluctant. Running her down and interrupting her lunch wasn't the way to get her talking.

Remy's cell phone rang in her pocket, and she pulled it out, distractedly glancing at the screen. She gave a little gasp of pleasure when she saw who it was.

"Well, hello, gorgeous. I knew it. You can't live without me, can you? Say, whose dumb idea was it to sleep apart—"

"Remy. Hey, I need you to come over to the lab when you can. Preferably now, if that's possible. Or sometime in the next hour, before people start getting back from lunch?"

Remy paused, realizing Giana was serious. "Uh, sure. What's going on?"

"It has to do with the Swaggett sample. I have some questions about it. It's, uh…Well, I don't want to get into it over the phone. Can you just get over here as soon as you can?" She was already heading for the car. "Of course. See you in a few."

* * *

Giana forced herself to stop pacing and take a seat. She glanced at the wall clock again, just as a rapid knock sounded at the door. Exhaling, she crossed the lab quickly, momentarily forgetting her anxiety when the detective stepped into the room. Remy looked good. She seemed rested, and she was wearing those harness boots with the square heel that Giana loved. They made her look about eight feet tall.

Remy's eyes returned the inspection. She glanced around the lab, obviously noting that they were alone. Before Giana could react, she was pulled into Remy's arms. The kiss was stolen, and delicious, and frustratingly brief. Remy released her, and Giana took a quick step back to steady herself.

"Um. That's not why I asked you to come over here, Detective." She turned and strode away before Remy could grab her again.

Remy followed close on her heels. "All business this morning, I see. I missed you, too, by the way." Her tone was light, unworried. "Hey, how is it that you're the one working on this Swaggett thing, anyway? I thought Curtis Mason did all the DNA stuff for the lab."

"He does. But with his workload, it would've taken him at least another two weeks to get to it."

"Cookie put you up to this, didn't he?" Remy protested. "I didn't tell him to do that. I'm pretty sure we're barking up the wrong tree with this guy, anyway."

Giana glanced back at her. "Is that why you neglected to mention it to me? You didn't think I could help to maybe move this process along at all?"

"Well, of course. But I didn't see the point of you going out of your way for something that isn't even—"

"The Swaggett sample is a match."

"What?" Remy stopped short.

Giana paused to look at her and nodded. Then she was in motion again, stealing the stool from a neighboring workstation to roll it over next to her own. She took a seat and glanced up at Remy's stunned expression. "Sit, please. I have some things I need to explain to you first. Before you do anything else."

Mute, Remy sat down beside her. She watched as Giana powered on a pair of twin color monitors that were set up on the countertop in front of them.

"First of all," Giana began, "I have a question about the procedures that are typically followed when you collect DNA from a suspect. Is the subject in question ever allowed to handle, or in any way come into contact with, the outer packaging of the container before it's sent off to the lab?"

Remy frowned. "You mean the actual box we send to you? Of course not. We collect the swabs and hair or whatever, and then we take it out of the room to wrap and label it. The perp never touches anything."

Giana nodded. "That's what I thought. And Swaggett's sample—that was handled while you were still in New Orleans, right? You didn't actually observe the collection process on that one?"

"That's right." Remy's brow had furrowed with a look of concern. "It was either Cookie or Pierce. They were both on it at the time."

Giana turned to face the monitors. "Okay. What we have displayed in front of us here are two examples of intact genetic profiles."

Remy leaned forward to peer at the colored screens. Giana glanced at her, realizing that, while she herself saw code and critical information, Remy probably saw the pretty peaks and valleys of a mountain range. She used her pen as a pointer.

"To grossly oversimplify things, there are six basic genetic markers we rely on to compare one genetic profile against another. These are the peaks you see here. When there's a discrepancy between two panels, it's usually pretty obvious."

She typed several commands into the keyboard and pressed enter. She watched as the two images began to merge. "Swaggett's sample is the one on the left. And that's me on the right."

Remy glanced at her. "You tested yourself?"

Giana nodded. "Well, I needed a control. And in this case, it didn't hurt to do a dry run first."

The images finished merging, one superimposed over the other. Giana used her pen to indicate multiple points on the screen. "You see? You can easily identify the areas where things don't line up. It's pretty obvious that these two are not a match, right?"

Remy glanced at her and shrugged. Giana clacked away at the computer again. Her own data disappeared from the display, and a split-screen image appeared on the right-hand monitor.

"Okay. Now, here we have the two hairs that were recovered from the bodies of Willard and Everett. You can see that the profiles are fragmented and incomplete." She placed her pen on the various areas of white space that interrupted the mountain ranges. "You can't make a meaningful comparison of one against the other because the critical markers are either missing or they don't correspond. *However.* When you're using a complete profile as your starting point—such as Swaggett's here on the left—you can compare each one against it and make your analysis that way."

She punched more commands into the keyboard and hit enter, folding her arms as both of the images on the right-hand monitor began to migrate to the left. They superimposed over Swaggett's profile, and Giana looked at Remy expectantly.

"I don't know what I'm supposed to be seeing here." Remy's tone was laced with frustration.

"Remy, they're a perfect match. Both of the hairs from Willard and Everett are a perfect match with Swaggett's."

Remy stared at the monitor for a moment. "I can't fucking believe this," she muttered quietly. She reached for her cell phone, but Giana laid a hand on her wrist to stop her.

"Wait. Just let me show you one more thing." She typed at the keyboard and brought up yet another profile on the right-hand monitor. "As I said, before I began this analysis this morning, I did a dry run first. I've only actually performed this procedure a few times, and frankly, I needed the practice. I wanted to run through all the steps once, from start to finish, just to make sure I had it down correctly, before I approached the actual evidence.

"I had my own sample, of course, but to make a proper comparison, I needed another guinea pig. There wasn't anyone else in the lab, so… I used saliva I recovered from the adhesive on the kit's labeling."

Remy looked at her sharply. Giana shrugged. "I was improvising." She nodded at the profile on the right-hand screen. "That's it right there." She hit the enter button on the keyboard and felt her heart begin to pound as the image migrated to the left monitor. It superimposed over Swaggett and Everett and Willard—in a perfect match.

Remy stared at the monitor. "Is that…" She glanced at Giana and then back at the screen. "That's a match? You're saying they all match?" Giana nodded, watching as comprehension dawned on Remy's face, followed by confusion, and then disbelief. "Wait. But that's not possible. How is that possible?"

Giana shook her head. "I'm afraid that's not my purview, Detective. I can't tell you who handled the kit. All I can tell you is this: the person who licked the seal on that package's labeling is the same individual who provided the samples inside it. As well as the hairs recovered from the victims' bodies. Those hairs are Caucasian, remember, so that eliminates Cookie."

They sat staring at each other, unmoving. The look on Remy's face told Giana she was right to feel the sense of alarm she'd been resisting up until now. A cold finger of fear wrapped around her as a picture of Nick's lopsided smirk sprang into her mind. She'd been alone with him. Multiple times. And the last time had been…harrowing.

Remy stood up abruptly from the stool. "Just…let me get this straight here. So what you're saying is, you think he swapped out the samples. You think he dumped Swaggett's and replaced them with his own?"

Giana didn't respond. The silence in the lab was oppressive. Remy raked both hands through her hair, clasping them at the back of her neck.

"Uh…Okay," she said after a moment. "We can activate the warrant on Swaggett now. That's the first thing we need to move on."

"But…" Giana started to protest.

"I have to, Giana. I know, it looks like he's being set up, yes. But I can't take the risk. In case something went wrong here and Swaggett really is our guy."

"And what about…?" Giana didn't want to say his name.

"I have to talk to Cookie," Remy said, beginning to pace. "I have to find out what happened with that sample. To see if maybe there was somebody else besides Pierce who could've had access to it. And then… Shit, I don't know. We take it to Bronson, and let him make the call. In the meantime, can you run these tests again? And maybe—"

"Get a second opinion? Of course."

"I'm sorry, Giana. It's not that I don't trust your work."

"No, I completely agree with you." She blew out an unsteady breath. "We have to be sure."

Remy suddenly pulled her into a tight embrace, and Giana squeezed her fiercely back. She was unable to control the tremor that ran through her body.

"You're okay," Remy whispered. "Everything's going to be fine, all right? I'm sorry, baby, but I have to go."

CHAPTER TWENTY-EIGHT

Remy slowed the car as Swaggett's address came up on the right. She cruised past the apartment building and spotted a good parking spot across the street and several houses down. Making a quick U-turn, she maneuvered the Charger into it and cut the engine. Cookie leaned forward to peer through the windshield at the building.

A narrow cut above dilapidated, the two-story structure appeared to hold maybe eight units. A rusted iron fence enclosed the property. The dented security gate came flush up against the broken concrete sidewalk in front.

"What a dump." Cookie checked his watch and drummed his fingers against his knee. "Did you get an ETA on that CSI crew yet? Where the hell are they?"

Remy lifted a shoulder. "They told me one hour. That was about an hour ago."

"We should go in," Cookie grumbled. "He could be in there right now."

A patrol car had been dispatched to Glide Memorial some hours ago. The officers were unable to locate Swaggett there.

Remy had opted not to send another one to his apartment building. Whatever evidence existed inside, she wanted it collected and carefully preserved. A couple of young boots kicking the door in was not the way to do that.

"If he's in there, we'll handle it," Remy said. "Let's just sit tight for now."

Cookie loudly exhaled and shifted in his seat. "I can't believe it really turned out to be this fucker. I mean, this cat was as cool as a cucumber when we brought him in." He shook his head. "Must be one of those freak nutbags. Could eat your brains right out of your skull and never bat an eye."

Remy kept her silence beside him. She hadn't decided yet how she wanted to broach the topic of Pierce. "That day you brought Swaggett in," she said after a moment. "You guys used the standard messenger service, right? When you sent his sample to the lab?"

Cookie glanced at her. "Hmm? No, uh, Pierce walked it over himself. Said something about needing to preserve the chain of custody."

"So he was the one who collected the sample too?"

"No, that was me. I did the swabs and everything and handed them off to Pierce so I could keep working on Swaggett. Kept him there for another hour and couldn't get a damn thing out of him. The guy is one cold fish, let me tell you."

"So you don't know if anybody else handled the kit after that. Besides Pierce."

Cookie turned to look at her. "No, boss. But I'm pretty sure it was all Pierce. What, uh…What are you getting at here?"

Remy shook her head as they both glanced out the window, distracted by a low-rider coupe cruising slowly down the street. The bass thumping from the car's stereo vibrated inside the Charger.

"That black Mustang that Pierce drives," Remy said. "Is that his only vehicle, do you know?"

"Naw, he's got a *nice* truck. F-250 SuperCab. Four-by-four, raised suspension, all terrain tires. Pretty fucking sweet. Uses it when he goes up to Sebastopol to fish. Keeps threatening to take me with him, too, one of these times, but…"

"Is it black?"

"The truck? Yeah..." Cookie was staring at her now.

"You mentioned he had that detail in the Tenderloin a while back. When was that again?"

"I don't know. Probably six months ago, I guess. Why?"

Remy didn't answer him. She was too busy tracking another vehicle as it rolled quietly past them on the street. She used her chin to point at the black Mustang. Cookie turned, and they both watched as the car came to a stop, then reversed into a parking spot halfway down the street. A moment later, Nick Pierce emerged from the driver's side.

Remy and Cookie watched in stunned silence as Pierce checked the street, peering first in one direction and then the other, his gaze slipping right past the Charger without seeing them. He shut the car door and quickly approached Swaggett's building.

"Hey. What the..." Cookie grabbed hold of the door handle, moving to get out of the car. Remy grabbed hold of his arm to stop him.

"It's a lot to explain right now, Cooks. But I need you to trust me."

Cookie released the handle and slowly leaned back in his seat. They both watched as Pierce reached the building's entrance and tried the gate. Finding it locked, he rapidly pressed at multiple buttons on the intercom, glancing down the sidewalk again in both directions. The jarring buzz of the gate release could be heard from where they sat.

Moving quickly, Pierce pushed opened the gate and moments later disappeared into the building. Cookie turned and gaped at Remy in confusion.

"We wait," she said. She glanced at her watch to mark the time.

Minutes later, Pierce reemerged from the building. He peered down the street again, then slipped out the gate and strode quickly back to his vehicle. Remy watched as the Mustang promptly pulled away from the curb and proceeded down the block. She forced herself to wait until the brake lights had disappeared around the corner.

She was out of the car then, Cookie exiting on his side a split second later. They crossed the street together and reached the security gate a moment after that. Remy didn't hesitate to use Pierce's technique to gain access. They were through the gate in seconds and found the front door to the building unlocked.

Inside, the hallway was narrow and dimly lit. The pungent odor of ammonia permeated the air. There were only four doors to choose from, and they halted in front of the one marked 3A. Remy flattened her back against the wall, her hand on the grip of her pistol, while Cookie put his ear up to the door. After a moment, he pounded his fist hard against the flimsy material.

"SFPD! We have a warrant to search the premises!"

They waited, listening for any sound from inside the apartment. Cookie looked at Remy with a question in his eyes. She nodded, and he stepped back and used the heel of his boot to deliver a powerful kick. The door shuddered, a deep split snaking through the cheap wood of the jamb. Cookie reared back and kicked again, and the door flew open, slamming back against the interior wall.

Guns drawn, they entered the unit with caution. She cast her eyes about the shabby room. A tattered blanket was hung across the only window. Sunlight struggled weakly in through the rips in the fabric. She held her position as Cookie silently departed to check the other rooms. He returned in seconds and gave the all-clear.

They holstered their weapons as Remy moved to the window and yanked the blanket off its hooks. Pale gray light fell into the room. There was a mangled couch that had seen better days. The coffee table was littered with beer cans and an old hubcap that served for an ashtray. It overflowed with a mountain of ash and cigarette butts. Notably, the floors of the apartment were bare. There were no rugs or carpeting to speak of—least of all in the shade of Sunflower Dreams.

A card table sat against one wall near the kitchen, and it was covered with all manner of drug paraphernalia. Sorting trays and a digital scale. Plastic bags and little squares of tin foil. A stack of blue milk crates sat on the floor next to the table, and Remy immediately recalled that day she'd first run into Swaggett at Glide. With his dolly stacked full of blue crates.

She pulled a small bundle of latex gloves out of her pocket and tossed two at Cookie. She wriggled into a pair of her own as she walked over and stood in front of the milk crates. They were all empty except for the one on top. She selected a carton and pulled it out, noting instantly that the weight wasn't right. Carefully, she worked open the seal at the top and peered inside. Inverting the carton, she shook the white brick out on the table. It was wrapped in plastic and duct tape, she estimated maybe half a kilo of heroin or coke. A vice cop's dream.

Remy left the drugs on the table and proceeded down the short hallway toward the rear of the apartment. The bedroom was small and equally drab, its window covered by a set of battered metal blinds. The bed was unmade, and a small dresser sat against one wall. Otherwise, the room was depressingly bare. Remy edged around the bed to get to the window, yanking at the cord on the blinds until the slats came up at a lopsided cant.

She turned to let her eyes roam the room, eventually coming to rest on the cluttered dresser top. There was a hairbrush, a bottle of cologne, and sundry personal items. But what snagged her gaze was the glint. A tiny fleck of gold in an otherwise grim canvas.

Barely breathing, she stepped to the dresser and stood staring down at the necklace. She lifted it, draped over the tip of one gloved finger, and held it up to the window. The cloverleaf pendant dangled at the end of its chain, turning slowly, like the rotating beacon atop a lighthouse, the sunlight peeking intermittently through the tiny H's punched in the metal.

* * *

Giana let the door swing shut behind her, hurrying into the kitchen as one of the grocery bags began a deliberate slide down her hip. It was the one with the carton of eggs inside. She barely made it in time, lifting up on her tiptoes to shove the bags safely onto the counter. With a relieved sigh, she glanced at the clock, wondering if it was too early to get started cooking dinner.

She hadn't heard from Remy since their meeting in the lab, but she was counseling herself not to be overly concerned about that. Things were heating up with the investigation—she was sure the detective had her hands full. There was no need to worry. This was all part of the territory when your girlfriend was a cop. She supposed she'd better start getting used to it.

She finished unpacking the groceries and paused to check her phone again. If she sent another text at this point, it was going to start to look needy. She forced herself to set the phone aside but swiped it off the counter immediately when it started to ring. "I was wondering when you'd call! I was just about to get dinner started if—"

"Giana. Are you at home right now?" Remy's voice sounded strange. "Stay there, okay? I'm on my way over."

"Uh. Okay. That's perfect. I was thinking I'd do a nice pasta—"

"Giana, listen to me. It's Nick."

"What?" Giana's heart began to knock in her chest, even before she fully understood what Remy was telling her.

"It's him. It's too much to get into over the phone, but we've got an APB out on him now. He's gonna know about it, of course, but I'm sure he'll be picked up pretty quick. Probably within the hour. Look, there's nothing for you to worry about, all right? But stay inside for now. And don't open the door for anybody but me."

"Remy…" Giana was having trouble breathing.

"Is the front door locked?"

"Jesus, Remy. You're scaring the shit out of me."

"Go and lock the door, Giana. Do it right now."

It was an order, and she felt her legs moving toward the front door. She locked the knob at the handle, then slid the deadbolt into place. Her hands were shaking. "There, okay? It's locked."

Remy exhaled into the phone. "I'm sorry, babe, I don't mean to freak you out like this. It's just a reasonable precaution, that's all. Until we can locate him. Look, Cookie is dropping me off and we're just a couple of blocks away. I'll be there in two shakes, all right? See you soon."

Remy clicked off, and Giana stood there with the phone to her ear. The evening had taken on an eerie surrealness that she wanted to wake up from. She would open a bottle of wine, that's what she would do. Remy would be here in a few minutes, and everything would be fine.

A loud knock sounded at the door, and she nearly shrieked. Her mind immediately began to rationalize, actually considering the possibility that Remy could have teleported from Cookie's car to the front door of her apartment in seconds. She concluded it was unlikely.

The knock sounded again, even more demanding this time, and she clapped a hand over her mouth. She watched as the doorknob jiggled. Her heart slamming in her chest, she held perfectly still. Several seconds passed in silence. Gingerly, on the balls of her feet, she stepped up to the door and peered through the viewhole.

Nick's image on the other side was distorted, like a funhouse mirror. His legs were too small for his body, and his head was oversized, looming above his chest like a balloon. He leaned forward and pressed his eye against the viewhole.

"Giana…" He called her name in a singsong voice. "I know you're in there, baby. You wanna come out and play?"

She backed away from the door. She didn't stop until she'd collided with the couch, so startled by the contact she nearly toppled over it. Her fingers trembling, she sent a text to Remy.

He's here.

"Giana!" There was a loud thud against the door. It sounded like Nick had kicked it. "I'm trying to fucking apologize here! Why won't you fucking let me do that?" The door shook again with a tremendous thud, and she jumped as the phone pinged in her hand.

Call 911. Stay on the phone with them. I'm almost there.

"I heard that!" Nick called through the door. "Who are you texting with in there? That fucking dyke whore? Tell her to get her ass over here. The three of us can have a little fun!"

Giana dialed 911, holding the phone to her ear as she numbly walked into the kitchen. She pulled a chef's knife out of the block.

"Nine-one-one, what is your emergency?" The dispatcher's voice was nasal and tinny. She sounded as if she were a great distance away.

"Hello? There's, there's…"—Giana swallowed—"there's an intruder trying to get into my apartment."

"Please verify your address, ma'am."

"What?"

"You're calling from a mobile phone, ma'am. I need you to verify the street address and the apartment number where you are."

Giana rattled off the information, walking back into the living room to stare at the door. It was a solid door, she told herself. It was made of solid, sturdy construction. She jumped as another loud crash shook it in its frame. "He's trying to break down the door."

Nick shouted from the other side. "What's that? Did you call the police, honey? Tell them I'm already here." He laughed. A strange, high-pitched cackle she'd never heard him make before.

The dispatcher was speaking to her. "…officers on the way. You're doing fine, ma'am. Don't hang up the phone, okay? Just stay here with me."

The door shuddered again, and Giana watched as the wooden frame dislodged. Chips of paint and plaster fluttered to the floor.

"Ma'am? Did you hear me? Is there another room in the apartment that you can get to and lock yourself in? Go there now."

Giana nodded, no longer able to speak. She remained where she stood as the door shook again with a heavy bang.

"Ma'am, are you there?"

"Mm-hmm."

"Is the intruder known to you?"

"What? Yes. He's, uh…"

"Can you tell me his name?"

"Yes, it's Nicolas Pierce. He's a police officer. He's, uh, he's wanted for murder."

"Nicolas Pierce. Okay, we've got it. You're doing great, ma'am. Are you in the other room yet?"

Giana tightened her grip around the handle of the knife. Her mind screamed at her feet to move. She stood motionless as the door shook violently once again and finally burst open.

* * *

The elevator doors glided open with a warbled ding. Remy stepped into the carpeted hallway, weapon drawn, a round in the chamber. She felt like she was underwater. Her movements were sluggish. Sound reached her ears in distorted reverberations. A figure stood midway down the hallway, and Remy focused on it, attempting to categorize its size and shape. She watched as it lifted one leg and kicked.

The sharp crack of splintering wood shattered the haze. She snapped out of her stupor, her senses zooming in with extreme acuity. The figure stumbled forward and regained its balance, and she trained her Glock on the center of its body mass. Her voice bellowed in the empty hallway. "Pierce!"

Nick straightened and turned his head. His body remained in profile, his firing hand hidden from view.

"Show me your hands, Pierce! *Now!*"

Remy barely caught the movement as Nick turned and fired. She registered the muzzle flash a split second before she squeezed off a round and dropped to the carpet. Several more shots exploded in the corridor around her. She rolled and came upright in a crouch against the wall. There was no cover. She took aim and fired again as Nick turned and sprinted in the opposite direction. He disappeared through the fire exit door at the far end. She rose to her feet and tore down the hall to Giana's apartment, careening to a halt in the open doorway.

Giana stood motionless in the center of the living room. Her eyes were the size of saucers, but otherwise she appeared unharmed. Remy quickly crossed the room and removed the knife from her hand. She stepped quickly toward the kitchen, leaning across the island to drop the knife in the sink.

"Don't go near that again," she said, returning to Giana's side. She was trembling uncontrollably now, and Remy pulled her into a close embrace. "Uniforms are coming," she said in her ear. "Just stay calm and answer their questions when they get here." She looked into Giana's face. "You know I have to go after him, right? Tell me you're gonna be okay." Giana blinked and nodded. Remy kissed her hard on the mouth, then turned to race out of the apartment. She nearly collided with Liz, who now stood gaping in the doorway.

"What just...? Were those gunshots?" Breathing heavily, Liz stared in confusion at the splintered doorframe then back at Remy again.

"It's all right. Cops are on the way." She kept her voice calm as she stepped around the stunned woman. "Take care of Giana, okay? I have to go."

She reached the end of the corridor in seconds and halted at the fire exit. Crouching low, she pushed the heavy door open a crack, then a little wider, and listened. Faint, echoing sounds could be heard from several stories below. She straightened and stepped into the stairwell, leaning forward to peer cautiously over the railing. The painted handrails spiraled like an Escher drawing eight stories down. She could detect no sign of movement.

She took the stairs at a trot, pausing periodically to listen, trying to control her breathing, straining to hear any sound that wasn't her own. She was alone in the stairwell until she hit the landing on the ground floor. The door burst open, and Cookie trained his firearm at her face, at the same instant that she drew on his chest. They both exhaled.

"He didn't come your way?"

Cookie shook his head, and they both glanced down the final flight of stairs. The garage level was below them. Cookie took the lead as they descended the steps, shoulders brushing against the wall. When they reached the bottom, he paused to listen at the door. With a nod, he quickly yanked it open, and they entered the garage together, Cookie scanning right, Remy covering his left. The concrete floor sloped downward in one direction, and Cookie pointed at his chest and silently headed that way. She took the ramp leading up to the street.

Distant traffic noises drifted in through the gated entrance. Remy trained her ears to focus on sounds from inside the garage. She moved forward on the balls of her feet, drawing deep breaths in through her nostrils, holding them a second before she breathed out again, willing her heart rate to slow. Her eyes scanned continuously, panning left to right, chest level to the floor and back again, watching for a shadow or any hint of movement as she passed row after row of parked vehicles. She made a quick about-face to check her rear, then continued forward. Police sirens could be heard approaching now. Flashes of blue and red light strobed into the garage, casting eerie shadows against the walls.

She had almost reached the end of the row when Nick came hurtling at her from the right. She turned as his body slammed into hers, her weapon discharging, the thunderous explosion reverberating in the garage. Nick's momentum took them both to the ground, Remy gasping as her elbow connected with the concrete. A white-hot flash of pain shot up her arm. The gun flew from her grip.

Nick's hands clawed at her throat, clamping around it like a vise, pressing down on her windpipe as she struggled under his weight. Lungs burning, she writhed and twisted beneath him, franticly kicking until she managed to wedge a knee between their bodies. Nick's arms straightened, but he held on, his grip like a python around her neck.

Remy felt the life beginning to ebb out of her, a black fog closing in around the edges of her vision. She drove her knee hard into his abdomen, pushing with the last of her strength. His grip loosened on her throat, and she sucked in a gasp of air, clawing furiously at his wrists, swinging blindly at his face.

She felt it when her fist contacted the bridge of his nose. She heard the dull pop of cartilage breaking. Nick grunted, and she gyrated her body like a madwoman, until at last she had wrestled free. Coughing, she scrambled across the pavement, moving in the direction she thought she'd heard her handgun go, dead certain in the next instant she would hear the blast, feel the searing heat as the bullet ripped into her spine.

She spotted her Glock and lunged for it, seizing it in her hands as she rolled onto her back. Her vision was clear when she took aim at the midpoint of Nick's sternum. He froze in a crouch, panting, his hands hanging poised at his sides. His weapon was still holstered. They stared at each other, unmoving, their breathing ragged, both of them fully aware that Remy had the drop.

She swallowed with difficulty. Her throat was on fire when she spoke, her voice a croaking rasp. "I'd like you to go ahead and try it, Nick. Please."

Time slowed again as she watched the cocksure grin slide into place. His hand reached for his weapon, and she fired two rounds into the center of his chest.

Almost simultaneously, the garage exploded with three more shots. Nick's body spun and dropped to the ground, and Remy's vision focused in on Cookie, who was standing a few feet beyond. They locked eyes, a faint haze of gun smoke drifting in the air between them. They were directly in each other's line of fire, and Remy forcefully exhaled, grateful their aims had been true.

Cookie holstered his pistol and came trotting over to help her, grabbing her by the hand as she struggled to a standing position.

"You okay, boss?"

She nodded, wincing as the agonizing throb in her right elbow finally began to register. She heard the drone of the garage gate lifting, then strained voices and footsteps rapidly approaching. She holstered her weapon, and she and Cookie both pulled out their badges, displaying them prominently as the cavalry came running around the corner.

CHAPTER TWENTY-NINE

Giana glanced up from her newspaper as Remy came into the bedroom, managing a loaded serving tray with one arm. The other arm was still immobilized in a sling. "What are you doing, you knucklehead? You should've let me do that for you." She tossed the newspaper aside as Remy bent at the knees and carefully lowered the tray onto her lap.

"Oh, don't be ridiculous," Remy groused. "I'm not an invalid."

"Well, you make a terrible patient," Giana scolded. She glanced up in time to catch the slight wince on Remy's face as she pulled the sling over her head. She tossed it on the chair in the corner, and Giana shook her head but held her tongue, surveying the collection of items on the tray in front of her. There was a stack of mail, two mugs of hot coffee, and a tulip in a little vase. A wicker basket held something mysterious bundled up in cloth.

Remy climbed into the bed beside her, holding her injured arm out at an angle. "Was that the article on Pierce you were reading?"

Giana nodded, releasing a heavy sigh. "That woman locked up in his cabin? She was trapped up there for something like four days. Can you imagine? She must've been scared out of her mind. Just sitting there waiting. Dreading the moment he would come back." She lifted a coffee from the tray and took a sip. The mug trembled in her hand. "You know, he kept trying to get me to go with him to that cabin. He must've asked me twenty times. I can't stop thinking about what would've happened if I'd said yes."

"But you didn't." Remy used her good hand to grab hold of one of Giana's. She interlaced their fingers and squeezed. "You didn't. And now you're safe here with me." The gray eyes were clear and steady. The bruising around her neck was almost gone.

"What about Swaggett? Did he have anything to do with it?"

Remy shook her head. "They're bringing him up on drug charges, but it looks like he's not connected to the murders in any way. I'm thinking Pierce found out that Swaggett was already on our radar—thanks to me, of course—and he decided to capitalize on that by swapping out their DNA samples and planting evidence in the guy's apartment." She looked at Giana with open admiration in her eyes. "He might've gotten away with it too, if it hadn't been for this brilliantly talented...smart... ridiculously sexy forensic scientist who stepped in and—"

Giana shushed her. "Oh, stop it. We do make a great team, I'll give you that. But you would've had the situation well in hand, with or without me."

Remy snorted softly, gazing into her eyes for a moment. "Hey, look at this." She pulled a postcard from the stack of mail on the tray and handed it over. The front side was a glossy snapshot of Max and Jerome. They were handsome and grinning, standing in front of a beautiful old greystone in Chicago's Lincoln Park.

"They got the house?" Giana was amazed. "Wow, that was fast."

"Well, Max had a connection, of course. And real estate is never a bad investment to hear him tell it. They'll be in escrow for a while, but yeah, the place is theirs. God, he is so excited. He actually believes he's going to talk Pappy into moving up there with them."

Giana gave her a dubious look as she handed the postcard back.

"Yeah," Remy agreed. Chuckling, she gathered the rest of the mail and dropped it on the floor on her side of the bed. "They want us to come visit, of course. As soon as they're done sprucing it up."

"Well, that sounds like fun." Giana kept her eyes on her coffee mug. "We could spend a few days in Philadelphia while we're at it. My aunt has plenty of room. We can stay with her." She waited, then finally glanced at Remy.

"You want me to meet your aunt?" Remy's eyes went wide with a look of mock horror.

"Among others," Giana replied. "I'm dying to see how you and my brother Anthony will get along." She watched Remy's eyes grow wider still. "Oh, come on. It's only fair. I put up with your relatives for an entire week. Like, *all* of them."

Remy snorted softly. She brought Giana's hand up to her lips and kissed her knuckles. Then she leaned over to nuzzle at her ear.

"I'm perfectly serious, you know," Giana murmured.

"Oh, I have no doubt that you are." Remy's voice was warm with laughter as she continued to nuzzle.

"Remy," Giana said quietly. "Will you do something for me?"

"Hmm? Anything."

"One of these days, when you're ready…I'd like you to talk to me about your mom."

Remy went still beside her. "You mean Sabine?"

"No, sweetie. I don't mean Sabine."

Remy straightened, facing forward in the bed. She lifted one of the mugs from the tray and took a sip. "Well, what do you want to know about her?"

Giana shrugged. "Anything. Everything. Whatever you want to tell me. I just want you to *want* to tell me."

Remy looked at her and held her gaze for a long moment. Ultimately, she nodded. "I can do that."

Giana nodded too. "Okay then."

Remy took another sip from her mug and glanced down at the tray. "I brought you something."

Giana widened her own eyes now as she remembered the wicker basket. She looked down and approached it with caution, using her fingertips to carefully unfold the cloth. She gave a little gasp when she saw the *cornetti* inside. They were still warm. "Oh my God, Remy, you didn't. Where did you *get* these?"

"I have my resources," Remy replied, obviously very pleased with herself.

Inhaling deeply, Giana selected one of the gorgeous pastries and took a bite. She closed her eyes as the flaky, buttery goodness filled her mouth. Then Remy's face was up against hers, nuzzling and kissing, licking at the crumbs on her lips. She gave a muffled protest, trying to chew at the same time that she kissed Remy back, torn between the pastry and her lover's lips, delighted that she didn't have to choose.

Bella Books, Inc.

Women. Books. Even Better Together.

P.O. Box 10543
Tallahassee, FL 32302

Phone: 800-729-4992
www.bellabooks.com